THE ISLANDS
OF THE BLESSED

ALSO BY THE AUTHOR

The Land of the Silver Apples

The Sea of Trolls

The House of the Scorpion

A Girl Named Disaster

The Warm Place

The Ear, the Eye and the Arm

Do You Know Me

THE ISLANDS
OF THE BLESSED

NANCY FARMER

A RICHARD JACKSON BOOK
Atheneum Books for Young Readers
New York   London   Toronto   Sydney

Atheneum Books for Young Readers

An imprint of Simon & Schuster Children's Publishing Division

1230 Avenue of the Americas, New York, New York 10020

For information about special discounts for bulk purchases, please contact
Simon & Schuster Special Sales at 1-866-506-1949 or business@simonandschuster.com.
The Simon & Schuster Speakers Bureau can bring authors to your live event. For more
information or to book an event, contact the Simon & Schuster Speakers Bureau
at 1-866-248-3049 or visit our website at www.simonspeakers.com.

Book design by Russell Gordon

The text for this book is set in Edlund.

Manufactured in the United States of America

First Edition

2 4 6 8 10 9 7 5 3 1

Library of Congress Cataloging-in-Publication Data

Farmer, Nancy, 1941–

The Islands of the Blessed / Nancy Farmer. — 1st ed.

p.   cm.

"A Richard Jackson book."

Sequel to: The Land of the Silver Apples.

Summary: Two years after their adventures in the Land of the Silver Apples,
the apprentice bard Jack and his Viking companion Thorgil confront the malevolent
spirit of a vengeful mermaid and begin a quest that casts them among the fin
folk of Notland (present-day Orkney Islands).

Includes bibliographical references (p.   ).

ISBN: 978-1-4169-0737-4

ISBN: 978-1-4391-6047-3 (eBook)

[1. Bards and bardism—Fiction. 2. Druids and druidism—Fiction. 3. Saxons—Fiction.
4. Vikings—Fiction. 5. Mythology, Norse—Fiction. 6. Folklore—Scotland—Orkney—
Fiction. 7. Mermaids—Fiction.] I. Title.

PZ7.F23814Is 2009

[Fic]—dc22   2008045415

To Harold

May we find the Islands of the Blessed together

—⟪⟫—

ACKNOWLEDGMENTS

Heartfelt thanks to the editors who picked me out of the slush pile and nurtured my career: Richard Jackson, Susan Hirschman, and Sharon November.

Especial thanks to Emma Dryden and Carol Chou for cheering me on while I was writing this book.

Warmest appreciations to my son, Daniel, and nephew, Nathan Stout, for their joint inspiration for the character Olaf One-Brow.

CONTENTS

	Cast of Characters	xi
1.	The Gathering Storm	1
2.	The Wild Hunt	8
3.	The Hazel Wood	17
4.	Seafarer	30
5.	A Scream in the Dark	41
6.	Fair Lamenting	53
7.	The Mermaid	65
8.	The *Draugr*	74
9.	A Plea for Justice	83
10.	The Hobgoblins Arrive	94
11.	Hazel Comes Home	106
12.	The Tanner Brats	117
13.	The Paths Open	127
14.	Schlaup	137
15.	All Aboard	148
16.	A Love Story	159
17.	The Pink Palace	167
18.	Pangur Ban	178
19.	Find Tanners	189
20.	The Quest	203
21.	Ethne's Cell	211
22.	Schlaup's Betrothal	225
23.	The Sacrificial Stone	232
24.	Bjorn Skull-Splitter	242
25.	Princess Thorgil	250
26.	The Hogboon	264
27.	Escape Plans	273
28.	Full Moon	287

29.	The Dead Wall	299
30.	The Water of Life	310
31.	Voyage to Notland	321
32.	The Fin Folk	328
33.	The City Under the Sea	335
34.	The Shoney's Feast	346
35.	The *Draugr*'s Tomb	359
36.	A Life for a Life	367
37.	Grim's Island	375
38.	St. Columba's Cave	383
39.	Odin	391
40.	A Joyful Reunion	400
41.	Rescue	408
42.	Flying Venom	417
43.	Sister Wulfhilda	427
44.	The Rune of Protection	436
45.	Departure	445
46.	Thorgil Silver-Hand	454
47.	The Islands of the Blessed	462
	Appendix	469
	The *Carnyx*	469
	Father Severus	470
	The Fin Folk	471
	Flying Venom	472
	Lorica	473
	Mermaids	473
	St. Columba	474
	Seafarer	475
	Sources	477

CAST OF CHARACTERS

HUMANS (SAXONS)

Jack: Age fourteen; an apprentice bard

Hazel: Jack's sister; age eight; stolen by hobgoblins

Lucy: Jack's foster sister; lost to Elfland

Mother: Alditha; Jack's mother; a wise woman

Father: Giles Crookleg; Jack's father

The Bard: A druid from Ireland; also known as Dragon Tongue

Ethne: Daughter of the Elf Queen and the Bard

Pega: An ex–slave girl; age fifteen

Mrs. Tanner: The tanner's widow; mother of Ymma and Ythla

Ymma and Ythla: The Tanner girls; ages ten and eight

Brother Aiden: A monk from the Holy Isle

Gog and Magog: Slaves of the village blacksmith

King Brutus: Ruler of Bebba's Town

Father Severus: Abbot of St. Filian's Monastery

Sister Wulfhilda: A nun

Allyson: Thorgil's mother; deceased

HUMANS (NORTHMEN)

Thorgil: Olaf One-Brow's adopted daughter; age fourteen

Olaf One-Brow: A famous warrior and Thorgil's foster father; deceased

Skakki: Olaf's son; age eighteen; a sea captain

Rune, Sven the Vengeful, Eric the Rash, Eric Pretty-Face: Members of Skakki's crew

Egil Long-Spear: Sea captain and trader

Bjorn Skull-Splitter: Olaf One-Brow's best friend

Einar Adder-Tooth: A pirate

Big Half and Little Half: Brothers working for Adder-Tooth

THINGS THAT GO BUMP IN THE NIGHT

The Bugaboo: King of the hobgoblins

The Nemesis: The Bugaboo's second-in-command

Mr. Blewit: Hobgoblin foster father of Hazel

*The **draugr***: Avenging spirit

The hogboon: Soulless being that feeds on life

OTHERS

The Shoney: Ruler of the fin folk

Shair Shair: The Shoney's wife

Shellia: Their daughter; also known as the *drauger*

Whush: A fin man

Man in the Moon: An old god; exiled to the moon

Yarthkins: Also known as *landvættir*; spirits of the land

Pangur Ban: Large white cat from Ireland

Odin: Northman war god; lord of Valhalla and the Wild Hunt

JOTUNS (TROLLS)

The Mountain Queen: Glamdis; ruler of Jotunheim

Fonn and Forath: The Mountain Queen's daughters

Schlaup Half-Troll: The Mountain Queen's son

Pangur Ban

I and Pangur Ban, my cat—
'Tis a like task we are at:
Hunting mice is his delight;
Hunting words, I sit all night.

Better far than praise of men
'Tis to sit with book and pen.
Pangur bears me no ill will;
He too plies his simple skill.

'Tis a merry thing to see
At our tasks how glad are we,
When at home we sit and find
Entertainment to our mind.

Oftentimes a mouse will stray
In the hero Pangur's way;
Oftentimes my keen thought set
Takes a meaning in its net.

'Gainst the wall he sets his eye
Full and fierce and sharp and sly;
'Gainst the wall of knowledge I
All my little wisdom try.

When a mouse darts from its den,
O how glad is Pangur then!
O what gladness do I prove
When I solve the doubts I love!

So in peace our tasks we ply,
Pangur Ban, my cat, and I.
In our arts we find our bliss;
I have mine and he has his.

Practice every day has made
Pangur perfect in his trade;
I get wisdom day and night
Turning darkness into light.

Written by an unknown eighth-century Irish monk in the margins of a manuscript, when he was supposed to be copying the Bible. Translated by Robin Flower in The Irish Tradition, *Oxford University Press, London, 1947.*

Chapter One

THE GATHERING STORM

Jack's fingers ached and blisters had formed on the palms of his hands. Once he could have done this work without harm. Once his skin had been covered with comfortable calluses, protecting him from the slippery handle of the sickle, but no longer. For three years he'd been freed of farmwork. He'd spent his time memorizing poetry and plucking away at a harp—not that he'd ever equaled the Bard. Or ever would.

Sweat ran down his forehead. Jack wiped his face and only succeeded in getting dirt into his eyes. "Curse this job!" he cried, hurling the sickle to the earth.

"At least you have two hands," said Thorgil, sweating and

laboring nearby. She had to hold the bracken ferns in the crook of her arm and slice through them with her knife. Her right hand was frozen, useless, yet she didn't give up. It both impressed and annoyed Jack.

"Why can't someone else do this?" he complained, sitting down in the springy bracken.

"Even Thor does inglorious chores when he's on a quest," said Thorgil, stolidly dumping an armload of bracken into a growing pile. She turned to gather more.

"This is no quest! This is thrall work."

"You'd know," retorted the shield maiden.

Jack's face turned even hotter as he remembered how he'd been a slave in the Northland. But he swallowed the obvious response that Thorgil herself had been a thrall as a child. She was prey to dark moods that rippled out to blight everyone around her. That was the word for her, Jack thought grimly. She was a *blight*, a kind of disease that turned everything yellow.

Nothing had worked out since she'd arrived in the village. It took the utmost threats from the Bard to keep her from revealing that she was a Northman, one of the murdering pirates who'd descended on the Holy Isle. Even as it was, the villagers were suspicious of her. She refused to wear women's clothes. She took offense readily. She was crude. She was sullen. In short, she was a perfect example of a Northman.

And yet, Jack had to remind himself, she had their virtues too—if you could call anything about Northmen virtuous. Thorgil was brave, loyal, and utterly trustworthy. If only she were more flexible!

"If you'd shift your backside, I could harvest that bracken. Or were you planning on using it as a bed?" Thorgil said.

"Oh, shut up!" Jack snatched up his sickle and winced as a blister broke on his hand.

They worked silently for a long time. The sun sent shafts of heat into the airless woodland. The sky—what they could see of it—was a cloudless blue. It pressed down on them like an inverted lake—hot, humid, and completely still. Jack found it hard to believe that a storm was on its way, but that's what the Bard had said. No one questioned the Bard. He listened to birds and observed the motions of the sea from his lonely perch near the old Roman house where he lived.

A rumbling sound made both Jack and Thorgil look up. The blacksmith's two slaves had arrived with an oxcart. A moment later the large, silent men crashed through the underbrush to gather up the bracken. They tramped to and fro, never speaking, never making eye contact. They had been sold by their father in Bebba's Town because they were of limited intelligence, and Jack wondered what kind of thoughts they had. They never seemed to communicate with each other or anyone else.

Even animals thought. As the Bard had instructed Jack, animals had much lore to impart to those who paid attention to them. What kind of lore did Gog and Magog, as the slaves were called, have to impart? Nothing good, Jack decided, looking at their brooding, averted faces.

When the oxcart had been loaded, Jack and Thorgil set off for home. Most of the time they lived at the Bard's house, but now, during the crisis of the impending storm, they had returned to the farm Jack's parents owned. It had grown a great deal in the last three years.

Beside the fields, farmhouse, barn, and winter storage shed was a new dairy Jack's father had built. This contained three sturdy black cows tended by Pega, whom Jack had freed from slavery. She also cared for the chickens, new lambs, and a donkey. But she was not allowed to touch the horses. The horses were Thorgil's domain and jealously guarded, particularly from the tanner's daughters.

At the edge of the property, where the land was too stony for crops, was a hovel constructed of peat. This was where the tanner's widow and her two daughters crowded together with hardly more room than three peas in a pod. They had arrived to help Jack's mother the year before and had never gone home.

"I *wish* this storm would arrive," cried Thorgil, throwing a stone at a crow. The crow eluded it. "The air's so heavy! It's like breathing under mud."

Jack looked up at the cloudless, blue sky. Except for the ominous stillness, it could have been any early summer day. "The Bard spoke to a swallow from the south. It told him that the currents in the air were disordered and all the migrating birds were confused. Why don't you ever talk to birds, Thorgil?" The shield maiden had gained this ability when she'd accidentally tasted dragon blood.

"They never tell me anything," she said.

"Maybe if you didn't throw rocks at them . . ."

"Birds are stupid," Thorgil said with finality.

Jack shrugged. It was like her to ignore the gifts she had and to demand what she could never achieve, a glorious career as a warrior. Her paralyzed hand had put an end to that. She also wanted to be a poet. Jack had to admit that she wasn't bad. Her voice was harsh and she had a fondness for bloody death scenes, but her stories held your attention.

During long winter evenings the villagers gathered at the chief's hearth for song and hot cider. The Bard played his harp, and when he wearied, Jack and Thorgil recited sagas. Brother Aiden, the little monk from the Holy Isle, joined in with tales of the god Jesus, of how He fed a thousand people with five fishes and performed many other diverting miracles. But the real draw at these gatherings was Pega. Her voice was so compelling that the very storm blasts hushed to listen to her.

"By Thor, those Tanner brats are meddling with my horses!" Thorgil broke into a run, and Jack hurried after to break up the inevitable fight. The tanner's daughters were fascinated by the horses, a gift from King Brutus the year before. Actually, it was unclear whose horses they were, since they'd been handed to the entire group of pilgrims returning from Bebba's Town. Jack thought they ought to be the Bard's, but Thorgil insisted that they were hers by right, since she was the only true warrior among them.

"Get off, you mangy curs! You'll ruin their training!" Thorgil whistled and the horses wheeled, throwing their small riders into the dirt. The animals came to a halt before the shield maiden, prancing nervously like the spirited creatures they were. Jack ran to pick up the howling girls. "Tell them to shut up or I'll really give them something to blubber about," snarled Thorgil, stroking the manes of the horses.

Jack checked the girls and found they had no real injuries. They were eight and ten, stunted from years of bad food and the noxious air of the old tannery where they had lived until their father died. "They're only children," Jack reproved, wiping the girls' dirty, tear-streaked faces with the tail of his tunic. "You probably did the same thing at that age."

"*I* was a shield maiden. I was the daughter of—"

"Careful!" Jack said sharply. The girls stopped crying and eyed Thorgil curiously.

"Who was your da, then?" the older one demanded.

"Probably a troll," the younger said, giggling. Thorgil reached down, but they sped off before she could wallop them with a rock.

"Filthy bog rats," Thorgil said.

"All it will take is one slip," Jack warned. "One hint that you are not a Saxon to someone who has reason to hate you, and the whole village will turn against you. And it will turn against my parents and me for sheltering you."

"That debt is the only thing that keeps me from flinging my true heritage into their faces." Thorgil embraced the neck of one of the horses, and it blew a long, horsey kiss at her. Jack was impressed, as always, by how much the animals loved her. Too bad she couldn't inspire the same sentiment in people.

"Let's go to the house," Jack said. "I'm starving, and we have to cut bracken all afternoon."

"Curse the bracken," swore Thorgil. "Curse the pointless, boring existence in this village. For one rotten turnip I'd throw myself off a cliff into the sea!"

"No, you wouldn't," said Jack, leading the way.

Chapter Two

THE WILD HUNT

Thorgil's bad mood followed them back to the house. She accepted Mother's food with a scowl and set about stuffing herself. "In this village it's customary to say thank you for food," Mother said. Jack sighed inwardly. It was a battle that never ended, trying to instill basic courtesy into the shield maiden.

"Why?" demanded Thorgil.

"It shows gratitude."

"I *am* grateful. I'm eating this swill, aren't I? Besides, it makes as much sense for you to compliment me for cutting bracken. If everyone started thanking everyone else for the smallest chores, we'd never get anything done."

"That's not the point," Mother said patiently. "People want to hear kind words. It's like saying 'Good morning' or 'How are you?'"

"What if it's a rotten morning or I don't give a flying flip how someone feels?"

"Oh, have it your way!" exclaimed Mother. "Sometimes I wish a Northman ship would swoop down and take you away!" She hurried outside and Jack raised his eyebrows. It was unlike Mother to lose her temper so completely. But then, Thorgil was capable of making even gentle Brother Aiden blot his manuscript when she was on a rampage.

Jack heard Mother and Pega discussing how to protect the livestock from the coming storm. Cows and horses would have to crowd together in the barn. The more aggressive sheep would have to fend for themselves outside.

"Even Olaf One-Brow wished people a good morning," remarked Jack, naming Thorgil's dead foster father.

"Only if it *was* a good morning. He never lied." Thorgil shadowed her eyes with her hand.

"Are you crying?"

"Of course not. It's the filthy smoke in this filthy hovel." The shield maiden continued to shadow her eyes.

"Do you want some of my bread?"

"Why would I want your weevil-infested leavings?" Thorgil said, though from the way she was eating, it was clear she was ravenous.

There was no point trying to be sympathetic, Jack thought. She only looked upon it as weakness. Her moods built up like summer storms, forking lightning in all directions, but if you were patient—and closed your ears to her insults—the clouds would eventually blow away. He wasn't sure which he preferred, Thorgil's glooms or her periodic episodes of joy. Sometimes she was seized by a kind of wild rapture in which colors, smells, and sounds overwhelmed her with ecstasy. Then she would grab him by the arm and force him to pay attention to whatever it was.

The Bard said this happened because Thorgil had been raised as a berserker, dedicated to death. Now she was controlled by the life force because of the rune of protection she wore. It was only natural that the two instincts were at war.

Pega came to the door with a hen caged in a basket, and Jack's heart lifted. Pega never made you feel rotten. She was endlessly thoughtful, always looking for ways to make people happy. She helped Mother with the cooking, weeded the Bard's herb garden, and stood over Brother Aiden, making sure he ate regularly. She had been born a slave and was touchingly grateful for any welcome anywhere. Jack thought she looked almost pretty, in spite of a disfiguring birthmark across half her face. It was her spirit shining through, the Bard said, just as Thorgil's simmering malice spoiled what could have been real beauty.

"We'll have to keep the chickens here," Pega announced, placing the basket against a wall. "You should see the sky to the south! It's weird and dark, but I can't make out any clouds."

"Do you need help?" Jack asked hopefully.

"I need you to take food to the workers in the fields," Mother said, bumping the door open as she carried in another hen. "From the look of that sky, there won't be time to cut more bracken. You can double-check the hives on the way back."

She didn't smile, and Jack felt unfairly included in Thorgil's disgrace. It wasn't *his* fault he couldn't keep the shield maiden in line. Even Olaf One-Brow used to hang her over a cliff, by way of getting her attention, when she acted up. Unfortunately, Olaf had been just as likely to reward her for nasty behavior. Northmen admired such things.

Jack and Thorgil loaded the donkey with baskets of bread and cider. Most of the villagers were harvesting hay as quickly as possible. A few, like Mother and the chief's wife, were supplying food to keep them going. The sky outside had indeed changed remarkably in just a few minutes. To the north it was blue, but it deepened to slate when you turned toward the south. And yet, as Pega had said, you couldn't make out any clouds.

"What's that odd smell?" said Thorgil.

"I'm not sure," said Jack. "It's a little like clothes drying in sunlight."

"It's . . . nice. Makes me feel like running or singing. Maybe this storm will be fun after all." Some of the gloom lifted from Thorgil's face. Jack thought it was typical for her to be cheered by something that worried everyone else.

"I've never seen a sky like that," he said.

"I have," said the shield maiden, "when I was very small. My mother carried me to a cellar where they stored vegetables.

She was trying to protect me, and I remember her lying on top of me. I heard dogs howling, or perhaps it was the wind—"

"We'd better get our chores done," Jack said to change the subject. Thorgil's mother had been a slave, sacrificed on the funeral pyre of her real father. All of Thorgil's memories from that part of her life were evil. When she could be persuaded to speak of them at all, they drove her even deeper into despair.

They hurried from farm to farm, delivering food to people in the fields and barns. The storage barns had floors of slate, over which was spread a layer of bracken. Bracken not only protected the hay on top from rising damp, but also cut into the mouths of rats and discouraged them from invading. Livestock depended on this fodder for winter. If it was spoiled by rain, it would rot and the animals would starve. The newly cut hay gave a rich, green smell to the air.

In each field Jack saw people bending, slashing, and bundling. When possible, the workers used the blacksmith's cart for transport. But speed was important, and for the most part, they had to carry the hay themselves. Those with no barns protected their haystacks with inverted cones of thatch, somewhat like giant hats, and hoped for the best.

Months ago Jack had tried to hitch Thorgil's ponies to a cart, but they fought the harness and were completely ungovernable. This was another fault held against him unfairly. Jack knew nothing about handling horses. It was Thorgil who had their trust, but she refused to train them for farmwork. They were warriors, she insisted, not thralls.

Thorgil. Jack saw how the villagers cautiously accepted food from her and turned away to make the sign of the cross.

They left the donkey in the last barn and walked on to check the hives. "We'd better hurry," said Jack, looking at the darkening southern sky. *Were* there clouds? Something certainly teemed in the distance, and yet the air was still and dead. Leaves on the trees hung straight down.

Even the bees knew something was wrong. They had stopped zipping to and fro in search of nectar, and warrior bees at the entrances danced around as though searching for a hidden enemy. The nests were protected by inverted baskets, somewhat like the hats over the exposed haystacks. The bees would have been far safer indoors, but moving hives confused them dreadfully. They would have to survive where they were.

Father had built a stone barrier around them early in the year, to keep sheep from grazing too close, and now Jack was glad of this extra protection. "They're acting as though it's night," he said, wondering. "They've almost all gone inside. Listen to that hum!"

"You know, I can almost understand it," said Thorgil, pressing her ear to one of the inverted baskets. "It's like a birdcall. Isn't that strange?"

"Bees *are* creatures of the air. What are they saying?"

"They're frightened. They feel death is near—ow!" Thorgil slapped her ear and jumped away.

"Move back. When one stings, the others join in," advised Jack.

But the bees stayed clustered in the hives. Jack and Thorgil crouched down some distance away to observe them. Whatever enemy the insects detected was too dangerous for them to confront.

"Look!" Jack yelled in sheer disbelief. The southern sky was filled with towering clouds. The dark haze had resolved into shreds of mist flying toward them at such speed that Jack instinctively threw himself to the ground, pulling Thorgil with him. A second later the storm hit.

From absolute stillness the air suddenly whipped into a hurricane that sent them skidding along the ground. One of the beehives lost its cone and fell over against the stone enclosure. The wind howled so loudly, Jack couldn't make himself heard. He wriggled across the dirt, with Thorgil at his side, making his way to a sheep byre he knew existed at the far end of the field.

He couldn't see it until a flash of lightning turned everything white and a clap of thunder shook the ground. "By Thor!" formed Thorgil's lips, brilliant in the light. They crawled furiously, freezing each time one of the bolts fell from the clouds. As yet there was no rain. They reached the byre and squeezed in with a trio of ewes who'd had the same idea. The wind tore across the top of the protecting ring of stone, but at the bottom, in a fug of sweaty wool, Jack almost felt safe.

"By Thor!" shouted Thorgil again, pointing.

Jack looked up to see a dangling cone of cloud unlike anything he had ever encountered. It roared like a thousand enraged bees, and his skin crawled as though ants were swarming over it. The mouth of the cone gaped open, and he saw ropes of lightning twisting around inside, with tree branches and what might have been part of a house. Then it was gone.

The ewes screamed and huddled closer together. Jack burrowed in with them, but Thorgil suddenly tried to climb out of the byre. The wind knocked her back. She pulled herself up again and raised her arms to the sky. Her voice was no louder than a cricket's chirp against the howling storm, but Jack could just make out the words: *"Take me with you!"*

"Get down!" he shouted, tackling her legs.

"No! No!" she protested. He dragged her down. She fought back, punching him in the stomach. He collapsed, trying to get his breath back, and she struggled up again. "Take me with you!" she screamed. Then the rain started, buckets of rain sluicing down and filling up the byre so that the ewes had to fight for air. They pummeled Jack with their hooves and one actually stood on top of him. The wind knocked her over the side and he heard her terrified bleating as she was swept away.

How long the rain poured down, Jack wasn't sure. It seemed to be for hours. The temperature dropped rapidly, and for a brief period hailstones bounced over his head, big hailstones that hurt and made the sheep bellow. When that ended, the rain began again. During all this time lightning came in bursts and thunder rolled around the horizon.

But eventually the heavens calmed. The flashes became infrequent and the thunder grumbled away to the north. The southern sky turned a pale and beautiful blue.

Jack stood up cautiously and saw a scene of utter destruction around him. Every bush had been beaten flat. Branches from the distant forest were strewn across the ground, and not far away the ewe that had stood on Jack lay dead.

Thorgil, too, was outstretched in the mud. He hadn't even been aware she'd left the byre! "Oh, Thorgil!" Jack cried, struggling out of the enclosure and rushing to her side. He lifted her onto his knees. "Oh, my dear! My love!"

Her eyes were wide open, staring. But they weren't glazed in death. Jack was so relieved, he hugged her and then worried about whether she had broken a rib. "He wouldn't take me," she said in a faint voice.

"Who wouldn't take you?" Jack said, thinking she was delirious.

"He saw my useless hand and knew I was no longer a warrior. He wanted me, but Odin wouldn't allow it. Oh, Freya, I wish I were dead!" Thorgil began to cry, which worried Jack even more than if she'd started cursing.

"Are you hurt inside?" he asked anxiously.

"Nothing that death wouldn't fix," she said with a touch of her old spirit. "Even then, I'll never see him again."

"Who? What are you talking about?" The sun was breaking out to the south and the clouds overhead had turned white, with patches of blue between.

"Olaf One-Brow," the shield maiden said, sighing deeply. "He was in the clouds, but he had to leave me behind."

Chapter Three

THE HAZEL WOOD

"How could she have seen Olaf?" said Jack. "She said Odin was leading a Wild Hunt, but I only saw clouds and that . . . *thing*, hanging out of the sky."

"That 'thing' sounds like a waterspout," said the Bard, casting a handful of dry pine needles over the hearth fire. A pleasant odor filled the air. Thorgil lay deeply asleep on a bed of dried heather. Thanks to the Bard's sleeping draught, she no longer thrashed about or tried to tear out her hair. It had been the longest hour of Jack's life, dragging her to the Bard's house while preventing her from doing herself damage.

Her hair had grown out in the past year, and it was surprisingly clean. No longer did it hang in an untidy fringe from being hacked with a fish scaling knife. It was a pale golden color, like sunlight on snow. In spite of the bruises—and Thorgil seldom lacked those—her face had a delicacy Jack hadn't noticed before. She'd changed in the last year, he realized, becoming taller and more beautiful.

Jack turned away, his cheeks burning with embarrassment. What difference did that make? She was the same foul-tempered Thorgil no matter how she looked.

"I've never known a waterspout to be so destructive," remarked the old man, rummaging in a chest. "It plowed a road through the forest and probably carried off Gog and Magog."

"It did *what*?" said Jack. After running home to check up on his parents, he'd spent yesterday afternoon helping the Bard prepare elixirs. It was now morning, and Jack hadn't been near the village since the storm.

"The blacksmith's son told me that Gog and Magog have disappeared."

"Perhaps they ran away," Jack suggested. The thought of the men being pulled into the sky was horrible.

"I fear not. The blacksmith said they liked to sit outside during storms. It was the only time he ever saw them smile, and since it was their sole pleasure, he left them to it. A mistake, it would seem."

Jack had seen Gog and Magog squatting in the mud during a thunderstorm. They'd sat together, swaying back and forth, with their faces turned up to the sky. Their teeth had gleamed in the lightning. They'd seemed possessed with a wild joy that Jack neither understood nor cared to see, and he'd hurried away as quickly as possible. He shivered. "Where are they now, sir?"

"That depends on who conducted the Wild Hunt." The Bard laid out a collection of pots, sniffed each one, and made a selection. He lifted down a large mortar and pestle from a shelf. "Oh, yes, the Hunt is real," he said, grinding the herbs. "Who leads it depends on who sees it. Brother Aiden was its quarry as a child, until Father Severus rescued him. Aiden was convinced he saw the Forest Lord and his hounds. Severus thought he saw Satan leading the damned."

"And Thorgil saw Olaf One-Brow," said Jack.

"If she's correct, Gog and Magog might have been taken to Valhalla. Wouldn't that make her cranky!" The Bard's blue eyes twinkled. "Ah well, Thorgil wouldn't be Thorgil if she wasn't cranky."

"If you say so." Personally, Jack wouldn't have minded if the shield maiden were pleasanter—more like Pega, for example. It was extremely wearing to mediate between her and the enemies she always managed to make. And yet, when he'd seen her lying next to the sheep byre, *dead* for all he could tell, like that poor ewe—

"She'll be fine," said the Bard, with that uncanny ability to know what was passing through Jack's mind. "Now I want you to mix the contents of this mortar with a lump of butter the size of a hen's egg. Knead a handful of flour with enough water to make a stiff paste, blend everything, and roll out pills the size of peas. Dry them before the fire."

"Which pot should I store them in?" asked Jack, who had done this before.

"The green one for headaches. Dear, dear, the garden is almost picked clean. I'm going to need plants from the forest."

Soon they were walking down the path, leaving Thorgil to sleep. The Bard had put on his better robe, belted up to protect it from mud. His white beard fanned out over his chest, and his feet were encased in tan leather boots that laced up the front. Old as he was, he barely needed to lean upon his black ash wood staff, though he needed Jack to carry elixirs and the harp.

Jack could feel the life force stirring in the air around the staff, and it filled him with longing. Once he too had owned such a magical thing. He'd owned the rune of protection as well, if you could say such a thing belonged to anyone. The rune passed from person to person, following its own destiny, which was beyond the understanding of whoever sought to possess it. Once gone, it could never return. Jack sighed inwardly, remembering its living gold engraved with the image of Yggdrassil. It had preserved the Bard for many long years before coming to Jack, and then—in a moment of weakness, he thought darkly—he'd given it to Thorgil.

The fields were strangely bare, like plucked chickens, and more than one house had its roof missing. Water oozed out of hillsides. Streams cut new channels into soil, and here and there sunlight flashed from ponds.

Jack looked back at the Bard's house, perched dangerously on a cliff over the sea. It had weathered the storm beautifully.

Whether this was due to luck or the old man's magic, Jack didn't know, but it clung to the rocks like a limpet.

They made their way through the village, dispensing medicine where needed, and good advice. At the blacksmith's house the Bard played music to raise the family's spirits.

"Gog and Magog were like my own lads—well, if they'd been brighter and more presentable," the blacksmith amended, looking fondly at his handsome daughters and sons. "I was that used to them. They slept in a heap with the cows, and if a wolf came near, they put up such a mooing, not one calf was ever lost. I'll miss them, by God I will, the poor, witless creatures."

You had a power of work out of them for the crusts of bread they were fed, thought Jack uncharitably.

The Bard played his harp. The blacksmith's wife tapped her foot to the rhythm, and Colin, the blacksmith's youngest son, performed an impromptu jig.

And yet if Gog and Magog hadn't come here, Jack mused, *who knows what fate might have been theirs? They might have ended up as slaves in a lead mine. At least they had some joy, mooing with the cows and worshipping lightning. What is happiness, after all?* He thought of Thorgil, whose hope had been to fall in battle; and of his father, Giles Crookleg, who relished disappointment; and of Father Severus, who enjoyed cold baths and fasting. The elves pursued an endless round of pleasure—much good it did them, doomed as they were to fade at the end of days.

Happiness is a puzzle and no mistake, Jack decided.

The Bard roused him and they set off again. Shreds of mist rose from a hundred rivulets left behind by the storm, and a scarecrow was bent double in a ruined field. "*He* didn't protect anything," Jack commented as they squelched past in the soft earth.

"Odin's crows take more than a heap of straw to be impressed," said the Bard.

Jack and the Bard trudged on, observing the devastated barley and oat fields. Half of the sheep were missing, according to the villagers, although most of them would probably turn up. The chickens and cattle had been protected indoors, and Thorgil's ponies had also survived. The Tanner girls had pulled them into their hovel when they saw black clouds approaching.

It was an amazing feat, considering that there was scarcely enough room for the Tanners inside. The girls had forced the horses to lie down and then lain on top of them with their mother between. It made a stifling crush of horse and human flesh, but all had lived.

"That means *we've* earned the right to ride them," Ymma, the older Tanner girl, declared when Jack and the Bard stopped by to check on their welfare.

"You'll have to discuss that with Thorgil," the old man said.

"Pooh! She thinks she owns everything. Who's her father, I ask you?" the girl said rudely. "Where's her family?"

"Everyone says she acts like a Northman," added her younger sister, Ythla.

The Bard turned on them so suddenly, the girls shrank away and their mother grabbed their arms. "What do you mean, talking back to the Bard?" Mrs. Tanner cried. "Go down on your knees at once and beg his pardon. Honestly, sir, I don't know what's become of them since their father died." She pushed the girls down and they apologized loudly.

Jack wasn't surprised. One look at the old man's face and you understood why he was known as Dragon Tongue and why even Northman kings were afraid of him. But the girls had only said what everyone else was probably whispering.

They found Mother sitting by the beehives. Only two colonies had survived. The rest were dying of cold and wet, the bees creeping over the ground or struggling weakly in the mud. Mother had built a fire nearby—not too close, for smoke could harm them as well—and had laid out chunks of bread covered with honey. The insects clustered eagerly around the food.

"They're the last of a royal line," she said sadly, "brought here by the Romans. The women of my family have guarded them since time out of mind. No Saxon bee matches them for strength and industry, but they will be lucky to live through this winter."

The Bard played his harp and Mother sang, using the small magic that calmed nervous animals. Her voice was not unlike a drowsy bee-hum itself. She told them of sunny days to come, of new flowers and warm breezes.

"How's your supply of candles?" the Bard asked when he had handed the harp back to Jack.

"I know what's in your mind," she replied. "The crops are ruined, and if we are to survive this winter, we must barter for grain. Whatever I have is yours."

"I can always count on you, Alditha," said the old man warmly, clasping her hands.

From there the Bard and Jack made their way to the hazel wood that lay in the shadow of the oak forest. This woodland, though littered with debris, had been spared. A tangle of branches and gnarled roots was crossed by odd little paths carpeted with bluebells. You might meet anything in the hazel wood—long-eared hares, badgers, a wolf folding itself into the twilight, or even a bear. It was a secret, knowing place, and you didn't enter it carelessly after dark. The leaves now shone with an eerie brightness, and the air was fresh and delightful.

"It's as though the storm never happened," Jack said with wonder.

"Hazel woods are protected," said the Bard. "At the School of Bards—where I was an outstanding student, by the way—a newcomer was left in a hazel wood overnight. In the morning the teachers asked him what he'd seen. You have no idea how some of those lads twisted themselves into knots, trying to say what they thought the old bards wanted. If the boys lied, they were sent away and never allowed to return."

"Just for that," murmured Jack, thinking of the times he had lied to avoid a thrashing from Father.

"Serving the life force is a serious business," the old man said.

"What did *you* see, sir?" Jack said daringly, for the Bard rarely answered questions about himself.

The old man pushed aside a downed branch with the tip of his staff. "Right now I see ceps." A cluster of fat mushrooms with white stems and brown caps crowded around the foot of a tree. "We're in luck, lad. They'll make an outstanding supper."

Jack crouched down to gather the ceps, and their rich, earthy odor made his mouth water.

"Hazel woods are brimming with the life force," the Bard continued, moving more branches out of the way. "They lie close to the boundaries between the nine worlds, and many a secret pathway lies hidden under their leaves. A true bard knows how to find them."

Jack felt a tremor of fear, which he quickly tried to suppress. His experience with other worlds had mostly been bad. On the other hand, there were moments—such as when he and Thorgil had found the Valley of Yggdrassil—so wreathed in glory that tears came to his eyes when he remembered them. And then an awful thought struck him: Suppose the Bard were testing him right now? Perhaps it was time to discover whether he was a true bard or whether he should be sent back to weeding turnips and chasing black-faced sheep.

Jack looked around, willing the leaves to dissolve and show him a secret path. But nothing appeared. It was an ordinary woodland full of moss and lichens. The trees nearest the fields had been coppiced, cut close to the roots to allow for the growth of straight branches that might be used for fences. A red squirrel scolded him from a high perch, and he saw it flick its tail with rage.

"What do you see?" the Bard asked in a soft voice.

Jack's throat constricted. Sunlight hovered over the sheltering leaves. A thrush opened its beak and sang. A spiderweb shivered delicately in a puff of air. "I see . . . oh, curse it! I don't see *anything*. No, that's not right. I can see a squirrel, a beetle, a thrush, a spiderweb, but nothing important. I'll never be a true bard!"

"And what could be more important than a squirrel, a beetle, a thrush, and a spiderweb?" insisted the old man.

"Why . . ." Jack looked up.

"Exactly. Ever since I took you on as my apprentice, I've been training you to see things as they are. Until you do that, you haven't a hope of looking farther. One night very soon, I want you to sleep here."

Jack swallowed nervously. The woodland appeared tranquil and safe by daylight, but he knew things could change after dark.

"You asked me what I saw when I was tested at the School of Bards," the old man said. "The first time I encountered the same sort of creatures as you—a hedgehog, a bat, a doe with her fawn. But the *second* time—" He fell silent.

What happened the second night? Jack thought wildly. The Bard walked on briskly, and the boy knew he wouldn't answer any more questions.

They followed one of the paths through the hazel wood.

Bluebells brushed against their ankles, and the sound of water rushing through an unseen brook came to them.

"Look there," commanded the Bard. Jack's breath caught in his throat. Where once there had been a dense mass of ancient oaks, a road had been torn out, as though someone had taken a giant sword and slashed right and left through the heart of the forest.

"Typical of Olaf and his thick-skulled bunch to leave a mess," remarked the Bard, looking out over the destruction.

"Was Thorgil right?" Jack asked. "Did Odin really lead a Wild Hunt here?"

"Something laid waste to these oaks."

The new road was littered with branches, and water pooled in the center where the ground had been plowed deeper. "If it was a Hunt," Jack said carefully, "what was it hunting?"

"Not Gog and Magog, poor lads. They were merely unlucky to be in its path," said the Bard. "The Wild Hunt drives misfortune before it. Plague, famine, and war follow behind. I believe we're in for an interesting time."

The sky was bright blue, as though nothing had ever disturbed it, and the air was warm with summer. Jack saw Brother Aiden picking his way through the branches like a small brown sparrow hopping from perch to perch. The monk held aloft a wooden cross and was chanting in Latin. Jack couldn't understand him, but it was clear that the words were filled with Christian magic.

"Aiden, my friend," called the Bard, "you'll be up to your ears in mud if you don't watch out."

The little monk looked up and almost slid off a branch. "I must sanctify this place," he said, bracing his feet. "Evil has been done here."

"Aye, and evil has been done to the farms as well. We must trade for grain before winter comes." The Bard strode onto the road—for an old man his step was amazingly sure—and helped Brother Aiden to firmer ground.

"I can mix ink. People always want to buy that," offered the monk. Brother Aiden was renowned for his magnificent colors, which were used to illuminate holy manuscripts.

"Excellent! I'll get Pega to help you. Jack and Thorgil can gather herbs for my elixirs. John the Fletcher has a stock of deerskins, and I'm sure I can pry a few coins out of the chief's wealth-hoard. My stars! That new road is so straight, you could almost believe it was made by Romans."

Jack looked through the opening to a distant meadow and the hills beyond. A lone bird fluttered from one side to the other of this opening. Its cries reached him from the shadows of a yew. "It sounds . . . so sad," he murmured.

The Bard cast a sharp look at him. "Indeed. It is mourning the loss of its young. Have you been taking lessons in Bird from Thorgil?"

Jack grimaced ruefully. "No, sir. The last thing Thorgil wants is to admit she understands it."

"Insufferable child. She's made a career of pigheadedness. Stay and help Aiden, lad. I'll expect you for dinner." The old man collected the harp and the basket of mushrooms and strode away, leaving Jack uncertain of what he was supposed to do next.

"I'd like it very much if you would sing for me," Brother Aiden said shyly. "My heart is heavy over the loss of those poor men." The little monk's eyes were filled with tears, and Jack knew he was remembering his own escape from the Forest Lord or Satan or whoever led the pack of hunters.

And so Jack sang of the earth when it was gentle and not wild, of the harp in the trees when wind played among the leaves. He sang of fair meadows where deer brought their young, knowing them to be safe, and of the cry of larks tumbling in High Heaven.

Gradually, Brother Aiden's face cleared and he looked hopeful again. "Thank you," he said. "Your voice is wonderfully healing, almost as fine as Pega's." He began once again to bless the raw wound in the forest.

Jack gazed down the passage, thinking, *This is the path Odin took with his warriors, if Thorgil saw truly. They passed her by, ignoring one who wanted to join them and taking Gog and Magog, who didn't. Why does everyone always compare me with Pega?*

Feeling slightly nettled, he bade good-bye to Brother Aiden and went home to see whether he could help with repairs.

Chapter Four

SEAFARER

The last rays of sunlight caught on the wings of swallows as Jack returned to the Bard's house. The sea, still troubled by distant storms, was lined with foam. The air was beautifully clear, however, with every sound carrying for miles. Jack heard Brother Aiden's bell from the little beehive-shaped hut where he lived. It trembled like a plucked harp string before dying away into the deepening blue sky—as different from a cowbell as nightingales were from crows.

King Brutus had found it buried in an old chest at St. Filian's Monastery. Since the monastery already had a bell, and this one was too small for such a grand establishment, he'd sent it to the village. Brother Aiden was delighted.

Until a week ago, he'd made do with a rusty instrument that clanked rather than rang.

This was the first time Jack had heard it, and it filled him with a longing he didn't quite understand. It sounded again. Brother Aiden would be kneeling in prayer; the bell was to call whoever wished to join him. Jack thought it odd that sound traveled farther than sight, for Brother Aiden was too far away for Jack to see even the fire outside his hut.

Thorgil said that sounds never really died. She said the Northmen heard their dead calling to them on nights when lights danced in the sky. Jack had never seen such a thing and didn't want to.

The bell rang a third time, and from the sea came a terrifying wail. Jack's hand went to his knife. The cry faded to a sob and then ceased altogether. He waited tensely, scanning the distant waves. He saw a long, discolored patch of sea moving toward shore, and then it was gone.

Probably seaweed, thought Jack. Still, he watched until darkness forced him to go on.

Inside the Bard's house, a cheerful fire sprouted green, red, and yellow flames as it burned driftwood. An iron pot bubbled with the enticing smell of mushrooms. Jack sighed with happiness. Everything was as it should be. The painted birds on the walls moved in the firelight, and a painted breeze appeared to ruffle the leaves of a flower garden.

Jack was about to ask the Bard whether he'd heard the cry when he saw the old man feeding scraps of dried fish to a large, bedraggled-looking bird. Thorgil was squatting beside him, engaged in conversation—to go by the croaks—with the bird. She didn't look pleased, and Jack guessed the Bard had bullied her into performing.

"Look what the storm has washed up," said the Bard. "Fetch us some of that stew while I put our friend to bed." He urged the bird to an alcove filled with straw. Jack noticed that it hopped unsteadily and that one of its wings dragged on the floor.

"What is it?" he asked.

"A great wonder," said the Bard enthusiastically. "He's called a—what did you say, Thorgil?"

"An albatross," she replied sullenly. She was pale and her face was badly bruised, but she seemed to have recovered.

"He's a visitor from the far south, and I do mean far," said the old man. "Imagine! There's a place even I haven't heard of. It's a land full of ice mountains that groan all winter long and break off into islands when summer comes."

"It sounds like Jotunheim," said Jack.

"I thought so at first, but Seafarer—that's the bird's name—says it's home only to birds and seals. It's so remote, I can't understand his speech. Fortunately, Thorgil can."

Jack took down a stack of bowls, placed a chunk of bread in each, and ladled stew over it.

"The poor fellow took a beating in the storm. Dislocated his wing. Thorgil found him struggling in the surf and carried him here." The Bard was delighted with his new guest, and Jack knew it was due to tales of a new land beyond the sky's reach. The Bard was always interested in new things.

Jack and Thorgil sat on the floor to eat. "I've never seen such a big seagull," the boy said, watching the bird fidget in his alcove.

"I haven't seen anything like him either," the old man said. "He wasn't at all friendly when he arrived—tried to peck out my eyes—but I soon put him straight with a fear-spell. We have an uneasy truce now. He needs my help, and I'll only give it if he behaves."

"I'd like to learn a fear-spell," said Thorgil, spearing a morsel of stew meat with her knife.

"I wouldn't dream of teaching it to you," the Bard said. "You'd terrorize the village every time you got into a snit."

The albatross clacked his beak. Jack held out a chunk of meat at arm's length, and the bird seized it before retreating back into the shadows.

"He trusts you," the old man said approvingly. "That's very interesting. Your powers have grown since you lost your staff."

Jack concentrated on his food. It still upset him to think about the staff. He'd cut it from a branch of Yggdrassil. It had been a true bard's staff, except that he'd had no time to learn its powers. He'd lain it across the barrier between life and Unlife to lift a curse from Din Guardi. Now it was gone, ashes on the wind.

"That deed opened a door into the unseen world for you," the Bard said, correctly guessing what was on Jack's mind. "Sacrifice, done rightly, is stronger than magic."

"Northmen sacrifice thralls," Thorgil said. "I never saw it do *them* any good."

"I'm not talking about the slaughter of hapless slaves. I'm speaking of a man who lays down his life so that others may live, or a woman who starves herself to keep food in her children's mouths."

"You sound like one of those mewling Christians," sneered the shield maiden. Jack raised his hand to caution silence. The Bard was slow to anger, but you didn't want to push him too far.

"I wouldn't dismiss Christians so readily, Thorgil Small-Brain," the old man said. "They may seem weak, and some of them are certainly rogues, but they have prevailed in situations that would slow the blood of the bravest hero."

"They're only fit to pull dung carts," Thorgil said carelessly. "The future belongs to the strong."

"That belief is why Northmen are going to disappear."

"Disappear!" Thorgil sprang to her feet. "My people will never be defeated! Our fame will never die!"

For an instant the hearth flames blazed and the shadow behind the Bard loomed. Thorgil sank to the floor, her eyes wide and frightened. The albatross moaned, and Jack was suddenly clammy with sweat. Then the flames subsided. The Bard was a kindly old man again, normal-size and a bit frail.

"Good fear-spell," murmured Jack.

"Thank you," said the old man. "I learned that one from a sea hag in the Orkney Islands."

The shield maiden struggled to a sitting position with as much grace as she could manage. Her eyes shot daggers at the Bard.

He continued, ignoring her. "Many strange things have been happening: the Wild Hunt, the loss of Gog and Magog, the arrival of Seafarer, that cry from the sea."

"You heard it too, sir?" Jack said.

"I could hardly miss it. I was on the cliff watching waves," the Bard said. "I was rather hoping to find another albatross. The cry came from directly below, and I was about to climb down to investigate when I saw a creature poke its head out of the water. It was as long as a Northman ship with a huge tail curled beneath it."

"A sea serpent?" cried Jack.

"A much rarer being. It was a Pictish beast."

"Now I know we're in for bad luck," Jack said.

"For shame," the old man scolded. "Not everything Pictish is bad. At any rate, this beast seemed drawn to whatever screamed. It made straight for shore, and I ran for my staff. You can never be quite sure whether a monster is hungry or merely curious. It was gone by the time I returned."

"And the creature below?"

"I couldn't find it," said the Bard. "You know, I've heard that cry before, but I can't quite remember where."

"We should hunt for it," said Thorgil. She drew her knife and held it up in the firelight. Her movements were much more polished after a year practicing with her left hand, but she would never regain her earlier skill. Her right hand looked completely normal, apart from a strange silvery hue, but it was as useless as a block of wood.

Jack wasn't sure whether Thorgil's paralysis was of the

mind or whether some dire ill had passed to her from the demon she had attacked. The Bard had tried to heal her. Even Brother Aiden (when she was asleep and couldn't spit at him) had prayed over her. Nothing helped.

"It's as black as a lead mine out there," the Bard said. "It's far more likely something would find *you* before you stumbled over *it*. Besides, I have new magic for you to learn, Jack."

The boy was elated. At last! Months had passed with only a repetition of the spells he'd already studied. He'd called up fire, calmed winds, and practiced farseeing, which had shown him meaningless beaches and gloomy rocks. The only new spell he'd learned was to separate grain from grit by calling to the life force within the kernels.

"What about me? Why can't I learn magic?" demanded Thorgil.

"I haven't chosen you as my apprentice, but if it's any consolation, you already have some powers. When you tasted dragon's blood, you became part dragon. That's why you can understand the languages of the air."

"Part dragon?" Thorgil said, interested. Jack could almost see the thought passing through her mind. If she were part dragon, she could fly over her enemies and blast them with fire.

The Bard smiled grimly, showing that he, too, understood. "Don't expect to sprout wings anytime soon. You've been given a useful skill, and through the sacrifice of your hand, I suspect you've gained even more. You might even turn into a healer."

Jack hooted with laughter before he could stop himself.

"Your wits have turned," Thorgil snarled. "I am no healer to mumble charms over weaklings. I'm a shield maiden and will fall in battle holding my sword, even if it's in the wrong hand."

"That path is no longer open to you," the Bard said. "I've seen how the horses come to you and follow your every command. I heard how you lifted that crow from the mud and breathed hope into his wings."

"What crow? Nobody saw me. I didn't do it," cried Thorgil.

"He came by the house and told me about it," the Bard said, amused.

"He was a follower of Odin. It was the least I could do," the shield maiden conceded.

"You needn't be ashamed of kindness, Thorgil. Even the great Olaf One-Brow once stretched out his hand to a girl-child nobody wanted. Now, I need to teach Jack a sleep-spell. We must put Seafarer's wing right before it sets permanently in that position."

"I could learn that," Thorgil said eagerly.

"No, you couldn't, but you can haul Seafarer out of his nest for me."

Seafarer was in no mood to let anyone touch his wing. He snapped and screamed when Thorgil tried to move him. In the end she had to lure him out with a trail of dried fish. He gulped down the treats, keeping one beady eye on the humans, and kept up a burble of hisses and grunts. Even

Jack, who knew no Bird, recognized them as insults.

"Now comes the hard part," the old man said when the bird had settled far from its lair. "I must pull Seafarer's dislocated wing back into line, and it's going to hurt like the very blazes. I don't dare give him poppy. The infusion is too strong and might kill him."

"Should I hold him down?" said Jack, looking doubtfully at the sharp beak.

"Too dangerous. Birds, even intelligent ones, panic when you try to restrain them. Thorgil, you must distract Seafarer. We need him relaxed while the spell works its power. Ask him about the land he came from. You can tell him about the Northland too."

Thorgil grinned, and Jack knew she had every intention of learning the new spell. She began speaking in Bird. It was a strange language full of groans and clicks, and Seafarer answered her with croaks and sighs. Sometimes his voice seemed to come from a great distance, like something you might hear on a night wind. Sometimes it boomed close to your ear. Whatever they were talking about, the great bird was entranced by it.

"Now, lad. Observe my hands," the Bard said quietly. "I'm going to weave a spell in the air as well as with words. Seafarer can't understand human speech, but with animals, music is far more important. Listen to the tone of my voice."

The Bard settled in front of Seafarer and began to move his hands like seaweed undulating in a gentle sea. It was a beautiful motion, so fluid and peaceful that you wanted to watch it for hours. Jack thought it was like music made visible. The Bard began to speak in a drowsy voice that made the boy feel warm and safe inside. The words didn't matter. The Bard could have been saying "tra-la-la" for all the difference it made, but in fact he was actually making sense:

You are floating on a still pond . . . floating . . . floating. . . . It's the softest bed you have ever known . . . floating . . . float-ing . . . softer than your mother's wings . . . safer than your father's shadow. . . . Nothing can harm you. . . . All is peaceful . . . floating. . . . You are getting very sleeeeepy. . . .

Jack's head jerked up. His vision had blurred and he had to force himself to focus. For an instant the Bard's hands looked *exactly* like seaweed, and Jack knew the magic was overwhelming him. He pinched himself viciously.

Seafarer sat with his beak half open. He slowly blinked that double blink of seabirds when a milky skin slides sideways before the eyelids come down. His legs gradually collapsed until he was sitting on the floor. Jack pinched himself again. *Warm . . . safe . . . floating . . .*

Thorgil fell over with a thump. She was going to have another bruise, Jack thought distantly, trying to keep his wits about him. Then Seafarer fell over.

"Quick, before he wakes," murmured the Bard. "Hold his good wing close to his body." Jack obeyed, and all the while the slow music of the old man's voice wove itself around them like a vast, shining coil. The Bard grasped the other wing and flexed it with a quick movement. There was an audible click. Seafarer shrieked, but his eyes stayed closed. He lay on the floor, sound asleep.

"That went well," the Bard said briskly, dusting off his hands. "I'll let him rest awhile. You might turn Thorgil on her side, lad. She's facedown, and if I'm not mistaken, she's got a straw up her nose."

Chapter Five

A SCREAM IN THE DARK

Thorgil did have a nasty bruise in the morning, but what annoyed her more was not remembering the sleep-spell.

"Some people can do it and others are unable to resist the magic," the Bard explained.

"I can resist anything," the shield maiden protested.

"We're all aware of that, but the sleep-spell is out of your control. It's just how things are. You couldn't fly, no matter how hard you flapped your arms."

"Olaf used to say that when I tried to make poetry," Thorgil said. "But after I drank from Mimir's Well, I could do it as well as Jack."

"That's what *you* think," said Jack. He was delighted by

Thorgil's failure. He remembered the music of the spell perfectly and was itching to try it out on a black-faced sheep.

"Well, I'm not giving up," she said. "Think how useful it would be to send your enemies to sleep—though it lacks honor to slay a sleeping man."

The Bard shook his head. "Your motives, as usual, are appalling. Kindly tell Seafarer that he isn't allowed to fly for a few days." The bird had retreated to the alcove after being awoken, and they could hear him grumbling inside.

Thorgil knelt and spoke to the creature. "He isn't happy about staying here. He says he must go in search of a mate."

"Where's he going to do that?" inquired the Bard.

Thorgil translated. "He says he saw lady birds south of here that were almost the right shape. They were a little small, though."

"*Almost*? Wolves are *almost* the same shape as lambs. Did he have any success?"

"No, but he's hopeful."

"Well, explain that his wing is extremely weak and he'll have to wait. Now, I need you two to gather plants in the meadows. I want comfrey, feverfew, mint, and valerian. If you run across henbane, I can use that, too. Mind, you keep it separate from the rest. Mugwort is always welcome. Look for it on sandy soil."

Jack fetched collecting bags, and soon they were walking through fields to the wild lands that lay beyond the village. The air was warm, and villagers were already planting stands of peas and beans for winter. Thorgil found a patch of wild lettuce and Jack gathered comfrey. By now they were at the edge of the hazel wood.

"Phew! It's hot," exclaimed Thorgil, throwing her bags down among the bluebells. She lay flat on her stomach by a stream and splashed water into her mouth. "Mmm! This tastes as good as mead!"

Jack shared out oatcakes left over from breakfast. "The Bard says we're going to Bebba's Town in a few weeks."

"I know. We have to buy grain. Isn't the light through those leaves marvelous? And those butterflies are like white flowers fluttering in the air."

Jack braced himself for one of Thorgil's good moods. "I wonder how we'll get the grain back. The road is so full of potholes, you couldn't possibly drive a cart over it."

"The Bard says we'll hire a ship," the shield maiden said, sitting up. "Just think of having a deck beneath our feet again, the waves crashing against the prow, the wind howling about our ears! Do you remember the color of the sea in a storm, all gray and green with the foam blowing off the crests of the waves? You could almost see into the halls of Ran and Aegir," she said, naming the Northman sea gods. "Do you remember?"

"Yes," said Jack.

"Well, you don't seem happy about it."

"Who could be happy about drowning? It's the only way you can visit Ran and Aegir."

"That's not the point!" the shield maiden cried. "It's the

beauty of those colors! And the cold spray in your face. And the slosh of water around your boots. And the feel of the ship keeling over in a sharp wind. Olaf used to hand out coins when we were in danger of sinking, so we'd have a gift for Ran when we came to her halls. The sea kingdom isn't as glorious as Valhalla, but it isn't bad, either—"

"Thorgil," said Jack.

"Yes?"

"Stop babbling."

"I'm not babbling," she said, too happy to take offense. "Perhaps we'll hire a *knorr* in Bebba's Town. They're not handsome, but they hold a ton of supplies and they make the loveliest sound all night—*knorr, knorr, knorr.* A *drekar* would be even better."

"If the villagers saw a *drekar,* they'd run for the hills," Jack said.

"And so they should! A dragon ship full of berserkers— what could be prettier?" Thorgil smiled up at the sunlight, shining green through the leaves.

"In my opinion, a barge loaded with grain."

"You're as dull as a slug. Tell me, Jack. I've been puzzling about something that happened during the storm. I remember climbing out of the sheep byre and the hailstones striking me. Then I was lying in the field with the dead ewe at my side. You lifted me up—"

"The mind can plays tricks in an emergency," said Jack, hoping she didn't remember what he'd said.

"I know, but it seemed I heard the words—clear as clear—

'Oh, my dear. My love.' Isn't that funny? I must have imagined it."

"You must have. The storm was too loud to hear anything."

"The words were really distinct."

"We should start collecting again," said Jack.

Thorgil made a face at him. "Oh, very well! But I want a bath in that stream first." She disappeared behind a clump of bushes, and soon Jack heard her splashing around.

He turned his back and occupied himself with whittling a Y-shaped stick. Thorgil emerged a few minutes later, having donned her clothes again.

"This is a dowsing rod," Jack explained, handing it to her. "It has to be made from hazel wood because hazels have their roots in the life force. You hold the dowser by its arms, see, and when you're near an underground stream, it dips down."

"You can't go five steps without finding a stream here," said Thorgil, laughing, "but thanks. I'll keep it for later." She tucked it into her belt. "Would you like to learn Bird?"

"Why—yes," said Jack, astounded. Thorgil had actually thanked him! She'd also offered to share her lore. And taken a bath without being threatened. She *was* in a rare mood.

"Very well: This is how you say hello to Seafarer. First, you have to compliment his wings." Thorgil cawed—something between a groan and a shriek.

Jack attempted to copy it and was corrected until he got it right. "Why do you have to compliment him?" he asked.

"Albatrosses are proud of their wings, and if you don't

praise them, they'll attack you. These are the words for getting him into the alcove. You offer to preen his feathers, but you don't have to follow through. It's a catchall phrase for 'please settle down.'" She produced a low burble, followed by a sigh.

Jack learned this one easily, for it was close to music. "How do you know this? Even the Bard had never seen an albatross before."

"It's simply . . . part of me," Thorgil tried to explain. "Since tasting dragon blood, I've had a fellowship with the creatures of the air. When we first returned to Middle Earth, I had to concentrate very hard to understand birds, but with the passage of time, their voices have become clearer."

"That's a wonderful gift," said Jack enviously.

"No, it isn't." Thorgil plumped down on the grass. A pair of thrushes caroled to each other from the trees, and Jack wondered what they were saying. All at once he became aware of the complex lives threading in and out of the hazel wood—the moles blindly pushing dirt, the fish with their mouths pointed upstream, the dragonflies darting through dappled sunlight. The wood was like one creature whose mind was bent to—what?

Thorgil interrupted his thoughts. "At first it was fun, knowing something others didn't. Then it became a curse. Birds never shut up, you know. You can't imagine how horrible it is, waking up every morning to yammering about earthworms and itchy feathers."

Her head drooped. She looked so woebegone that Jack

forgot her dislike of sympathy and impulsively put his arm around her.

"Don't pity me!" Thorgil snarled, shoving him away so roughly, he banged his head into a tree.

"What's wrong with you! I'm only trying to be nice!" Jack said.

"You're treating me like a stupid girl."

"You are a girl," Jack said.

"I'm a shield maiden, not a sniveling Saxon cow."

"Why don't you stop yowling about how awful *my* people are and look at yourself," cried Jack, stung. "You have no more gratitude than a bog rat. You insult everyone six ways to Sunday."

"I don't lower my standards just because I live in a pigsty," said Thorgil haughtily.

"*Pigsty?* How dare you say that about my parents' house! I remember when you slept with dogs in the Northland because they were the only ones who'd have you."

"Even a Northland dog has more honor than a cringing Saxon."

"Really? Well, even a cringing Saxon dog has more honor than a half-Northman thrall!" shouted Jack.

"I'm not a thrall!" shrieked Thorgil, grabbing her collecting bags. "And I'm never entering your parents' house again!" She stormed off before he could reply.

So much for Thorgil's good mood, thought Jack, rubbing his bruised head. He went off in a different direction.

❖ ❖ ❖

After a while Jack's temper cooled and he began to regret his hasty words. But Thorgil was so infuriating! Even Olaf One-Brow used to knock her flat when she got into a snit. Of course, Olaf had knocked everyone flat, including Jack, at one time or another. It was the Northman way.

Jack sat in the shade of a tree trying to regain that odd impression he'd had earlier, of the woodland being a creature with one mind. Perhaps it was the pooling of the life force, or perhaps—a cold finger touched Jack's heart—the hazel wood was a corner of the realm where the Forest Lord held sway. He remembered the subtle whispering among the leaves in that realm and the way a root humped up to catch an unwary ankle.

This isn't the Land of the Silver Apples. I'm being foolish, he thought. The Forest Lord would never have allowed his trees to be cut back as these were. This was Jack's country, where folks were sensible. No Pictish gods here.

He cleared his mind to call to the life force. *Come to me. Reveal yourself. Show me the paths by which you travel.* The wood remained as before, with birds darting to and fro, frogs cheeping, and spiders connecting the spokes of their webs in the branches above.

The sun began to incline to the west, and Jack remembered he hadn't collected the herbs the Bard had asked for. He began exploring along the border between the hazel wood and the oak forest. He found a bed of mint and chewed a few leaves to stave off hunger pangs. He gathered elecampane for coughs, fennel for stomachaches, and valerian for troubled sleep. He picked mugwort to use against the flying venom that traveled from house to house, bringing fever in its wake.

Under a birch tree Jack discovered *atterswam*, a beautiful but very dangerous mushroom. It had a bright red cap spotted with white, and the Bard said Northmen sometimes used it to go berserk. "It gives them visions, and occasionally it kills them," the old man had said. "Too bad it doesn't work that way more often." Jack wondered whether Thorgil had ever taken it.

Where was she? She'd make good on her threat to stay away from Jack's house. Once declared, a threat was as good as an oath with her. He'd have to explain to Mother and Father why she didn't visit anymore, but they'd be pleased. Everyone was growing weary of Thorgil's constant battles with the Tanner girls. Where would she go? John the Fletcher might put her up in his barn. He admired her skill with horses. When winter came, she'd have to move in with the Bard.

Jack collected a few of the red mushrooms, making sure to keep them separate from everything else. A squirrel scampered up a tree with an *atterswam* in its mouth. Jack threw a stick at it, trying to make it drop the poisonous fungus, but the squirrel climbed beyond his reach and continued eating. *Perhaps squirrels like visions,* he thought, hoping the creature wouldn't fall dead from its perch.

The sun slid behind the hills. Darkness flowed into the woodland and a mist fumed from the boggy ground, making the trees appear as though they were floating in a white sea.

And suddenly, the birds stopped calling. The boisterous chatter that accompanied sunset vanished as though an unseen enemy had appeared under the trees. Dusk became darker, cold deeper, earth danker.

Jack stood perfectly still.

Was it a wolf? Or, God forbid, a bear? Oddly enough, he smelled seaweed, though the breeze had died. *Has one of those paths between the worlds opened?* Jack thought, both excited and afraid. If so, what had stepped through?

A cold presence spread through the mist. It enveloped him with such malevolent force that he gasped and almost dropped the collecting bags. Such chill he had not felt since confronting Frith Half-Troll. It was like a door into the heart of winter. His body grew numb and his mind went blank.

In the distance Brother Aiden rang the prayer bell. It was a frail sound, hardly louder than the call of a chick, but so pure that it pierced through the gathering gloom. The spell was broken. Jack clutched the bags to his chest and fled down a long, pale avenue of bluebells, now gray with twilight. Mist swirled about his legs. His heartbeat thundered in his ears. His feet sank into pockets of mud, almost sending him sprawling, but he kept going until he broke out into a field.

He ran until the hazel wood was only a shadow against the oak forest. The sky outside was still blue, with wisps of clouds catching the sunlight from beyond the hills. The field, although ruined by the storm, had a normal, friendly look about it. Jack bent over to catch his breath.

Brother Aiden struck the bell a second time, and a scream erupted from the woodland. It went on longer than any creature could possibly scream and finally died away into a low, shuddering moan. But by that time Jack was at the other end of the field. By his side ran a fallow doe so panicked that she paid no attention to the human within arm's reach of her.

They both collapsed at the same time. The doe turned dark, appealing eyes toward him, and he put his hand on her warm flank. "It's all right," he whispered. "It will not come into the light." He fervently hoped this was true. She stared at him, her sides heaving with terror. Brother Aiden's bell sounded again, and both boy and deer turned toward the woodland.

But nothing further happened. After a while the doe rose to her feet and walked away. Jack rose too, perplexed about what he should do. Normally, he would return to the Bard's house. The old man was waiting for his herbs, and Thorgil might be there too.

Jack looked back at the forest. The shield maiden had been headed toward the fields when he last saw her. She would have put distance between herself and him, and that meant she would have gone to the sea. Thorgil always went there when she was upset. When she recovered, she would probably return to the Bard.

The thought of the Roman house and the old man waiting inside was very attractive. That scream, though, had been aroused by Brother Aiden's bell. Last night the creature had been on the beach. Tonight it was in the woodland, much closer to Brother Aiden's hut. Its intent was most certainly evil. The cry from the woodland had been steeped in hatred. It wasn't the hunger call of a predator, but the voice of something exiled from all earthly joy.

Sighing, Jack turned toward the village. He ran through the darkening meadows, past outlying sheds and houses, until he saw the little monk kneeling by a fire outside his hut.

Chapter Six

FAIR LAMENTING

Jack knelt too, not wishing to disturb Brother Aiden. He couldn't understand the prayers, yet the words soothed him. Pega often said it felt like summer near the monk's hut, no matter how cold the winds were elsewhere. There was something so angelic about Brother Aiden that even the frost giants walked carefully around his dwelling.

Now Jack felt a calm descend on him, as though the creature in the hazel wood hadn't been so terrible after all. It was merely a lost wolf howling for its companions or a seal that had wandered from the coast. He *had* smelled seaweed.

"I should teach you Latin," said Brother Aiden. "Then you might not fall asleep during prayers."

Jack sat up abruptly. "I'm sorry, sir. It's the warmth and quiet. I've been working all day."

"No offense taken," the monk said cheerfully. "I'd invite you in, but there's no room." He waved at the door of his beehive-shaped hut. Jack had been in there once or twice and knew it was hardly more than a man-made cave. There was space for a tiny altar, a storage area for parchment and ink, and a heap of dried heather for a bed. Anyone taller than the monk couldn't even stand up.

A table and stool sat outside where Brother Aiden illustrated his manuscripts. Dishware and food were stowed in a heavy wooden chest beneath. The bell was suspended from a wooden frame near the fire.

"I can offer you some of Pega's excellent eel-and-turnip stew," the monk said, laying out bowls, spoons, and a knife for himself. Jack, like most villagers, carried his own knife. His was especially fine, for it had been a gift from the Mountain Queen in Jotunheim. "Let me ring that bell a last time—good heavens! What's the matter?" Brother Aiden cried as Jack grabbed his arm.

"Begging your pardon, sir," the boy said, "but you can't do that. At least not tonight."

"Why ever not?" said the monk, rubbing his arm.

"I—I'm not sure. Only, there's a *thing* in the woods that screams when you toll it. Last night the thing was on the beach, and now it's closer. We'd better ask the Bard what to do."

"Have something to eat, lad. You can explain more clearly

on a full stomach." Brother Aiden ladled stew from a pot on the fire and unwrapped a small loaf of bread. "I can't imagine anyone screaming about that bell. It has such a lovely tone that it has been given its own name: Fair Lamenting."

"Fair Lamenting?" said Jack, his mouth muffled by bread. "That doesn't sound good."

"It depends on what you're lamenting," said Brother Aiden. He took less stew than Jack and only the thinnest slice of bread. "There's a longing that comes over you when you see something so perfect, it must be divine—a lamb standing on its feet for the first time, for example, or a swallow diving out of a cloud. The moment is so beautiful that you want to hold on to it forever, but you can't. And so you lament and feel joy at the same time."

Jack struggled to understand. It seemed yet another puzzle to do with happiness. He doubted whether Gog and Magog had done much "fair lamenting" when they mooed with the cows. For that matter, the cows seemed pretty happy too. There were no worries about whether the mooing was going to go on forever.

"What you really see is a glimpse of Heaven, for in Heaven such moments last forever," explained the monk. "The sound of Fair Lamenting reminds us of the joy that lies beyond the sorrow of this world. Did you know that this is the very bell St. Columba brought from Ireland?" Brother Aiden reverently lifted the instrument from its hook and set it on the table. "It's what drew the Picts from their hills."

"I heard that they swarmed out to kill St. Columba, and he

scared the daylights out of them by threatening to send them all mad," said Jack, who had been told this by hobgoblins.

Brother Aiden frowned. "I'm sure that's wrong. It doesn't sound saintly at all."

"Perhaps it's only a rumor," said Jack, who didn't want to upset the gentle monk. He explained about the monster in the hazel wood, but Brother Aiden didn't seem concerned.

"There are many poor beasts astray after that storm. I've been frightened myself by a cow bellowing for her calf. It's all too easy to deceive oneself, especially when it's dark and you're alone. Once when I was walking at night, I saw a pair of big, glowing, blue eyes by the side of the road."

"Crumbs! What did you do?" said Jack.

"There was precious little I could do. The moon had gone behind a cloud, and I could hardly see where to put my feet. I sent a silent prayer to St. Columba and edged forward, clutching the cross at my neck. Then—not five paces away—another pair of glowing eyes appeared on the other side of the road." Brother Aiden took a mouthful of bread and chewed slowly. He was almost as good a storyteller as the Bard and knew when to pause, to hook his audience.

Jack waited impatiently for the monk to swallow.

"I took a few more steps," Brother Aiden continued, "and what did I see but a *third* set of eyes squarely in the middle of the road. Would you like some cider? Your mother sent over a bag this morning."

"No! I mean no, thank you. Please tell me what happened," said Jack. The monk smiled happily.

"Well! I stood perfectly still, unable to go forward. If I turned away, the creatures might leap upon my back. I sent a prayer to St. Christopher, who protects travelers. Next, I commended my soul to Jesus, in case St. Christopher didn't come through. Someone must have been listening, though, for all at once the moon came out from behind the clouds. The road was bathed in beautiful light. And behold! The eyes disappeared. In their place were sheep—perfectly ordinary sheep. I had wandered into the middle of a flock. So you see, the mind plays tricks on us when we're frightened. I'm sure your creature is just as ordinary."

Jack stifled the urge to argue. He was unusually sensitive to the forces that lay beneath everyday life. Sometimes doing magic actually made him sick, and the Bard said that was because his defenses were too weak. It took years of training to endure some kinds of knowledge, and Jack had been exposed to it before he was ready. The malevolent hatred surrounding the strange beast had been very real. He didn't have to see it to know it was an enemy.

The boy tipped the bell on its side, being careful to muffle the clapper. It was a quadrangle with rounded corners, and it threw back the firelight with a reddish glow. In spite of its simple design, it had a richness that spoke of palaces and kings. "This *is* nice," he said.

"Bronze covered in gold," Brother Aiden said proudly. "Gives it that deep, musical tone."

"The clapper looks like iron," said Jack, moving it into the light.

"Very observant. Bronze would be too hard and would damage the bell."

"Why is it shaped like a fish?" the boy asked. For indeed, the long pendant was a magnificent work of art, with fins and scales and a pair of round, fishy eyes staring down at the mouth of the bell. It was slightly battered from use.

"Father Severus said it symbolized the church. Would you like more stew?"

"No, thank you," Jack said politely, though he could have cleaned out the pot. He knew the stew was meant for the monk's breakfast. They tidied up, Jack polishing the bowls with sand and Brother Aiden storing leftover food in the chest.

The moon, half full, washed the earth with enough pale light for Jack to make his way to the Bard's house. He gathered his belongings and replaced his knife in the scabbard that hung from his belt. "Why don't you come with me?" he suggested. "I know the Bard likes your company."

"I'll come in the morning," Brother Aiden said. "I've much to think about tonight. I must consider that scream you heard."

Jack looked up, startled. So the monk did suspect something he wasn't telling. "Are you safe here?" he said, suddenly aware of shadows all around and the distance to the nearest house.

"No one is entirely safe in this world," Brother Aiden said. "If God chooses to call me in the night, I hope I may answer bravely. I will stay. However, there's no point leading whatever-it-is into temptation. I'll take the bell inside with me, though the Lord knows where I'll find space for my head."

Jack looked back frequently as he made his way through the fields, to see whether the monk was still outside. He thought he saw the door of the hut close and the fire dim as though something had flitted in front of it. *Huge, glowing, blue eyes,* he thought, searching the darkness. *Why blue?* For some reason the color was the creepiest part of the story.

To the right of the path Jack saw long, gray breakers advance to the shore and withdraw. To the left was the black, meandering path of a stream. He smelled seaweed and meadowsweet and felt a fine salt mist. The sea was hidden on the last part of the trip, though he could hear it hissing and rattling over pebbles. At last he came to the Bard's house and entered its warmth gratefully.

"It's about time," complained the Bard, sitting by the fire with Seafarer at his feet. "I was about to send a bat to look for you. Where's Thorgil? Don't tell me she's off gathering moonbeams too."

"I warned you about picking fights," said the old man, fastening lengths of twine across the room. "She's like a ship without ballast, always at the mercy of the wind."

"I didn't pick the fight," Jack said sullenly, hanging herbs to dry on the lines. He'd described the events of the day, ending with the scream and the visit to Brother Aiden.

"No, but you kept it going. Only Freya knows where she's hiding out." The Bard opened the bag with the *atterswam* and sniffed. "Excellent! I meant to ask you to look for these." He threaded the mushrooms on a string.

"You aren't . . . planning to eat them?" Jack asked hesitantly. He remembered how the Northmen took them to go berserk.

"My stars, lad, I'm not insane. Once these are dried and powdered, they're going into one of my best potions: Beelzebub's Remedy Against Flies. I discovered the recipe while fumigating King Hrothgar's hall. You have no idea how nasty a place can get after a monster's been rampaging through it. Did I ever tell you how I saved Beowulf's life?"

"Yes, sir," said Jack. He liked the story, but he was more interested in *atterswam* now.

"Hrothgar nailed the monster's arm to the wall as a kind of trophy. Foolish man! It attracted flies like you wouldn't believe. I went out to the forest for fresh air, and what did I come across but a patch of *atterswam*? As I watched, a fly settled on one of the caps. One minute later it keeled over dead. That was all the hint I needed. I mashed up the mushrooms in milk, soaked balls of wool in the mixture, and hung them from the ceiling of Hrothgar's hall. You know how flies like to circle around the center of a room. When they get tired, it's natural for them to land on the nearest resting place, but they only land once on Beelzebub's Remedy."

"That's brilliant," said Jack.

"Yes, it is. I used to sell the potion as Dragon Tongue's Revenge, but Brother Aiden suggested the other name. He thought Beelzebub would appeal more to Christians."

Jack helped himself to a bowl of stew from the Bard's constantly replenished pot. After a second (and larger) dinner, he swept the floor and laid out a bed by the door. He fluffed up the straw in the Bard's truckle bed at the far end of the house. This resembled an oval coil of rope, and the old man fitted himself inside as snugly as a cat in a basket.

But the Bard wasn't ready to sleep yet. "Shoo Seafarer into his alcove. We have one last chore to perform."

Jack reproduced the burble/hiss Thorgil had taught him. It must have been correct, because the great seabird warbled pleasantly before ambling off to bed.

"It seems you didn't spend the entire day fighting with Thorgil," the Bard observed.

"That's probably the last thing she'll ever teach me," Jack said.

"Don't count your dragons before they're hatched. She may be less angry than you expect." The Bard unpacked a metal flute from a chest. Jack had seen ones made of wood, but this was crafted with far more artistry.

"It looks like the clapper in Brother Aiden's bell," the boy said, wondering. The same fins and scales decorated the sides, and the same round eyes gazed at the world from behind a wide, fishy mouth.

"Ah! So you had a look at that," said the Bard. "I suppose Aiden told you it's a symbol of the church. He's wrong. It's the salmon that spends half the year in the Islands of the Blessed and returns to the pools of its youth in the fall. Some call it the Salmon of Knowledge, for it knows the pathways between this world and the next."

"Brother Aiden says the bell is called 'Fair Lamenting.' When people hear it they are reminded of Heaven," Jack said.

"It reminds them of what lies beyond the setting sun. Call it Heaven if you like." The Bard polished the flute with the hem of his robe. "The bell was named Fair Lamenting long before any monk set foot in Ireland. It was made for Amergin, the founder of my order. Through time, it came to St. Columba, who was top of his class for that year."

"St. Columba was a bard?" said Jack.

"One of the best. It was he who moved my school to the Vale of Song to protect it from Christians. He himself became a Christian, yet he did not entirely forget the ancient lore. He could call up winds and calm storms, draw water from the earth, and speak to animals. When he was old, a white horse came to him and laid its head against his breast. Then he knew that the wind blew to the west and that it was time to go. It is said that St. Brendan the Navigator took him to the Islands of the Blessed."

For a moment Jack could find nothing to say. The vision of the horse saluting the old bard moved him in a way he couldn't explain. In his mind he saw the ship waiting to bear St. Columba away. It would be a humble vessel, as befitted a Christian saint, but its place in the sea would be assured.

"I thought . . . saints went to Heaven," he said at last.

"Perhaps they do. Eventually. But the Islands are a way

station for those who are not yet finished with the affairs of this world. The old gods live there, as do the great heroes and heroines. Amergin is there, unless he sought rebirth. Now, it's getting late and we have work to do."

They went outside. "Cast your mind into the wind," commanded the old man. "Feel the lives in the air."

The boy had often followed birds in their flight, sensing the steady beat of their wings. He had amused himself by making them swoop and turn. He could even, though this was forbidden, have called a fat duck down to its death. Now he searched the black sky for whatever might dwell within. High above he detected a skein of geese. Lower down an owl coasted the breeze, its eyes scanning for mice. And lower still—

Jack heard a thin, peeping call, and his attention wavered enough to see the Bard blowing on the flute.

Eee eee eee, it went. A simple call and yet not simple. It had layers and layers of meaning, the same way a leaf-stained pond reveals first the surface and then more depths as one continues to gaze. *Eee eee eee* went the air from a hundred different places.

And suddenly the sky was full of bats swirling and dipping around the old man. The Bard played his flute, and the bats answered. Jack could detect variations of pitch and intensity in the cries, but he had no idea what they meant.

The Bard put down the flute. With a dry rustle the bats dispersed, and in an instant they had disappeared. "They've gone in search of Thorgil," the old man explained. "I'll leave the door ajar in case one of them comes back."

"Is that what the flute is for? To call bats?" whispered Jack. He wasn't sure why he was whispering.

"You can call many things with it, some of which you would not care to meet. On the way to Bebba's Town I'll show you some of its uses." The old man said nothing more, but Jack was elated. He was going to learn new magic. He'd already learned a few words in Bird and how to cast a sleep-spell. Things were looking up.

He shifted his bed to the other end of the house. He didn't care to spend the night next to an open door with bats coming and going and a monster wandering in the hazel wood. He kept his knife ready and had his eye on a hefty branch smoldering in the fire in case of an emergency.

But the Bard slept peacefully all night and woke refreshed, just as Jack finally managed to close his eyes.

Chapter Seven

THE MERMAID

It was Brother Aiden who roused Jack some time later. The little monk banged the door open with his foot because his hands were holding the bell. "There *is* a monster," he said, panting as he placed the bell on the floor. "Something killed John the Fletcher's fighting cock and all the hens. The chief found a dead lamb outside his door."

"Sit down and catch your breath," the Bard ordered. "Jack, fetch our guest some cider."

The boy sat up and brushed bits of straw from his hair. He quickly found a bag and filled a cup.

The monk downed the cider and held out his cup for more. "I could take a bath in this, I'm that lathered. Jack was right about a creature attracted to Fair Lamenting. It was all over the village hunting for it."

"Or the attack was a coincidence. The damage could have been done by a bear," suggested the Bard.

"A bear kills to eat. This thing tore animals to shreds and scattered the remains. Thank God it didn't find a child." Brother Aiden put the cup down. "The chief has ordered women and children to stay indoors, and John the Fletcher is organizing a hunt party."

"They won't find anything," the Bard said quietly. A significant look passed between him and the monk.

"Thorgil!" cried Jack. "She was out all night!"

"She's fine," the old man assured him. "A crow spied her early this morning, sitting on a beach."

"I'll look for her."

"She'll come when she's ready," the Bard said firmly. "Now, Aiden, let's discuss this monster of yours."

Jack was torn. He wanted to know about the monster, but he was worried about Thorgil. She had to be very cold and hungry. She couldn't even start a fire with that paralyzed hand of hers.

"Stop fidgeting, lad. She's guarded by the rune of protection," the old man said. "Now, to begin—"

The rune only helps you endure pain. It doesn't save you from it, Jack thought bitterly, remembering the blows he'd received from Olaf One-Brow.

"—something was awakened by Fair Lamenting that should have remained asleep."

"I don't know how it could have heard the bell so far away, or why it chose this moment to emerge," argued Brother Aiden.

It? thought Jack. *What on earth is he talking about?*

"The bell of Amergin is heard in all worlds, and remember, it hadn't been used for a long time," said the Bard. He set the bell upright and a faint chime sounded. All three listeners flinched. "I'll have to wrap this in wool."

"Father Severus has much to answer for," Brother Aiden said sadly.

"Indeed he does. For one thing, he should have left the bell on Grim's Island."

Grim's Island! Where's that? thought Jack.

The little monk sighed, running his hand over the bright gold of Fair Lamenting. "The abbot himself insisted on bringing the bell. Remember, it had been owned by blessed St. Columba."

"And hidden by him," reminded the Bard.

"Yet Fair Lamenting was one of the few things to survive the destruction of the Holy Isle," said Brother Aiden. "Surely that means the bell is holy. Who could have guessed it would travel the long miles?"

"They say such beings can swim through rock," said the Bard.

Jack couldn't hold it in any longer. "What are you talking about? What's 'it'? Where's Grim's Island? How can anything swim through rock?" He looked down, his face hot with embarrassment. The Bard had often lectured him about demanding quick answers. Most things worth knowing took time, the old man said. One had to wait, let the answer reveal itself. Forcing an explanation before it was ready was like picking an apple blossom and expecting it to taste like an apple.

"I'm surprised you waited this long," commented the Bard. "I could see the questions piling up, but for once, I sympathize. This is a secret we've kept too long, and we must move swiftly to contain the damage." The old man sat down on the chest where he stored the silver flute. "You go first, Aiden. You're the one he trusted with the tale."

"You must understand that Father Severus is the most unselfish man alive," began Brother Aiden. "He has done many, many acts of kindness."

Jack nodded. He remembered the gloomy priest in Olaf One-Brow's ship lecturing everyone about sin and later giving tongue-lashings to the elves (who thought it great fun). But the man had shown compassion for three imprisoned children. Without him they would have died.

"In other circumstances Father Severus could have been a great king," the monk said. "He inspires obedience. People follow his orders without question."

Jack recalled the wicked monks of St. Filian's cringing before Father Severus like whipped hounds. The citizens of Bebba's Town accepted his leadership instantly and thus obeyed his order to make Brutus their king. Without the priest's guidance Brutus would never have accomplished anything except to look adorable.

"Let's not forget, your hero has a few blind spots," said the Bard.

Brother Aiden smiled apologetically and continued his tale. "Grim's Island is a cold, nasty place and so far north that sunlight barely touches it in winter. In summer it's either shrouded in fog or lashed by arctic storms. But to Father Severus it was a paradise for the soul. He had grown weary of the soft life on the Holy Isle."

"I thought the monks worked hard," said Jack.

"Oh, we did. When we weren't digging rocks out of fields, we were repairing roofs, mending fences, and chasing sheep. We prayed seven times a day and twice in the middle of the night. We slept on the ground and in winter meditated in snowdrifts. But there were pleasures too." The little monk's eyes softened at the memory.

"I remember singing in the chapel, and the beautiful stained-glass window. I spent many happy hours mixing inks in the library—such beautiful colors! I rolled out sheets of gold to decorate the manuscripts. And the food! We had chicken on Sundays, and bread and beer every day. We made wonderful syllabubs for saint's days. As for the flummery . . ." Brother Aiden closed his eyes in ecstasy.

"The best kind, with nutmeg and cream," Jack murmured. "Father told me."

"I can see why Severus wanted to leave," the Bard remarked dryly.

"Yes, well, he's a very spiritual man," Brother Aiden said. "Grim's Island was made for heroes like him. It's the most forbidding chunk of rock imaginable, and even Father Severus was taken aback by the sheer bleakness of the place. He arrived in a little coracle with only a sack of seeds and a few tools. He had to hunt all over the island for loose stones to build a hut. The only trees were on a mountain in the middle and beyond his strength to reach.

"At night Father Severus curled up in a sandstone cave hardly big enough for a family of foxes. By day he toiled unceasingly, digging seedbeds. He lived on seaweed and limpets. He drank rainwater caught in the rocks.

"Winter came early. By then all the limpets had been eaten and the crops had withered from the cold. The hut was unfinished, and so Father Severus moved into the cave. He didn't expect to survive. This would have depressed a lesser man, but he looked upon it as a chance to enter Heaven early."

"I remember," said Jack. "He used to say the longer you lived, the more chance you had to sin."

"I'll never understand Christians," the Bard said, shaking his head.

"There was one chore Father Severus never neglected, no matter how ill he felt," said Brother Aiden. "He always said his prayers—seven times a day, though it was difficult to tell time in such darkness. In between, he chipped away at the sandstone to enlarge the cave. One day his knife lodged in a crack, and when he worked it loose, a rock fell out of the wall. Beyond was a small chamber.

"Father Severus felt something inside, wrapped in layers of wool. He hauled it out and carried it to the beach. It was one of those rare nights when the stars were not hidden by clouds and a full moon shone everywhere. The wool was of very fine quality, white in the moonlight and embroidered with gold. Father Severus unwrapped it and found—"

"Fair Lamenting," said Jack.

"Exactly. It was enfolded in a robe far too grand to have belonged to a monk."

"It was Columba's robe when he still ruled my order," said the Bard. "He was leaving his magic behind in a place where he thought it would do no harm. Little did he know a bumbling idiot would root it out."

"I would call it honest ignorance," Brother Aiden protested mildly, "which we all fall prey to—but to go on, Father Severus rang the bell. The sound rolled out over the sea, and all at once the waves became as smooth as glass. The wind died and a warmth like summer spread over the beach. It was as good as a feast to hear that music, Father Severus told me. All hunger, cold, and fear fled before it. In spite of his weakness he prayed for a long time, full of joy, and that night he slept like an infant. When he awoke, he found a fat salmon lying outside the cave, next to a stack of driftwood."

"It was his first encounter with the mermaid," said the Bard.

Jack came alert at once. He'd heard vague rumors of a scandal between Father Severus and a mermaid, but no one would tell him the details. Pega thought there had been a love affair. She guessed there was a family of little half-monks living on a beach somewhere.

"You can put that fevered idea out of your mind at once," the Bard said, reading his expression. "The truth is more dreary."

"For several weeks Father Severus woke to find food and kindling by the cave," said Brother Aiden. "His strength returned and so, gradually, did the sunlight. He went out to work on the hut and discovered, to his amazement, that it had been finished. It wasn't a beehive shape—more of a long spiral such as a sea snail might construct—but large enough to be comfortable.

"Father Severus assumed that angels were taking care of him. He built an altar of driftwood and thanked God for His mercy. Then he built a frame for the bell. When it rang, he heard a fair voice crying in the distance, but again he assumed it was an angel. This went on until spring, when it was time to plant.

"One afternoon, after hours of backbreaking labor, he turned gratefully to prayers. He rang the bell. It was answered, as usual, from the sea. He rang again, and there, just beyond the line of seaweed where the water grows deep, a creature rose from the waves. The sun was behind it, making it difficult to see, but it had the shape of a human. It raised an arm in greeting.

"It slithered over the seaweed, and when it reached the sand, it squirmed onward like a seal. Father Severus retreated. This was no angel, nor was it a seal, for its skin was as white as a child's and long, golden hair streamed from its head. Just below its waist the skin gave way to silver scales, and the rest of its body ended in a fish tail. Then Father Severus realized he was looking at a mermaid.

"The mermaid wriggled closer and, quick as thought, peeled off her fish scales. She dropped them as a lady might drop a skirt onto the sand and stood before him on two normal human legs—except her legs were thin and weak, for she'd had little use for walking. 'I have cared for you these long months,' she said. 'I love you. Come with me to my father's kingdom and we will be wed.'

"'*Retro Satanas!* Begone, Satan!' cried Father Severus, making the sign of exorcism.

"She came toward him, naked as an eel. 'I was drawn by Fair Lamenting, for it calls to the heart of all things. But when I saw you lying helpless in the cave, I knew my fate was entwined with yours. Come with me now. Beyond the waves lies a kingdom of surpassing beauty, where all is delight.'

"'*Retro! Retro!*' shouted Father Severus, trying to fend her off.

"She pursued him as best she could, but her feet were tender and she couldn't move swiftly. Father Severus climbed into the rocks where she couldn't reach him.

"'I shall return,' she conceded finally. 'For seven days I shall return, and on the eighth I shall take you, willing or no.' Then she wriggled back into her scales and swam off as swiftly as an otter."

Chapter Eight

THE *DRAUGR*

The late morning sunlight flooded into the open door of the Roman house and woke Seafarer in his alcove. The bird hopped to the floor, stretching his wings experimentally and making little grunts of pain. "You can't expect to get better in a day, my friend," said the Bard. He opened a bag of dried fish and threw some on the floor. Seafarer, with one beady eye fixed on Brother Aiden, edged forward and snatched up the treat.

The monk's mouth fell open in amazement. "This is true magic to tame such a creature."

"He's not tame. Watch your eyes," warned the Bard. The monk recoiled as the albatross made a vicious stab at him.

"Take our friend for a walk, Jack, before he does harm. Aiden and I will prepare breakfast." The boy sighed inwardly, but he knew better than to complain. The Bard could not be hurried and would ask Brother Aiden to finish the story in his own good time.

Jack and the bird walked along the cliff above the sea with Seafarer ahead, eagerly craning his neck at the bright blue sky. They sat down to rest after a while. The albatross screamed a challenge and a dozen seagulls tumbled off the cliff.

"Feels good, doesn't it?" Jack said companionably. "There's nothing like a good threat to start the day." Seafarer burbled back. The boy could smell oatcakes toasting in the distance. "I'd like to see a mermaid," he confided, "though I don't know about marrying one. Seems like you'd drown if you moved in with her. How do you think she breathes underwater?"

Seafarer made a sound between a purr and a croak. Jack was almost certain it was an answer to his question. Suddenly, the bird gave a whoop and soared off the cliff. He almost succeeded in flying, but his bad wing collapsed and he dropped. Jack slid down the rocks as fast as he could. At the bottom he saw the bird staggering drunkenly over the sand, shrieking and clacking his beak.

"You idiot!" cried Jack. "You'll ruin all our work!" And then he saw Thorgil running toward them. She was cawing in Bird and scattering her carrying bags on the beach. Presently, she met up with Seafarer and the two danced around each other in a frenzy of joy.

"Oh, Jack! You'll never guess what happened!" she yelled.

"Skakki is here! My brother! He dropped anchor at the inlet where we left you and Lucy. He's promised to take us to Bebba's Town."

"You say there's a *Northman ship* anchored near our village?" said Brother Aiden, his eyes wide with horror.

"Skakki has taken an oath not to pillage us," Thorgil said carelessly. "He might pick up a few slaves elsewhere, but I don't see the harm in it."

"No harm?" cried the monk. "Can you not hear the cries of children being torn from their parents' arms? Is your heart made of stone?"

"We don't usually steal children," said the shield maiden. "They're not durable, and anyhow, the market for brats is poor."

"Stop needling him," warned the Bard. Thorgil grinned evilly and fished an oatcake from the ashes. She held out a tidbit to Seafarer, who took it carefully. He had become wary of hot things.

"Has the whole crew returned?" said Jack. All at once a great longing swept over him to see the Northmen again.

"Most of them," the shield maiden said after cramming her mouth with oatcake. "There's Skakki and of course Rune, Sven the Vengeful, Eric Pretty-Face, and Eric the Rash. Schlaup is new. Eric Broad-Shoulders was eaten by trolls."

"Oh, my," said Brother Aiden.

"My foster father, Olaf One-Brow, tried a slice of troll once. He said it was nasty."

"Thorgil!" thundered the Bard. "Don't make me turn you into a frog."

She laughed and helped herself to another oatcake. Jack was delighted to see her so happy. She had apparently forgiven their quarrel in the hazel wood, for she'd greeted him with warmth. She had, as he'd suspected, fled to the beach. Once she began walking north, it seemed reasonable to continue. The waves calmed her mind and the smell of the sea raised her spirits. After a while she cut cross-country to the old Roman road and found her way to the inlet.

"Skakki never believed I was dead," Thorgil said. "Early this year he returned to the beach where he'd left me and saw my runes carved into a tree. When he couldn't find me, he guessed I'd gone to the only place where I might find welcome. He's much bigger. I thought he'd had his full growth, but he's practically a giant now. Like Olaf." A shadow crossed the shield maiden's face.

"So he's willing to take us to Bebba's Town," said Jack, to keep her from brooding.

"Once he's finished with business farther south. You don't want to know what that is, Brother Aiden—all right! I'll shut up!" Thorgil ducked as the Bard raised his staff.

They made a second breakfast with fresh bread from the village and a roast goose Thorgil had brought from her shipmates' dinner. Brother Aiden retold the tale of Fair Lamenting for her benefit. "I did hear a woman weeping as I walked on the beach," mused the shield maiden. "I couldn't find her. Skakki thought he saw a *draugr* when they dropped anchor."

"Draugr?" inquired Jack.

"You know. An undead spirit. We ringed the camp with silver coins to keep it away."

"That's exactly what I feared," said the Bard. "Tell the rest of Severus's story, Aiden. We need to make plans."

"For seven days Father Severus tried everything he could think of to get rid of the mermaid. He chanted exorcisms, waved crosses, and cursed her, but she was relentless. Each afternoon she pursued him. She was amazingly strong. She could lift boulders and throw them as easily as you toss a pebble. She wasn't trying to kill him, of course, but to frighten him into giving up.

"The mermaid could also command the waves. On the next-to-last afternoon she called up a wave so powerful, it reached the rocks where Father Severus was hiding. It almost pulled him into the sea. Then he knew how she planned to capture him on the last day. That night he struggled to climb the mountain at the center of the island. He could almost do it, but there was a sheer cliff partway up that was impossible to pass.

"He went down to the water, sunk in despair and lamenting the day he'd left the Holy Isle. And then it came to him. What if she lived on the island with *him*?

"He couldn't marry her, of course. Not because he was a priest—some priests did take wives, though it was frowned on in Rome. He couldn't because she was a beast, plain and simple. Oh, she might look human, but underneath she had no more spirituality than an ox."

"'An ox,'" he mused thoughtfully.

"She was enormously strong. He'd had ample evidence of that. She was talented—just look at the hut she'd constructed. She could fish and gather driftwood. *She could farm.*

"On the last afternoon Father Severus built a great fire next to the water. He tolled Fair Lamenting, and the mermaid rose from the waves. She came to shore swiftly and dropped her scales on the beach. 'Nice day for a swim,' Father Severus commented.

"'*You do not flee,*' said the mermaid.

"'What's the point? You'd only catch me.'

"'I would prefer that you come willingly,' she conceded. 'It's a poor marriage that begins with force.' She held out her arms to embrace him.

"'I have one thing to attend to first,' Father Severus replied, smiling. He darted past her, snatched up the scales, and threw them into the heart of the fire.

"The mermaid screamed. She raised a wave to put out the flames, but it was already too late. Her fish tail had burned to ashes. 'You have severed me eternally from the sea,' she cried. 'Oh, cruel, cruel man! How could you have treated me so after all my care? I can never swim the long miles back to my home.'

"'Then I suppose you'll have to live here,' said Father Severus.

"He trained her to dig seedbeds and to carry water from a stream flowing out of the mountain. She built a wall to keep the north wind from blowing soil away. She lured salmon to her hand by singing. Father Severus had to teach her to cook, however, for her kind prefer to devour food raw. At night she slept naked on the beach. After several months her hands became rough and her hair grew matted and filthy. Father Severus didn't mind. You don't ask for beauty in an ox."

"By Thor, that's a fine tale," interrupted Thorgil. "He tricked the mermaid and turned her into a thrall."

"You're supposed to feel pity for her," Brother Aiden said.

"Why? She threw rocks at him."

"Thorgil has a point," said the Bard. "Severus's crime was not in forcing her to work for him, which she richly deserved, but in thinking she had no soul. He treated her like a chair or a cup, to be discarded when it was broken. Go on, Aiden."

"Father Severus was contented with life," continued the monk. "He could pray and meditate whenever he liked. The mermaid no longer bothered him with talk. In fact, she became entirely silent. The garden prospered and he could store food for the winter. When he had a craving for meat, he sent her fishing. There was always enough driftwood for his fire.

"The mermaid, however, had a hatred of fire. She curled up in the little cave, winter and summer, without a scrap of cloth for warmth. Father Severus supposed she was like a seal and didn't feel the cold, and so he put it from his mind. He didn't notice the gradual change that came over her.

"One day he sighted a ship in the distance, making its way to Grim's Island. It was the abbot of the Holy Isle, coming to check on his welfare. 'Delighted to see you looking well,' said the abbot, coming ashore. 'Good Lord! What's that?' The mermaid was shuffling to and fro with loads of driftwood.

"'Just a sea creature I trained to work,' said Father Severus.

"'But it's female! And it's naked!'

"'It isn't human,' Father Severus said reasonably. 'Many a monk lives with a cow and nothing is said.'

"'It has the form of a human,' said the abbot, squinting to make her out more clearly. 'By blessed St. Bridget, it's the ugliest woman I ever saw.'

"Then Father Severus took a closer look at her too. The mermaid had changed so gradually, he hadn't paid attention. She was much larger, and the nails of her feet and hands had grown into claws. Her skin was rough, her teeth yellow, her hair was beginning to fall out and the clumps remaining were a rat's nest. Her movements, never graceful on land, were now totally bestial. 'She looked better when I got her,' Father Severus admitted."

"That is the way of fin folk," the Bard put in. "When the females are immature, they are surpassingly beautiful. If they wed a human, they remain so all their lives. But if they marry one of their own kind or are spurned by a human, they change into the adult form: a sea hag."

"A sea hag," said Jack, full of wonder. He could make a magnificent poem out of this tale, as good as *Beowulf* or Olaf One-Brow rescuing Ivar the Boneless from trolls. Thorgil's eyes were shining too.

"Unfortunately," said Brother Aiden, "the abbot thought

there had been quite enough meditating and praying on lonely islands. He accused Father Severus of shirking his duties to the monastery and ordered him to return at once. And so they packed up Columba's robe and Fair Lamenting and departed.

"The mermaid—now sea hag—dived into the water and tried to follow them. The sailors rowed for all they were worth. Gradually, the sea hag fell behind, and the last they saw of her was a mop of dirty hair bobbing up and down in the waves."

Everyone was silent after that. The Bard put more wood on the fire, and Thorgil, deep in thought, stroked Seafarer's feathers. Brother Aiden bowed his head. Finally, Jack said, "That's terrible. They abandoned her to die."

"I was never sure whether she'd had the strength to return to Grim's Island," said the Bard. "Now it seems she drowned and became a *draugr*."

"An undead spirit," said Thorgil.

"And she's here," added Brother Aiden.

Chapter Nine

A PLEA FOR JUSTICE

As the Bard had suspected, John the Fletcher and his hunting party could find nothing. The *draugr* had vanished like morning mist. "She's still out there, though," the old man said as he and Jack mixed potions for sale in Bebba's Town. "I instructed everyone to surround the houses and animal pens with holly branches. She won't like walking on thorns. Once a sea hag has lost her tail, her feet are her weakest point."

Jack lined up pots, which were colored to show what kind of pills they contained: red for fever, green for headaches, blue for stomach problems, and black for Beelzebub's Remedy Against Flies.

"*Draugr*s can swell up to four times their size, you know," said the Bard. "One climbed onto King Ivar's hall while I lived there and almost brought the place down. It hammered on the roof with its heels. That sort of thing happens a lot after funerals in the Northland—they call it 'house riding.'"

"House riding," echoed Jack, carefully measuring pinches of dried wormwood into an elixir.

"On that occasion it was Ragnar Wet-Beard—he got the name from all the beer he swilled. One night he fell into a barrel and drowned. Add honey to that elixir, would you? The wormwood makes it bitter."

"Yes, sir," said Jack.

"Ragnar was simply lonely, poor soul. He'd wandered out of his tomb and seen his friends holding a wake. Once we realized the problem, we stocked his tomb with beer. And tied his big toes together so he couldn't get far."

Jack put his finger into his mouth before he remembered it was covered in wormwood. He ran outside to spit. *House riding!* It was typical of the Northmen to tolerate *draugrs* banging holes in their roofs. He was heartily glad nothing like that had happened while he was in the Northland.

Jack rinsed out his mouth and shaded his eyes, looking for Thorgil. She had taken Seafarer for a practice flight. The albatross had grown extremely attached to her, and Jack suspected he didn't want to leave. She had taught Jack more Bird, but he knew he would never be as fluent as she. Still, he could say *Come here* and *Stop that* as well as *Are you hungry?* Seafarer generally was.

Somewhere to the south, Skakki and his shipmates were

conducting business, as the shield maiden put it. Pillaging, probably. Burning down villages. Jack didn't know how he could face them again, knowing the evil they had done. He went back inside.

The Bard was tying lids onto filled bottles of potions. "Nasty stuff, wormwood," the old man said. "Personally, I don't think it adds much, but people trust a medicine that tastes foul."

"Why was Ragnar Wet-Beard still there?" asked Jack. "I thought warriors went to Valhalla."

"Only those who fall in battle." The Bard transferred the wormwood bottles to a basket for transport to Skakki's ship. Jack thought that if you didn't have a stomachache before you tasted the elixir, you'd have one soon after. "Poor old Ragnar missed his chance. He hung around for a few months, moaning and rapping on doors. He couldn't hop far with his toes tied together. Finally, he pushed off to Freya's Heaven—or, considering that he drowned, he might have gone to Ran and Aegir's hall at the bottom of the sea."

"He doesn't sound that bad," the boy said. Practically all the herbs he'd collected were used up. Ten baskets were lined up against the wall, but there were another ten still empty. That meant another trip to the hazel wood, something Jack had hoped to avoid.

"Ragnar? He was gentle as a kitten, except when he ran berserk. Our *draugr* is another problem altogether. For one thing, she's a sea hag and they're always dangerous. For another, she has a genuine grievance."

"We didn't do anything to her," said Jack.

"Fair Lamenting drew her from the grave. Now she won't rest until she's taken revenge, and we're the easiest to find." The Bard sat down and motioned Jack to do the same. He was silent for a few moments, stroking his beard and gazing at the Roman birds painted on the wall. "We can't buy grain in Bebba's Town until they bring in the fall harvest. Skakki's away, anyhow. I'd planned to draw the *draugr* after us when we left, but the village needs protection now."

Jack didn't like the way this conversation was going. He'd assumed the Bard could cast her out with a spell. What was this about drawing her away?

"There are laws in this world that I cannot bend," the old man explained, reading Jack's expression. "Because the sea hag has a genuine grievance, I cannot use magic. She has earned the right to seek justice. That's why you and I are going to the hazel wood tonight to bargain with her."

"You and I?" Jack almost shouted, he was so surprised.

"Odin's eyebrows! You didn't think being a bard was all singing and picking wildflowers?" The Bard's eyes flashed with indignation and Jack felt ashamed. But going into the hazel wood at night? If he heard that howl again, he'd be out of there faster than a scalded cat. "You faced a dragon and Frith Half-Troll," the old man reminded him. "You broke the spell that held Din Guardi in the grip of Unlife. Don't sell yourself short, lad. By tomorrow you'll be snapping your fingers at sea hags."

If I'm still alive, Jack thought resentfully. Then Thorgil returned with Seafarer and there was much croaking and self-congratulation. Seafarer had frightened a young pig from its hiding place and Thorgil had brought it down for dinner.

"Hold it tightly," the Bard warned as they made their way across the dark fields. "We don't want to meet the *draugr* here. In the hazel wood I can draw strength from various sources."

Jack clutched the well-wrapped bell closer. It was an awkward shape to carry. *What absolute lunacy*, he thought. If it were up to him, he'd sink Fair Lamenting in the deepest part of the ocean, but the Bard said it was too late for that.

A lapwing whirred up from beneath Jack's feet and he leaped back. The bell made a faint *clink*, like a seashell falling on rock.

"Be careful!" The Bard whirled and put his hand on the bundle. "The slightest sound echoes through the nine worlds."

They hurried on. The ground was boggy and streams appeared where Jack didn't expect them. Water seeped into his boots. He also felt an itch in the middle of his back, which he was desperate to scratch.

The moon was slightly more than half full. It shone over the distant oak forest, picking out gaps in the trees, in particular the road torn by Odin and his huntsmen. No gaps were visible in the hazel wood, though Jack knew a few small meadows existed. He wished that they could have had Thorgil with them. She wouldn't jump every time a bird flew up. Also, and Jack hated to admit this to himself, he was far less likely to bolt if she were there.

But the Bard had said this task had to be handled carefully. They couldn't afford one of Thorgil's rash decisions.

The hazel wood loomed before them. They halted, still in moonlight, before its shadow. "Shouldn't we have brought a torch?" began Jack.

The Bard silenced him with a wave. "Observe and learn. You may need to do this one day on your own. Now cast your mind out to the life in this woodland. There are paths unseen to the daytime eye."

Great, thought Jack. *I'll probably meet a troop of ogres out for a stroll. I hope they eat* draugrs. He breathed deeply. The air under the trees was rich with damp earth and hidden flowers. He felt for the life force and found it easily. Everything in the woodland seemed nervous. Jack felt a hare slip carefully from a hollow in the ground, and then he found himself in the hollow, where four tiny copies of their mother huddled.

This was so comfortable, Jack lingered. He could almost feel tiny paws twitching, a tiny mouth open in a yawn.

"Do not allow yourself to enter an animal's body," the Bard's voice came from far away. "It's a dangerous trick and one for which you are not ready."

Jack backed off. So *that* was what he'd been about to do! He'd always envied the Bard's ability to fly with hawks or run with deer. He'd even tried to do it without success, but tonight the skill came naturally. Perhaps it was the hazel wood.

Jack sensed a hedgehog snuffling among the roots of a tree. All at once it shrieked and rolled into a ball.

"Did you hear that?" the Bard said softly. "The animals know something dangerous has come into their forest."

Jack found the mother hare again. She was cowering in a clump of grass in a meadow. She wanted to flee, but even more strongly she wanted to return to her young. She looked up and saw a pair of big, glowing, blue eyes.

"Ha!" shouted Jack, pulling himself out of the hare's body. He was standing next to the Bard with the bell clutched so tightly to his chest, it was certain to leave a bruise.

"Remind me to leave you at home when I want to creep up on something," the Bard said.

"I—I saw eyes," stammered Jack. "They w-were glowing." Then he remembered Brother Aiden's story. "Oh, crumbs, it was only a sheep."

"Aiden told you that tale, did he?" the Bard said. "It happens that you did see a sheep in the meadow, but what frightened the hare lay *behind* it." All at once they heard frantic baaing and the sound of bushes being trampled. The noises faded away into the distance. "It appears the *draugr* isn't interested in sheep," remarked the Bard.

"I'd l-like your permission, sir, to put down the bell and d-draw my knife," said Jack, unable to stop the trembling in his voice.

"In a moment. Your knife will make no impression on the *draugr*, by the way. You might as well try to cut stone." The old man listened attentively. "Most intriguing."

"Wh-What?" said Jack.

"A path has opened and some extremely interesting visitors have stepped through. We can't have *them* meeting the sea hag. Take out the bell, lad, and ring it."

"*What!*"

"Do it quickly. We need to draw the *draugr* to us."

Jack almost dropped the bell as he fumbled it out of its wrappings. He knew he had to obey before he thought about the consequences. He swung Fair Lamenting. The clapper struck the sides and a golden chime rolled out through the hazel wood, driving all fear before it and filling the boy with rapture. No music had ever been so sublime.

It was like all the best moments of his life happening at once, like the time he watched Father build their house and when Mother sang to the bees. It was when the Bard asked him to be an apprentice and when Thorgil, Pega, and he hugged one another under the grim walls of Din Guardi. But it was also a memory of his grandfather sitting by Jack's bed when he had a fever and of John the Fletcher's sister making him an apple tart after he fell into a pond. Those people were dead. Now, in the glory of this music, they rose up before him.

Jack dropped the bell to the ground. He found, to his amazement, that his face was wet with tears.

"That's why they call it Fair Lamenting," the Bard said quietly. "Hark, now. You must be alert. *She* approaches."

They heard weeping. It sounded like a woman sobbing as though her heart would break. It drew nearer and the air became chill. A mist swirled along the ground, and the smell of unnameable rotting things surrounded them. Jack drew his knife.

The Bard raised his staff in the moonlight at the edge of the wood. "I command you by root, by stone, by sea!" he cried.

A darkness solidified under the trees. *Who calls?* said a voice filled with stones scoured clean of life.

"I am the heir of Amergin," said the Bard. Jack looked up, amazed. "I am here to listen to your plea for justice."

Deep was my love; bitter was my fate, said the *draugr. My bones washed up on my father's shore, and great was his grief as he laid me in a tomb. He did not seal it, for he knew I could not rest. Until justice is done, I may not be born anew into the world.*

"Fair enough," said the Bard, "but you can't go around killing things. That only ties you more firmly to this existence."

The mist on the ground thickened. Tendrils of it reached up to brush Jack's legs, and he unconsciously felt for the rune of protection that no longer hung around his neck.

I don't believe you, said the *draugr.*

"It's the truth," the old man said. "Each murder carries its own cry for justice against *you.* Already you have forfeited the right to Father Severus's life—do not dispute it!" he shouted as the darkness swelled and branches snapped.

Who are you to stand in my way? I will take my revenge where I will. The trees groaned as they were forced apart. A portion of sky over the woodland turned black.

"I am the emissary of the life force! I stand against Unlife! If you wish to return with the sun, you must listen to me!"

The mist billowed up, pressing against Jack's chest until he struggled to breathe.

The Bard raised his staff. "Do not force me to subdue you!"

A howl as terrifying as the one Jack had heard before filled the night. Deer crashed out of the hazel wood. Badgers, foxes, a wolf, and three figures that looked almost human bounded over the fields. Jack wanted to run as well, but he couldn't desert the Bard.

The old man lifted both arms and lightning flickered around his body. He towered up fully, as large as the darkness. Now it was impossible to tell which was more terrible. For a moment the two faced each other, and the ground trembled, and the air shook. Then the howling stopped. The mist evaporated, and the darkness shrank until it was no taller than a woman.

Good fear-spell, thought Jack, dimly aware that he had fallen to his knees. The Bard was his normal size again, but a light still glimmered about his robes.

"That's better," the old man said. "In a few weeks' time I shall be traveling north to see Severus. Justice demands that he pay for what he did to you, but the form of his punishment is yet hidden from me. It will happen as it is meant to happen."

I have waited so long, said a voice no longer full of death, but like a young and sorrowful woman. *I loved him deeply*.

"You must be patient, child. No more killing. Lie still under the wandering clouds until I summon you. I swear before the councils of the nine worlds that I will see you safely to your long rest."

A sigh like a wave gently withdrawing from a sandy beach flowed over the hazel wood. The darkness thinned until it became only an ordinary tangle of bushes and trees. A frog cheeped from a hidden stream. The Bard lowered his arms, groaning slightly with the effort. "What I wouldn't give for a cup of hot cider right now," he muttered, leaning heavily on his staff.

"That was wonderful!" Jack cried, rushing to help him.

"It was, wasn't it? Haven't lost the old touch, thank whatever gods and goddesses are listening," said the Bard. "I'm able to walk on my own, lad. You carry the bell, and for Heaven's sake, don't let it ring. You can come out now, my friends," he called over the dark fields.

In the distance Jack saw two blobby shapes pop out of the ground.

Chapter Ten

THE HOBGOBLINS ARRIVE

"Festering fungi!" yelled one of the shapes. "What kind of company do you keep, Dragon Tongue? I thought the Great Worm and her nine wormlets had come to devour me!" A creature with large eyes shining in the moonlight and a wide, lipless mouth bounded up to them.

"The Nemesis?" said Jack, hardly daring to believe his eyes.

"Who else would I be?" the hobgoblin snarled. "Certainly not his Royal Stupidity there. 'Let's visit Jack's village,' he said. 'Let's see if darling Pega has changed her mind about marriage.' Idiot! Why would a winsome girl like that want an oaf like him?"

Jack laughed in spite of himself. The Nemesis went on spouting insults as the Bugaboo appeared, filthy and dripping. "Any port in a storm, eh?" the hobgoblin king said cheerfully. "When I heard that howl, I ducked into the nearest hole. Too bad it was full of mud!"

"You can bathe in a stream on the way home," the Bard said.

"Delighted to see you again, sir," the Bugaboo told the old man. "And you, too, Jack. What a treat! Tell me, is Pega, um, her lovely self? Does she miss me?"

Jack didn't know what to say. Pega thanked God on her knees every day that she hadn't married the hobgoblin king and gone to live in a musty cave full of mushrooms.

"I'm sure she'll faint dead away when she sees you," sneered the Nemesis.

"It might be a good idea to limit the number of people who do see you," the Bard suggested. "Folks here might mistake you for demons, and we wouldn't want them to take after you with rocks and rakes."

"It's our traditional welcome," the Bugaboo said, sighing. "What was that horrible cry we heard in the woodland?"

"Such a tale is best left for daytime." The Bard hunched over his staff, and Jack realized that the old man was completely exhausted.

"We should go home now," the boy said. "I'm sure we can find room for a pair of old friends."

"More than a pair, actually," said the Bugaboo. "You can come out now, Blewit. It's perfectly safe."

A skinny hobgoblin appeared from behind a bush, struggling with a bundle. Jack was amazed to see the long, gloomy face of Mr. Blewit. The bundle wriggled free and dropped to the ground.

It was Hazel, Jack's long-lost sister.

The little girl bounded over the grass exactly like a sprogling, or young hobgoblin. "Oh, goody! Mud men! My favorite treat," the child squealed.

Jack lifted her into his arms, intending to swing her around, but she weighed twice as much as he'd expected. He put her down again.

"I'm along to make sure you don't steal my baby," growled Mr. Blewit. "This is a visit, mind you. Don't get too used to her."

Get used to her? Jack wasn't sure he could ever do that. He loved her, of course. She was his sister. But she'd been stolen as an infant by hobgoblins. When he'd found her in the Land of the Silver Apples, Hazel didn't even know she was human. She imitated the hobgoblins' froggy ways, blinking her eyes one after the other as they did. She attempted to snag moths out of the air with her tongue. She even gleeped, making an ugly plopping sound that indicated joy.

"Stop nitter-nattering, Blewit," the Nemesis ordered. "Our feet will have put down roots by the time you finish moaning. I'll carry Dragon Tongue." The hobgoblin hoisted the Bard as easily as a man picking up a kitten. Jack was relieved that the surly Nemesis had realized the old man's exhaustion. Being carried like a baby wasn't the most dignified way to travel, but the Bard didn't complain. With Jack leading the way, the group set off for the old Roman house.

"I remember this place," said the Bugaboo as they reached the top of the cliff. "It's lasted well, but then, the man who built it was an excellent architect."

"You know who built it?" asked Jack, who recalled that until recently the hobgoblins had scarcely aged at all. The Bugaboo could be very old indeed.

"I *saw* who built it," the hobgoblin king said. "He was a poet exiled for writing rude poetry about his emperor. He painted the walls to resemble a Roman garden to cheer up his wife. There used to be a bathhouse over there before part of the cliff crumbled into the sea."

"He had a pair of brats who threw stones at me when I surprised them in the woods," the Nemesis said, grinning wickedly.

Jack felt a chill that was something like being in the presence of a *draugr*, but not as deep or dire. It was more of a passing sadness, a faint memory of a beloved dwelling, now lost in time.

The Nemesis put the Bard down and steadied him as the old man found his feet. "Thanks, old friend," the Bard said. "Magic tires me out more than it used to."

"Stuff and nonsense," the hobgoblin said gruffly. "Fighting monsters always takes it out of you, no matter how old you are." Jack was surprised by how respectful the Nemesis was.

Hazel darted past them. "Da! It's the ugly mud woman," she called. "Where's the pretty one?"

"If you touch those baskets, I'll kill you," came Thorgil's voice from inside.

Hazel laughed like a hobgoblin; the sound resembled someone choking on a piece of gristle. *Dear God*, thought Jack. *What are Mother and Father going to think of her?*

Mr. Blewit hurried inside and snatched up the little girl before she could get into trouble.

Jack saw to his consternation that Thorgil had gone hunting and made a stew with the results. She usually avoided such work, but her good mood must have impelled her to cook. She could no longer use a bow and arrow, but her skill with a spear or a sling was excellent. The shield maiden's cooking methods were basic, however, and she tended to leave shreds of fur in the mix. Jack saw what looked like squirrels bobbing around.

"Smells interesting," said the Bugaboo, opening his nostrils very wide. "Perhaps it would benefit from a few mushrooms—"

"There you go, criticizing the cook before you've properly greeted her," the Nemesis complained. "I apologize for my rude companion, Thorgil, and for dropping in on you so unexpectedly—great toadstools!" The hobgoblin leaped out of the way as Seafarer made a stab at him. Jack had forgotten how very nimble hobgoblins could be. The Nemesis clung to the ceiling by his sticky toes and fingers.

Thorgil laughed merrily. She said something in Bird to the albatross, and he slouched off to the alcove. "I, at least, welcome you," she said. "Seafarer has never seen anything like you before."

"I've never seen anything like him either," said the Nemesis, dropping down. "Is he a troll-seagull or what?"

"An albatross from the far south. Seafarer says there are thousands of his kind there."

"Let's hope they stay there," muttered the Nemesis.

"Greetings, noble shield maiden," the Bugaboo said, bowing deeply. "It is a pleasure to see you."

They sat around the fire with bowls of stew, which wasn't as bad as Jack had feared. Fortunately, there was a good supply of bread, for the hobgoblins ate ravenously. Hazel licked out her bowl and clamored for more. After they had finished, the Bard explained about the trading journey to Bebba's Town.

"You're low on food! You should have told us," exclaimed the Bugaboo. "The Nemesis and I will go fishing. There's nothing like hobgoblin toes to attract a fat fish." He held out his foot, wriggling the long toes temptingly in different directions. Hazel clapped her hands with glee.

The Bard jerked himself awake. "My stars, I'm about to fall off my perch. If you'll forgive me, dear friends, I'll go to bed." The hobgoblins apologized for keeping him up late, and Jack helped him to the truckle bed at the far end of the house. "See to the bedding, lad," the Bard said. "There should be enough straw in the storeroom."

Jack moved baskets and chests next to the wall to make space. The Nemesis and Mr. Blewit helped him make up beds, and by the time they were finished, the floor was wall to wall hobgoblins and humans. If anyone else visited, Jack thought, they would have to hang him from the ceiling.

Mr. Blewit covered Hazel with his cloak. It was made of motley wool, and when it was in place, all you could see was the top of her round little head. The rest of her seemed to vanish. The melancholy hobgoblin stroked her hair, and she gleeped faintly.

Jack had a hollow feeling in the middle of his heart. The Blewits loved Hazel deeply. They would never give her up. But Mother and Father wanted her too, and they certainly deserved to keep her. It was a problem for which there was no good solution.

Jack packed Fair Lamenting in one of the Bard's chests. By the time he'd finished, he was almost falling off the perch himself. He settled gratefully into a heap of bracken and straw.

"Tell me what happened with the *draugr*," whispered Thorgil, crouching beside him on the floor.

Jack listened to the night wind fiddling with the thatch overhead and watched the shadows flicker at the far end of the house. "Not tonight," he said, remembering the chill mist pressing in against his chest. "The Bard says such tales are best kept for daytime," he said. "I think he has a good reason."

The Nemesis sprang from his bed with a roar. "That monster tried to eat my toes!" he shrieked, quivering with rage. Seafarer looked up, thoughtfully clicking his beak.

"Is it morning yet?" said Thorgil, burrowing deeper into her straw.

"Your pet tried to kill me and that's all you can say?" screamed the Nemesis.

Jack got up swiftly and opened the door. The sun was just below the margin of the sea and wisps of clouds had turned pink in the dawn. *Come*, he said in Bird. The albatross ignored him.

"You have to compliment his wings first," Thorgil muttered. When Jack had repeated the correct formula, the great bird reluctantly turned away from the hobgoblin's toes and followed the boy outside.

"They are like fishing worms, aren't they?" Jack said, leading Seafarer down to the water. He sat on the sand, enjoying the fresh air after the musty atmosphere in the house. Hobgoblins always did smell of mushrooms, he remembered. "What are we going to do with you when we go north?" Jack said.

Seafarer spread his wings and tested the breeze. One of them drooped. He did a practice run along the sand and fell over in an ungraceful heap.

"Don't feel bad," Jack said to encourage him. "It's early days still. If worse comes to worst, I suppose we could take you with us. I wouldn't trust the Northmen too far, though. They'll think you're a seagoing chicken."

Seafarer had discovered a tide pool full of crabs and proceeded to clean it out. By then Jack could smell food, and he rose and ambled up the path. He heard the sound of pattering. Seafarer was running after him as fast as he could.

"I wouldn't desert you," the boy said, touched. He stroked the bird's feathers and was rewarded with a soft whistle that meant contentment. "I wish I knew more Bird. It comes naturally to Thorgil, but I have to work at it. Never mind. I once learned to communicate with giant spiders, and nothing could be harder than that." He kept up the one-sided conversation, not knowing whether Seafarer understood a single word. But the Bard said animals responded more to music than speech. Seafarer certainly seemed interested in Jack's voice.

"Keep that behemoth away from me," the Nemesis said as they entered.

"Now, now, you could easily spare him a toe," the Bugaboo said. "It isn't as though it wouldn't grow back."

Jack put Seafarer in the alcove and sat next to the fire with the others. The Bard had already recounted the story of the *draugr*, leaving out the grimmer parts because Hazel was listening.

"We've come across a *draugr* or two in our travels," said the Nemesis. "Jenny Greenteeth, for example. *There's* someone you don't want to find at the foot of your bed. Do you remember that night we camped in the Hall of Wraiths?"

"Oh, my!" The Bugaboo's eyes bulged at the memory. "A deer would have had trouble keeping up with us after she appeared—but we mustn't get bogged down in old tales. My dear Dragon Tongue, do you think it's safe to lure the sea hag away? You have to keep several hops ahead of something like that."

"Of course it isn't safe," the Bard said, stirring the embers of the fire with his staff. Jack had often noticed that it never burned, no matter how long the old man poked around with it. "I can't leave her here. She'll become a permanent resident, like Jenny in the Hall of Wraiths. Jenny's grievance happened so long ago that she can't remember what it was. If you don't fix wrongs in time, they never go away."

"Well, you can't have a *draugr* trailing after you forever."

"No," said the Bard thoughtfully, stirring the flames. "Everything depends on what fate has in store for Severus. He isn't a bad man, you know, just an incredibly pig-headed, narrow-minded idiot. He feels guilty."

"Fat lot of good that does," said the Nemesis.

"He won't escape punishment, but it will probably take the form of some penance. I doubt whether the *draugr* will be satisfied with anything less than his death."

"What happens if she isn't satisfied?" demanded the Nemesis.

The Bard's eyes looked into the distance, seeing beyond the wall to someplace Jack could only guess at. "Then . . . I suppose . . . I must find another solution."

All this while Seafarer had been talking to himself. Jack had noticed that the albatross liked to join conversations. They must have reminded him of the sounds a flock made when birds nested together. Seafarer clicked, whistled, snapped his beak, and moaned, for all the world like someone offering an opinion. Hazel had been growing steadily more restless. She was irresistibly drawn to the dangerous bird and more than once had to be kept from pulling his feathers.

Now she wriggled off Blewit's lap and made a beeline for the alcove. Blewit caught her just in time. "Let's go down to the beach, dearest, and see if your old da can snag a fish," he whispered. She nodded happily and waggled her stubby toes in imitation of his long ones. Jack was relieved when they left.

"Excuse me for interrupting, sir," he said, anxious to take advantage of Blewit's absence. "I need to ask whether Hazel is here permanently."

"No!" cried the Nemesis before the Bard could respond.

"He's right. It would kill the Blewits to give her up," the Bugaboo said. "And anyone can see that tearing Hazel away from them would cause *her* untold harm."

Jack bowed his head. He didn't know what to say.

"I know we're responsible for the problem," said the hobgoblin king. "I'll do everything in my power to solve it. We'll visit every summer and give Hazel a chance to know her human family."

"Why not stay all the time?" Jack said.

The Bugaboo and the Nemesis exchanged glances. They seemed reluctant to answer.

"Because the villagers would mistake them for demons," the Bard said. "It's foolishness, of course—no one is more kindhearted than hobgoblins—but old habits die hard. We can't even admit that Hazel was raised by them. She'll have a hard enough time fitting in."

"There's also—*you* know," the Bugaboo said hesitantly.

"What?" said Jack.

"Getting *mudstruck*." The hobgoblin king whispered as though it were a shameful secret.

Jack looked to the Bard for explanation.

"Hobgoblins are irresistibly drawn to humans, or as they

put it, mud people," the old man said. "From the first minute they saw us, hobgoblins fell in love. You've seen how they copy our houses and clothes. The trouble is, if they stay around us too long, they can't bring themselves to return home. It's a kind of addiction, like the craving for strong drink among Northmen."

"Many a Christian house has its resident hobgoblin," the Bugaboo said sadly. "He watches over the family and secretly does small chores, like cleaning out the fireplace or rocking the baby's cradle. Gradually, he wastes away out of loneliness. He's never appreciated, though he would give his life for his humans. If he's discovered, he's pelted with rocks."

"So that's being mudstruck," murmured Jack.

"Please! We don't use the word in polite company," the Nemesis growled.

"And now it's time for me to introduce the child to her real parents," the Bard said, standing and brushing a few flecks of ash from his robe. "Jack and Thorgil will accompany me. You hobgoblins can stay here, if you wish."

"Blewit would never let his darling out of his sight," said the Bugaboo. "He'll insist on following, and we, of course, must support him. But never fear. No human ever sees us when we want to remain hidden."

Chapter Eleven

HAZEL COMES HOME

Hidden they were, from farmers planting fields and from John the Fletcher hunting for the *draugr* that had killed his hens. None of the women traveling to the baker's house, from which the warm smell of bread radiated, saw the hobgoblins. Not one of the boys playing Bull in the Barn noticed the speckled shapes flitting from shadow to shadow. Of course, the motley wool cloaks helped, but even without such cover, the hobgoblins blended into the background with remarkable ease. Jack could detect them because he knew what to look for.

Everyone noticed Hazel. *How could they not*, Jack thought miserably. She puffed out her cheeks and wiggled her ears with glee. This was a grand adventure! She was seeing more mud people than she had ever dreamed possible and thought they were pleased with her as well. They raised their eyebrows and opened their mouths into an *O*, exactly like a hobgoblin when he was happy.

"Who is this lassie?" inquired a farm wife, after watching Hazel snap at a butterfly.

"Jack's relative from the north," the Bard said blandly. "His great-aunt's brother's granddaughter. Doesn't she look exactly like Giles Crookleg?"

"Why . . . yes," said the woman, trying to work out the relationship.

"We'll have to teach her manners," hissed Jack when they were alone again. Hazel was hopping down the road. She did it extremely well, aided by her sturdy legs and lots of practice. "Everyone will think she's demented."

"I disagree," Thorgil said unexpectedly. "Everyone will think she's simply playing. She's no different than a puppy trying out its paws."

"Very wise, shield maiden," the Bard said.

If the hobgoblins were invisible to people, the animals could certainly see them. There was much baaing and bellowing as black-faced sheep scurried out of their way. A cat arched its back and spat when the Nemesis grinned at it. Chickens fled in panic when Mr. Blewit's long, unhappy face peered out of a gooseberry bush.

They arrived at the path leading to Jack's farm, and he unconsciously slowed down. Now was the moment he dreaded. Now he wished they could return to the Bard's house, spend more time preparing for this meeting, and train Hazel to be more like . . .

Lucy.

Lucy was the daughter his parents had loved all those years Hazel was missing. Lucy was like a ray of light dancing over a pond, the joy of Father's eyes from the first moment he saw her. Her hair was as golden as sunset clouds, her eyes as blue as forget-me-nots. People caught their breath when they saw her, for no child in the village had ever been so beautiful. How could stocky, earthbound Hazel ever take her place?

Pega came out of the barn with an armload of hay. Hazel whooped and ran to her. "The pretty lady!" she squealed. She collided with Pega, sending hay in all directions.

"Why, it's—it's—how did you get here?" gasped Pega, trying to catch her breath. She waved distractedly at the others.

"Da brought me," cried the child. "Please say you'll be our queen! The Bugaboo is most dreadfully unhappy."

"Dear saints in Heaven, is he here too?" said Pega, looking around. She tried to walk, but Hazel had clamped her sturdy arms around the girl's legs.

"The hobgoblins have promised to stay out of sight," the Bard said, amused. "I presume Giles and Alditha are at home? Good. Wipe that glum expression off your face, Jack, and unhook your sister."

Jack pried one of Hazel's hands loose and dragged her away, but the little girl kept a firm grip on Pega's skirt. "You *are* a strong little lassie, aren't you?" said Pega, following to keep her clothes from getting torn.

"I shall wait in the barn," Thorgil said haughtily. "I have taken an oath never to enter that house again." Jack didn't argue with her. He had more than enough problems.

Everyone was sitting in the sunny herb garden. Mother was weaving, and Mrs. Tanner was twisting wool into yarn. The Tanner girls were riddling seeds, shaking them in baskets to see which were heavy and might still grow. Father was mending a milk pail.

Mother's hand flew to her mouth and she stood up abruptly, knocking over the loom. "Oh, Giles! Oh, Giles, look!"

Father turned and for a moment seemed utterly bewildered. He reached out and then yanked his hand back as though he'd touched a live coal. "By all that's holy, she looks like my old da," he whispered.

Hazel dropped Pega's skirt. Her eyes grew very big.

"She's the image of you, Giles," said Mother.

Jack realized that his father had forgotten how he himself looked. He'd never looked in the chief's mirror, the only one in the village, and only rarely at his reflection in a puddle. He often said that thinking about one's appearance was wicked vanity. In fact, Hazel was exactly like him. She had the same gray eyes and brown hair, the same sturdy frame and determined expression.

"Well, Hazel, what do you think?" the Bard said. "Do they meet with your approval?"

Hazel shrank against Pega. "They're all right for mud people," she said. Mother looked up, puzzled.

"That's what her foster family calls people in this part of the world," the Bard said. Jack noticed that he didn't use the word *hobgoblin*.

"Then she is . . . who I think she is," said Father. The old man nodded.

"My dear, dear child," Mother said, holding out her arms. "I'm so glad you're home."

The little girl recoiled. "This isn't my home, and you're not my mumsie!" she cried. "My mumsie is pretty. You're an old mud woman. Da says you want to steal me and never let me go!" She began to hiccup, and then she screeched the way a young sprogling did when it was distraught.

"Hey!" shouted Pega, rapping Hazel on the head with her knuckles. "What a rotten thing to say! You ought to be glad to have more than one mumsie. I never even had one, or else I don't remember her. She probably sold me for a loaf of bread."

Hazel looked up, her eyes blinking erratically. She had never seen Pega so angry.

"Pay attention, you brat. You've got *two* mothers and *two* fathers. You should thank God on your knees for such luck. Now march over there and apologize to that nice lady."

Hazel snuffled and wiped her nose on Pega's skirt. "Really? You can have more than one?"

"Of course, you ninny."

The little girl turned toward Mother. She still clung to Pega, but she had stopped crying. She made a hobgoblin curtsy, somewhat like a frog lowering itself onto a lily pad. "I'm sorry, nice lady."

Jack looked at Pega over Hazel's head, and she nodded slightly. He knelt beside the little girl and smoothed back her springy hair. "You have only one brother, I fear, but he loves you as much as two. Welcome home, little sister."

She studied him very seriously from head to foot. Jack thought for a moment and decided to risk it. "Long ago I asked you to look at my hands. Do you remember?"

Hazel grimaced. "Maybe."

"I said that our hands were shaped alike. Our fingers weren't long and sticky like . . . the others. It showed that you belonged with me. Have you thought about that?"

The little girl hung her head. "After you went away, I looked into a pail of water. I saw . . . I saw . . ." Her lip quivered and she looked ready to cry again.

"It's all right," Jack said softly. "You don't have to talk about it if it upsets you."

"I saw *him*!" She jabbed her finger at Giles Crookleg. "I saw my face and it was like *him*. Then I knew I was the ugliest sprogling that ever lived!" She howled and buried her face in Pega's skirt.

"We have our work cut out for us," said the Bard.

Jack was exhausted by the time evening came. The Bard and Thorgil had departed; Pega had gone to stay with Brother Aiden, hoping to avoid another marriage proposal from the Bugaboo. Jack was left alone to shield Hazel from trouble.

The Bard had cautioned Hazel not to mention her past, but the Tanner girls had already been alerted that something odd was going on. "What's a sprogling?" they asked at the first opportunity.

"It's the Pictish word for 'child,'" Jack replied quickly. It had been decided to say that Hazel had been stolen by Pictish traders and raised in the far north. He worried that the little girl would blurt out the truth, but she was more mature than he'd realized. Hazel only looked like a five-year-old. She was actually eight. Though the Blewits had frequently taken her to Middle Earth, she had not aged in the Land of the Silver Apples.

"Is that why she's so tiny? Because she lived with Picts?" demanded Ymma, the older Tanner girl. She had grubby, blond braids and a wiry body like a stoat's.

"Ma says she was born the same year as me," said Ythla, the younger. "That means she's eight, and she's a runt." Ythla was like a fox with a sharp nose and reddish hair.

"Picts are small because they eat small food," Jack said, improvising rapidly. "Dwarf cabbages, dwarf apples, chickens the size of sparrows. It's all that grows in Pictland." His head was beginning to ache from all the lies he had to tell.

"Do giants get fed giant cabbages?" said Ymma, interested.

"Gog and Magog must have eaten them," giggled Ythla. "They were huge. And stupid. I'm glad the Wild Hunt carried them off."

"That's an evil thing to say," Jack said. "Gog and Magog are probably dead." The Tanner girls only laughed.

Mother and Father had tried to be welcoming, but they were unsure how to treat this odd daughter. Hazel was so very active and her behavior so bizarre. Because they were rare and valued, hobgoblin sproglings were outrageously spoiled. They squalled constantly for attention. They grabbed the best bits at mealtimes and insulted anyone who got in the way. Jack had to say, over and over until he thought he'd go mad, "Please, Hazel. Don't do that, Hazel. That's rude, Hazel."

Father would raise his hand to cuff her, as he'd cuffed young Jack, and freeze. "It's what I deserve," Giles Crookleg muttered to himself. "It's my fault, the sin of pride." Jack knew he was remembering how he'd brought Lucy home because she was beautiful and concealed the fact that she'd been switched with Hazel.

Mother gently tried to correct the little girl—"No, Hazel. You can't cram whole apples into your mouth"—and Hazel would stop whatever she was doing. A moment later she'd forgotten. Hobgoblin habits were too strong to change quickly.

"More! More! More! More!" droned the little girl after the evening meal was finished.

"There isn't any more," Mother said.

"Don't care! Gimme more!" screamed Hazel, until Jack grabbed her arm and dragged her outside.

"You can't shout at Mother like that," he scolded when they were in the dark herb garden. "It's disrespectful and it hurts her feelings. Do you understand?" Hazel struggled to get away, but Jack—barely—managed to hang on to her. She was very strong. "You don't talk that way to your hobgoblin mumsie," he said.

"I do so. All the time," Hazel declared.

Jack sighed. "Well, you shouldn't, and you definitely can't do it here. Anyhow, we don't have much food. A Wild Hunt destroyed most of our crops."

"What's a Wild Hunt?" asked Hazel.

"Odin and his warriors rode among the clouds and tore a road through the forest. I'll show you tomorrow." Jack retold the story the way a bard would, first describing the dark sky and the ominous stillness. When he got to the part where the wind carried off the ewe, Hazel was hanging on to him as though a wind might carry her off too. Jack was pleased with his storytelling. He ended the tale on a high note with everyone safe. Hazel fell asleep while leaning against him. He wondered how he would ever carry her back into the house.

"*That's* proper nightmare material," complained Blewit, popping up from behind a rosemary bush. "Totally unsuitable for a delicate sprogling. I wouldn't be surprised if she wakes up screaming."

"She's not delicate, and she loved every minute of it," Jack said.

"She's my dainty little toadflax blossom, yes she is," crooned the hobgoblin, taking one of Hazel's chubby hands. She didn't stir. Like most sproglings, she was used to sleeping through parties where young ones might be whisked up at any moment and admired.

"I heard her begging for food," accused Blewit. "You're letting her waste away."

"I am not," Jack said.

"Liar."

"Calm down, Blewit," said the Bugaboo, suddenly appearing from the darkness with the Nemesis. "We all know Hazel eats as much as the Great Worm and her nine wormlets." Blewit grumbled under his breath, but he didn't contradict his king.

They sat together under a nearly full moon. The odor of crushed mint rose from the ground where they were sitting, and a nightingale began to sing from a tree. The village seemed so peaceful—and had once *been* peaceful, Jack thought. He longed for those days again. Season had followed season with comforting regularity—plowing, planting, harvesting, a pause for winter. No surprises.

All had been predictable until the Bard arrived.

That was when the world had waked up and noticed the sleepy little village on the shores of the North Sea. First the rider on the Nightmare thundered in from across the sea. Jack still shivered to remember the Rider's thorny legs gripping the belly of its horse and the white blood dripping down. Then the Northmen missed the village by only a hair, though they didn't miss Jack and Lucy. They had carried the children off as slaves.

This year alone, in only a few days, the village had been visited by a Wild Hunt, a *draugr* had taken up residence in the hazel wood, and now a troop of hobgoblins was camped in

Jack's garden. He sighed inwardly. He was the Bard's apprentice and, as the old man had said, such a calling wasn't just singing and picking wildflowers. It was a bard's job to deal with things that went bump in the night.

"I have to go in now," the boy said. "I don't know whether I can lift Hazel."

"Weakling!" sneered Mr. Blewit. He swept the little girl up easily and carried her to the door. The motley wool robes of the hobgoblin shifted eerily like the shadows of bushes dancing in the wind.

Jack was suddenly reminded of the Bugaboo's mission. "Did you ask Pega again if she would marry you?" he asked.

"I don't want to talk about it!" the Bugaboo cried, flinging his cloak over his head and disappearing completely.

"That means yes, and that means she said no," said the Nemesis. Then all three creatures bade Jack good night and vanished into the darkness.

Jack dragged Hazel inside and rolled her onto a pile of heather and straw. She didn't stir as she was bumped along and she didn't wake up screaming in the night, as Blewit had predicted. She slept as soundly as a sprogling, which was very sound indeed. The first Jack heard from her was a monotonous "Food . . . food . . . food . . ." around dawn.

Chapter Twelve

THE TANNER BRATS

During the next few weeks, when Jack wasn't helping the Bard, he was trying to keep peace at home. Pega returned and was of great help, but even she was becoming irritable. Hazel threw unexplained tantrums. Father spent most of his time in the fields or drinking ale with the blacksmith. Mother found fault with everything. The only good thing was that Thorgil stayed away. Jack didn't know what he would have done if she'd been added to the explosive mix.

"It's those Tanner brats," said Blewit at one of Jack's nightly meetings with the hobgoblins. "They've decided to move in permanently, and they're trying to drive out Pega and Hazel."

"Are you sure?" said Jack. He knew Blewit complained about everything, even that the sun rose in the east and disturbed his sleep. Blewit, like all hobgoblins, was happiest underground.

"He's right," said the Bugaboo. "We can hear everything they say." He unfurled his ears to demonstrate how very keen hobgoblin hearing could be. "They've been unforgivably cruel to dear Pega. I was within a heartbeat of taking steps, but the Bard said I had to get your permission."

Jack wondered what "taking steps" involved. Hobgoblins, if threatened, could stand up to dragons. "I haven't noticed Ymma and Ythla doing anything bad," he said.

"Blistering beetles! The first thing Dragon Tongue taught you was how to observe and melt into the background," exploded Blewit. "What good is it spying on animals when you've got people at home that need watching?"

It had simply never occurred to Jack that the same skills he used to study animals could work on humans. The Bard called it "being cloaked in the life force." You became part of the landscape, no more noticeable than a tree or rock. Jack had become so good at this, mice perched on his feet to nibble seeds and birds landed on his shoulders.

"I suppose I could spy on them," he faltered, thinking that there was something low about the activity when it involved people.

"Well, you'd better do something fast," Blewit said. "They're making my Hazel miserable, and I won't put up with it much longer."

So Jack began observing the activities in his house. When he stood next to a wall, he became wall. When he stood in the shadows, he became shadow. It surprised him how effective the magic was. Even Mother, who was a wise woman, couldn't detect him.

Ymma and Ythla had always seemed ready to help with tasks, and yet they didn't accomplish much. Jack saw that they did chores so carelessly, Pega often had to redo the work. The Tanners frequently stole small items to carry back to their hovel. Turnips and apples, a cup, a piece of leather, and a horn spoon found their way into the girls' pockets. Nothing large was taken, but all together, the theft was considerable.

Mrs. Tanner seemed honest, but she must have known what was going on. Occasionally, in a halfhearted way, she tried to discipline her daughters. She never went so far as to return any of the ill-gotten goods.

Now Jack was watching as the Tanner girls cleaned house. As usual, when they thought they were alone, they spent most of the time poking into corners and trying to open chests. When Pega came through the door with a pail of milk, Ymma whispered, "I hope the milk won't turn sour," just loud enough to be overheard. Pega flushed.

This was another game Jack had discovered. Pega had been born with a birthmark covering half her face. She had ears that stuck straight out through wispy hair, and her mouth was as wide as a frog's. Jack no longer noticed her looks, Thorgil had never noticed them, and the Bugaboo thought she was positively ravishing. But most people didn't want Pega around. Her ugliness might mark unborn babies. *She might turn milk sour.*

The Tanner girls subtly and continuously drew attention to the girl's disfigurement.

Hazel bounded in, and Pega quickly put the milk pail on a shelf before the child could knock it over. "I do love you," said Hazel, hugging the older girl.

Ymma and Ythla whispered together. Jack heard the word *half-wit.* This was another game, to make Hazel feel stupid.

"I love you, too, but I've got work to do." Pega pried Hazel's arms loose and covered the milk with a cloth. She pointedly ignored Ymma and Ythla.

"Please, please, please, take me for a walk."

Pega started to object and then, seeing the little girl's anxious face, relented. "Oh, very well. While the cream rises, you and I can hunt for bugs in the garden. I'll let you feed them to the hens."

"Make sure she doesn't eat them herself," said Ythla slyly.

"Make sure you don't find them in your hair," retorted Pega, sweeping Hazel through the door.

The house fell silent as Ymma and Ythla finished tidying and sweeping. They worked silently, each anticipating the movements of the other like a pair of wolves. Ymma gathered a handful of dirt and moved swiftly to the milk pail, and Ythla whisked off the cover.

"What are you doing?" said Jack, stepping out of the shadows.

Ymma screamed and dropped the dirt on the floor. "Where did you come from?" she cried. Ythla's face had turned white.

"I'm a bard. I come and go where I will." Jack strode forward and restored the cover to the milk.

"You're a damned wizard!" Ymma spat at him. Then, perhaps recalling that Jack was the son of the house, she smiled sweetly. "It *was* a clever trick, though, wasn't it, Ythla?" Her sister nodded enthusiastically. "I'm truly sorry. I shouldn't have lost my temper."

Jack watched coldly as they left. He'd observed them teasing Hazel and then sitting back contentedly as she was scolded for bad behavior. One of their favorite tricks was to hold food in front of the little girl and then snatch it away.

"Oopsie!" sang Ythla on one occasion, yanking a piece of cheese away for the third time. The little girl reacted with the ear-piercing screech that only a sprogling could produce. Mother ran in.

"I want my cheese," wailed Hazel.

"You really, really must learn not to cry every time you have a hunger pang," Mother scolded, taking her into her arms.

"But they took my cheese!" Hazel pointed at the Tanner girls.

"Don't make up tales, darling. It isn't nice," said Mother. By now Ythla had popped the morsel into her mouth. "I think you'll feel a lot nicer with a nap."

"No, I won't," grumbled Hazel, but she followed Mother up the ladder to the loft. This was a huge improvement on the little girl's behavior from when she first arrived. Pega had drummed the importance of obedience into her head.

Blewit was right. I haven't been paying attention, thought Jack. He'd discovered why Hazel had so many tantrums and why everyone was so short-tempered. The Tanner girls might even have been responsible for some of Thorgil's evil moods earlier.

Jack waited until the Tanners had departed for their hovel. Pega and Hazel had fallen asleep in each other's arms at the far end of the house. In a low voice he described everything he'd observed to his parents.

"Ymma and Ythla are mistreating Hazel?" said Mother. "You must be mistaken. Why, only this morning Ymma told me she'd never seen a more adorable child."

"She's lying," Jack said bluntly.

Mother looked upset. "As for stealing, I've noticed a few turnips go missing, but the Tanners have been dreadfully poor. I'd hate to punish them for a crime born of hunger."

Jack's hopes fell. He'd been counting on her support.

"Just how did you find this out?" said Father.

Jack knew he couldn't admit to using magic. Nothing was more likely to start a lecture about demons dragging wizards down to Hell. "I've simply been around more. The Tanners are making Pega unhappy as well."

Father yawned deeply and removed his shoes. "It's only women's fiddle-faddle," he said.

"They might drive her away."

"Where would she go?" Father said comfortably. "It isn't

as though people are lining up to hire such an ill-favored lass. The Tanners have been useful and the girls are excellent Christians. They join me for prayers, which is more than I can say for you."

Jack was praying at that very moment—for patience. "Doesn't it bother you that Ymma and Ythla lie, steal, and play nasty tricks?"

"Seems to me"—Father cast a glance at the loft where his bed lay—"that you're mightily free with advice for a lad. Seems to me you've learned a few nasty tricks yourself, hanging about in shadows and doing wizardry." And Jack knew that the Tanner girls had got to his father first and that there was no more point to arguing. "Clean up your own sty before you come squealing to me," Father advised. He lumbered to his feet and climbed the ladder. Mother, with an apologetic look, followed.

Jack kicked the straw of his bedding and slammed his fist into the wall, only hurting himself. Fearing to wake Pega and Hazel, he went outside to cool off.

The sky was strewn with a thousand stars, shining so brightly that he could make out the shapes of trees and bushes. A faint, tinkling sound came from all around. It was as though the stars themselves were whispering, but Jack had heard that sound before. It was when he was recovering in the hall of the Mountain Queen in Jotunheim. Her palace had been so huge that when he looked down from a high window, all he could see were swirling clouds of ice crystals. It was this, striking against the ice walls, that made the sweet chiming.

"On nights like these—," said a voice next to his ear. Jack jumped straight up and came down ready to fight. "Whoa! I'm not an enemy," cried the Bugaboo, dodging the boy's fists.

"Then don't leap out at me!" Jack yelled.

"Take a deep breath, laddie," said the Nemesis, popping up on the other side of him. "We're not the ones you're angry with." Blewit stepped out from behind a bush.

Jack sat down on the ground. "No, you're not," he admitted.

"We were listening to the argument," the Bugaboo said. "You can't blame your parents. To them you're still a sprogling."

"But how can they allow Pega and Hazel to suffer?"

"They don't see what they don't want to see. Let's sit awhile and enjoy the sky. I was about to say, before you performed a leap that would do a hobgoblin proud, that on nights like these the walls between the nine worlds grow thin."

Jack gazed up, listening to the faint echo of ice falling on ice in far Jotunheim. The trolls were folded inside their mountain, taking refuge from summer. Yet each year the sun shone more brightly, and each year more of their realm melted away. It made him sad to think of it. "Look!" he cried, pointing. A streak of light crossed the heavens like a spark. Then another and another.

"Now, that *is* a treat. They're leaves falling from the Great Tree," the Bugaboo said.

"From Yggdrassil," Jack murmured, remembering how the Tree had reached up higher than the moon. At the top lay a heavenly green field around a hall so enormous, a thousand men could stand side by side in its doorway. It was Valhalla. He shivered. "Thorgil says the Northmen hear their dead calling to them when lights dance in the sky."

"Many things happen when the walls between the worlds grow thin. Once I heard waves breaking on the Islands of the Blessed," said the Bugaboo.

Jack thought of the gifts the Mountain Queen had given him: the marten-fur coat, cow-skin boots, and tunic. They had been stored away because he'd outgrown them. Only her knife was still useful.

And the cloak. It had been a very long time since Jack had thought about the spidersilk cloak. He'd given it to the Bard along with the wealth-hoard he'd used to buy Pega's freedom. It was probably in one of the old man's chests.

"Thank you for showing me this," Jack told the hobgoblins. "My problems don't seem so important after watching leaves fall from the Great Tree." He stood up.

"You can't be thinking of going to bed yet," said the Nemesis. "The night's entertainment has just begun."

"Excuse me?" said Jack.

"We haven't forgotten about the Tanners. We're only waiting for your permission to take steps."

Jack remembered how dangerous hobgoblins could be, and he wasn't sure he wanted to involve them. "You wouldn't do anything *drastic*, would you?"

"Of course not," scoffed the Nemesis. "Only a harmless bit of hobgoblinry, no worse than saying boo at a birthday party."

"Dragon Tongue thinks it's an excellent idea," the Bugaboo added.

"I suppose . . . if the Bard agrees, and if you promise not to hurt them . . ."

"Never!" The Nemesis's eyes gleamed in the starlight.

"Well . . . all right."

"At last! I get first crack at Ythla," cried Blewit, jumping up.

"I get Ymma for what she did to dear Pega," said the Bugaboo.

"Wait! Wait!" shouted Jack as the hobgoblins bounded off like giant frogs, but they paid no attention. He followed them as best he could in the darkness, with the streaks of light falling from the sky and the stars shaking as though they would come loose.

Chapter Thirteen

THE PATHS OPEN

Jack fell several times on the way. His eyes weren't as good as the hobgoblins', and they were used to traveling in the dark. He was anxious to get to the Tanner hovel before anything happened. But by the time he arrived, the hobgoblins had already got inside. "Phoo! Filthy in here," he heard the Nemesis say. Then out they came, each one carrying a Tanner. They leaped over the fields, and every time their feet touched earth, Jack heard a scream.

"We've come to take you away!" the hobgoblins shrieked, tossing their captives into the air and catching them.

"No! Not Mrs. Tanner!" Jack shouted. They were too swift for him.

"We've got a lovely dark hole full of earthworms," Blewit warbled. It was the first time Jack had ever heard him sound happy. "We're going to put you inside and feed you spiders and all kinds of nasty, oozy things."

Ythla sobbed and begged for mercy.

"Mercy! Not likely, after you stole from people who took you in."

"We're sorry! We won't do it again!"

"Oh, you won't. Not where you're going," gloated Blewit.

By now the hobgoblins had passed beyond the village and were approaching the hazel wood. Jack's side hurt from running and his legs threatened to give out. Now he understood why his father hadn't been able to catch the hobgoblins when they stole Hazel all those years ago.

The creatures raced through the hazel wood, zigging and zagging along paths Jack could only guess at. *The* draugr *is in here somewhere,* he thought. But he had no time to be afraid. He stumbled after the sound of running feet, more often than not colliding with bushes or tripping over roots. By the time he got to the other side, he was at the end of his strength. He collapsed onto the ground.

He was lying in the broad road carved out by the Wild Hunt. The starlight had grown brighter, as though light were leaking from some unknown source. The hobgoblins had put down the girls and their mother. It was the first time the Tanners had got a good look at their captors.

"Oh, dear God! They're demons," groaned Ymma.

"We're demons! We're demons!" screeched the Nemesis,

doing a cartwheel around the terrified group. "We've come to take you away!"

"Stoke up the fires!" sang the Bugaboo. "We've got a load of sinners to deliver!"

"We repent!" cried Mrs. Tanner.

"Too late." Blewit stuck his long face close to hers, and she screamed. "You stole, you lied, you cheated—and you hurt little girls."

"We'll never do it again. We'll leave the village." Ythla tried to hide behind her mother, but the Nemesis pulled her out by one leg.

"You *are* leaving the village," he said, grinning dreadfully.

Jack by now had got back his breath. He was satisfied with the girls' punishment, but he felt the hobgoblins were being too hard on Mrs. Tanner. "Stop that at once," he called, getting to his feet.

"Eek! It's the young bard!" shrieked the Nemesis, bouncing into the air with exaggerated terror.

"Please, oh great one, don't turn us into stone!" cried the Bugaboo, falling to his knees.

Jack understood then that the hobgoblins were inviting him to rescue the Tanners. "I might or I might not turn you into stone," he said carelessly. "The girls certainly deserve to be dragged down to Hell, but you've gone too far with their mother. She's innocent."

"She is not!" Blewit said indignantly. "I heard her plotting to drive Hazel and Pega away—and you, too, if she could manage it. I say let's sharpen the pitchforks and roast them all."

"Submit, demons!" cried Jack, raising his arms the way the Bard had when he battled the *draugr*. The Nemesis rolled into a ball, and the Bugaboo unfurled his ears to their fullest extent—*fwup!*—and furled them up again. Blewit merely folded his arms and waited. "I've decided that these sinners should be spared—for the moment—on condition that they leave the village as soon as possible."

"We'll do it. We'll be good," whimpered Mrs. Tanner.

"Very well. You demons can go," Jack said grandly.

"Oh, can we? Oh, thank you, great bard," said the Nemesis, groveling in a way Jack knew was sarcastic.

"But if we see one scrap of bad behavior," growled Blewit, "if you make Hazel cry or upset Pega, we'll be back!"

All three of the hobgoblins popped out of sight, but their voices still resounded: *"We'll! Be! Back!"*

The Tanners clung to one another, not daring to move, until Jack took Mrs. Tanner's arm. He still felt sorry for her, although he believed Blewit. She wasn't innocent. She had probably trained her daughters to be thieves. "I'll take you home," he said. The Tanners followed him docilely, and at the edge of the hazel wood he cast his mind out to feel what creatures were abroad in the darkness.

To his amazement the scene before him cleared, as a muddy stream does when clean water flows into it. He could see exactly where the paths were, and he knew that the *draugr* had hidden herself elsewhere. "Hold hands and follow me," he commanded.

On the other side Ymma, very hesitantly, said, "I'm sorry I

called you a 'damned wizard.' It was foolish of me. We would have been lost"—she swallowed hard—"if you hadn't rescued us. How did you know we were in trouble?"

"I'm a bard," said Jack. "I know these things."

"You do realize what you've done," said the Bard the next day. He and Jack had set out to inspect the inlet where Skakki and his crew would land. The stones of the old Roman road were covered in moss and shaded by a canopy of beech trees so thick that the twilight never lifted. The air was hot and still. The only thing moving was a haze of mosquitoes. "You do realize that in forcing the Tanners out, you've taken responsibility for their move."

"I couldn't leave them here. They'd be up to their old tricks in no time," Jack said sullenly.

"I'm not criticizing you." The Bard stopped and wiped sweat from his brow. "Whew! It's as hot as a dragon's belly in here. I wouldn't be surprised if we had a thunderstorm tonight." Which meant, Jack knew, that they *would* have a thunderstorm tonight. The Bard was never wrong about such things.

"The Tanners will be far better off in Bebba's Town," the old man went on, "where their troublemaking won't be so noticeable. There are many places they can find work. Really, lad, you've done them a favor."

"So . . . how will they get to Bebba's Town?" the boy asked, guessing he wouldn't like the answer.

"On Skakki's ship, of course. Will you look at that road!

Straight as an arrow and hardly a rock out of place. The Romans were amazing builders. Unfortunately, they didn't have a speck of sympathy for nature. A road had to go from here to there by the shortest way possible, and if a tree was in the way, they cut it down. If there was a hillock, they leveled it. That's why the Romans aren't here anymore. Nature doesn't take kindly to being pushed around."

They continued walking, with the Bard stepping sure-footedly on the slippery moss with hardly any help from his staff. The air changed as they neared the inlet, becoming cooler and mixed with the smell of seaweed. In the distance Jack heard surf. "Perhaps there won't be room for the Tanners," he said hopefully.

"I sailed on this ship with Olaf," the old man said. "He could ferry a herd of horses with it—well, to be accurate, he could *steal* a herd of horses with it. Our cargo isn't large, and we'll only have you, me, Thorgil, and Seafarer for passengers. There's plenty of room for the Tanners."

Wonderful, thought Jack. *Ymma, Ythla, and Thorgil crammed in together like a box full of spiders.* Not to mention Sven the Vengeful, Eric Pretty-Face, and that new fellow, Schlaup. Thorgil said Schlaup could lift an ox over his head with one hand.

Northmen loved picking fights better than swilling ale, and they were extremely fond of ale. Jack remembered how Olaf had kept order with blows and threats, and wondered whether Skakki was tough enough. "Isn't Brother Aiden going?" the boy asked. By now they had reached the path that led from the road to the sea.

"Aiden would die rather than set foot on a Northman ship," said the Bard. "He saw his friends murdered by some of the very people we're going to travel with."

Jack, too, had seen Northmen run berserk, and the memory still haunted his dreams.

A tongue of land formed a shallow bay and made an ideal place to anchor. It was well hidden from view, and on either side was a beach of clean white sand. The Bard found a rock to sit on. "Swallows have reported seeing Skakki's ship a week to the south. You can stop furrowing your brow, Jack. He's trading amber and sea ivory this time, not slaves."

"This time," Jack said bitterly.

"I've told the villagers we're taking an Irish merchant vessel and have been vague about where it's to be anchored," the old man said. "You understand that we can't let them catch sight of the crew. You and Thorgil will have to do all the loading."

"What about the Tanners?" said Jack.

"I'd rather they didn't know who we're sailing with until it's too late."

They sat for a while, watching the waves break beyond the tongue of land. Green sandpipers scurried along the beach, running for safety when the water foamed in. A flock of black-and-white eider ducks sailed overhead.

Brother Aiden had told Jack that eider ducks had once befriended St. Cuthbert. They had attended his sermons, and the mother eiders trusted him so much, they had let him pick up their chicks. When St. Cuthbert became abbot of the Holy

Isle, he forbade anyone to hunt the birds. But a wicked monastery servant had killed one and thrown the evidence into the sea. The very next day the sea had coughed up bones and feathers onto the chapel doorstep. For even the sea, Brother Aiden said, knew better than to lie to a saint.

Jack had heard many stories about St. Cuthbert and animals. Otters kept him warm when he meditated, sea eagles dropped fish when he was hungry. Once, the saint scolded a pair of ravens for stealing thatch, and they brought him a lump of fat to oil his boots with, by way of apology. It was Christian magic and, as far as Jack could see, not that different from the Bard's magic.

The old man said the life force flowed in streams deep in the earth. If you understood its workings, you could call it forth—or rather *it* chose to listen to your call. This was where the power to do magic came from. Jack didn't understand much of this explanation, but he knew the power was difficult to control. And sometimes things happened that weren't supposed to happen.

"I could see the paths in the hazel wood last night," Jack said aloud.

"That's excellent," said the Bard.

"But I don't know how I did it."

The Bard smiled. "Quite a lot of what we do is a mystery, even to us." Jack's heart warmed to the word *us*. "Learning magic is like knocking at the same door again and again. For a long time no one answers. You imagine that the tenant is at the other end of the garden pulling weeds, or perhaps he's in bed. After a while you decide no one's at home. You turn to go, but knock one last time and lo! The door opens."

"Does that mean I can see the paths whenever I want now?"

"It means you won't be kept waiting as long next time." The old man reached into a sack tied to his belt and removed his silver flute. "I thought it was time you practiced this. Have you ever played a flute?"

Jack's mind went back to the years before the Bard had arrived. When John the Fletcher had shot a swan, he'd made whistles from the hollow wing bones. All the village children had received such gifts, but only Jack had shown talent. He'd been able to create a tune with the crude instrument while the others had been satisfied with blasting one another's eardrums. When the huntsman had seen Jack's ability, he'd made him a real flute out of apple wood.

The boy had been transported by its music. He'd played and played until Father, who thought such activities were a waste of time and probably wicked, had cast the instrument into the fire.

Jack was swept with anger as he remembered. He reminded himself that Father had changed since the trip to Bebba's Town. There were fewer lectures on sin and more opportunities for fun. But still, the memory of that beautiful instrument burning—

"An acorn for your thoughts," the Bard remarked.

"Oh! I'm sorry!" Jack was startled out his reverie. "I have played a flute, sir, but not one so fine."

"There *are* none finer. This was made for Amergin. We

won't call bats now because it's unfair to drag them into the sunlight. Let's start with field mice."

"Field mice?" echoed Jack.

"You never know when you might need something chewed. Watch where my fingers go and listen to the sound." The Bard put the flute to his lips and his fingers covered seven of the eight holes. Jack heard a faint squeaking, such as one might detect near a haystack on a summer day. The old man repeated it several times, with the boy watching intently, before handing the flute over.

The first sound came out as an alarming buzz.

"Stop!" cried the Bard, covering his ears. "You're calling up hornets!" He demonstrated the method again, and gradually, Jack got the idea. It wasn't the same as playing a harp. It was more like talking to one person in a crowded room. He or she could pick out your voice from all the others because only you were trying to communicate. In this case, the field mice were like a single, listening ear among a thousand ears in the forest.

Jack looked down to see dozens of beady little eyes observing him from the leaf litter. Some mice had crept onto his feet and a few bold ones had climbed onto his lap. Jack kept playing, elated and a little frightened, until the Bard gently took the flute from his hands.

"That's enough, lad. We must let them go before a hawk discovers them." The old man waved his hand and the tiny creatures pattered away. The sun had turned toward the west and the predicted thunderclouds had begun to build. They hurried home along the moss-covered Roman road.

Chapter Fourteen

SCHLAUP

A week had passed and the inlet was wrapped in fog so thick, dawn barely penetrated it. Jack and Thorgil had traveled by the light of a horn lantern, and now they waited together on the chilly sand. Thorgil was barely able to sit still for excitement. "We're going to take ship again. I'm going home. Isn't it wonderful?" she said.

Jack pulled his woolen cloak tighter. Water droplets beaded his hair. His backside was as wet as a frog's bottom.

"Well, isn't it wonderful?"

"I suppose so," he grumbled. "What's taking them so long?" Only a foot or two of water was visible and a pale ribbon of foam moved in and out of sight.

"They have to be careful in fog," said Thorgil. "Eric the Rash has to stand at the prow with a weighted line to call out the depth. Listen! I think I can hear him now."

Jack listened. All he could hear was surf muttering along the coast. Gradually, the sky paled and the sea turned a faint gray-green. The tongue of land appeared like a stain against the fog.

"Four oars deep," floated a voice over the water. Jack had to strain to understand the words. It had been almost two years since he'd spoken the Northman language. "Three oars deep . . . slowly, slowly, I can see land. Two oars deep. Slow down, you *kindaskitur*! It's as shallow as a miser's purse!"

Kindaskitur*s*: *sheep droppings*, translated Jack. And then he saw it: the long graceful outline, the sail reefed against the mast, the shaggy shapes leaning on the oars. The prow was oddly shortened, and he remembered that the great dragon head, carved by Olaf One-Brow, had to be removed when they came to shore. Otherwise, it would anger the land spirits.

"Drop anchor!" roared a new voice Jack recognized as Skakki's.

"We're here! We're here!" screamed Thorgil, jumping up and down.

Jack heard splashing and thrashing as oars were unshipped and heavy shapes dropped into the water. Jack found that his heart was thudding. It was hard not to feel fear at the arrival of Northmen. The first shape waded to shore, taller than any man had a right to be, and swung Thorgil around in a bear hug.

"Little sister!" cried Skakki. "You're as welcome as sun after storm! Scrawny as ever, I see."

"I am not!" protested Thorgil, laughing.

"It's that feeble Saxon food. I'll put you on the outside of a couple of roast oxen to fatten you up. Who's this runt?"

Jack looked up, appalled. Skakki had grown more than a foot since he'd last seen him, and the man's shoulders and chest had broadened out. He was a true son of Olaf One-Brow now, except for the eyes. Where Olaf had peered out at the world with cheerful brutishness, Skakki had his mother's depth of mind.

"I am Dragon Tongue's assistant," Jack said, drawing himself up as tall as possible.

"Ah! The skald," Skakki said, using the Northman word for *bard*.

"He's really only an apprentice," said Thorgil.

Jack let it pass. He was more interested in the other shapes that appeared from the fog: Sven the Vengeful, Eric the Rash, Eric Pretty-Face, and other men he didn't know that well, but who were as villainous-looking as the rest. Eric Pretty-Face had horrific scars and ears that were almost chewed off. "IT'S JACK!" he roared, and the boy remembered that the man was nearly deaf and always shouted. "GOOD TO SEE YOU, SKALD. DO YOU HAVE A CHARM AGAINST HANGNAILS? I'VE GOT ONE THAT'S DRIVING ME CRAZY."

How can you be bothered by a hangnail after being chewed on by trolls? thought Jack, but he said he would ask the Bard for help. The Northmen welcomed him with playful punches and insults, and the boy was moved in spite of himself. He knew they were murderous thugs. They had destroyed the Holy Isle and driven Brother Aiden mad. They'd sold slaves and burned down villages. They'd almost sacrificed Lucy to the goddess Freya. And yet . . . he couldn't bring himself to hate them.

"Where's Rune?" Jack asked.

"These days he needs help getting to shore," Skakki said. "Hey, Schlaup!" A sound somewhat like the grunt of a wild boar came from the ship. "Bring Rune."

Something large dropped into the sea. A shape loomed in the dove gray fog. If Jack had thought Skakki was enormous, he was nothing compared to what was approaching. Fully seven feet in height, the creature was made taller by bristly hair sprouting from his head. His brow jutted forward in a way Jack had seen before, and two fangs lifted his upper lip into a permanent snarl.

He's a troll, he thought, amazed because Jotuns and Northmen were bitter enemies. As Schlaup came forward, Jack saw that he was actually smaller than a troll. He seemed, in an odd way, more refined. He had a troll's clawlike fingernails, flat teeth, and eyes the color of rotten walnuts, but these features were softened by something vaguely familiar.

"Good Schlaup. Put Rune down," said Skakki. And then Jack noticed the emaciated Northman the creature carried in his arms. Time had not been good to the old skald, and constant exposure to icy winds couldn't have been healthy either. But Jack knew Rune would have it no other way. He would not die in bed like a cowardly thrall. When his time came, if the gods were kind, he would hold a sword in his hand and fall in battle.

"Oh, Rune," said Jack, feeling an ache in the back of his throat. "I'm so glad to see you."

"I wouldn't have missed this voyage for the world," said the skald, standing carefully. "We found Thorgil alive, and now Dragon Tongue will take ship with us. By Thor, I'm looking forward to seeing the old rascal!"

Sven the Vengeful and Eric the Rash had chopped open logs to get at the dry wood inside, and soon a merry fire was blazing on the beach. "You warm up," said Schlaup, urging Rune toward the fire. Jack was startled, for he hadn't expected the creature to speak. Trolls had trouble forming words and usually communicated with one another by thought. Those who did make the effort had harsh, unmusical voices. Schlaup's voice was completely human.

They sat around the fire, exchanging news and making plans on how to load the ship. Thorgil and Jack would move the trade goods halfway and crew members would meet them. No one wanted the Northmen—especially Schlaup—spotted near the village. Jack kept glancing at him.

"Go on, ask," Thorgil said. "I did, the first time I saw him."

"Ah, but I didn't tell you the whole story, little sister," said Skakki, who was lounging on a log with his long legs stretched out before him. "I told you he was a half troll, but I didn't say where we got him."

"Did you say 'half-troll'?" said Jack. The offspring of troll/human marriages were almost always doomed. They were forever torn between two worlds and either went mad or turned vicious. Frothi had devastated King Hrothgar's hall and tried to murder Beowulf. Her sister, Frith, had sent a Nightmare to kill the Bard. When Frith fell into a snit, even berserkers climbed the walls to escape.

Skakki grimaced. "Not all such beings are evil. Much depends on the parents. Frothi and Frith's father had been rescued from an avalanche by the Mountain Queen and imprisoned in her harem. He spent the rest of his life bitterly regretting his captivity. He hated the sight of his daughters. Schlaup had a different father."

"I can see that he is a handsome lout," said Thorgil, using the troll word for *male*. "I look forward to taking ship with him." Schlaup turned a bright orange, the troll equivalent of blushing, and ducked his massive head.

"Go on," said Jack, but Skakki, to his annoyance, insisted on having breakfast first. Bread and cheese was brought from the ship and toasted before the fire. It was excellent bread, and the cheese was strong enough to bring tears to your eyes. Jack, who'd had nothing to eat that morning, was grateful, although he wished Skakki would tell the story *and* eat.

But the Northmen weren't like that. They preferred to do only one thing at a time. If pillaging, they gave their whole attention to it. If feeding, all conversation stopped until their bellies were stuffed.

Skakki produced a large pot of salty black berries that had

come from across the sea. He called them "olives," and Jack thought they were delicious. So did the Northmen, who were besotted with anything salty and jostled one another aside to get at the treat.

The sounds of chomping and slurping filled the air. Sven the Vengeful passed around bags of cider, with a large one reserved for Schlaup. A quarrel broke out over who had eaten the most olives, and Skakki clouted the crewmen nearest him. That was how his father had kept order, Jack remembered, except that when Olaf smacked someone, he stayed smacked for at least ten minutes.

When the food was gone, Skakki suggested a burping contest. Thorgil eagerly joined in, and Jack drummed his fingers with impatience. He knew what the young sea captain was up to. Northmen loved to drag out a story until you were ready to scream and half the fun was making the listeners beg for the conclusion.

When the burping contest was over—Schlaup won with a sulfurous belch that was pure troll—Skakki insisted that Rune produce a poem to celebrate their arrival. "Stop fooling around!" exclaimed Jack. "I want to know Schlaup's history."

Everyone guffawed, with Schlaup producing a deep *wuh-huh-huh*, and Jack knew they had only been waiting for him to lose his temper. "Do you really, really, really want to know?" cooed Skakki.

Jack sighed. "I really, really, really want to know."

Skakki paused for effect, and everyone leaned forward, though all of them, except Thorgil, must have known the tale.

"One dark, snowy night," began the young captain, "we heard a knock on the door of our hall. Everyone stopped what he was doing, for we knew few beings ventured out in the dead of winter. The ships were drawn up onto land, the sheep were locked into their pens. Honest folk, and even the dishonest ones, were sheltering inside their houses.

"We listened. One knock meant a *draugr* was lurking outside. You definitely don't want to open the door to a *draugr*, because—"

"Don't change the subject," said Jack.

Skakki smiled evilly. "I thought you were interested in *draugr*s. Thorgil says you've got one in the village."

Jack restrained himself with the greatest difficulty. Nothing entertained Northmen more than making you lose control.

"Very well," Skakki went on. "We waited and listened. Whoever it was knocked *three* times. We waited again and the sound was repeated. Yet you don't want to be hasty, for all kinds of things are abroad in the dark. The men took up their weapons and sent the women and children to the back of the hall." Skakki paused to gulp down cider, taking his time about it. Jack wanted to upend the bag over his head.

"I opened the door a crack. Outside, the snow was coming down in flakes as big as my hand. Before me, almost invisible, were two huge creatures wrapped in cloaks of white wolf skin. 'Trolls!' I shouted. I tried to close the door, but one of them shoved it open so forcefully that it ripped off its hinges.

"'Put down your weapon, son of Olaf One-Brow,' the creature said. 'I bring greetings from Glamdis, the Mountain

Queen.' And she—for it was a female—held out a carving of an elk. Do you remember how Olaf loved to make toys out of wood and how he decorated our hall with wolves and bears? No one could make better animals. I recognized his work.

"'I am Fonn, daughter of the Mountain Queen,' the troll announced. 'This is my sister Forath. I speak for both of us, because she cannot use human speech.' It was then that I felt the muttering of troll-thought in my mind," said Skakki. "Meanwhile, the snow was blowing inside in great drifts."

"'Olaf made this elk for us on one of his visits,' said Fonn. 'And once, while he was visiting our mother, he made Schlaup.' She stepped aside, and I saw a third, smaller shape behind her. It was a young lout."

"Wait!" said Thorgil. "You mean Schlaup is Olaf's son?"

"Indeed, he is. When you get used to him, you'll see the similarity," said Skakki.

"Another brother," cried Thorgil, transported. "I knew he was quality the minute I saw him."

"Glamdis was so deeply in love with Olaf, she didn't try to imprison him in her harem," Skakki said. "That was most unusual, for Glamdis likes to enslave her louts and they, by all accounts, enjoy being enslaved."

"No one was ever able to control Olaf," said Rune.

Jack was appalled, not so much by Schlaup's existence, but by Olaf's part in it. Jotun females were eight feet tall with bristly orange hair sprouting from their heads and shoulders. Their fangs, though daintier than the tusks of the louts, weren't what most men found attractive in a wife.

"HE MADE A TROLL QUEEN FALL IN LOVE WITH HIM. WHAT A HERO!" bellowed Eric Pretty-Face.

"Then why did she cast out his son?" Jack asked.

All eyes turned to Schlaup, who seemed embarrassed by the attention. "Because I can't think straight," he said.

"Nonsense," said Skakki. "There's nothing wrong with your brain. You just can't pass thoughts through the air like the trolls. Neither can I." He turned to Jack. "Fonn explained that Schlaup's disability made him too isolated. She and Forath cared for him, but after Olaf died, there was no one who could carry on a real conversation with him. No troll-maiden ever selected him to dance. No lout invited him to play Dodge the Spear. It was decided that Schlaup had a better chance of happiness with his father's kin."

"And so he does," Thorgil declared warmly. She sat next to him and laid her head against his massive chest. "I, too, have a disability," she said. "My right hand was paralyzed when I fought Garm, the Hound of Hel. At first I was devastated and wanted to die, but I remembered what Olaf always said: You must never give up, even if you're falling off a cliff. You never know what might happen on the way down."

Schlaup rumbled deep in his chest like a gigantic cat.

Jack was amazed. After all those months of lamenting about her hand, all those tantrums and fits of despair, Thorgil seemed perfectly at ease with her handicap. It must have been the presence of the Northmen and her brother—*brothers*, Jack corrected himself. Dear God, *he* was having trouble getting used to Hazel. She was at least human, not a seven-foot monster.

But the Northmen didn't judge people by their looks. They might be brutish, violent, and dangerous, but they were also loyal and courageous. If someone possessed those virtues, it didn't matter that he had bristly orange hair and a belch that smelled like a dead whale. Of all the people in the village, Jack remembered, only Thorgil had never commented on Pega's ugliness. And that was because she simply couldn't see it.

Chapter Fifteen

ALL ABOARD

Jack and Thorgil ferried baskets to the ship until he thought they must have walked the distance to Bebba's Town three times over. Even with the donkey's help, the process was exhausting. They met the Northmen halfway, handed over their burdens, and returned for yet another load.

After two days another Northman ship, captained by Egil Long-Spear, anchored in the little inlet. Egil had gone on raids with Olaf, but he was not a berserker. His heart wasn't in killing, and in better times he would have made a good farmer. Unfortunately, the Northman lands were barren. Most years the only source of food was plunder, and Egil, making the best of a bad lot, combined pillaging with trade. He much preferred trade.

Of all the Northmen, he was the most presentable. He had an easy, friendly manner, spoke fluent Saxon, and genuinely liked Saxons. He had sailed from the Northland in a broad-beamed ship designed for transport, not battle. Jack had wondered how Skakki could have traded with anyone, but now he understood.

Good-natured Egil had been the one who sailed into port, while Skakki lurked in the shadows. Egil traded furs, sea ivory, reindeer antlers, and amber from both ships. He returned with silver, casks of olives, salt blocks, Spanish wine, and, for his own ship, a flock of sheep.

Jack found the sheep extremely interesting. They clustered together in a docile herd, and their wool was so thick, he could sink his hands in it up to the wrists. Egil said they had come from the same land as the olives and were called "merinis."

On the last night Jack's parents threw a farewell party. Brother Aiden, the Bard, and the Tanners were invited. Mother baked honey cakes, Pega made an eel stew, and Father roasted a large salmon in the coals. Unknown to him, the salmon had been provided by the Nemesis, who had dangled his wiggly toes in the sea while Mr. Blewit waited nearby with a club. Also unknown to Father was the hobgoblins' parallel party in the fields.

The hobgoblins feasted on mushrooms and salmon, and toasted each other with Brother Aiden's excellent heather ale. After dinner they began skirling. They puffed up like giant frogs and let the air out slowly, closing first one nostril, then the other to vary the pitch. The result was such a horrid wailing that villagers in houses all around clutched their crosses and prayed for deliverance. Some of them implored Thor and Odin for mercy, in case Jesus was busy.

"You may need these in your negotiations," Brother Aiden said, handing a parcel to the Bard.

The Bard felt the package and nodded. "I hope it will not come to that."

Come to what? thought Jack. All day mysterious signals had been passing between the two men. They could not discuss the *draugr* openly, nor could they admit that Skakki's ship was in port. That would have caused so much curiosity and so many expeditions up and down the coast that the secret of the Northmen would have been out. As far as the villagers knew, the trip was going to take place next month.

Everyone at the party knew of the departure, of course, and Pega got teary-eyed when she gave Jack a basket of her special scones. The dough to make them had been pounded repeatedly with a mallet to preserve the finished product for weeks or even months. "I know you'll come back before then." Pega sniffled. "You *must* come back."

"I'm not going to die," Jack said.

"You never know what's around the corner," the girl said, wiping her eyes. "One of my owners went to the henhouse to gather eggs and was trampled by a bull. I was beaten because I was supposed to collect the eggs."

"If you had gone, you would have been trampled," pointed out Hazel, who was in her usual place by Pega's side. Her behavior had improved enormously since the Tanners had retreated to their hovel.

"I didn't count," Pega said.

Jack hated it when she spoke of her owners. It reminded everyone that she'd been a slave. "Nothing's going to happen to me," he insisted.

"That's what people always say."

"You count with me," said Hazel, snuggling against Pega. The older girl stroked her hair, and it seemed to Jack that his sister was much fonder of Pega than she was of her own mother. Not that Mother didn't try. But there was always a slight hesitation before she hugged Hazel. Father didn't hug her at all.

It will all come right somehow, Jack thought.

"Would you like to see us off?" the Bard asked Brother Aiden.

"Oh, no—I couldn't," said the little monk, turning pale. "The very sight of—"

"Careful," warned the Bard as the Tanner girls left off stuffing themselves and came over to listen.

"Why doesn't everybody come with us to say good-bye?" demanded Ymma. "We deserve a nice send-off."

"I don't know why you're all so hush-hush about it," Ythla said. "People keep asking when we're going, and I have to keep telling lies."

"Don't nag the Bard," Mrs. Tanner scolded. "Honestly, sir, I don't know what's become of them since their father died."

"I know what *might* become of them if the wrong ears

are listening," said Jack, and he was gratified to see all three Tanners flinch.

He spent the last night at home. He tried to keep the peace by attending Father's prayer session, something he hadn't done for a long time. It wasn't that he disliked prayers. He enjoyed listening to Brother Aiden even though he couldn't understand Latin. It merely seemed that praying was a form of Christian magic, and some people were better at it than others. Father dwelled too much on grievances and sins. If Jack had been God, he would have preferred more appreciation for the things that did go right.

When Jack rose before dawn, Pega was already waiting for him, pale and woebegone. Breakfast was a mostly silent affair, with Father exhorting him to avoid temptation and Pega quietly weeping. Hazel picked up her mood and started to cry too. Mother stared down at her hands. Jack couldn't wait to get out of the house.

"It's only a short trip," he protested as Mother accompanied him as far as the beehives. "I don't know why everyone's making such a fuss about it."

"You're going off with Northmen," Mother said. "Even if, as Thorgil swears, they've taken an oath to help us, Northmen attract danger as oak trees draw lightning."

The bees were flying to and fro, making use of the long summer days. The two surviving hives had grown into four, after careful watching to follow and capture new swarms. "I looked into the water," Mother said.

Jack tensed. Mother was a wise woman, though she took

care to conceal it from Father. One of her arts was to gaze into a bowl of still water until the surface deepened, showing distant places and things that would come to pass. These visions were rarely clear. She might see a stag walking through a forest or a woman standing on a cliff. The meaning would become clear only later.

"I saw you—you and Thorgil—in a little boat," Mother said. "It was evening and the sun had marked out a path of shining gold on the water. I tried to call to you, but you raised your arm in farewell. You were holding a bard's staff. That's all."

"What does it mean?" said Jack. His staff had been lost when he freed Din Guardi from the grip of Unlife.

"I don't know, but . . ." She paused, and Jack was appalled to see tears on her cheeks. "It felt as though you were going on a far longer journey than to Bebba's Town. It felt as though you were never coming back."

"Of course I'll return!" cried Jack. "I fought my way out of Jotunheim and survived the dungeons of the elves, didn't I? You must stop listening to Pega's stories."

Mother smiled ruefully. "I suppose I have been listening to her. She told me about a man dying from a bee sting and someone else falling down a well."

"Her ex-owners all seemed to have bad luck."

Mother laughed, and Jack was able to leave her with a lighter heart. But he puzzled over the vision. He and Thorgil in a small boat? That wasn't surprising. But the sun setting over water to the west wasn't possible on this coastline. The sea lay to the east.

The Tanners had large bags filled with clothes and cooking utensils, some of which Jack suspected came from his house. As they walked along, Ymma called out to a farmer that they were off to Bebba's Town.

The farmer cupped his hands. "What's that? Is the ship here?"

"Not yet!" Jack called, and turned on the girl. "I told you to keep your mouth shut."

"Why should I?" Ymma retorted. "Anyone would think we were going *pillaging*, like you did with those nasty Northmen."

"I didn't go with them willingly and I never, ever, pillaged. If you knew anything about it, you wouldn't suggest the possibility." Jack was struggling to keep his temper.

"*I* know what pillaging is," Ythla chimed in. "It means having lots of nice things."

"It means killing and burning," said Jack.

Ythla shrugged, and her mother made no attempt to scold her daughter. It suddenly occurred to Jack that the Tanners were about to encounter real experts on pillaging. He felt a small glow of happiness inside.

Most of the Bard's cargo was already aboard, but important items had to be carried personally. The old man had the mysterious parcel Brother Aiden had given him, as well as a bag of his more important tools. Jack was in charge of Fair Lamenting, the Bard's harp, and the great bird Seafarer. The Tanners complained bitterly when they realized Jack wasn't going to help carry their belongings.

"You can leave things behind," he said. "I'm sure Pega could find a use for them."

"Not on your life!" said Ymma.

"We're being driven into the wilderness," moaned Mrs. Tanner. "How can we abandon anything that might stand between us and destruction?"

"You *are* heartless," said Ythla.

For a moment Jack wavered—he was genuinely sorry for Mrs. Tanner—but he knew he couldn't take on any more burdens. And so they set out, with the Bard going first to show the way. Jack stayed behind long enough to close up the Roman house.

We go north, he explained in Bird to Seafarer as he checked to be sure nothing had been left behind. He'd learned enough of the language for simple conversation. *Maybe catch fish.*

Fish are good, said Seafarer, fluffing his feathers. *Maybe find female.*

Jack didn't know. He'd never seen an albatross before this one, but where a storm blew one such creature, it might blow two.

When he closed the door for the last time, he felt a strange presence. Out of the corner of his eye he saw a man dressed in a white tunic, holding two children by the hand. The children laughed and pointed at something in the distance, but when Jack turned, the vision was gone.

He didn't worry about leaving the house unguarded because the hobgoblins were going to move in. Any villager who decided to explore the apparently empty dwelling would get a horrid surprise. Hobgoblins could make themselves invisible to human eyes, but their long, sticky fingers felt entirely real.

Seafarer flew better than Jack had expected, and they managed to catch up with the Bard and the Tanners. Thorgil had already warned the Northmen of Seafarer's size. "He's lord of the southern skies," she had told them. "He travels with us to visit the ravens of Odin." This wasn't true, but it insured that no one would try to put the albatross into a cooking pot.

"By Asgard, you're a sight for these old eyes!" cried Rune when he saw the Bard. "I thought the fishes had eaten you after we set you adrift. No hard feelings, I hope."

"None whatsoever," the Bard replied. "It was Frith's doing." The Northmen gathered around, for all knew Dragon Tongue except Schlaup. He hung back shyly until the Bard beckoned him forward. "Schlaup Olaf's Son! Tell me, has the Mountain Queen forgiven me for melting a hole through her wall?"

"Not yet," said the giant, shuffling his feet.

Meanwhile, Jack was having a complicated time keeping the Tanners from fleeing. The only thing that helped was that they were unwilling to let go of their belongings. "It doesn't matter who sails the ship," Jack said desperately. "You don't need to talk to them. We'll be in Bebba's Town in no time."

"Those are Northmen," hissed Mrs. Tanner. "You've sold us into slavery! *Dear God, what's that?*" Schlaup had turned around at the sound of her voice. He grinned, showing jumbled teeth.

"It's a troll!" shrieked Ythla.

"Half-troll, actually," Jack said.

"He's going to eat us! Help! Help! Let me go!" cried Mrs. Tanner, trying to wrench herself away.

Skakki was watching with amusement, but when the Tanners looked as though they might actually escape, he turned to Schlaup. "Bring them," he ordered.

The giant lurched forward like an eager hound, swept up all the Tanners and their bags, and waded out to the ship. "Don't drop us!" wailed Ymma. "We can't swim!"

"Drop us!" begged Mrs. Tanner. "It's better to drown than be eaten."

But Schlaup did neither. He plopped them onto the deck and sat down next to them. He lifted the tip of Mrs. Tanner's untidy braid between his fingers and sniffed it.

Soon the long, graceful ship was loaded and slid from the inlet onto a bright, sunlit ocean. The waves settled into a regular pattern, and the red-and-cream-striped sail bellied out above. Thorgil sat in the stern to manage the rudder.

Once they were away from land, Sven the Vengeful climbed onto the prow and reattached the wonderful dragon's head, carved from real life by Olaf. Again the craft became a noble *karfi*, the streamlined battleship that Jack remembered. The Northmen began to sing:

From whence comes the wind
That stirs the sea,
From where the force
That fans fire to flame?

On the great Tree sits an eagle.
His wings drive the foam-tipped wave
Over the ale-horn of the sea.

The air of this world
Flows from his wings.
Marvelous are the winds made,
Yet never seen.

In the distance a small speck marked out the position of Egil Long-Spear's craft. The fat *knorr* was ideal for carrying trade goods, but it was also easy to overtake and plunder. Thus Egil depended on Skakki's protection, while at the same time he provided cover for the berserkers.

One thing Jack had forgotten was the smell of the ship. The Northmen's boots stank like carrion and their clothes reeked of sweat. Bilge sloshed beneath their feet and the very timbers of the craft were soaked with ancient fish blood and worse. The breeze carried away some, but not all of it. The Tanners were draped over the side, throwing up, and Jack, to his shame, soon joined them.

Chapter Sixteen

A LOVE STORY

They passed small islands inhabited only by gulls, eiders, and puffins. To the left the mainland was a green smear, and to the right endless waves came out of the east and rocked the ship. It was a calm sea, although the Tanners complained loudly and feared they would be sent to the bottom at any moment.

"Wait till they see a real storm," said Thorgil, who was watching the distant shoreline with Jack.

"Let's hope we get to Bebba's Town before anything happens," Jack said. They were moving slowly to keep pace with Egil. The Bard and Rune had settled in the stern, and from time to time one of them would take up his harp and sing.

Then crew members would gather around and the rear of the ship would sink perilously low while the prow lifted.

That evening they camped on a bluff overhanging the sea. The two ships bobbed side by side, for there was no good place to draw up on land. Egil's sheep bleated plaintively as they eyed the shore, and tenderhearted Schlaup waded out to them with armloads of grass. Egil's men built a bonfire. The Bard told the story of how he spent a week on an ice floe with a bear. Rune recounted the saga of Olaf One-Brow rescuing Ivar the Boneless from trolls, but not before Ivar had married Frith Half-Troll.

"What a huge mistake that was," said Sven the Vengeful.

"You can't really blame Ivar," Eric Long-Spear argued. "She was very beautiful when she was in a good mood."

"You know what happens when half-trolls lose their tempers—," Sven began.

"Careful!" Eric glanced toward Schlaup, but Schlaup wasn't paying attention. He was sniffing Mrs. Tanner's braid, and she was smiling girlishly.

Jack was astounded. The giant couldn't possibly—it wasn't thinkable that—"Does he *like* her?" Jack whispered to Thorgil.

Thorgil laughed. "Why not? Mrs. Tanner is sturdy. That's important to a troll. She's already proven she can have children. *And* she orders him around."

Which was true, thought Jack. Once Ymma and Ythla's mother had realized that Schlaup could be bullied, she gave him a constant stream of orders. The giant was sent hunting for snacks, furs to rest on, bags of cider. He stood obediently in the sun to provide her with shade. It was what louts were used to from their females.

"What can she possibly see in him?" said Jack.

"I'm surprised you can even ask that question about my brother," replied Thorgil indignantly. "He's big, he's strong, and he's clearly a good provider. She needs someone to take care of her and the children."

It made sense, Jack conceded, but he still wasn't convinced. It suited Mrs. Tanner to have a willing slave for as long as the voyage lasted. He doubted whether she wanted a half-troll trailing after her when they reached land. Thorgil might not be able to see Schlaup's defects, but any normal person would. "By the way, where are Ymma and Ythla?" he asked.

Thorgil looked around. "On the ship, I suppose. They can't swim and they refused to let Schlaup carry them ashore." Then the Bard called for Thorgil to recite poetry, and she rose gladly to perform.

Seafarer, who had been sitting at her feet, rose too and gave a loud scream that everyone had learned was a victory cry. His irritability and willingness to fight had charmed the Northmen from the very beginning. Seafarer, for his part, considered the crew to be part of his flock. *I am great; I am powerful; I am terrifying,* he screamed.

Be still. Pecks-from-Afar speaks, said Jack. For a while he had wondered how to say Thorgil's name in Bird, but the albatross had renamed her after watching the shield maiden throw a spear. Seafarer settled down with a grunt of satisfaction.

Thorgil gave one of her usual bloodthirsty sagas in which everyone died messily. Jack listened with only half an ear. He wondered what Ymma and Ythla were up to on the ship.

But the next days passed peacefully—or as peacefully as time ever passed on a Northman ship. Rune told Eric Pretty-Face to shut up because he was making him go deaf, and Eric punched Sven the Vengeful to sooth his feelings. Sven the Vengeful threatened to rip his head off, and Skakki said, "Calm them," to Schlaup, after which Eric and Sven woke up at opposite ends of the ship without quite remembering how they got there.

The final campsite, close to Bebba's Town, was a small inlet cut off from the mainland by high cliffs. Northmen had visited it often enough to build a small dock, huts, and permanent corrals for horses and sheep. Egil off-loaded his cargo. Skakki made camp, for the berserkers couldn't show themselves so close to the Holy Isle. Some people in Bebba's Town might recognize them. Thorgil gave Seafarer over to the care of Rune until she returned.

The plan was this: Egil would take the Bard and his companions to town and wait for the old man to buy grain and settle the problem of the *draugr* with Father Severus. Afterward Egil would take them back to the village while Skakki waited at the secret port.

In the morning Jack and Thorgil changed into the magnificent clothes the Lady of the Lake had given them. Jack wore a white tunic and a blue cloak embroidered with silver moons and stars. Thorgil had a dark blue tunic and a leaf green robe with vines around the edge. They had both grown in the past year, yet curiously, the clothes had grown with them. The Bard said that the cloth had been woven from the hair of goats that fed upon the leaves of Yggdrassil. Thus, it renewed itself as the Great Tree did.

They would visit King Brutus first to ask for lodging. "I don't fancy sleeping at the monastery after confronting Severus about the *draugr*," the Bard said.

"Are you going to summon her?" asked Jack.

"It depends on how Severus reacts. First, I very much want to know what's become of my daughter. I regularly send swallows to check up on her. They report that she has become increasingly unhappy."

Jack wasn't surprised. Ethne was half-elf and had spent most of her life enjoying pleasures humans could only dream of. He couldn't see her living as a nun.

"For the past two months the swallows haven't been able to find her at all. I tried farseeing and had only a brief vision of her in a small, dark room. It's worrying."

But when Egil's ship cast off, a crisis developed. Schlaup suddenly realized that the Tanners were departing and demanded to be taken along. "No, Schlaup. Stay," ordered Skakki.

"I want my troll-flower," the giant bellowed. "I want her for a wife."

Mrs. Tanner and her daughters were hiding behind a heap of baskets on Egil's ship, and Jack realized she had hoped to slip away before Schlaup noticed.

"You can't go into Bebba's Town. They'll kill you," Skakki explained.

"Not me," said the giant, thumping his chest.

"Yes, you. And me. We can't stand against a whole town."

"Then she stays!" Schlaup suddenly seemed a lot larger. Jack remembered how Frith shape-shifted when she fell into a snit and worried about what form the giant was capable of taking. The Northmen backed away. The Bard raised his staff. But it was Mrs. Tanner who saved the day.

"Bad Schlaup!" she screamed from the ship. "I'll come back when I've finished my shopping trip. If you cause any more trouble, I'll come over there and box your ears!"

This would take some doing, Jack thought, because she could hardly reach them.

Schlaup gave in at once. "I'm sorry, troll-flower. Don't be mad." His lip quivered.

"That's better," said Mrs. Tanner. "If you're a good lout, I'll bring you a treat from Bebba's Town. Now sit down and behave." The giant crouched obediently on the dock as the ship pulled away, and Jack could see his shape long after the other people faded from view.

He found the Bard standing at the prow, gazing at the waves dividing to either side. "Excuse me, sir," he said. "What's going to happen if Mrs. Tanner doesn't come back? I don't think she means to."

"I imagine Schlaup will be upset," the Bard said.

"Yes, but what will he do?"

"He won't harm us. It's not in his nature." The old man sat down on one of the chests from the Roman house. It was filled with jars of Beelzebub's Remedy Against Flies.

"On the shore just now," the boy said, unsure how to describe it, "Schlaup looked different. Bigger. I remembered Frith . . ."

"Ah! So that's what you're worried about. The answer is yes, Schlaup can shape-shift if he falls into a snit, but he would never attack friends. He's anchored by Olaf's solid character. He has his father's openheartedness and his troll mother's inability to lie. It's bad luck that he's managed to fall in love with someone who doesn't know the meaning of truth."

"Love?" said Jack, appalled.

"I'm afraid so. And you're quite right: Mrs. Tanner hasn't the slightest intention of coming back. Schlaup may well fall into a snit when he discovers he's been lied to, but we'll have to deal with it when the time comes. Do you know how he earned his name?"

Jack shook his head. He sat down across from the Bard and felt the mist being cast up by the prow. Egil's figurehead, an eagle with wings upraised and beak opened to scream, was circled by a delicate rainbow where the sun shone on the spray.

"There's an island in the far north with a mountain completely encased in ice," said the Bard. "Rivers that flowed down its sides have frozen, and snow adds to its height every year. The peak can be seen for many miles, and even when it isn't visible, it casts a bright reflection against the sky."

"Rune told me about that island. He said the Northmen use it for navigation."

"I've been there," said the old man. "Rune has visited it several times in search of sea ivory. But this mountain has a fire inside. Rune says it contains a dragon, but I'm more inclined to think there's a crack leading down to Muspelheim, the world of fire."

A seagull floated idly past, did a double take, and turned back to land by the Bard. It settled down as tame as you please, and the old man stroked its feathers. *Just like St. Cuthbert*, thought Jack.

"At any rate, the fire occasionally breaks through," the Bard continued. "It melts the ice from below until suddenly the whole side of the mountain comes loose and roars down in one glorious, gigantic avalanche. That's what the Northmen call a *schlaup*. And that, apparently, is what our friend looks like when he falls into a snit. I'd like time alone now to think, lad. We're getting close to Bebba's Town."

On the way to the stern, Jack passed the Tanners, who were huddled in a tight group with their many bags around them like a fortress. They reminded him of a flock of ravens guarding the carcass of a deer.

Chapter Seventeen

THE PINK PALACE

The first thing Jack saw on land was the fortress of Din Guardi rising from a shelf of rock. He had to rub his eyes to make sure he wasn't dreaming. A year ago the fortress had been so utterly destroyed that not one stone had been left standing on another. Yet here it was again, grander than before. The old walls had been gray and pockmarked as though they were suffering from some disease. Now they were a delicate pink. The battlements, once so forbidding, were decorated by green stonework so cleverly made that it looked like vines scrolling along the top. At each corner was a pink tower with the prettiest flags imaginable fluttering in the breeze.

Perhaps it had looked so in the days of Lancelot, King Brutus's ancestor, Jack thought. In those days it had been called Joyous Garde and had been the home of music and laughter. But when it fell into Unlife, all joy fled. The halls became icy all year round, and not even weeds could grow in Din Guardi's grim, gray courtyards.

"How in Middle Earth did Brutus do it?" said Thorgil, standing beside Jack.

"He was helped by the Lady of the Lake," said Jack. "She must have used magic."

"Then I wouldn't trust the floors in that place. I saw the magic of Elfland fall apart," the shield maiden said.

"He had the monks of St. Filian's to do the heaviest work, and they don't have any magic at all."

The ship turned toward the port of Bebba's Town and Egil's crew guided it in. The men had been carefully picked. There wasn't a berserker among them, for such warriors were impossible to control, and they had exchanged their leather armor for tunics. Each of them knew enough Saxon to pose as someone from another part of the country. There were differences. Egil's crewmen were taller than the local people and their blue eyes sometimes had a wolfish gleam. An observant man would have noticed the calluses that indicated the use of weapons, but most people weren't observant.

The broad *knorr* edged its way to the dock and was soon tied up. Many people watched to see what sort of cargo this unusual ship carried. Egil brought out only a few trade

items—soapstone bowls, frying pans, and copper cauldrons—
for he had already done the bulk of his trading. The Bard's
goods would be kept on board until market day.

"You can sleep here until you find a place to stay," Egil
told Mrs. Tanner.

"I've had enough of ships," she spat at him. "Death traps,
that's what I call them. Besides, I have a brother in this town
and it's his duty to do right by us." Without a thank-you
or even a good-bye, Mrs. Tanner started off with Ymma
and Ythla in her wake. They dragged the bulky bags behind
them.

"Good riddance," muttered Jack.

His spirits rose as they walked along the road to Din
Guardi, even though he had to carry Fair Lamenting. The
bell was wrapped in many layers of cloth and the resulting
bundle was too large to tuck under his arm. Townspeople
stood aside, impressed by Jack's and Thorgil's clothes and
even more so by the Bard in his spotless white robe. The
old man had added a wreath of oak leaves. That, along with
the blackened ash wood staff, told everyone that he was an
important wizard.

There was no longer a border of hedges around Din
Guardi, for which Jack was grateful. It had formed a barrier
between the fortress and the outside world, but its purpose
had not been for protection. The Hedge had been like a silent
army of closely massed trees, ever watchful at the boundaries of Unlife. When you passed through the tunnel linking
the fortress with the outside world, branches reached out to

catch your feet or scratch your face. When Unlife failed, the Hedge had torn apart the old Din Guardi and the men who were caught within had not been seen again.

Now the new building was open to the sea and sky. Jack thought it made an impressive sight, but he was surprised to see no sentries. The front gate stood open. "Isn't that dangerous?" he said.

"*Hall built of stone, sword close to hand, yet all fails when vigilance wanders,*" quoted Thorgil.

"Quite right, shield maiden," said the Bard. "Brutus is a weak king, more suited to singing love ditties, but he's all we have to work with." They went inside and wandered around until they encountered a servant carrying a tray of meat pies. "Announce our arrival," the old man ordered. "Tell King Brutus that Dragon Tongue has arrived with two friends. We request lodging." The servant didn't question the Bard's authority and hurried off to obey.

"The floor plan is different from what I remember," complained the old man. "It's not intelligently laid out for defense. I believe Brutus has forgotten that this building is meant to house an army ready for battle. I ask you, who ever heard of *pink* as a proper color for a fortress?"

Presently, the servant returned and led them to the throne room. Brutus was lounging on a couch, and all around him, on floor cushions or standing by his side, were ladies in long, flowing gowns. Some held musical instruments and others held trays of food. All of them were vying for the king's attention. He lazily accepted their tribute—a honey cake, a morsel of chicken—and waved languidly at whichever musician he wished to hear.

"Wasting your time as usual, I see," said the Bard, rapping his staff smartly on the floor.

"Dragon Tongue!" cried Brutus, rising to his feet. "What a pleasure to see you! And you, too, Jack. Thorgil, you've turned out to be quite a charmer."

Thorgil blushed and Jack felt annoyed. The shield maiden always ignored his compliments, but she was smiling now.

"I must disagree, dear Dragon Tongue. Ladies are *never* a waste of time," said Brutus. The court women giggled and fluffed their hair.

"Try to remember you're a king. Your business is to rule," the Bard snapped, but Brutus wasn't the slightest bit embarrassed.

"Father Severus attends to the ruling," he said. "He's much better at keeping order, and he positively *enjoys* hearing dreary old court cases. He's the abbot of the monastery now, you know. My job is to inspire."

The old man shook his head. "You're hopeless, like all the rest of the Lancelot family. But I've come here on business. Our village has been devastated by a Wild Hunt, and I must trade for grain. Is there a corner in this pink monstrosity where an old man and a couple of children can rest their heads?"

"Of course!" Brutus said. "Let's see . . . the Amethyst Suite is available, or you might like the Swan Room. It's all in white. My goodness, you'd melt right into the background!" The king was overcome with mirth.

"Any place with beds will do," the Bard said.

"We must have a feast to celebrate your arrival. I have the most inventive cook. Last night he served roast pig stuffed with lamb stuffed with goose stuffed with pigeon stuffed with lark. We were all placing bets on what we would find in the next layer." Brutus sent ladies off with various orders. Servants dragged in chairs.

"I'd hoped to see Ethne here," the Bard said. "She's completely unsuitable for a convent, and in my opinion, you couldn't ask for a lovelier queen. Do you ever look in on her?"

For the first time Brutus seemed uneasy. "You haven't heard?"

"I live in a tiny village. I have trouble hearing anything. Is she ill?"

"Not exactly," the king said.

"Well, where is she? I'll go at once to help her."

Brutus nervously laced his fingers together and nibbled his lower lip. It would have looked silly in most men, but it only made him more adorable. One of the lady musicians sighed. "It isn't allowed—I mean, Father Severus wouldn't allow it," stammered the king. "It has something to do with church rules. I *did* tell him it was a bad idea. I meant to send you a message, but . . ." He spread his hands helplessly.

"But you couldn't be bothered!" roared the Bard. "By Odin's eyebrows, you're a king. *You* give the orders to Father Severus, not the other way around. Now where's my daughter?"

"It's awkward . . ."

"If you don't tell me what happened this instant, you're

going to be hopping around a marsh full of hungry herons!"

The air crackled with electricity and the tapestries on the walls billowed out. A court lady fainted into the arms of her companions. Brutus quickly laid out the tale with many a glance at the old man to see how he was taking it. It seemed that Ethne had gone mad—well, not mad exactly. She heard voices. Hearing voices might be insane, except when you really did hear them. And Ethne did. It was her elvish relatives trying to get her to return.

They came to Ethne's room every night. They filled her ears with the glories of Elfland and offered to take her home, if only she would give up her quest to gain a soul. "Father Severus couldn't hear them, but I could," said Brutus. "The elves have never hidden from me, and the queen has always fancied me."

"I know," said the Bard, disgusted. "This is what I feared from the beginning. My poor child is caught between two worlds, and she's chosen a path too difficult for her. I wanted to immerse her in the life force, and that rascally priest has walled her off from it. Wait till I get my hands on him! Where is she?"

"That's the problem," the king said miserably. "He really did wall her up. I mean, she's alive, but he put her into the one place the elves dared not approach. There's a tiny room next to the chapel. It's full of Christian magic, and the Fair Folk can't endure it. Father Severus put her there and the monks bricked up the door. The only opening is a narrow window."

"You mean she can't get out?" Jack cried. He'd seen the

room. It was hardly wider than a bed and not much longer.

"Death would be better than such an existence," said Thorgil.

"Ethne agreed to it," said Brutus. "She was suffering so from the voices, and she truly wanted to earn a soul. Food and drink are handed through the window and she isn't entirely without entertainment. She can listen to the monks pray. Several times a week the abbot—Father Severus—gives a sermon. Oh, and he let her keep the cat."

"Thank Freya," breathed the Bard. "She still has Pangur Ban."

"Is that what he's called? He goes in and out the window and brings her all sorts of things from the outside world." The king looked relieved by the old man's apparent approval, but in the next instant the Bard's staff came crashing down and the walls trembled.

"You have much to answer for," the old man said. "You should have taken Ethne away and married her. Love would have driven away the illusions of Elfland, love and the presence of honest sunlight. But I have graver concerns than punishing you. I must go to St. Filian's now, for there is a debt that has fallen due. I fear that all the treasure Father Severus has laid up in Heaven will not cover it."

King Brutus gave them ponies to ride, for it was a long walk to the monastery. He insisted on providing them with a basket of meat pies for the road. The Bard angrily waved it away, but Thorgil accepted it. The king held her hand just a little too long when he gave her the basket.

Neither Jack nor Thorgil dared speak to the Bard. He rode silently ahead, and the air around him rippled like a heat haze over a summer field. But when they reached the grove of pines overlooking the monastery, the old man turned aside and found a grassy meadow. "If I go to St. Filian's in this state of mind, I'll bring the whole place down around our ears," he said. "Does that sound familiar, Jack?"

The boy grimaced. The year before, he'd accidentally called up an earthquake when the monks threatened to throw his sister into St. Filian's Well.

They let the ponies graze while they picnicked. In the distance Jack could see the walls of the monastery. The earthquake cracks had been filled in and a brilliant layer of whitewash had been applied. All around lay an extensive garden, and a new white building stood at the edge of the Lady of the Lake's territory. Father Severus must have driven the monks hard to accomplish so much.

"That, I believe, is the convent," the Bard remarked, looking at the new building.

Jack lay down the bundle containing Fair Lamenting, and Thorgil handed around meat pies. The pastry was crisp, the lamb meltingly tender, and the whole flavored with pepper, Jack's favorite spice. Also in the basket was a flask of mead. "I'll save this for later," the Bard said. "I need my wits about me." His mood seemed to have improved with the good food and fresh air.

"I've often told you," the old man said, "that one should never use anger to reach the life force. Yet that was what I was about to do." He shook his head. "I've lived a long, long time, but mortals still have the ability to make me lose my temper."

Mortals? thought Jack, but he didn't dare ask what the Bard meant.

"I need advance knowledge before I approach St. Filian's." The old man felt in the bag he always carried and drew out the silver flute of Amergin.

"That's pretty!" exclaimed Thorgil.

"Wait till you see what it does," said Jack.

The Bard played a tune first, a rippling, lilting melody like a mountain stream pattering over rocks. Birds landed on the branches above him and cocked their heads to listen. Then the music became solemn, not sad exactly, but very serious. It was the kind of music an ancient forest might make. It spoke of time passing and beauty fading. All things ultimately returned to the earth, even trees that had seen the Romans arrive with their mighty plans. But the Romans had gone into the earth with the trees. They had rested awhile and then had returned with the sun, as creatures immersed in the life force did.

The Bard put down the flute. Thorgil quickly wiped tears from her eyes. "There," the old man said. "I needed to remind myself what's important, or I might have lost my temper and called lightning down on that idiot Severus. Now I'll play something else." He put the flute to his lips and produced a sound so deep that Jack felt it in his chest.

The sound rolled through the grove of pine trees, and the birds fled before it. It was like the purr of an immense, self-satisfied cat. It made Jack sleepy, and he thought about how nice it would be to curl up in front of a fire. Suddenly, a large, snow-white cat sped out the monastery door and bounded up the hill as fast as it could go. It arrived at the top of the hill lickety-split and threw itself at the Bard.

"You old rascal! You're so heavy, you must have made off with half the chickens in the neighborhood," cried the old man, fending the creature off. The cat paraded back and forth, rubbing itself against the Bard and meowing. "Yes, yes. I missed you too. It's been a long time since the Vale of Song. Sit down, old friend."

The cat obeyed and regarded the children with intelligent blue eyes.

"This is Jack, my apprentice," said the Bard. "And this is Thorgil Olaf's Daughter of the Northland. Jack and Thorgil, allow me to introduce Pangur Ban."

Chapter Eighteen

PANGUR BAN

Pangur Ban yowled melodically with what Jack supposed was a greeting.

"A very good day to you too," the boy replied, and Thorgil added her respects.

"He's so big and white," she said, "I'd think him a troll-cat if he weren't so friendly."

"You can speak directly to him," said the Bard. "Pangur Ban understands every word."

"Well, then, I'm sorry I called you a troll-cat," the shield maiden said courteously. The creature sniffed her. His tail quivered and he gave a staccato, panting cry.

"Yes, she is allied with the creatures of the air," the Bard explained. "She drank dragon blood by accident, but that doesn't give you the right to hunt her. I apologize, Thorgil. Pangur goes quite distracted when he smells Bird."

"If he tries to hunt me, he's going to wind up as a rug on my floor," said Thorgil.

Jack quickly fed the cat a meat pie. He stroked the white fur and was rewarded by a deep, hypnotic purr. "It's lucky you gave him to Ethne, sir," he said.

"You may call it luck," said the old man, "but as you know, these things happen for a purpose. Pangur had arrived on an Irish ship before I even knew of Ethne's existence. He asked me for a soft berth in a monastery because he loves monasteries. They never run out of food, and the monks dote on him. When Ethne declared her intention to gain a soul, I thought, 'Nothing could be better for my girl's soul than a worldly old cat like Pangur Ban.'"

The Bard then questioned the cat about Ethne. How was she faring? Did she get enough to eat? Would she like her old father to knock down the wall and carry her off to King Brutus? The cat yowled with mirth. "I know he's a poor excuse for a husband, but he would cherish her," the old man said.

Little by little, Jack gleaned the situation as the Bard translated Pangur Ban's words. Ethne had fallen into a kind of trance. On the one hand, she was grateful to be free of elvish voices. On the other, so little happened that she spent most of the time staring into space. Twice a day food was thrust through the window and refuse taken away. No one spoke to her. She could hear the muffled prayers of the monks and Father Severus's sermons, but she no longer listened to them.

She prayed when she thought of it. She paced to and fro in the narrow space between the bed and the wall. The rest of the time she slept. Pangur Ban was at his wits' end trying to find activities for her—there's only so much petting a cat can endure. He brought her treats from the outside world. He raided the kitchen for pies, fruit, roasted birds . . .

Pangur Ban licked his lips and glanced at Thorgil.

Of course the monastery was no longer the luxurious place it had been before Father Severus arrived. Half the time the monks lived on bread and water, and self-flagellation was epidemic.

"Self—what?" asked Jack.

"The monks beat themselves with whips," the Bard said. "It's supposed to make them virtuous. I'll never understand Christians."

Jack found it difficult to understand too. He'd been knocked six ways to Sunday by Father, and all it made him was resentful.

Most important, Pangur Ban brought Ethne fragments of the outside world. He would drag in a vine covered with leaves, or a rose, or a mouthful of acorns. He brought her mice and small birds, and she'd begged him to take them away and free them. Once he brought her a dead mole, and she wept for the pity of it.

"That wasn't nice," objected Jack.

"I disagree," said the Bard. "The worst thing that can

happen to Ethne is that she loses her ability to feel. Then she will become all elf and soulless as they are. Sorrow is a part of life."

"We can't leave her in that prison," Thorgil said.

"No, we can't." The old man gazed into the distance, going far beyond the monastery, the lake, or even the bright sky beyond. "Unfortunately, we have two problems. I must rescue Ethne, but I must also attend to the *draugr*. If the *draugr* emerges before I've found a solution, she'll start killing again."

They sat and looked down at the monastery. The ponies ambled closer and nudged Thorgil with their noses. Horses always favored Thorgil, Jack thought, even ones who'd never seen her before. Pangur Ban stretched out his long body and appeared to sleep, but the tip of his tail moved ever so slightly. "I'll have to deal with the *draugr* first," the Bard finally decided. "I know Ethne is suffering, but I hope she can endure a while longer. I dare not allow the *draugr* to emerge."

He picked forget-me-nots and wove them into a garland. Laying a hand over them, he chanted something in a language Jack didn't know. But Pangur Ban did. The cat rolled on the ground and purred ecstatically, finally coming to rest at the Bard's feet. The old man wound the garland around the cat's neck. "I have called life into these flowers," he said. "They will not fade for many a day."

Pangur Ban sped away.

"What language was that, sir?" Jack asked. "You've often used it to work magic."

"It is the speech they use in the Islands of the Blessed," said the Bard. "I learned it as an apprentice."

"But Pangur Ban understands it."

The old man gazed after the cat, who was just then reaching the monastery door. A monk bent down to pet him and received a crisp bite. The cat fled through the door. "Remember my telling you about how dangerous it was to trade places with an animal's spirit?" the Bard said.

Jack nodded. He remembered how the old man had hidden in the body of a crow and been unable to leave.

"The longer you're in an animal's body," the Bard said, "the more you forget about being human. They didn't teach the skill at the School of Bards until the final year, and some apprentices never made it out of their animal's body. Pangur Ban was one."

"He's a *bard*?" cried Jack.

"A failed one. You have to be very sure of your own identity before attempting such a feat. I always suspected that Pangur preferred being a cat rather than a human. There are no responsibilities and endless chances for fun, and he was always a happy-go-lucky lad."

"But still . . . never to be human again." Jack was appalled. "What happened to his body?"

"It was inhabited by the cat's spirit and wandered away. To outsiders the cat/lad appeared to be simpleminded, but of course he wasn't. I heard that he became a rat-catcher in Dublin and was very good at it."

Thorgil called the ponies, and Jack packed up the remnants of the lunch. He mounted, settling the awkward bundle containing Fair Lamenting before him. "Now comes the hard part," said the Bard.

As they drew near the monastery, Jack noted the extensive fields and newly planted orchards all around. Monks were busy weeding, setting up trellises, and digging seedbeds. He recognized some of them. They were thinner and better-muscled than before, and it was clear that Father Severus's discipline had been good for them. The boy also recognized the former criminals by their missing ears and slit noses. These seemed to have been freed from slavery, for they were dressed as monks and were working alongside the others.

Yet the faces were as shifty and brutal as before. The monks had never been much more than thieves, and the criminals had been condemned murderers. Whatever sermons they endured didn't seem to have reformed them.

"What's going to happen here, sir, if Father Severus is removed?" Jack said in a low voice.

"An excellent question," the Bard replied. "I'd hate to see this lot run wild again."

They were shown into the courtyard Jack remembered from his first visit. It had been repaired after the earthquake, but the fountain barely trickled. Instead of rosebushes and lavender, the yard was covered with gravel, and the pleasant wooden benches had been replaced with cold, hard stone.

"Severus does like his penances," remarked the Bard, lowering himself carefully.

They waited. The abbot—Father Severus—was meditating,

they were informed by a villainous-looking monk with a withered hand. Jack knew the man had endured a trial by ordeal and had been forced to carry a glowing piece of iron for nine feet. When the wound festered, he'd been found guilty.

"His Future Sainthood always spends the afternoon on his knees," the monk said. "That's after a good fast in the morning and a light scourge for lunch."

"What's a scourge?" Jack said after the man left.

"A special kind of whip," the Bard said. "It leaves deeper scars."

Jack felt repelled and disgusted. What kind of madness was going on here? It was impossible to believe that these monks had any kinship with gentle Brother Aiden or St. Cuthbert.

"The Northmen endure pain gladly," Thorgil said, "yet they do not inflict it on themselves. I see no honor in such wounds."

"You're correct there, shield maiden," said the Bard.

The sun had inclined to the west and shadows had begun to fill the courtyard when Father Severus strode in. He was as thin as ever, but underneath, Jack sensed an iron strength. The boy looked for the kindness he'd seen in the dungeons of the elves and found it missing.

"You! Wizard! Why have you come?" the abbot said.

"And a very good afternoon to you too," said the Bard. "Do you remember Jack and Thorgil?"

Father Severus cast a piercing look at the two. "Oh, yes.

The pair that brought down Din Guardi. It's back again, you know. My monks built it."

Jack felt uneasy at the words *my monks*.

"With help from the Lady of the Lake," said the Bard.

"That vile witch," swore the abbot. "It should have been a proper fortress, and her mincing sorcery turned it into a playground."

"It isn't as though Brutus is a warrior," the old man remarked.

"He does nothing. Nothing! Parties all night, sleeps all day. If anything needs doing in Bebba's Town, the people come to me."

"I'm sure you tell them what to do," the Bard said.

Father Severus glared at him. "So what if I do? These people need a firm hand, and most of them are pagan backsliders. I've gotten rid of naughty practices like Yule singing and dyeing Easter eggs, but they still sneak into the woods for May Day. Well, why are you here? I have confessions to hear and penances to hand out."

Jack couldn't believe the change that had come over Father Severus. What had happened to the man who'd sheltered them in Elfland and given them hope when all seemed lost?

"I, too, have important business," the Bard said quietly. "Something to do with mermaids."

For an instant Father Severus looked startled, but just as swiftly he recovered. "That matter was concluded years ago. It was bad judgment on my part, but no harm was done."

"Much harm was done," said the Bard. He recounted the arrival of the *draugr* and the havoc she had wreaked.

"How can you expect me to believe that tale," the abbot scoffed. "A wolf slaughters a lamb, a cow bellows in the woods, and everyone panics."

"I saw the *draugr*. So did Jack."

"Oh, that's a fine source of information—a wizard and his apprentice."

Jack was beginning to dislike Father Severus. "Brother Aiden believes in her too," he broke in. "He says a wild animal wouldn't kill things without eating them."

The Bard put his hand on the boy's shoulder. "That'll do, lad," he murmured. He looked up at the abbot. "Severus, you were responsible for the mermaid's death. Did you think there'd be no consequences? She has appealed for justice before the councils of the nine worlds."

"This gets better and better." Father Severus laughed, a hollow, cheerless sound, and Jack remembered that he had never been good at laughing. "There are only two worlds: this one and the world to come. Now I'm supposed to worry about a creature with no soul coming back from the dead. She complains to councils that don't exist, and a wizard with nonexistent powers comes along to threaten me."

"You take that back!" Jack shouted. The Bard held out his staff, and the boy felt a wave of heat.

"Stop wasting my time and run along," snarled the abbot.

"You leave me no choice," the Bard said quietly. "Jack, unwrap Fair Lamenting."

The boy's hands trembled as he put the bundle on the floor and fumbled with the cords binding it. Thorgil bent down and cut them with her knife. "This will be fun," she whispered. Jack wished he were as calm about calling up the *draugr*, but then, he'd actually seen her and Thorgil hadn't.

"Fair Lamenting," murmured Father Severus, and for once he didn't look so confident. "It has been long since I heard it. If it hadn't been St. Columba's sacred bell, I would have sunk it in the depths of the sea."

"You would have done better to sink yourself," the Bard snapped. "Last chance, Severus. Shall we discuss how to deal with the *draugr*, or should Jack ring the bell?"

The abbot drew himself up, tall and proud. The man had courage, Jack conceded unwillingly. He'd faced down Northmen and the Elf Queen. He'd offered himself as a sacrifice in place of Pega. He had confronted Hell itself, and if he'd fallen to his knees in terror, it didn't lessen his nobility. They had all cowered.

"There is no *draugr*," Father Severus said. "I am a Christian. I do not believe pagan lies."

The Bard nodded. Jack quickly unwrapped the layers of cloth, and the object within rolled over the floor with a clanging and clanking.

It was a small copper cauldron with a stone inside.

Father Severus barked a startled laugh. He bent over with mirth, slapping his knees with his hands. "By blessed St. Bridget, there's no Fair Lamenting, either! This is a fine joke, wizard! Did Brutus put you up to it?"

The Bard, Jack, and Thorgil could only stare, thunderstruck, as the cauldron came to a halt against a wall.

"Nothing to say?" the abbot jeered. "Then be off with you!" He clapped his hands, and a pair of hefty monks came through the door. The Bard, Jack, and Thorgil left with as much dignity as they could muster.

Chapter Nineteen

FIND TANNERS

"The Tanners did it," Jack said at last, after they had traveled several miles. The Bard had gone ahead and the air around him had swirled, and his pony had laid back its ears in fear. But finally the air cleared. The pony's ears went up, and Jack dared to break the silence. "We know they're thieves. No one else would have done it."

"They stayed behind when we camped on the beach," Thorgil said. "They claimed to be afraid of Schlaup, though anyone with sense could see his good character. I wonder what else the Tanners took."

"I should have brought Fair Lamenting ashore with me," said Jack. "The minute Ymma and Ythla thought they were alone at the farm, they went through everything. I should have known they'd do the same thing on the ship."

"I don't blame you, lad," the Bard said. "I was also entirely too trusting." They stopped at a flowery meadow beside a rushing stream. Thorgil took off her boots and led the ponies into the water, where they drank noisily and sloshed their hooves. After a while she led them out to graze. The Bard broke the seal on the flask of mead and drank morosely.

It was getting close to sunset. Long shadows stretched across the grass and swallows dipped and fluttered in the upper air. "Mrs. Tanner said she was going to her brother," Jack said. "Perhaps King Brutus could help us."

"Brutus couldn't find his crown with both hands," said the Bard. "There are a thousand people in this town—farms and houses everywhere. We don't know what her brother does for a living; to go by her, he's probably a pickpocket. We don't know what he looks like."

"The arrival of a widow with two daughters can't be that common," Jack pointed out. "King Brutus could send out searchers. In time—"

"In time! We don't have time, lad. If someone rings that bell, we've had it. Which brings me to the question, how did the Tanners know where it was?"

"Ymma and Ythla were always lurking about," Jack said bitterly. "They saw me carry a mysterious bundle to the ship and decided to look inside. They knew enough to substitute one of Egil's copper cauldrons."

"I hate the sight of that wretched pot," said the Bard, swigging more mead. Jack had brought the small cauldron back with them. It belonged to Egil, after all, and was valuable. It was a rich red-gold color, reflecting light from a dozen surfaces made by the artisan's hammer. Egil said it had been made by men burned dark by the sun, the same ones who had traded *merini* sheep to him.

Thorgil returned from tending to the ponies and settled herself on the grass. She, at least, was in a good mood. The long ride and misadventure at the monastery had amused her. Her cheeks were rosy and the sun had brought out a spray of freckles on her nose. She was as finely dressed as a young knight. But where a year ago she had been easily mistaken for a lad, subtle changes had occurred. Her waist was more defined, her mouth was softer, her chest—

Jack looked away. No matter how hard Thorgil attempted to hide it, her chest definitely hadn't stayed the same.

"An acorn for your thoughts," the shield maiden said.

Jack felt his face grow hot. "I was trying to think where the Tanners might be hiding."

"They'll be easy to find," Thorgil said.

"Easy! Where in this rats' nest of a town do we start looking?" cried the Bard.

"We don't have to look. Remember, Mrs. Tanner practically promised to marry my brother. *He* certainly thinks so." Thorgil pulled up strands of grass and began chewing on them.

"*Schlaup?*" said the Bard, sitting bolt upright. "My stars! You're a genius, Thorgil!"

"I know," said the shield maiden, idly chewing.

They galloped back to the harbor in the gathering dusk. Egil and his crew had made camp on the beach. By day the men could pass for Saxons, but now, roaring songs and cavorting around a giant bonfire, they were clearly something else. A few women they had managed to lure from town huddled together in a frightened group. One of the crewmen swung a woman around in a wild dance, ignoring her screams.

"Haw! Haw! Haw!" laughed the Northmen. "She's playing hard to get!" Kegs of beer, half buried in sand, were strewn around.

"Dragon Tongue," cried Egil, rising as the ponies were reined in. "Have you found lodgings? You're so late, we were beginning to worry about you."

"Turn those women loose!" said the Bard, dismounting. "Thor's thunderbolts! Do you want the whole town down on us? Go on, shoo, you silly geese!" He pointed his staff at the women and they fled. He pulled the dancing crewman away from his captive.

"I was only flirting," the man grumbled. The last woman sped after the others.

The Bard sat down on a beer keg and mopped his brow. "Once and for all, get it through your heads: *No pillaging.* This is a trading mission. You can't just carry off anyone you take a fancy to. Egil, I expected you to have them better trained."

The captain grinned, not the least repentant. "Yes, sir. I'll have a talk with them. I have to say, though, that those ladies were eager to come here when it was still light."

"I'm sure they were," the Bard said, sighing. "There's feather-heads in every port. Now we have a very serious problem." He explained about the loss of Fair Lamenting and the dire consequences if it were rung. "We need Schlaup's assistance."

"Schlaup?" echoed Egil. "Begging your pardon, Dragon Tongue, but if you think a little innocent pillaging is going to stir things up, wait till the townsfolk see a half-troll walking their streets."

"I know," the old man said, shaking his head, "but he's our best hope. If we're lucky, the whole thing can be accomplished under cover of darkness. Any late-night drunk who encounters Schlaup will think he's hallucinating."

With much complaining, and threats and blows from Egil, the crewmen unloaded the ship's cargo. Half of them remained behind to stand guard and the other half took up the oars. This would be a dangerous voyage in near complete darkness. The Bard stood at the prow to navigate.

The night was moonless. Sandbanks and islets lay in their path, but when the Bard held out his staff, the sea was covered by an eerie glow. Waves foaming against rocks shone whitely. The water was as clear as glass with the sand below a pale green.

The Northmen had started out in a mutinous mood, but when they saw the strange light, they quieted down. Jack felt the fear radiating from them as they pulled the heavy oars. A bard that could do this kind of magic could turn them all into dolphins and order them to tow the ship.

When they reached the hidden inlet where Skakki's ship lay, Egil blew a loud blast on a ram's horn. Torches suddenly flared on the shore. Men scrambled for their weapons. Grinning with satisfaction, Egil guided his craft to shore.

"You rotten pile of fish guts!" screamed Skakki. "What do you mean sneaking up on us in the middle of the night? What's the matter? Did the ladies of Bebba's Town get a whiff of you and throw you out?"

"On the contrary, he threw the *ladies* out," Egil said, pointing at the Bard. "But we have a problem and we need Schlaup." After a quick conference it was decided to take Skakki's ship. Speed was necessary, for they would need to ferry the half-troll there and back again before sunrise. Soon the swift, sleek *karfi* left the dock, with the Bard providing directions and Jack and Thorgil crouching beside Rune in the stern. Jack and Thorgil had changed into sturdy work clothes and were bundled up in cloaks. The midnight air had turned cold.

Rune manned the rudder. He might be crippled by old age, he told Jack and Thorgil, but his sense of place in the sea was as good as ever. Even without the Bard's light, he could have remembered the way. "You feel that breeze?" he said. "It comes from a stream that cuts through hills on the mainland. It's like a warm current in the cold sea air. Directly opposite is a tiny island. You can feel the breeze reflected back, along with the smell of bird poop."

"I didn't have a chance to ask the Bard," Jack said after a while. "What's so special about Schlaup?"

Thorgil laughed. "Everything's special about my brother."

"Schlaup has a skill the rest of us lack," explained Rune. "You've noticed how he's riveted on Mrs. Tanner. Love-smitten he is, the poor ignorant lout, while she's as winsome as a box full of adders."

"I think the whole situation is disgusting," said Jack.

"Aye, you're right there," Rune said. "Our Schlaup deserves better. Did you notice how he kept sniffing Mrs. Tanner's braid?"

"Yes . . . why, he's like you," said Jack as the realization dawned on him. "He has a memory for smells."

"Schlaup's ability beats me hollow," admitted Rune.

"He inherited the gift from his mother," Thorgil said proudly. "A Jotun can track an elk through fifty miles of forest."

"He can sort Mrs. Tanner's musty stench from a thousand others," Rune said, turning the rudder to avoid an islet. The sound of crashing waves passed to the right. "Things should get interesting when we reach Bebba's Town."

Amidships, where there was less danger of capsizing the vessel, the large shape of the half-troll loomed. He had not yet been told what his task would be and so he sat, humming a tuneless song through his front teeth. All around, the green glow from the Bard's staff fell into the sea and landed on the sand far below.

They reached Bebba's Town and slid into a berth. Schlaup

lumbered ashore, causing the dock to creak dangerously and Skakki's ship to sway.

"Schlaup Olaf's Son, I have a little chore for you," the Bard said. "Do you remember Mrs. Tanner and her daughters?"

The giant bobbed his head enthusiastically. "Nice," he rumbled.

"That's a matter of opinion, my friend. Do you think you could find them?"

"Oh, yes!" said the giant.

"Now I want you to listen very carefully," the Bard said. "Jack is coming with you." The boy looked up, startled. "He's my apprentice and will tell you what to do. Jack, your task is to search for Fair Lamenting. Find it quickly, and for Freya's sake, don't ring it. You must return before dawn. Is that clear?"

"Yes, sir," said the boy.

"Oh, and, Schlaup? Carry Jack on your shoulders. He won't be able to keep up."

The half-troll scooped up the boy. Jack suddenly found himself seated behind Schlaup's bristly head and tentatively touched an ear. It was as scaly as it had looked from a distance. Schlaup swayed back and forth, snuffing the breeze, opening first one nostril and then the other as the hobgoblins did. Thorgil had explained that this gave trolls depth of smell, much as two eyes gave a man depth of vision. It was one reason why Jotuns were such excellent trackers.

"*Gaaahhhh,*" sighed Schlaup.

"That means he's located Mrs. Tanner," Skakki said. He handed the giant a flaming torch to light the way. "Go with good fortune, my brother, and may Heimdall's eyes aid you, young skald," he said, invoking the Northman god who guarded Asgard. *"Find Tanners!"*

Schlaup was off like a hound after a fox. He bounded through darkened streets and across the small gardens many of the townspeople maintained. His feet flattened cabbages, lettuces, and broad beans. Around and through the warren of houses he went, with Jack clinging on desperately and the flames of the torch streaming back.

They passed beyond the edge of town and entered an area of widely spaced hovels. It smelled vile, and Jack realized they had reached the dwellings of those who worked at trades normal folk wouldn't tolerate nearby. The reek of tanneries, the eye-watering tang of chicken manure, the choking fume of smelters were almost unbearable even at this time of night.

Schlaup stopped abruptly and emitted a sigh of pure happiness. He plucked Jack off his neck, shoving the torch into the boy's hands. "She's in there," he whispered, pointing at a structure surrounded by steaming pits.

Jack shaded his eyes, trying to see what kind of place they'd come to. It seemed to be a wasteland, far from other buildings. The hovel in front of them was slowly collapsing on one side, like a giant beast frozen in the act of lying down. The pits, to go by the stench, were filled with hides soaking in urine. A tannery, then. It wasn't surprising. Mrs. Tanner's husband had followed that craft until he staggered out drunk one night and drowned in one of his own pits.

This dwelling wasn't even as tall as a man. Jack guessed you'd have to crawl through the door to get to bed, though he couldn't glorify that entrance with the word *door*. It was merely a hole with a leather curtain in front of it.

Schlaup didn't bother with the curtain. He peeled back the roof and felt around inside. "Troll-flower," he warbled, lifting a shrieking Mrs. Tanner in his hands. More screams erupted from the darkness.

"All of you, be quiet!" ordered Jack. He didn't want the neighbors aroused. "Your lives depend on silence. I'll call up demons if you don't behave."

The screams stopped, and Jack heard muttering and rustling from inside. "It's that wizard," a voice whispered. All at once the leather curtain fell back and Ymma and Ythla scuttled out.

"Fetch Tanners," Jack commanded.

Schlaup scooped them up easily and held all three in a hearty embrace. "Nice," he cooed.

A man attempted an escape, and Jack held him at bay with the torch. "If you move one inch, I'll tell my friend to bite off your head," the boy said. The man fell to his knees.

"I didn't know it was stolen," he blubbered. "My sister showed up and demanded I take her in. She's that pushy, her and her brats. What was I to do? It's not my fault."

"You didn't know *what* was stolen?" Jack demanded.

"Shut your mouth!" said Mrs. Tanner.

"You shut yours, you hag!" the man retorted. "That bell, sir. Beautiful it was, all red-gold and shining. I should have known it wasn't a gift as she said. I thought about selling it to the monastery, but Father Severus is merciless. If he knew the bell was hot goods, we'd be flogged within an inch of our lives."

"I thought you didn't know it was stolen," Jack said.

"Oh, I didn't! I was only trying to avoid the appearance of evil." The man rocked back and forth as though praying.

"Where is it?" Jack said.

"In there." The man gestured at the hovel. "I'll fetch it—"

"*I'll* fetch it."

The man crawled inside and Jack followed him, holding the torch away from anything flammable. "In there, sir. Under that heap of sheepskins."

Almost gagging from the smell, Jack removed the skins one by one. They hadn't been cured yet, and the odor of rotten meat filled the air. The boy carefully pulled up the last pelt and there, shining in the leaping torchlight, was Fair Lamenting. It bore no stain, though the skins had been coated with blood. It was as pure as when it had been first smelted.

Jack looked for something to wrap the bell in, but nothing was clean, so he used his robe. As he felt within, to still the clapper, his hand met only air. "Where's the clapper?" he said.

"Well, sir." The man started to back away. "This morning I gave the bell a couple of shakes, just to check its quality you see, and Ymma screamed that it was magic. It would call up a monster—"

"*You did what?*" Jack shouted. Schlaup was attracted by

the noise and leaned over the ruined roof to see what was happening.

"Don't let him eat me, sir! I just dinged it a couple of times, and it made the prettiest sound. I felt like an innocent lad again with my whole life ahead of me. But Ymma, she grabbed the bell and yanked its clapper out. Used my pliers. I can get another one, sir. There's metalworkers all over this town—"

"Where's the original?" Jack felt sick. There was no way to make a replacement. No mortal had the skill to craft the beautiful Salmon of Knowledge or open the way between this world and the others.

"Ymma thought it was silver. She took it to a blacksmith, but he said it was only iron."

"Then what happened?" Jack was beside himself with fury. If it had been the old days when he still possessed his bard's staff, he was sure he could have called up an earthquake.

Ymma was hanging over the roof, clutched tightly in Schlaup's arms. Her sister and mother were wedged beside her. "You'd better tell him," Mrs. Tanner said.

"Oh, be gone with you," the girl said rudely. "You're only trying to shift the blame."

"You pounded it," her mother snarled.

"You told me to," Ymma retorted. "She said people would recognize the fish and we should beat it flat. So I did. The blacksmith traded me onions for it."

Jack felt dizzy with dismay. This was the worst thing that could possibly have happened. That marvelous work of art had been turned into an ugly lump of iron. Could it still call up the voice of Fair Lamenting? And could he tell it apart from all the other lumps of iron the blacksmith probably had?

Suddenly, he realized this wasn't his only problem.

The bell had been rung.

A couple of dings, Mrs. Tanner's brother had said. It had been enough to make that scoundrel feel innocent. Had it been enough to call the *draugr*? Was she already on her way?

Jack heard a crow call somewhere in the distance. He looked up to see that the rim of the eastern sky had turned blue. "It's almost dawn," the boy said with a groan. "Schlaup, can you carry all of us? We'll leave the man behind."

"Sure," said the giant.

Jack crawled outside and threw the torch away. He felt desperately tired and discouraged. "Put me on your shoulders, my friend, and don't drop any of the Tanners."

The giant easily balanced his captives while hoisting Jack up. The boy cradled the bell against his stomach and put his arms around Schlaup's forehead.

"What do you think you're doing!" cried Mrs. Tanner. "You can't send us back to those pillaging Northmen!" Jack ignored her.

"I always said he was a nasty wizard," Ymma said.

"It's not Christian to take revenge," Ythla added, weeping.

A breeze stirred, wafting away the noisome smell of the tannery. More birds called—sparrows, larks, wrens. "You'll have to hurry, Schlaup," Jack said wearily. *"Find ship!"*

The giant bounded away with the Tanners wailing and

the wind whipping through Jack's hair. They passed a farmer checking his hens, and the man ran away, leaving the cage door open. Schlaup narrowly missed stepping on a drunk sleeping in an alley. Other than that, they encountered no one.

It may not be Christian, Jack thought when he saw the harbor and Skakki's men waiting to cast off, *but it's very, very satisfying.*

Chapter Twenty

THE QUEST

"You're right," the Bard said when they were safely out to sea. "Ringing the bell was the worst possible thing that could have happened."

"There wasn't time to hunt for the clapper," Jack said. Moodily, he watched Schlaup. Amidship, where he couldn't capsize the vessel, the giant contentedly fiddled with Mrs. Tanner's braid. Her daughters were draped over the side, as far away as they could go.

"It might not have made a difference," said the old man. "The artwork was part of the clapper's magic."

"So what do we do?"

The Bard gazed out at the gray-green sea. The sun had just

risen, and the tops of the waves seemed lighted from within as they peeled away from the prow. "I'm not sure, lad. Those two 'dings' may have been enough to awaken the *draugr*, but not enough to provide direction. That's very worrying. She may be prowling the village."

Thorgil brought them some of Pega's special scones and a pot of butter. She spread the butter with her fingers and licked them. "It's not all loss," the shield maiden said. "My brother has found a wife." Jack noticed that Mrs. Tanner had reestablished her control of the giant. She had pushed him away, and he was apologizing to her for being an oaf.

"Do you honestly think that's going to be any kind of a marriage?" Jack said.

"It's no worse than what most people have. They say it's better to fight than to be lonely."

"And you believe that?" Jack asked.

"I shall never marry," Thorgil said scornfully. "Shield maidens have all the power and status of men. If they wed, they lose it. They can no longer go a-hunting or bring home fine plunder. They are bound to the house, cooking, cleaning, and chasing after smelly brats. There is no honor in such a life."

The Bard smiled for the first time since their humiliation at the monastery. "In a life as long as mine," he said, "I've learned that 'never' is a dangerous word to use. We may yet see you blushing and giggling, Thorgil."

The shield maiden sprang to her feet as though she'd been stung and stalked off to the stern of the ship. She joined Eric Pretty-Face in a loud discussion about how to gut sheep.

They spent the day resting in the hidden Northman harbor. Jack and Thorgil packed away the Lady of the Lake's gift and wore their old clothes again. Skakki, Egil, Rune, and the Bard conferred, and when evening fell, they called everyone together around a fire. It was a beautiful night, with a clear, starry sky and a warm breeze from the mainland. Pinewood burned fragrantly with many a pop from the pinecones Thorgil tossed in. They feasted on wild boar, goose, salmon, and the brambleberries that grew abundantly near the inlet. Seafarer ate half a salmon by himself, with Thorgil finishing the rest of it.

As was usual with Northmen, they gave themselves wholly to the task at hand. All conversation ceased while they stuffed themselves, but Skakki had limited the number of beer kegs. He needed clear heads later. After a while he stood up and commanded their attention. "You've all heard about the *draugr* and Fair Lamenting," he began. Everyone turned to look at Mrs. Tanner, and she sniffed contemptuously.

"Dragon Tongue is certain the *draugr* will emerge again," Skakki went on. "She may already be abroad." The Northmen glanced nervously at the forest ringing the shore, and Eric the Rash, who was afraid of the dark, moved closer to the fire. "Now we must repay a debt to Dragon Tongue. Some years ago we Northmen set him adrift to die—"

"It was Frith's order. I hold no grudge," the Bard interrupted, "yet I would not refuse aid from friends."

"Aid shall be gladly given," Rune declared.

"Quite right," said Skakki, "but all should agree before we take this quest."

What quest? thought Jack. He hadn't been present at the conference.

"Egil and his crew will return to Bebba's Town," the young captain continued. "They will help Dragon Tongue sell his wares and buy grain. That should take about a week. Then they will drop him off here before going on to deliver the grain to the village. After which they'll wait here for the rest of us to return from the north."

"What are we going to do?" said Thorgil.

"Patience, little sister." Skakki grinned. "You're going to love this. We're taking Dragon Tongue to Notland, to lure the *draugr* back to her tomb."

"Notland!" exclaimed half a dozen voices.

"Nobody goes there," said Eric the Rash, fear evident in his voice. "It's all dark and spooky."

"IT'S FULL OF SEA HAGS," bellowed Eric Pretty-Face.

"As well as sea ivory, pearls, and gold," added Rune. A thoughtful silence fell over the gathering.

The Bard rose. "I would not lure you to your deaths, dear friends. I ask only that you set me adrift in a coracle as you did before. Jack and I will enter the realm of the fin folk alone."

"You're not leaving me behind!" yelled Thorgil. "I'm not cowering on the ship while you risk your lives."

"Your presence would be most welcome," the Bard said warmly. "But I must warn you that the fin folk are as trust-worthy as moving mist. They're bad friends and worse enemies. I won't think less of you if you choose to remain with your brothers."

"*I* would think less of me," the shield maiden said proudly, her face flushed with emotion.

"Very well, my child. Skakki and the others will wait in the open sea for us. If we don't return within seven days, they may take it that we haven't survived and leave."

There was an uproar as Northmen shouted that they never abandoned comrades, that Odin would spit in their faces if they did such a deed. Even Schlaup, who was feeding slivers of roast goose to Mrs. Tanner, added his mighty voice to the turmoil.

"I'm touched," said the Bard, holding his hand up for silence. "You are most noble companions, but you have duties at home. Even Olaf didn't wait for ships that had been taken into the halls of Aegir and Ran. It is the way of the whale-road," he said, using the Northman expression for *sea*.

Skakki opened a keg of mead to toast the adventure, and the Northmen gathered around, eagerly holding out their drinking horns. Jack wandered off down the beach. He always felt uncomfortable around such parties, for the tempers of berserkers were uncertain. He could hear their drunken revels in the distance.

The men had begun a *flyting*, a recreational insult session. Someone accused Egil of using seagull poop on his beard and someone else roared that Eric the Rash spread it on bread. Each Northman strove to top the others, inventing practices that Jack found difficult to picture, let alone understand.

Eventually, as all such contests did, the insults degenerated into a free-for-all, until Skakki shouted, "Calm them!" to Schlaup. Afterward things became very quiet indeed.

Jack sat on the sand and listened to the waves. It seemed that no matter how hard he tried, something always messed up his plans. Now he couldn't go home. He'd have to sail north to some dark, spooky place inhabited by sea hags. It might take months. Pega would think he was dead. Father would think he'd deserted them. The hobgoblins would take Hazel away. And there wasn't a thing he could do about it. The more Jack thought, the more depressed he became. Why couldn't he lead a safe life like John the Fletcher or the blacksmith?

"No one's life is safe," said the Bard, appearing out of the darkness. Jack shivered. It was eerie the way the old man always knew what he was thinking. "The world is ever dying and being reborn, like the great tree Yggdrassil. Most people hide from such knowledge, but even they have moments of revelation. When John the Fletcher's sister died, he was shaken out of his daydreams for an entire afternoon."

They sat together. The old man wedged his staff in the sand and said words Jack didn't recognize. A gentle light radiated from the staff and turned the foam on the waves pearly white. "Was that the language of the Islands of the Blessed?" the boy said.

"Indeed, it was the Blessed Speech. Someday I'll teach it to you."

A fox trotted out of the woods. It waded into the water

and snapped up something that looked like a small crayfish. It caught a few more before returning to the trees. On the way back, it nodded politely to the Bard.

"Why was Father Severus so unfriendly?" Jack asked. "Thorgil and I helped him escape the dungeons of Elfland. We camped on the beach for weeks until he was well enough to travel. He acted as though he'd never seen us before."

"Severus is an able and courageous man, but he has a fatal weakness," said the Bard. "He loves power. He can't resist forcing his will on others, whether they be mermaids, monks, or kings. He has made himself the real ruler of Bebba's Town. Brutus is too lazy to resist him—which is a great shame, for Brutus has a generous heart. The abbot didn't want to recognize you, lad, because you reminded him of when he was unimportant."

Jack thought this over as the waves hurried along the shore and the night wind brought them the odor of pine trees. After a while the Bard took up his staff and they made their way back to the inlet. Northmen were sprawled in untidy heaps here and there on the sand. Eric Pretty-Face lay with his legs half submerged in water. It looked as though nothing short of Ragnarok could awaken these warriors, but Jack knew this was a illusion. He'd seen Northmen go from a drunken stupor to full battle readiness in seconds. Whether their brains were awake was another matter. Berserkers didn't need brains to fight.

"So many duties, so little time," murmured the Bard, gazing at the collapsed warriors. "The *draugr* must be laid to rest and grain delivered to the village—two tasks that pull us in opposite directions. In the middle lies Ethne. My heart cries out to rescue her, and yet the greater good demands that I wait. It's only for a while, of course. I'm sure she'll be all right if we provide her with supplies before we leave Bebba's Town. Pangur Ban can keep an eye on her. . . ."

Jack had never heard the old man sound so uncertain, and it worried him.

"Promise me this, lad," the Bard said. "If things don't work out in Notland, you must return and rescue my daughter."

"Of course I will," said Jack, deeply moved. "You don't need to ask."

"I know," the old man said, looking off into the darkness over the sea.

Chapter Twenty-one

ETHNE'S CELL

The Bard, Jack, and Thorgil returned to Din Guardi. King Brutus sulked charmingly because they had missed his party, but he soon forgot and planned another one. Each day the Bard and Jack went to the market square to sell their goods, while Thorgil was hired to train the king's horses. "They're shockingly behaved," she complained. "All they do is roll on the grass and eat daisies."

"Somewhat like their master," the Bard remarked. With the money they made, Egil's men bought grain and loaded it onto the ship.

Beelzebub's Remedy Against Flies sold out because everyone was plagued by flies in the heat. The potions for locking and unlocking bowels were also popular, along with salves for rash, pinkeye, and the traveling itch. The Bard sat under a tree and people whispered their ailments to him. He would tell Jack which medicine to fetch.

Some folk whispered that they needed curses, and the Bard sent them packing. "Be off with you! I don't deal in curses," he shouted. "Go ask at the monastery. I'm told they have curses to spare." He was still smarting over his reception by Father Severus.

They rode out to meet Pangur Ban in the evenings. Ethne was slightly more cheerful, the cat reported. She liked the flowers the Bard sent her. She had begun to sing again. She could almost, but not quite, touch a ray of sunlight that came through the chapel door and landed beneath her narrow window. Jack's heart burned with indignation at her imprisonment even though it had been her choice.

When everything else had been sold, the Bard thrust aside his pride, and he and Jack approached Father Severus again. "I don't have time for your foolishness," the abbot said angrily. "I've got someone who's come down with flying venom in my infirmary. We had to burn his house to keep it from spreading."

"This won't take long," the Bard said. "I have a selection of Brother Aiden's inks to sell." He placed a basket on the floor.

The abbot had signaled a hefty monk to remove the intruders, but at the mention of Brother Aiden he sent the man away. "Is that the ink they used on the Holy Isle?"

"The same," said the Bard. "Rose red, heavenly blue, leaf

green, the yellow of morning sun. It is as though you looked through a stained-glass window."

Jack smiled, remembering the window in the monastery storeroom. It had been small, made up of fragments of the original on the Holy Isle, but even those shone with a glory not altogether of this world.

"No one ever made finer colors than Brother Aiden," said Father Severus. "I'd pay handsomely if he were willing to part with the formula."

"Let me tell you a story," the Bard said. "Aiden, like all Picts, holds the secret to making heather ale."

"I've tasted it," the abbot said. "If you were burning in Hell, one drop would soothe your entire body."

"A Scottish king captured one of Aiden's ancestors and threatened to kill him. But he promised a hoard of gold and the hand of his daughter if the man would reveal the recipe for heather ale. The man preferred to die. That's the resistance you're up against if you want to learn how Aiden mixes ink."

Father Severus sighed. "What outrageous price do you demand?"

The Bard named a sum and added, "I want to see my daughter."

The abbot laughed. "I'm afraid that isn't possible. Ethne chose her penance willingly and her immortal soul depends on it. No male speaks to her, not even me."

"I'm her father!"

"A mere accident," said Father Severus. "A year ago you didn't even know she existed."

"But I do now!" The two men faced each other, and Jack felt a thrum of power from the Bard's staff. Equally, he sensed a cold wall of resistance from the abbot. Where had he encountered that force before? Was it when he saw the powers of the living world dash themselves against the walls of Din Guardi? Was it Unlife he felt?

"Thorgil could visit her," Jack said before the confrontation could come to blows. Both men turned to look at him. "She could check on Ethne's welfare."

"It's true," the abbot said unwillingly. "Thorgil isn't a male, though you'd have to look twice to prove it."

The Bard nodded. "Very well, Thorgil can take my place, but with these conditions: The bricks sealing up my daughter's cell must be replaced by a door. I don't want Ethne trapped should there be an earthquake or a fire. I also insist that you store jugs of water in her room in case of an emergency."

"The door must remain locked at all times," bargained Father Severus, "and I alone shall keep the key. I want no misguided rescue attempts. Also, Thorgil must come unarmed and in women's clothes." The abbot smiled and Jack's heart sank. He had yet to see the shield maiden unarmed or in a dress.

The two men shook hands, and it seemed to Jack that the Bard winced when Father Severus touched him.

"I swear," fumed the old man as they rode to Din Guardi, "I'll come back and wipe the smile off that pompous ass's face. If I wasn't so worried about the *draugr*, I'd do it right now. But with Thorgil's help, Ethne's existence should at least be bearable until either I or Skakki return to free her."

Either? thought Jack, depressed. *Why not both?* It seemed the Bard wasn't all that confident about returning from Notland. The boy puzzled over the change in Father Severus's behavior. The man had always been inflexible and grim, but there had been a real core of kindness in him. He'd rescued the child Aiden and taken him to the Holy Isle. He'd cared for Jack, Pega, and Thorgil in the dungeons of Elfland. What had happened to him?

Jack braced himself for a fight with Thorgil about the dress, but she surprised him. "It's a good trick," she said, "like the time Thor put on a dress and pretended to be Freya. He went right up to the gate of Jotunheim. 'Oo, let me in, you big strong Jotuns,' he said. 'I think you're all so cute!' Of course, once he was inside, he beat the snot out of them. How we used to laugh when Olaf told that tale!"

"I know you did," said Jack, thinking, *All Northmen are crazy.*

The next morning Thorgil, dressed in the finest robes King Brutus could supply, set forth on a white palfrey to visit the daughter of the Queen of Elfland. She wore a long, green dress and sky blue tunic. Around her waist hung a belt decorated with gold coins, and on her head was a white veil. Brutus had found her a diadem of amethysts for her brow. She could use only one hand, but she rode as well as any warrior with two. Horses instinctively obeyed Thorgil.

Jack and a pair of knights rode by her side, for it would have been dangerous for a lady to set forth in such finery without protection. "I hope you don't have a knife concealed somewhere," Jack said, knowing the shield maiden's habits.

"Why on earth would you imagine such a thing?" cooed Thorgil. "Besides, none of those monks is going to search me."

"Just don't do anything awful."

They came to the monastery and Father Severus observed Thorgil suspiciously. "You've changed a lot," he said.

"*Haven't* I?" warbled Thorgil. Jack closed his eyes and waited for a sarcastic follow-up, but she held out her arms to him instead. He helped her dismount.

"Don't think I trust you," the abbot said. "I've seen what your kind do. You're not visiting Ethne alone, and if you try anything stupid, I have a dozen monks around here who used to be murderous felons." He clapped his hands and a grim-looking nun appeared. It was the first time Jack had seen a nun, though he'd certainly heard about them. She was a great, strapping woman who could have wrestled an ox to the ground. Jack noticed a large scar on the palm of her hand. She had been subjected to a trial by ordeal.

"Sister Wulfhilda will escort you, Thorgil. She has the key to the door."

"Why, thank you, Sister Wulfhilda," the shield maiden said sweetly. Lifting the corner of her gown as elegantly as any lady of King Brutus's court, she followed the nun into the chapel. Jack and the knights were forced to remain in the courtyard.

They waited. And waited. Father Severus went off to discipline a few monks for gluttony. He returned, glanced irritably into the chapel, and excused himself for prayers. The bell clanged for lunch. Father Severus hurried back to invite Jack and the others to join him.

Jack remembered the dining hall vividly and looked forward to a feast, but the menu had changed drastically since the year before. Gone were the juicy slices of ham, the roast capons, the oysters nestling on beds of lettuce. Now they were served barley bread mixed with ashes, to remind the monks of mortality, as well as nettle soup and cider that was well on its way to becoming vinegar. Each man was allotted a tiny hard-boiled egg, except those who were being disciplined for gluttony. They sat in a mournful row, following every bite with their eyes.

Father Severus spoke at length about the reforms he had made at St. Filian's. "The monks attend prayers seven times a day, and the rest of the time they work. Every afternoon I counsel them on obedience. Wherever they walk, their heads must be bowed and their eyes cast down. They must be content with the most menial treatment. They must admit they are inferior and of less value than the vermin crawling upon a dog's belly. Also, laughter is forbidden."

Jack stifled a laugh of his own. How could anyone feel lighthearted after being told he was lower than a louse crawling on a dog's belly? "Doesn't fasting weaken you?" he said, looking at the line of mournful monks.

"Don't be ridiculous," scoffed Father Severus. "I've gone a month on seaweed and water alone. Those men's bodies may be lean, but their souls are as fit as greyhounds. Or soon will be," he said.

Jack dipped his bread into the nettle soup to make it soft enough to chew. "I'm curious about Sister Wulfhilda's hand. Did she undergo a trial by ordeal?" he asked.

"You always were an observant lad," the abbot said, not entirely pleased. "Wulfhilda fixed her husband a dish of forest mushrooms, and he died. She was accused of poisoning him."

"It could have been an accident."

"That's why we have trials by ordeal, to sort accidents from evil," said Father Severus. "I ordered the iron heated— using the large-size metal bar because of the seriousness of the charge—and Wulfhilda carried it the required nine steps."

"*You* ordered it?" Jack said, horrified.

"You can't think Brutus did," said Father Severus. "That sorry excuse for a king couldn't discipline a puppy for piddling on his foot."

"But—" Jack was about to say, *But you aren't king* when he remembered the Bard had said that Father Severus was the ruler in all but name. "It was so cruel."

The abbot laughed cheerlessly. Apparently, laughter wasn't forbidden for him. "Murder is cruel. Some of these monks are felons of the worst order, pardoned by the grace of God. If I relaxed my hold over them, they'd be at one another's throats in no time. As it happens, Wulfhilda's hand didn't fester and she was proven innocent. I admitted her as a nun because she had nowhere else to go."

And perhaps she could no longer earn a living, Jack thought.

He'd become aware of the restrictions such an injury caused from watching Thorgil. You couldn't milk a cow or sew. You couldn't spin thread, shuck peas, or braid hair. Much of what you did became slower and clumsier. It seemed insane that an innocent person had to maim herself just to prove she'd picked the wrong mushroom in the woods.

When they returned to the chapel, Jack saw Thorgil and Sister Wulfhilda laughing and talking in the distance. The abbot's eyes narrowed, but by the time he got closer, all laughter had stopped. The nun's head was bowed and her eyes were respectfully fixed on the ground. Thorgil perched on a bench, swinging her foot.

Father Severus produced a bag of silver from his sleeve and handed it to Jack. "You may tell Dragon Tongue I've fulfilled his conditions. Now he must fulfill mine. He must never ask to see Ethne again. Give me the key to her door, Sister Wulfhilda, and when you return to the convent, tell Sister Hedwigga to give you six strokes with the light cane. You know why." With that, he turned and strode away.

"Pig," said Thorgil under her breath. "You come with us, Wulfie. You'll have much more fun."

The nun shook her head. "I couldn't go off with Northmen, not after what they did to the Holy Isle. But I'll keep an eye on Ethne for you."

The knights brought out Thorgil's palfrey. The shield maiden rode away from the monastery looking as dignified as a court lady, until they reached the top of the hill. Then she hitched up her skirts and screamed, "Go for it!" The palfrey broke into a gallop and thundered down the other side. Jack had all he could do to keep up with her. The knights on their larger horses almost collided with the trees, but Thorgil zigged and zagged through them with ease. She pulled up at a cross-road where one road led to town and the other to Din Guardi. A noisy stream flowed along one side.

"Oh, Freya! What an awful place!" she cried, and then she screamed at the top of her lungs, making the palfrey dance sideways with alarm. "There! I feel better." She leaped to the ground. "You can't imagine how bad it is, Jack. Ethne's body is crawling with lice, and her hair looks like a bramble bush. She's so thin, I didn't even recognize her. Her skin is covered in sores. I know I'm not the cleanest person around, but I would never, ever, allow myself to get into such a state. And she thinks it's good for her soul!"

"Perhaps it is. She has to try harder than the rest of us," Jack said.

"I don't know what it takes to make a soul, but I'm sure it's not providing a free lunch for lice," Thorgil said passionately. "And Wulfie! Do you know what they did to her?"

"I heard about the trial by ordeal," said Jack.

"The monastery confiscated her husband's land, and when she was proven innocent, they didn't give it back. I'm so glad we pillaged the Holy Isle."

"Be quiet," Jack said, glancing at the knights, but they were busy sharing a skin of wine by the stream. "The Holy Isle wasn't like St. Filian's," he said in a low voice. "They were gentle folk who helped all who came to them. St. Filian's was always stocked with renegades who were hardly better than pirates."

"I know," Thorgil said. "Brother Aiden is so decent, he makes even me feel sorry for burning the place down." She took off her shoes and cooled her feet in the rushing stream. "What I don't understand is why Father Severus is so changed."

"The Bard says that power has corrupted him," said Jack.

"Wulfie says he goes out during the dark of the moon," the shield maiden said. "He walks in the forest, and when he returns, he locks himself in his cell and flogs himself with a whip."

Jack went cold. He remembered the Bugaboo's mother speaking about the Man in the Moon. *He's one of the old gods,* she said. *He's doomed to ride the night sky alone, and being with him is like being lost on an endless sea with no star to guide you. He visits the green world only during the dark of the moon, and his conversation is both cheerless and disturbing.* It was the Man in the Moon who had made an ally of Unlife.

But Father Severus didn't believe in the old gods. He would surely ignore any voices he heard on his walks.

"Not only that, someone died in the infirmary and Father Severus ordered the monk who cared for him flogged. That's his cure for everything."

"There's nothing we can do about it. We'd better go on to Din Guardi," Jack said.

The Bard was sitting in the Swan Room, writing on a wax-coated tablet of wood with a metal stylus. It was a method Brother Aiden had shown him for organizing tasks. When the

Bard had finished the list of chores, he smoothed out the wax so he could make another list.

King Brutus had been correct. The walls and curtains of the Swan Room were so white, the old man's robes almost disappeared against them. Only his ruddy face and hands were clearly visible. He looked up expectantly.

"It's as bad as you thought," Thorgil told him. "Filthy, depressing, and dark. But Ethne still refuses to leave. I *was* able to smuggle everything in."

"Smuggle?" said Jack.

The shield maiden grinned. "You'd be surprised by how much you can hide under a skirt—packets of dried meat, cheeses, the rest of Pega's special scones, a knife, a small mirror, a comb. With all the buckets of water Ethne has stored at the back of her cell, she could withstand a siege. The nun Wulfhilda has promised to check up on her."

"Excellent work!" the Bard complimented her. "Ethne may not want to leave now, but by the time we return from Notland, she'll be ready. And if we don't survive Notland, Skakki has promised to free her. I don't think Father Severus will enjoy how he does it, and I don't much care."

Jack looked from one to the other, annoyed that they hadn't included him in the plan. "How do you know Ethne will be ready?"

"We Northmen have much experience with hunger, especially during winter," Thorgil explained. "At first you crave food all the time. You can't think of anything else. But after a while you fall into a kind of trance and feel nothing at all.

At the end of winter Olaf used to go around to the farms and wake people up. That's what's wrong with Ethne. She's been eating that wretched monastery food for so long, her spirits are in a deep sleep."

"The comb and mirror?"

"Those were my idea," said the Bard. "My daughter isn't the most imaginative creature alive, and I'm fairly certain she has no idea how much her beauty has faded. When she looks into the mirror, she's going to get the shock of her life."

"She already has." Thorgil chuckled. "She was running her fingers through that rat's nest of hair when I left."

That evening King Brutus threw one of his parties. The central courtyard was filled with lanterns, and musicians played sweet music from bowers around the edge. Tables were set with roast salmon, suckling pig, green peas flavored with mint, apples cooked with honey, and many other delights. Jack thought of Ethne and wished he could send something to her.

Much of the entertainment was provided by Nimue, the Lady of the Lake, whose tall figure sent a memory of pain down Jack's spine. She had paralyzed him with elf-shot at their first meeting. The Lady danced with her nymphs around a fountain, she in shimmering white robes with her pale gold hair floating like a mist, the nymphs in glittering scales. Afterward they twined around the king's throne, and Nimue insisted on feeding bits of marzipan "to her dear Brutie-Wootie."

"I think I'm going to throw up," said Thorgil.

"If she keeps feeding Brutie-Wootie that gooey stuff, *he's* going to throw up," Jack said. They both laughed.

The air was soft and warm. Unseen flowers wafted perfume over the courtyard, knights danced with ladies, pages went around with trays of sweets, and as the daylight faded in the west, a full yellow moon rose over the fortress wall. Jack suddenly came alert.

"The moon was only half full last night," he said.

"That means this courtyard is full of glamour," said Thorgil, wrinkling her nose. "I told you those floors were unsafe. All Nimue has to do is turn the glamour off, and everything falls into the cellar."

"I think—hope—most of this is real." Jack looked around for the Bard and found him sitting against a far wall, observing the festivities. He was shadowy, as though he were sitting under a half-moon rather than a full one. The old man wouldn't be taken in by glamour, the boy thought. He'd know what was real and what wasn't.

"I hated this place when it was in the grip of Unlife," Jack said, "but I don't like it much now, either. Why can't people enjoy things as they are?"

"We'll soon have a ship under our feet and a wind at our backs. You can't get realer than that," said Thorgil. For the first time Jack felt a stir of interest in the adventure they were about to have. Up till then he'd been eaten up with chores—selling potions, bartering, packing, feeding horses, running errands. Now they were about to turn their backs on the safe, predictable world and go off into the blue. Who wouldn't be happy about that?

But first they had to settle the problem of the Tanners.

Chapter Twenty-two

SCHLAUP'S BETROTHAL

"You like Mrs. Tanner, don't you?" said Skakki for the fifth time.

Schlaup shuffled nervously from foot to foot. "Sure," he said, also for the fifth time. The Bard, Jack, Thorgil, and Skakki were meeting with him in a secluded corner of the secret Northman harbor.

"And you've said you want her for a wife," prompted Skakki. Jack closed his eyes. This had to be the most insane idea ever, trying to get a declaration of marriage out of a tongue-tied lout, but the Bard had said it was their best option. Troll males fell in love only once, and it was clear that Schlaup was besotted with Mrs. Tanner.

"Sure, I want to marry her, but . . ." The giant wrinkled his browridge in perplexity.

"Well, what?" demanded Jack. They'd been going at this for an hour, trying to extract a response from the bashful lout. If it were up to him, he'd dump the Tanners on a lonely beach and make them walk back to Bebba's Town. But Thorgil had pointed out that they knew the location of the secret Northman harbor. They would most certainly sell that information.

"It wouldn't be decent," Schlaup mumbled.

"Of course it isn't decent! We're talking about the Tanners here," cried Jack, losing his temper.

"Now, lad, we don't have a lot of choices," said the Bard. "We can't free them and we can't kill them. The only other possibility is to take them along."

"I know a man in Edwin's Town who'd buy them as slaves," offered Skakki.

"Never!" roared Schlaup with more energy than he'd shown so far.

"Then you have to make a decision, big brother," said Thorgil. "I don't know what you're so worried about. If one wife doesn't work out, you can always get more. Olaf had three—four, if we include your mother."

"I know how these things are done," Schlaup burst out suddenly. "Just because I'm not smart doesn't mean I don't know how marriages happen. First, the troll-maiden asks you to dance. She brings you presents: elks, bears, that sort of thing. Then she weaves you a cloak out of spidersilk, which she has pulled herself from the spinnerets of a giant spider.

Lastly"—he blushed deeply, turning a bright orange—"she drags you into her cave. The next morning everyone looks to see how many scratches she's left on your browridge."

Everyone stared openmouthed at the giant. They had never heard him talk so much.

"So *that's* the problem," exclaimed Skakki. "I don't know why I didn't think of it before. Schlaup, my brother, humans don't get wives the same way. That's why your sisters handed you over to us. You couldn't talk with your mind, and the troll-maidens ignored you."

"You don't have to rub it in," the giant said.

"I'm not trying to be insulting. You have to learn how to court women the Northman way. Now, Olaf won my mother, Heide, in Finnmark," Skakki explained. "She was the daughter of the village headman and an important wise woman. He traded many furs for her. She also demanded an amber necklace, silver bracelets, and her own personal wealth-hoard."

"What about Dotti and Lotti?" said Jack, naming the other two wives.

"They were bargains. Olaf threw them over his shoulders during a raid and made off with them."

"That's all the courtship they got?" said Jack.

"Pretty much," admitted Skakki. Thorgil laughed and the Bard shook his head.

"Don't listen to them, Schlaup," the old man said. "A true Northman marriage requires a woman's consent."

Schlaup's ears swiveled forward to better concentrate

on the Bard's words. His eyes closed until only a strip of dark showed between the lids. His lips moved silently. Jack suspected that the giant wasn't stupid at all but that he had trouble with human speech. He'd spent most of his life surrounded by silence.

"The kind of marriage Dotti and Lotti had was very close to slavery," said the Bard.

"Olaf was always good to them," Thorgil protested.

"Olaf was many things. He made toys, he loved music, he played stupid practical jokes, he liked to roll in a meadow like a horse. He was loyal, brave, and kind. But he was also a berserker. He carried Dotti and Lotti away from a burning village after killing their families."

Schlaup nodded to show that he understood. "Trolls burn villages too," he said.

"It's a favorite pastime with bullies all over the world," said the Bard. "Now, *your* marriage, Schlaup my lad, should not involve carrying off a shrieking woman. Pillaging is wrong."

"Oh, bother! And I was so looking forward to Mrs. Tanner's screams," said Thorgil.

"You must gain your future bride's consent," the old man continued, ignoring her. "I would begin by offering her a share of whatever pearls, amethysts, topazes, amber, and silver you acquire on your travels."

"*What?*" cried Jack and Skakki at the same time.

"You should also build her a hall of her own and let her run your affairs while you're at sea."

"She'll rob him blind!" said Jack.

Schlaup, meanwhile, was bobbing his head enthusiastically. "I can do that! I can do all of that!"

The Bard smiled. "I'm sure you can. Well, Skakki, I think it's time to announce a betrothal party."

Skakki went off to do this, and Schlaup returned to the ship to find a present for Mrs. Tanner. Thorgil moodily drew triangles in the sand with the tip of her spear. They represented the *valknut*, the mind-fetter Odin cast over warriors doomed to die. Jack watched a pair of ants trying to drag a dead beetle to their nest. "It's not fair," he said at last. "The Tanners lie, cheat, and steal, and they get rewarded."

"Think about it," said the Bard. "Schlaup has little chance of finding a wife either here or in Jotunheim. He has fallen in love with Mrs. Tanner, who we all agree has the soul of a bog rat, but *she's* the one he wants. He will always want her, for louts fall in love only once. We know Mrs. Tanner will agree to anything if she thinks she can get her hands on pearls, amethysts, topazes, amber, and silver. Problem one solved: a willing bridegroom and a willing bride."

"Yes, but—"

"Now, whether Schlaup actually brings home anything valuable is another matter. Wealth means little to him. Lay on the roast elk and a few barrels of beer, and he's perfectly happy."

Jack grinned as he saw where the Bard's argument was going. "What about the new hall?"

"We certainly can't have the Tanners moving in with Skakki and his large household. Heide would have their skins tacked to the wall in no time. Problem two solved and domestic squabbles avoided. As for stealing, exactly where would the Tanners go with their ill-gotten goods in the middle of an isolated Northman village surrounded by icy mountains, trolls, and storm-lashed seas?"

Thorgil laughed so hard she fell off her rock. "By Balder's backside, you're crafty! Remind me never to cross swords with you."

"Most people who have crossed swords with me," the Bard said with a gentle smile, "are no longer among the living."

That night they had the betrothal ceremony. The actual wedding would take place in the Northland. There would be feasting and gift-giving aplenty once they arrived there, Skakki said. King Ivar, whose wits were somewhat addled since losing Frith, could be talked into donating his great hall for the ceremony. It was as grand as a palace, Skakki said, what with all the carvings and tapestries.

Jack could see he was laying it on thick for Mrs. Tanner—or Ydgith. For the first time everyone learned her first name. At the mention of *king* and *palace*, her eyes grew very round. She was even more impressed by the promise of pearls, amethysts, topazes, amber, and silver, and dazzled by the necklace of heavy gold links Schlaup placed around her neck.

"It's part of the wealth-hoard the Mountain Queen sent with him," Skakki whispered to Jack. "I brought it along in case he wanted to barter, but Schlaup doesn't understand the value of gold. When he gets tired of admiring its color, he simply drops it on the ground."

The betrothal was celebrated with gusto. Rune recounted the love story of Balder and Nanna, the god and goddess of spring. Jack gave them the tale of the Irish god Aengus, who fell in love with the Elf King's daughter in a dream. Thorgil was discouraged from singing at all because she only liked battle scenes with bodies piling up.

They feasted, danced, and drank toast after toast to the new couple. The only discordant note was when Ymma and Ythla threw themselves on the sand and vowed to kill themselves rather than be dragged off to the Northland. "Stop whining, you little beasts," said their mother. "You're not spoiling the first good thing that ever happened to me."

But Schlaup, alarmed that they might carry out their threat, found them each a gold ring to wear.

Chapter Twenty-three

THE SACRIFICIAL STONE

Little do land folk know, who hide in safe houses,
Of what we suffer on storm-wracked seas.
Our sails hung with ice, our faces lashed by hail,
We ride the salt wave with only the scream of wind
For song and biting frost for fellowship.

Jack pulled his cloak tighter and listened to Thorgil declaim poetry at the prow of the ship. They wore thick woolen mantles treated with oil to keep the rain out. All day they had encountered storms. None of these lasted long, but no one could settle into a steady work rhythm. It was "Up oars," "Down oars," "More sail," "Less sail," and "Aegir's armpits! That was a big wave!" They were in a sunny period now, but the wind was full of ice.

"You can count on Thorgil to make bad weather worse," Jack observed.

"Northmen believe in facing things head-on," said the Bard. He was comfortably wrapped in fleece over his usual white robe. The wind had burnished his face to a rosy glow.

They had left the hidden port two days before, after the betrothal ceremony. Egil's cargo had been stored there with half of Egil's crew to guard it. Egil's ship and the rest of the men had gone south to deliver the grain.

Ydgith had established herself as queen of this tiny outpost, with Ymma and Ythla as her princesses. By the time Egil had gone south and Skakki north, she had managed to get her own hut, a supply of food, and new clothes for herself and her daughters. Her last words to Schlaup were, "Remember to get me freshwater pearls up north. I understand they're common there."

Thorgil continued to describe the miseries of sailing until Eric Pretty-Face bellowed, "BLOODY HEL! THAT'S THE THIRD TIME YOU'VE DESCRIBED FREEZING TO DEATH. SING ABOUT SOMETHING ELSE!" The shield maiden stalked off to sit by Schlaup in the middle of the ship.

"I like frost," the giant said to cheer her up. "Fonn and Forath used to take me on picnics in the frost."

"You miss them, don't you?" Thorgil said.

Schlaup nodded. "When I marry . . ." He paused to marshal the words in his head, then continued, "I will take Ydgith to Jotunheim. To meet Mother."

Jack choked back a laugh. He could imagine Mrs. Tanner's reaction to her new mother-in-law, a nine-foot-tall mountain queen with bristly orange hair and fangs.

The shadow of the great bird Seafarer crossed the deck, made a lazy circle, and floated north again. The albatross had proven to be a most valuable crew member. He could see the coast when they couldn't. He brought back information of islands, lonely villages, and inlets where they might spend the night without being discovered.

The Northmen's knowledge of the coast was imperfect. Even Rune's memory contained information only about the few places he had visited, and so Seafarer guided them most of the time. On the first day he directed them to a run of herring so dense, the ship was unable to move until the run passed. The Northmen dipped the fish out with nets, and Seafarer gorged himself until he was too heavy to fly.

That night they ate to their hearts' content and fell asleep around a roaring fire. But the next it rained, and they shivered under oilskins until dawn.

Thorgil pointed out a few of the places she recognized. "Those are the old strongholds of the Picts," she said, pointing at solitary round towers on the distant hills. "Rune thinks they're deserted now." It was a wild and forbidding coast, with many cracks opening up to the sea. The waves sent spray high into these channels, while between them cliffs jutted out like teeth.

"I have seen lights in those towers when all else was asleep," the Bard said, shading his eyes against the afternoon sun. "I have heard the *huushayuu* call to arms where no army has marched for countless years."

"What's a *huushayuu*?" said Jack, repressing a shiver. The word had a breathy sound that recalled evil memories.

"The Pictish war trumpet," the old man replied. Jack remembered darkness falling over a slave market long ago and men whose bodies seemed to writhe with vines. "The *huushayuu* was half as tall as a man, and its voice carried over vast distances. There was never only one of them. The Picts always had ten or twenty trumpeters, for the sound alone made an enemy's heart melt within him. The Romans called it a '*carnyx*.'"

"Olaf had an old *carnyx* hanging on his wall," Thorgil recalled. "It was shaped like a striking snake with a boar's head. He refused to let anyone touch it because he'd found it in a tomb."

The Bard gazed with dislike at the distant towers gliding by. "That was a Roman copy. A true *huushayuu* has the head of a Pictish beast. The jaw is hinged with a metal tongue inside."

Seafarer returned with the report that a deserted bay lay just ahead, and Skakki gave the order to turn toward land. The Bard quickly canceled that order. "We should go north until the light fails," he said. "If we don't find a harbor, it is still better to lie out at sea than approach that shore."

They left the round towers behind, and the cliffs became ever steeper and more jagged. Finally, just as the last band of red faded in the western sky, they came to a white sandy beach. It lay before a peaceful valley ringed by hills, and the Bard pronounced it fit for habitation.

Schlaup dragged the ship above the high tide mark all by himself. He was hopeless at many chores. He rowed too powerfully to work with others and couldn't navigate across a mud puddle. But where strength was concerned, there was no matching him.

"What does a *carnyx* sound like?" Jack said later, when they had eaten and were stretched out under the stars. He was unwilling to use the Pictish word *huushayuu*.

"That's not a question one should ask in the dark," the Bard said. "I will tell you this: The sound of a *carnyx* is like the cry of a Pictish beast. You'll hear it soon enough on the borders of Notland." The old man turned his back and refused to speak any more.

In the morning they came to the port where Jack and Lucy had almost been sold as slaves. Jack had been so sunk in misery at the time that he hadn't noticed much about the place. He was amazed to learn that this was Edwin's Town. All his life he'd heard about it—how grand it was, how it had a king. Now he saw that it wasn't much larger than Bebba's Town. It even had a grim fortress like the old Din Guardi before it was destroyed.

Next to the water were extensive wharves, and these accounted for the greater wealth of Edwin's Town. It was a trading center. Ships came from the south with salt, fine cloth, glazed pottery, hunting dogs, and cheese. From across the sea sailed Frisian traders with spices, oil, and wine. From the north came amber and furs. And, of course, slaves. Everyone traded in slaves.

When Skakki first docked, a number of townspeople asked him what he had "in stock." "Nothing now," he said, glancing at Jack. "See me next year."

The boy went for a long walk by himself to cool his temper. He knew what kind of stock the Northmen carried. Three years ago—was it only three years?—he'd been washed in the cold sea and scrubbed with vile-smelling soap that almost took his skin off. His hair had been combed for lice. Then his skin had been rubbed with oil to give it a healthy sheen, just as a horse might be currycombed for market. He'd been given as much bread and stew as he could eat. A slave bloated with food, Olaf often said, was easier to sell.

Jack shivered with disgust at both the Northmen and himself. By now he was beyond the wharves and among houses. The land went up into a shallow valley with mountains on either side. Long, narrow fields were separated from each other by ridges or hawthorn hedges. Birds flew in and out, chirruping and warbling.

Jack sat on a long, tumbled-over stone by a hedge. To his right a cone of rock, sliced off at the top, bore the dark fortress. The Bard said it was called Din Eidyn and was a companion to Din Guardi. It, too, had existed since time out of mind. It had been built when the Forest Lord still ruled the green earth and the Man in the Moon had not been banished to the sky.

A mist began to gather, the kind of sea fog called "*haar*" that could roll in swiftly and unexpectedly. Jack didn't move. He liked it here in the clean air above the smell of dead fish and Northman boots. He drew his cloak tighter and covered his head with the hood. A honeybee landed on his knee, struck down by the sudden cold. He moved it gently to the hedge.

Between him and the fortress loomed a ravine. Now it was filled with *haar*, so that the rock cone appeared to float on a milky lake. Jack heard the clank of cowbells and the distant call of herdsmen. The animals must have been wending their way from higher pastures to the safety of barns. It must have been later than he thought; certainly the sky was growing darker.

The fog overflowed the ravine and crept up toward Din Eidyn. It was advancing up the valley behind him too. By now the wharves and sea had entirely vanished. Yet Jack still preferred to stay where he was. His arms and legs felt heavy.

The *haar* drifted over him, dewing his face with cold droplets. He was enclosed in a room of air, for a few feet away in any direction lay fog. All he could see was the fallen stone, a corner of the hedge, and grass.

The stone. Jack felt it with his fingers. It wasn't merely a chunk of rock; it was richly carved with symbols. He recognized a mirror and a comb—odd things to carve, he thought. There was also—the light was growing faint and he had to bend down to see it—a strange beast with a long mouth and legs curled beneath it. And another beast that reminded him of the *carnyx* the Bard had described. At the far end was an ornately decorated crescent moon intersected by a broken arrow.

Jack turned even colder than the chill that surrounded him. He'd seen that symbol before on Brother Aiden's chest. Father Severus had said the crescent stood for the Man in the Moon and the broken arrow for the Forest Lord. The two together meant Brother Aiden, then only a lost child in a forest, had been chosen for human sacrifice.

Jack tried to get up, but the *haar* was pressing in on all sides. He struggled to breathe. Cold tendrils of fog reached into his mouth and filled his throat. He lay facedown on the stone. The rough granite pushed up against his chest and a weight pressed down on his back.

A small creature crept over the stone. Jack could just make it out from the corner of his eye. It was the honeybee. It was no longer than a fingernail, yet with a bee's yearning for sunlight it strove to escape the deadening cold. It moved slowly, laboriously, and when it reached Jack's face, he smelled honey. It climbed upward until he couldn't see it anymore. It reached his temple and stabbed down.

Pain roared through his senses. He sprang up, all sleepiness gone, and saw that the mist directly above him had opened up. The sky was full of stars. Jack sucked in air until he thought his lungs would burst. He heard heavy footsteps pounding up the valley. In the next instant Schlaup grabbed him and sped away with the boy tucked under his arm.

Jack saw only a blur of houses and streets before they were back at the wharves. Schlaup jumped aboard, making the ship tilt so violently that the sailors had to grab boxes to keep them from sliding off the deck. "I got him! I got him!" the giant cried, putting Jack down.

Skakki shouted to cast off, and the Northmen pushed away with their oars. The Bard crouched beside Jack, feeling his head. "Thank Freya he found you before the tide turned," the old man said. "We couldn't possibly hide Schlaup for another day. Too many people kept looking at the ship and asking what we were carrying."

Jack found that his throat was sore, as though he'd been shouting for a long time. "How did you hide him?"

"We threw a tarp over him," said Thorgil. "Skakki told everyone he was a heap of grain bags."

"I'm cargo," Schlaup said, pointing at his chest.

"You're much more than that," said the Bard. "What possessed you, Jack, to go off without telling anyone?"

Jack saw that the first streaks of dawn were appearing in the eastern sky. He realized he'd been gone most of the previous day and all of the night. "I went for a walk. . . . I'm not sure what happened next."

The Bard felt his head again. "That's better. Warmth is coming back. Did you fall asleep in a field, or what?"

Jack described the stone and the sudden appearance of *haar*. The sea and sky had by now lightened to that predawn color that makes it impossible to tell where one ends and the other begins. It was like sailing through dark blue air. "I thought only an hour had passed," he said.

"When you didn't appear, we began to worry," the Bard

said. "We searched everywhere, and at midnight I gave Schlaup a whiff of your old boots. He came back straightaway, saying he'd lost the scent near Din Eidyn. I sent him out again. It was an unusually clear night with no fog at all. Are you sure about the *haar*?"

"Very sure." Jack felt something small lodged in the neck of his tunic and felt with his fingers. He drew out a tiny, furry body. "The honeybee," he remembered. "It stung me and I woke up."

The Bard cupped the insect between his hands and whispered to it in the Blessed Speech. "Now fly you safely home with the gods' protection," he said aloud. He opened his hands and the bee flew away, or perhaps it was only blown away by the wind. Jack wasn't sure. It was such a little creature.

Chapter Twenty-four

BJORN SKULL-SPLITTER

"The year grows late," Skakki said, watching the distant shore that afternoon. The air was warm and the sky cloudless. Most people would have said the weather was ideal, but the Northmen were too experienced to be taken in by it. Ran, the goddess of the sea, and her nine daughters lay in wait for the careless. Her net was ever ready to take advantage of sudden storms. "There aren't many weeks of good sailing left."

"All I ask for is seven days' grace," the Bard said. "If we return in that time, you can take us to the nearest port. We'll make our own way south. If we don't return, you and Egil must turn east and leave us to our fate."

"I'd never do that," said the young sea captain.

"But he will," the Bard said privately to Jack later. "He's no fool. People are lost at sea all the time, and the survivors have to abandon them."

There's a thought to cheer oneself with on a dangerous journey, thought Jack. He'd inspected the little coracle they would take to Notland. As small as the ship felt on a vast, gray ocean, the coracle would be like a flyspeck compared to it. They might as well be floating in a bucket.

To save time, Skakki no longer followed the coast, for it was riven by a huge gulf. Instead, they went northwest out of sight of land, navigating by the star the Northmen called the Nail. By day Rune kept their direction with his memory of the sun's position at that time of year. The Bard helped by calling on the wind. Thus, they were blown along steadily for two days with the great sail always filled and the waves neither too high nor too low.

"I've been thinking about what happened in Edwin's Town," the Bard said as he and Jack rested in Schlaup's shade. "To someone like Severus the world is idiotically simple. There's only one way to do things, and it's always his. My stars! You have no idea how much he and the other Christians squabble about when to celebrate Easter. The ninnies don't realize Easter is one of the old goddesses, and she couldn't care a fig about when anyone celebrates her."

Seafarer returned from one of his forays and settled on the deck next to the old man. The bird reported that he'd seen no islands or ships ahead. Jack gave him a dried herring as a reward.

"Gods, if they're neglected, tend to fall asleep, but they never really go away," the Bard continued. "It is the Christians themselves who keep Easter's memory green and who, unwittingly, disturb her slumbers. A long time ago the Forest Lord and the Man in the Moon ruled these lands. Then people arrived with new deities: Odin, Thor, Freya, Jupiter, Mars, Jesus. Each new layer covered the old, but the old is still there. When you lay on that sacrificial stone, lad, something woke up. I'd be willing to bet that if the bee hadn't stung you, you'd be six feet under by now."

"Why would something want to kill me?" Jack asked.

"Why does fire burn and water drown? It's what happens when one falls into their power."

"And the bee?"

"Ah! There's the interesting part," said the Bard. He stroked the head of the albatross, and the great bird purred deep in his throat. "That small creature sacrificed itself to save you. It was no more random than Pega *happening* to have a candle in the dungeons of Elfland, or Severus *happening* to be in the forest when Aiden needed rescuing. Think of the momentous events of the past three years. The Holy Isle was destroyed and the Northmen learned that easy plunder was to be found in monasteries. You'd think this would prove the end of Christianity, but it hasn't."

"Northmen have been raiding more monasteries?" Jack said. He hadn't heard about it.

"Oh, yes. But at the same time, odd things have been occurring in the realms of the old gods. Elfland was laid bare to the light of truth, hobgoblins returned to Middle Earth, Unlife was driven from Din Guardi. It looks to me as though a profound shift has taken place in the life force. I'd guess that you have some purpose to fulfill and that is why you were saved. But don't get a swelled head over it. A cabbage has a purpose when someone needs to make soup."

The next day Seafarer returned with news of islands. The albatross was only interested in certain things and so they learned a great deal about fish. *Much food*, Seafarer exulted. *Many birds. They fear me. Feels good.*

Are there houses? Thorgil asked in Bird.

Don't know, Seafarer said. But when they came to the first island, they did find houses of a sort. Domes of turf bulged on the rocks, and the folk within hissed in a strange language and refused to come out.

"I think they're Picts," said Skakki. "Olaf arrived at some sort of trading agreement with them, but he said it was more trouble than it was worth. Farther on is Horse Island, ruled by Bjorn Skull-Splitter. He's one of my father's best friends. It's an excellent place to camp while we're waiting for you to return from Notland."

Of course he's called Skull-Splitter, Jack thought moodily as he watched the greenish depths of the sea. *No friend of Olaf's could possibly be called Bjorn the Beloved.* And he wondered what mayhem the man had committed to earn his name. The water was amazingly rich with life, from long, trailing forests of seaweed to teeming shoals of fish. Dolphins swam alongside the ship, diving in unison. Otters floated on their backs, munching crabs in their paws. They looked like humans eating chunks of bread.

The ship passed many small islands, some no more than rocks jutting out of the sea. All of them seemed deserted, although Jack saw standing stones in odd patterns and, once, a windowless tower. Horse Island was large and treeless with a few rugged cliffs topped by wiry grass. Jack thought it dreary compared to the sea.

Rune steered the ship to a bay with a beach and a village beyond the coarse sand. A crowd began to gather at their approach, and Skakki blew his father's horn in welcome. The crowd didn't react.

"They're too quiet," said Thorgil.

"They don't recognize the ship," Skakki said.

"That shouldn't make a difference. We sent them a traditional greeting and they didn't answer it," said the Bard. "Let's stay out of arrow range for a while." Skakki ordered the oarsmen to halt their forward movement.

Jack observed houses made of turf that blended so well with the ground, at first he thought he was looking at tiny hills. The Northmen inhabitants wore turf-colored clothes and turf-colored boots. With their hair the color of dry grass, they could have been fragments of island that had awakened and decided to walk around. Even the smaller, darker Picts among them faded into the background like noonday shadows.

Jack found their continued silence oppressive. He had little experience of Northman settlements, but his memory of Olaf's

village was of wild celebration when anyone showed up. They
welcomed visitors with trade goods and fresh gossip.

"Blow your horn again," suggested the Bard.

"I'll call them," said Schlaup. He stood up before anyone
could stop him and roared, "HEY, YOU! WE'RE OLAF
ONE-BROW'S PEOPLE! TALK TO US!" His voice boomed
like a clap of thunder, and to all appearances he was a villager's worst nightmare: a huge, dangerous troll. Everyone
fled and in a moment the beach was deserted. The Bard was
laughing so hard, he had to wipe his eyes with his sleeve.

"You got their attention all right, Schlaup," he said, wheez-
ing. "Oh, my! They're probably swimming to the next island
by now."

"At least they know who we are," said Skakki with a rueful
smile. "I'm sure Bjorn won't be so skittish." He gave the order
to land, and when everyone had disembarked, Schlaup dragged
the ship onto the sand. "I came here when I was twelve and
we were treated like kings," Skakki remembered. "Olaf saved
Bjorn's life during a sea battle, you see. There's nothing Bjorn
wouldn't do for him, or any of us, either."

"Sea battle?" said Jack. It hadn't occurred to him that you
could fight on water.

"Einar Adder-Tooth sank Bjorn's ship, and Olaf jumped in
to save him because he couldn't swim. Poor Bjorn has always
been scared spitless of water. He panicked and fought when
Olaf tried to rescue him, and Olaf had to knock him out. By
the time they got to safety, Adder-Tooth had disappeared into
the fog."

Close up, Jack could see many more houses clustered together like giant molehills. They formed a barrier to the rest of the island, and he thought they could provide a good place for an ambush.

"Bjorn's hall is that way," Skakki said.

"Wait a moment," cautioned the Bard. "He may be a dear friend, but you haven't been here for six years. We look like a band of berserkers—excuse me, most of you *are* berserkers. It wouldn't be the first time someone raided an island."

Sven the Vengeful, Eric the Rash, and Eric Pretty-Face looked uncomfortable. Jack knew they were thinking of the Holy Isle.

"I suggest that the crew be left here to guard the ship," the old man said. "Skakki, Jack, Thorgil, and I will make contact with Bjorn. He won't be alarmed by a small group, and it will give him time to recognize Skakki. You're twice the size you were last time," he told the young sea captain. "They won't be afraid of an old man leaning on a staff, although they should be, and Jack doesn't look at all alarming."

I beg your pardon, Jack thought. *Are we forgetting I overthrew Frith Half-Troll and broke the spell of Unlife on Din Guardi?* But he realized that his victories came about through magic, not brute force, which was what the islanders would be looking for.

"As for Thorgil, who would suspect a young lady dressed in the finest Din Guardi has to offer?"

"*What?*" cried Thorgil.

"Brutus sent along the dress you wore to the monastery,"

the Bard said. "I can't think of a better disguise for a dangerous warrior."

The shield maiden blushed. "You think I'm dangerous?
Truly?"

"Like a coiled dragon."

And so Thorgil hid behind the ship to change clothes
while the others waited. They set out with the Bard going
first. Jack had been correct. The village was like a maze with
paths going everywhere and each dwelling exactly like the
others. Once inside, it was impossible to see landmarks, and
they soon found themselves back on the beach. Thorgil called
to Seafarer for help.

The great albatross floated lazily overhead. *Many two-
legged beasts*, he called out. *Hide like crabs.*

"I thought so," muttered the Bard. But the hidden villagers
didn't attack, and with Seafarer as beacon, the group easily
found its way through.

Chapter Twenty-five

PRINCESS THORGIL

Beyond lay a sweep of uninhabited land covered with grass, heather, and a few marshes. It was beautiful in a desolate way and a relief after the closely packed houses. The wind blew unhindered across this open space, bringing with it the smell of the sea, and a well-trodden path told them the direction of Bjorn's hall. "It's made of stone." Skakki raised his voice to be heard over the wind. "He built it with the remains of old ruins he found lying around. Very impressive."

"And very foolish," said the Bard so that only Jack could hear. "Some old ruins have an evil past. He'll be lucky to wind up with only a ghost or two."

Seafarer flew above, diving occasionally to terrify gulls.

After he scattered them, he would loudly proclaim his superiority and insult the gulls' ancestry. Seafarer, Jack decided, was ideally suited to living with Northmen.

"Horses!" Thorgil cried suddenly. A herd of small but powerfully built beasts had suddenly appeared—or perhaps they had been there all along. They were earth-colored, the brown of turf and gray of chalk. Their skins were mottled like rocks flecked with lichen. Standing still, they could have faded into a hillside, but they weren't still now. A stallion screamed and pawed the ground as the mares gathered into a tight knot with the foals at the center.

"By Thor, they've gone completely wild," exclaimed Skakki. "I'm sure they're part of Bjorn Skull-Splitter's herd, because there were no horses on the island before he got here."

"Be careful!" called Jack, for Thorgil was advancing on the stallion. Jack started forward, but the Bard put his hand on the boy's arm.

"They won't harm her," he said.

Jack wasn't sure. The stallion snorted and stamped. He backed up slightly as if unsure how to deal with this human who didn't understand her danger.

The shield maiden halted. She held out her hands, palms up, and chanted:

> Man byþ on myrgþe his magan leof:
> sceal þeah anra gehwylc oðrum swican . . .
> Horse is a joy to princes in the presence of warriors,
> a steed in the pride of its hoofs . . .

Jack was astounded. It was a charm his mother had used to calm one of John the Fletcher's horses after a thunderstorm. Thorgil continued to speak softly and earnestly to the stallion. Jack couldn't hear everything because of the wind, but he could see the horse calm down and the knot of mares relax their protective circle around the foals. Finally, the stallion came up to the shield maiden, and she breathed into his nostrils. He lowered his head.

"There's something I haven't seen for many a long year," said the Bard.

Thorgil swung herself onto the stallion's back. Jack braced himself for a battle between the two, but the horse accepted her weight as though he'd known her all his life. "Now I look like a proper lady going on a visit," she announced.

"Pull your skirts down. You'll make a better impression," said Skakki.

They went on, leaving the herd of mares behind, and when Jack looked back, he could see nothing but heather and mottled rocks. He tried to touch the stallion, and the beast snapped viciously at him. "He's not tame," Thorgil warned.

"Where did you learn that charm?" Jack asked.

A shadow of pain crossed the shield maiden's face, and she paused before speaking. "My mother taught it to me. She said she was taken captive while clearing weeds from an outline of a horse carved into a hill. It was a holy place, she said, but I never bothered to ask her about it. My father carried her off . . . not Olaf—the one before." Thorgil fell silent. Jack knew it was difficult for her to remember her real father, the terrible Thorgrim, who had killed her brother in a berserker rage. When Thorgrim fell in battle, he demanded that Allyson, Thorgil's mother, be sacrificed on his funeral pyre.

"You carry the blood of the horse lords," the Bard said. "I suspected it after seeing how readily the steeds of Din Guardi obeyed you. Your mother must have been a descendant of King Hengist, who was said to take the form of a horse when he went into battle. Tell me, why did you blow into the stallion's nostrils?"

"Why . . . it seemed the right thing to do," said Thorgil.

"Exactly! Horses recognize one another by scent, and you knew it without being told."

"So I could be royal," said the shield maiden.

"Or part horse," Jack added. She danced the stallion sideways, making him jump out of the way.

They continued at a slow pace, enjoying the fresh air. It was wonderful to be on solid ground after so many days at sea. Voles ran for cover when Seafarer soared overhead, and blue butterflies drifted ahead of their feet. Loons took wing from pools of water, uttering weird cries as the group approached.

The land went up for a long while and then sloped down to a promontory high above the sea. A high wall stretched from side to side of the promontory, cutting it off from the rest of the island. There was only a single gate.

"Bjorn never needed a wall before," said Skakki. "I wonder what sort of trouble he's gotten into."

"He *is* called Skull-Splitter," Jack reminded him.

They left the Bard and Thorgil behind and went forward to gauge what kind of reception they would have. Skakki sounded his horn. After a while a large man with numerous scars on his arms and head opened the gate. "You're the lot down by the beach," he said. "My master says you can't bring the troll in here."

"That troll is my brother," Skakki said. "But I've left him with the ship. Kindly announce to Bjorn that the son of his best friend, Olaf One-Brow, is here."

The man looked startled. "You're Olaf's son? You were no bigger than a bog rat the last time I saw you."

Skakki narrowed his eyes. "And you haven't gotten any handsomer, Big Half."

"Aye, everyone says that." Big Half scratched his bristly cheek. "Come out here, Little Half. See what the tide washed up."

Another man squeezed past and stood, hands on hips, observing them. Jack was enchanted. He was no taller than the boy's shoulder, but his head was unusually large. To support it, his body was thickset and strong. "You're a dwarf!" Jack cried.

"I've kneecapped men for saying less than that," said Little Half.

"I didn't mean to be rude," Jack apologized. "I've always heard stories about dwarves living in hills and making gold rings. They gave the Mountain Queen a throne of gold and diamonds."

Little Half spat not far from Jack's feet. "If I could get my hands on gold and diamonds, do you think I'd be living in this pesthole? I'm just an ordinary man concentrated into a small area."

"He's my brother," explained Big Half. "Mother always said I was so big, there wasn't enough left over to make him."

"Garm's fangs! Do you see that?" cried the dwarf, pointing excitedly. "It's Bjorn's best horse come home again—and who's that riding him?" Thorgil was approaching slowly, keeping pace with the Bard. Jack hadn't paid much attention to the shield maiden's looks, but now he saw her through Little Half's eyes.

She wore a sky blue tunic over a green dress and soft leather boots. Her legs were visible because she rode astride, but they were cased in purple leggings that had certainly caught the dwarf's attention. Around her neck was an amethyst necklace, most certainly a gift from King Brutus. Thorgil had chosen not to wear a veil, and so her fine, wheat-colored hair flowed in the breeze and her cheeks were rosy with sunlight.

"Oh, the pretty creature," murmured Little Half, clasping his hands. Thorgil allowed Big Half to help her down, and Jack noticed that the man's face had broken out with sweat. Thorgil thanked him sweetly. She whispered something into the stallion's ear, and he turned and galloped back to the heath.

"That was Bjorn's best horse," Big Half protested.

"He'll return when I call him," Thorgil said. "This is Dragon Tongue, whose fame is renowned throughout the nine worlds." She nodded grandly to the Bard, who looked faintly surprised by her behavior. Jack certainly was. They were trying to allay the fears of the islanders, not remind them of the Bard's well-known powers.

"I've heard of Dragon Tongue," Little Half said uneasily. "They say that he can drive men mad by blowing on a wisp of straw. They say he melted a hole in the Mountain Queen's fortress."

Jack was intrigued. This was a tale he'd been trying to pry out of the old man without success.

"That was in my youth," the Bard said, sighing. "Alas, age falls upon us all." He leaned on his staff as though it were the only thing holding him up. "It would be good to rest somewhere," he said pointedly, looking at the gate.

"You can't spend the night here," Little Half said rudely.

"But, brother, only the other day the king said he wanted visitors—"

"Shut your face," snarled the dwarf. Jack was amazed by his hostility, and Skakki looked surprised too. Hospitality demanded that a Northman offer lodging, especially to an old friend.

Big Half looked unhappy, but he went back inside and dragged out a stool. "Rest yourself on that, Dragon Tongue. I'll fetch you something to eat, and something for you, too, pretty lady."

"Allow me to introduce Thorgil, my heart-sister," said Skakki, indicating that she had been adopted. The brothers bowed and Thorgil accepted their homage as though it were the most natural thing.

"I am heart-daughter to Olaf One-Brow, but my mother was of the line of King Hengist," she said proudly. Now Jack understood what she was up to. She'd always felt shamed because her mother had been a thrall. Thorgil herself had been a thrall most of her life, and the bitterness of it had eaten into her soul. She wasn't going to pass up a chance to act like royalty.

"A princess!" cried Big Half. "Oh, my, my, my! To think that we'd be so lucky. Wait till I tell the king."

"I told you! No visitors tonight," objected Little Half.

"But a princess—" The brothers went off to confer, and Jack caught fragments of the conversation: *enemies*, *dangerous*, *hogboon*, and now and then, *princess*. Finally, they came back and Little Half said they would ask the king for permission.

"I didn't know Bjorn was a king," Jack said when the brothers had gone.

Skakki shrugged. "If he wants to call a group of turf houses a kingdom, I don't see the harm in it."

The Bard had settled himself on the stool and was examining the wall closely. "There are markings here, Jack. Do you recognize them?"

The stones were extremely weathered and covered with lichen, but the boy could make out the faint outlines of animals. One of them was a serpentlike creature standing on its tail. "Is that a *carnyx*?" he asked.

"It's what the *carnyx* was copied from. It's a male Pictish beast. The females have legs of a sort; the males have none.

I'd guess this wall was made from an old Pictish tower. Speaking of claiming kingship, Thorgil, do you think it wise to pose as a princess?"

"That was *their* conclusion," she said. "I only said I was of the line of Hengist. Besides, dressing up and mincing around is a surprisingly effective battle strategy."

The Bard laughed. "I know that strategy. It's called 'flirting.'"

"Flirting?" said Thorgil, puzzled by the word. But before the Bard could explain, Big Half and Little Half returned.

"His Majesty bids you welcome," the dwarf said with a deep bow.

When they were through the gate, Big Half closed it with nine bolts. *That's a lot of bolts for one gate*, thought Jack. The wall was as deep as his outstretched arms and higher than Skakki's head. What kind of enemy was Bjorn expecting? He remembered the words the brothers had used: *enemies, dangerous, hogboon*. What on earth was a hogboon?

Inside, a courtyard separated the wall from the large hall beyond. Jack had expected the same landscape that existed outside, but here was no grass or heather. The ground was completely dead in spite of a spring bubbling up in the middle. The water had carved a deep channel, but it didn't flow more than a few paces before it disappeared into a rift in the ground.

The courtyard reminded Jack of the old fortress of Din Guardi, where nothing grew. It didn't have the cold despair of that place, however. Rather, it seemed filled with active resentment, a simmering rage that would wither the leaves of any plant brave enough to sprout. Jack felt sweat trickle down the back of his neck.

"You feel it too," the Bard said in a low voice. "It's the wall. The stones have been stolen from a Pictish tower, and those towers are not like other buildings. They draw their strength from the blood of men buried alive beneath them."

"What's that you say?" said Little Half, walking behind them. He was so short, Jack hadn't noticed him. "I told the king it was a rotten idea to tear down that tower. The horses bolted rather than carry the stones, and not one of them came back until today."

The entrance of the hall was secured by an iron door. Jack had never seen such a thing and wondered about it. The heavy door creaked dismally as it was dragged open, but when it was closed behind them, the simmering rage vanished. That explained why Bjorn had used such an expensive substance.

The hall itself was a simple structure, somewhat like King Ivar's dwelling in the Northland. A long fireplace ran down the middle, unlit at the moment. On either side were tables with benches, and along the walls were narrow sleeping cupboards. It was cluttered, as such places were, with chests, bedding, and stacks of peat to be used for the fire. The floor was covered by an ankle-deep layer of straw. At either end were openings leading to other rooms and possibly other ways to get into the courtyard. Jack knew from the Bard that such establishments sometimes had escape routes in case of an invasion.

On the seaward side two small windows let in the late-afternoon light. They would be blocked with bundles of hay at night or in bad weather.

A farther, open door led to a spacious area between the hall and the cliff's edge. Here were the features one usually associated with a large household: kitchens, barns, a granary, and an herb garden. Men were preparing game, cooking, or mending fishnets. Women sat weaving in the mild sunlight, and children drove seagulls away from drying fish. Yet there was a curious lifelessness about the place. The children didn't play or laugh.

"Hey, you! Get some water," bellowed a man at a pair of scullery boys.

"We did it last time," one of the boys dared to say, and he received a blow.

"Get moving or I'll lock you into the courtyard," threatened the man. The boys quickly gathered buckets and hurried to the iron door.

"The stream is our only source of freshwater," Little Half explained. "People don't like going out there because . . . well, you felt it. Sit down, honored guests, and I'll get you bread and cheese. The king will be with you as soon as he's finished combing his beard."

"Combing his beard?" whispered Jack, amused. "How long does that take?"

"Perhaps he's trying to impress me," Thorgil said, fluffing her hair.

"No, Bjorn would never put on airs like that," declared Skakki. "He's just getting the nits out."

The dwarf returned with food and excused himself. They ate. The silence of the hall settled over them. The sun lowered until it shone directly inside, and a haze of dust motes drifted through the light. "How do all those people fit in here at night?" Jack said at last.

"I imagine most of them return to the village before dark," said the Bard. "I suggest we do the same. There's something wrong here, and I can't quite put my finger on it."

"I should get Bjorn's permission to camp on the beach," Skakki argued. "Besides, he may have useful information about Notland."

"The only information he could possibly have is a warning to stay away from the wretched place." The Bard was getting tired and cranky. He thumped his staff on the floor. "Where *is* that so-called king?"

As if by magic, Little Half appeared. "I'm dreadfully sorry, honored guests. The king was called away to tend to a dead sheep. A terrible bird came out of the sky and frightened it into a ravine. They've gone off to retrieve the body. He sends his most sincere apologies and hopes you will accept his hospitality tonight."

"Unfortunately, we must return to our ship," said the Bard, rising to his feet. But at that moment a horn sounded and servants streamed into the hall bearing platters of food. They began setting the tables with trenchers of bread, wheels of cheese, pots of yellow butter, and a variety of roasted meats. A drinking horn was set up on a metal stand at each place.

At the same time, the village workers filed past and disappeared through the iron door. But when the Bard, Skakki, Jack, and Thorgil tried to follow them, they found a row of grim Northman warriors blocking their way. "Where did they come from?" said Jack.

"I've been a fool," the Bard said. "All that waiting was a trick to keep us here. I don't know why, but the reason can't be good."

"Bjorn was Olaf's best friend," protested Skakki.

"We'll see," the old man said. There was nothing to do except sit down and try to look cheerful about it. The tables were laden with food, yet no one arrived to eat it. The sun slid below the cliff. Seagulls wheeled in great flocks before going off to wherever they would spend the night.

The servants lit the fireplace and set fish-oil lamps in alcoves along the walls. They fitted bundles of straw into the windows and fastened sheepskins over them to keep out drafts. The air quickly became stale.

At last, just before sundown, the iron door opened. A tall man wearing a leather helmet and vest came in. The helmet covered most of his face, so Jack couldn't tell what he looked like, but he guessed it was Bjorn Skull-Splitter. Behind the king came several men carrying the flayed carcass of a sheep.

"By Thor!" cried the king to Big Half, who quickly ran to help him. "I never saw a bird of its like. It could have scared *me* into a ravine."

"Did you manage to shoot it?" Big Half said.

Jack held his breath. He was certain the giant bird was Seafarer, who was only trying to find them.

"The rotten thing kept the sun at its back," said the king. "I shot at it but kept getting blinded. Never mind! I'll kill it tomorrow." Big Half unlaced his master's vest and removed his boots. The king himself took off the helmet and shook out his hair. "So you're Olaf One-Brow's brat," he said, turning to Skakki. "If you've come here for vengeance, you're seeking an early grave."

"I thought you said he was a friend," whispered Thorgil.

"Bjorn Skull-Splitter was a friend," said Skakki, rising to his feet. "Einar Adder-Tooth wasn't."

Chapter Twenty-six

THE HOGBOON

"I've taken you by surprise," said Adder-Tooth, "but never fear. The rules of hospitality hold. I never kill a man without giving him a good meal." He clapped his hands, and a servant darted out with an ale-horn. The silent warriors sat down at the tables, and now all the ale-horns were filled. The men set about carving themselves chunks of meat and cheese with the knives people carried for this purpose. Servants ladled stew onto the trenchers.

"Eat up! You never know where the next meal is coming from—or if you'll be here to enjoy it," Adder-Tooth said heartily. He dug his thumb into a pot of butter and smeared it on a chunk of bread. "Bjorn thought his last moment had come when I dumped him into the sea. He lived to eat many a fine meal, thanks to Olaf, curse him, but no longer."

Skakki laid his hand on his knife. "Kindly refrain from insulting my father. He died a hero's death in Jotunheim and was given a funeral pyre worthy of the gods themselves."

"Oh, I heard about it. No one's questioning his honor. Bjorn, on the other hand, would have been better off drowning. At least he'd be feasting with Ran and Aegir instead of roaming the icy halls of Hel."

"I knew Bjorn," said Skakki. "He would not meet a coward's end."

Adder-Tooth waved his ale-horn at him. "Sit down! You're making me nervous, and that isn't good for your health."

The sea captain glanced at the Bard, who nodded. Skakki sat down, but neither he nor the others took food. The king ate heartily and so did his followers, although Jack noticed that Little Half seemed to have no appetite. The boy watched Adder-Tooth carefully, trying to gauge what sort of man he was. Like all Northmen, he would be a bully. He obviously enjoyed killing, but the laws of hospitality forbade him from slaying an enemy who had been given sanctuary under his roof.

For that matter, why *had* Adder-Tooth invited them in? Jack caught a glimpse of the king tearing apart a joint of mutton. His front teeth had been filed into points.

The wind rose outside and buffeted the straw bales in the windows. The iron door rattled as though someone were trying to pull it open. One of the warriors jumped to his feet.

"Sit down," the king said irritably. "The hogboon can't pass the wall."

For the first time the Bard spoke. "Don't tell me you've been foolish enough to have dealings with a hogboon."

Adder-Tooth laughed so explosively, bits of food flew over his chest. "I've been waiting to see how long it took to get a Dragon Tongue scolding. Ivar the Boneless used to cringe waiting for them."

"You may laugh if you like," the old man said, nettled, "but there's a reason you hide behind that disgraceful wall."

"I do not hide!" shouted the king, knocking over his ale-horn and causing his neighbors to recoil.

"Now who's cringing?" the Bard said. Jack held his breath. He expected the hall to break into open warfare, but after a moment Adder-Tooth settled down.

"The one who begged to have a sword in his hand at the end, but was too weak to grasp it, was Bjorn."

Little Half swung his short legs off the bench, went to the far end of the hall, and turned his back on the assembly. After a moment his brother joined him.

"I had sworn an oath to destroy Bjorn," Adder-Tooth continued, "but he shut himself into this hall and I couldn't reach him. What was I to do? My honor was at stake. And so I found a wise woman who was willing to help me."

"You mean you threatened her," the Bard said.

"So what if I did? She was a poisonous old hag and not fit to live anyhow. She demanded silver and free passage to another island. I had to find her a cloak dyed blue with woad.

She needed a hood and gloves made of catskin. She had to sit on a cushion filled with feathers so her spirit could fly. Paugh! *Seiðer* makes me sick!" Adder-Tooth said, naming the magic women used.

"Not sick enough to stay away from it," remarked the Bard. The king glared at him and drank another horn of ale. It was his sixth or seventh, Jack thought.

"The ceremony was done under the full moon. The hag sat on an old grave and chewed one of those red mushrooms that grow under birch trees."

"*Atterswam,*" murmured the Bard.

"Yes, that. She went into a trance. I had expected her to contact spirits and tell me how to break into Bjorn's stronghold, but something unexpected happened. She began to scream. Her body writhed and she flopped around like a hooked salmon. I didn't touch her. I don't meddle with *seiðer* even when I'm paying for it. Her form began to change, and suddenly she wasn't there at all. In her place was the hogboon. It had eaten her all up."

A hush fell over the hall. Wind burrowed through the straw and made the lamps in the alcoves flutter. The followers of the king had stopped eating. Beyond the howl of the wind and the sea crashing below the cliff, Jack heard voices. They were like men caught in a deadly trap—a sinking ship or a fire. They shouted for help, but no aid was coming and they knew it. They raged against their fate.

"Shouldn't we try to help them?" Jack said, fearful and yet unwilling to ignore them.

"They are not living men," said the Bard. Nothing he said could have been more dreadful.

Little Half moaned and buried his face in his hands. "I knew we shouldn't have touched that tower."

"Shut up! It was either that or the hogboon!" shouted the king. "We need music. Wake up my skald! The swine is probably drunk, but he'll sing the better for it. More ale! More mead!"

Servants hurried to obey, and soon a bedraggled young man stumbled into the hall carrying a harp. He ran his fingers through his hair. "What kind of song—?" he began.

"I don't care so long as it's loud!" roared Adder-Tooth.

It was evidently a request the skald had heard before. Shouting rather than singing, he recited the tale of King Siggeir, who captured a rival's ten sons and left them, bound and helpless, in a deep, dark forest. Each night a giant she-wolf appeared and devoured one of them. On the tenth night the youngest son, who was named Sigmund, clamped on to the wolf's tongue with his teeth and ripped it out. After which, Sigmund was rescued by his sister and went on to have many other nasty adventures.

Jack tried not to listen. It was the usual Northman entertainment. The warriors cheered every time Sigmund did something appalling. Much ale was drunk. Someone got sick in the straw. Eventually, most of the men crawled into sleeping cupboards along the walls and passed out. But a few stayed awake to guard the gate. Adder-Tooth was carried by servants to his private bedroom.

The Bard, Skakki, Jack, and Thorgil remained seated. "We must leave tomorrow," said Thorgil, who had been silent for a long time. She had dropped all pretense of being a delicate princess. Her gray eyes raked over the squalid hall and found nothing to her liking. "Gods! I'd forgotten what a drunken revel was like."

"This was no revel," said the Bard. "They were drinking to hide fear."

Big Half and Little Half appeared, with the young skald fluttering behind them. "You should eat," Little Half said. "I have cheese and bread in the pantry that hasn't been mauled."

"Is this how these men spend every night?" said the Bard, disgusted.

"I'm afraid so."

"I can't tell you how honored I am to meet the great Dragon Tongue," gushed the skald.

"So you should be," the old man said absentmindedly. "Thank you for your offer, Little Half. We would welcome food that hasn't been slobbered on." Soon everyone was enjoying a peaceful meal. If it hadn't been for the drunken snores and the guards lurking by the gate, it would have been almost cheerful. The terrible cries in the wind had vanished.

"Much as I hate to bring up an unpleasant subject, I need to know what happened with that hogboon," said the Bard when they had finished.

"What's a hogboon, sir?" Jack asked.

"Do you remember my telling you about Jenny Greenteeth?"

"The ghost who haunts the Hall of Wraiths?"

"Yes. She's a perfect example of what happens when you don't fix wrongs," said the Bard. "Long ago something terrible happened to Jenny and her spirit was unable to rest. The problem is, she can't remember what it was. She comes after anyone who strays into her territory, moaning *whooo . . . whooo . . . whooo* like a demented owl. My guess is that she's asking 'Who killed me?' Now, of course, no one can tell her. Jenny's fairly harmless, apart from causing the odd heart attack. A hogboon is far worse."

"This one came from an ancient barrow," said Big Half.

"I saw it when it came for Bjorn." Little Half shivered. "It was a tall presence wreathed in cobwebs. Its body was like the mold you find on bread. Soft-looking. It left gray footprints."

"Let's start at the beginning," the Bard said. "Adder-Tooth forced the wise woman to go into a vision trance. Unfortunately, she chose a barrow containing a hogboon, and it awakened. It saw an opportunity to take over a living body, except that hogboons are not alive. The best they can manage is to use up the life force within a host, and when that was gone, the woman dissolved into dust. Am I correct?"

"Yes, sir," said Little Half. "That's what Adder-Tooth told me. He himself didn't realize what had happened until the creature spoke. '*That was a dainty meal you prepared for me,*' it said. '*Ask of me any boon and it shall be granted.*' Well, of course Adder-Tooth only wanted one thing: the destruction of Bjorn. He immediately demanded that without asking whether payment would be involved."

"There's always a price for such favors," said the Bard.

"When Bjorn was alive . . ." The dwarf swallowed and wiped his eyes. "When Bjorn was alive, this hall rang with laughter. Women and children still lived here, and on that night we were posing riddles."

"I remember," said Big Half.

"Bjorn had given us this puzzle," said Little Half.

Its shaping power passes knowing.
It seeks the living one by one.
Eternal, yet without life, it moves
Everywhere in the wide world.

"The answer, of course, was Death. The riddle had no sooner been set when a gray presence drifted through the wall. The lamps grew dim and the smaller children began to cry.

"'*I seek Bjorn Skull-Splitter,*' it said in a ghastly voice. We were all terrified, but Bjorn bravely drew his sword. 'I am the one you seek. Why are you here?'

"'*I am the answer to your riddle,*' replied the hogboon.

"Our leader grew pale. 'Take the women and children from the hall,' he ordered. 'Now begone, foul creature, or I will be forced to kill you.'

"'*None may slay me,*' the hogboon whispered, and leaped at him. Bjorn sliced it in two with his sword, but the parts came together like smoke, and it laid its hand on Bjorn's chest. Our poor leader groaned and dropped his weapon. In an instant his face had aged ten years.

"'*Take up your sword, Bjorn Skull-Splitter. This battle is not over*,' said the hogboon. Bjorn, may Odin remember him, fought on. Each time the hogboon touched him, he aged. It was like watching a cat play with a mouse. At the last Bjorn could only lie helplessly on the floor. He tried to lift his weapon, but by then his hand was so gnarled, he couldn't open his fingers. He crumbled away into dust before our eyes. The next day Einar Adder-Tooth's army invaded."

"By all the gods of Asgard," swore Thorgil, "this crime cries out for vengeance."

"So it does, princess," said the dwarf, "but much happens for which there is no remedy. The living must go on." Jack had a moment of satisfaction when Thorgil looked startled. She had completely forgotten she was supposed to be a princess.

By now exhaustion was falling over all of them, particularly the Bard. They had walked a long way and the night's revels had been wearing. "We can continue this conversation in the morning," said Little Half, noting the old man's tiredness. "I'll bring fresh straw and you can sleep out here. I don't recommend the sleeping cupboards. They've been thrown up in too often."

"I could sing for you, to help you sleep," offered the skald.

"I'd rather listen to Pictish beasts howling at the moon," said the Bard. "There's one more question, Little Half. Why does Adder-Tooth want a princess?"

"Ah!" The dwarf looked embarrassed. It was he, after all, who had carried that information to the king. "Why does any ruler want a princess? He needs a wife."

Chapter Twenty-seven

ESCAPE PLANS

Jack thought Thorgil would never calm down. She stormed about, kicking straw and swearing bloodthirsty oaths until the drunken warriors began to stir. Skakki kept telling her, "I won't allow it, little sister. You have my word."

"You have my word too," said the Bard. She screamed at both of them.

"How can she be forced into marriage?" said Jack. "I thought Northmen brides had to consent."

"That's the ideal situation," the old man said. "But Adder-Tooth needs a princess to insure his kingship. He has no right to the title."

"I'll kill myself before I let that slime bucket near me!"

Thorgil snatched up a knife someone had left on a table, but it slid from her hand. She bent to retrieve it and her knees buckled. She collapsed on the floor. "Curse that rune of protection! Curse it! It won't let me die!" She thrashed about in the straw.

"Perhaps I could bring her a calming drink," said Little Half, who had dodged her fists several times.

"Something hot. No wine or mead," said the Bard. He laid his hand on her forehead and murmured words in the Blessed Speech. She shuddered and lay still.

"We should leave now," Skakki said in a low voice. He nodded at the iron door, where a few bleary-eyed guards squatted.

"I don't relish a long, dark walk to the village with a hogboon wandering about," said the Bard. "It may prefer to feed on full-moon nights, but it's clearly restless. Only the spirits in the wall are keeping it out. I wouldn't like to encounter them, either."

"Would they attack us?" Jack thought about the hogboon slowly devouring the life of the wise woman and Bjorn Skull-Splitter.

"Probably not," the old man said. "The spirits in the wall are innocent sacrificial victims. They strive to defeat the one who slew them, but if aroused, they might lash out at anyone who came near."

Great, thought Jack, hugging himself against the growing chill in the hall. The more he learned about spirits, the less he liked them—Jenny Greenteeth, the *draugr*, hogboons. But there was also the gentle ghost who had stood outside the old Roman house with his two children. Restless spirits weren't all bad. Perhaps most people noticed only the ones that were.

The dwarf returned with herbal tea for them all. Then he and his brother made comfortable beds of straw in the cleanest part of the hall and fetched sheepskins for the coldest hours before dawn.

Jack fell asleep quickly and slept like the dead until after the sun rose. The workers from the village had already passed through and the servants had opened up the windows. A chill breeze ruffled his hair.

Jack sat up and blearily looked around. The hall had seemed halfway decent in the dim light of the night before. Now it showed itself an utter ruin. Ale-horns were strewn everywhere with gnawed bones and half-eaten trenchers of bread. Servants were turning over the straw with pitchforks and tossing the riper bits into the fire. The warriors were crawling out of their cupboards. To go by the groans, they all had filthy hangovers, and they staggered outside to urinate over the edge of the cliff.

"I'm sorry, my lady," apologized Little Half, flinching at Thorgil's murderous glare. "You really must get up so we can put this place to rights. It's much nicer on the cliff."

"Oh, leave me alone," she muttered.

Jack helped her outside. They sat upwind from the warriors on stones overlooking the water. The sun was just breaking over the hills to the east, and the bay below them was still in deep shade. The water was dark blue with a frosting of seagulls.

"My head feels like trolls have been playing knucklebones with it all night," Thorgil moaned. "Ohhh, everything is moving."

Jack turned his head sharply and found that his vision was swimming too. "That tea Little Half gave us . . . ," he said.

"What?" the shield maiden said faintly.

"That drink we had just before going to bed. I think it was drugged."

"You can't trust anyone in this snake pit," she said.

"Apparently not." Jack was annoyed at himself. He should have been more suspicious of Little Half. He liked him because he'd been a friend of Bjorn, but the dwarf was in the service of Einar Adder-Tooth now.

Little Half brought out hot cider and oatcakes. "Traitor," snarled Thorgil.

"Now, princess, it isn't as bad you think it is." The dwarf knelt by her and placed her fingers around the warm cider cup. "Everyone suffers changes of fortune, and sometimes they turn out better than you think. My brother and I felt terrible when Bjorn died, but Adder-Tooth is no worse than most masters."

Thorgil looked up, surprised. "You've had many masters?"

"We're wandering entertainers. We go from hall to hall, and when one group gets tired of us, we move on. We used to visit Bjorn regularly, but we've also worked for Grimble the Sullen, Leif Lousy-Beard, and Ragnar the Ravenous. There aren't many jobs for a man like me. I'm too small to be a warrior, and my singing voice would curdle the milk inside a cow. But I know how to lighten a dull evening with lively tales and games. I'm also an excellent servant. I give good advice without appearing to do so, and I perform chores a king can't trust to others."

"Such as drugging people," said Jack. His head ached dully and he had trouble concentrating. The dwarf shrugged.

"What does Big Half do?" asked Thorgil.

"He juggles knives, but he usually winds up cutting himself. He does acrobatic tricks. Most of the time he falls flat on his face, and the warriors seem to find that amusing. I'm afraid my brother isn't the swiftest deer in the herd. Without my care, he would have starved long ago. He also plays Bonk Ball."

"What's that?"

"My own invention," Little Half said proudly. "You need a wooden ball wrapped in leather and a stick of wood called a 'bat.' A player throws the ball at Big Half as hard as he can, and he knocks it away with the bat. If he misses, it goes *bonk* on his head."

Jack smiled grimly. Big Half definitely wasn't the swiftest deer in the herd if he let his little brother talk him into such a game. "Tell me more about that wall outside."

Little Half hunkered down and helped himself to one of the oatcakes. "When you ask for anything from a hogboon, it expects to be paid back. The night after Adder-Tooth took over, the hogboon took shape in the hall. I can tell you, every one dived for cover. Warriors were fighting one another to get into the sleeping cupboards. They knew swords were no use against it.

"'*I have granted your wish, Einar Adder-Tooth,*' the creature said. '*Now I have come for payment. Each full-moon night I expect a living human left for me on my barrow. If you do not provide this, I will take you in its stead.*' Then it turned into a mist and disappeared through the wall.

"The full moon was just past," the dwarf continued. "Adder-Tooth asked the Picts about the body that lay in that barrow, and they said it was an ancient king who had also built a haunted tower at the other end of the island. He had buried thirty men alive beneath its stones. Some years later, on his wedding day, relatives of those men slew him and carried off his bride.

"Adder-Tooth reasoned that you had to fight ghosts *with* ghosts and that thirty vengeful spirits should be enough to fight off one hogboon. He ordered the tower dismantled and brought here. He didn't need to fortify the seaward side because hogboons can't travel through water.

"The minute we started dismantling the tower, the voices started. You couldn't understand the words, but the rage was unmistakable. The horses bolted. Men had to drag the carts themselves. They didn't complain, though, because fear drove them, and they got the wall up before the next full moon."

"If hogboons can't travel through water," Jack said with a yawn, trying to gather his thoughts, "why didn't Adder-Tooth simply go to another island?"

"He had always been landless," Little Half said simply.

"Bjorn's island, fine hall, horses, and sheep were more wealth than Adder-Tooth had ever dreamed possible. And he could call himself a king. You have no idea how much that means to a third-rate pirate. The first thing he did was hire a third-rate skald to sing his praises."

Jack saw the third-rate skald stagger out of the hall and collapse with his face in a trough of water.

Little Half stretched his arms and legs as the sun flooded the cliff over the sea. "Once the wall was up, the hogboon battered against it, and the spirits of the dead men battered back. If you thought last night was noisy, wait till you see what happens during the full moon."

"I have no intention of waiting for the full moon. I'm not staying here," Thorgil said.

The dwarf laughed. "You'll get used to the idea." He gathered up the cups and left.

Jack surveyed the edge of the cliff. It was at least a hundred feet down with no handholds and only a narrow beach at the bottom. The warriors had ambled away, and the villagers worked silently at various chores. Now Jack could understand their gloom.

"We have to find some way through that iron door," said Thorgil. She leaned against his shoulder. "Curse this dizziness."

"We'll ask the Bard what to do," Jack said, and suddenly froze. Where *was* the Bard? They hurried back to their sleeping site. Servants had raked it clean and provided fresh straw. The hall was deserted except for guards sitting by the iron door. "Where are our companions?" Jack demanded.

"Them? They were carried out at first light," one of the men said. "Had a bit too much to drink if you ask me, but didn't we all?" The other men guffawed.

"They were drugged! What have you done with them?" cried the boy.

"We took them back to the village," said Big Half, who had been drawn by the commotion. "Please don't cry, little princess. They can visit you after the wedding."

"There won't be any wedding!" shouted Thorgil. "I'm a shield maiden and my kind do not marry. Where's Adder-Tooth?"

"He left at first light too," said the guard. "If you'll pardon me, little lady, you're far too cute for a shield maiden."

"If I had an axe, I'd bury it in your thick skull!" screamed Thorgil.

"Feisty little morsel," the guard said to his pals.

Jack pulled her away before she resorted to mayhem. "We can't fight our way out," he said. "We'll have to use strategy."

"Like Olaf used to do," said Thorgil, wiping tears of frustration from her eyes. Jack smiled inwardly. Olaf One-Brow's idea of strategy was to run downhill with an axe, screaming at the top of his lungs.

"Skakki won't abandon you," he said. "Nor any of the others. They're probably thinking of a battle plan right now."

"I know that, but they're badly outnumbered," said Thorgil. "Oh, Jack, what are we going to do? Can't you call up an earthquake or something?"

Jack wished, not for the first time, that the Bard had taught him useful magic, such as how to knock holes in walls or make everyone go blind. "I'll think of something. Don't worry."

But the morning passed and he wasn't able to think of anything. Creating a storm wasn't any good. Farseeing was useless, and besides, it took concentration. Thorgil kept interrupting him. He tried to cast a sleep-spell over a woman plucking a hen, and she asked him if he was feeling ill.

Thorgil's scheme, which she repeated many times, was to kill the guards and make a run for it. There were five gate guards, Jack pointed out, each one weighing twice as much as they did. They would have to use strategy. She called him a weakling.

At midday they both sat with their legs dangling over the sea cliff. "I'd throw myself off if it weren't for this wretched rune of protection," Thorgil said, clutching the invisible pendant at her neck.

"You're lucky to have it," said Jack unsympathetically. He remembered how the talisman had made him feel. No matter how grim things were, it reminded you of how precious life was.

"Perhaps I could give it away. I think Little Half would like it." Thorgil was taunting him, one of her favorite activities when she was frustrated. The only person she couldn't give the rune to was Jack, and he was the only person who really wanted it.

"The Bard says the rune decides when to go," Jack said. "It won't let you do something so totally stupid."

The shield maiden grasped the pendant and tried to force

it over her head. Her hand opened involuntarily. The rune fell back into place. "I hate you," she said.

"I hate you too," replied Jack. He was thoroughly tired of her insults.

With a loud cry, Seafarer dropped onto the cliff, scattering the children who were guarding drying fish. The bird immediately fell upon the fish and started stuffing himself. *Seafarer! Fly away!* cried Thorgil in Bird. Already the warriors were scrambling for bows and arrows.

Fire! said the albatross, after choking down what he had in his beak. *Fire! Fire!* An arrow whizzed by. Thorgil shielded the bird with her body.

Fly! she screamed.

Fire! shrieked Seafarer, plunging over the edge and swooping away. A flock of seagulls exploded from below and unwittingly formed a barrier between the albatross and his hunters.

"Don't be frightened, little lady," said one of the men. "We'll protect you from that nasty bird."

"I'm not frightened!" yelled Thorgil, but they grabbed her by the arms and dragged her inside, along with Jack.

Adder-Tooth had returned and was sullenly drinking at a table. "Keep them here where we can watch them," he ordered. He called for Little Half to bring him more ale.

The shield maiden fumed and cursed, but it only made the guards laugh. One of them tried to chuck her under the chin. She slapped him, and Adder-Tooth shouted for them to leave her alone.

"Do you see how women are treated? Do you see?" Thorgil raged when she and Jack had retreated to the center of the hall. "That's why I will never marry."

For someone who wanted a princess, Jack thought, Adder-Tooth hardly looked like an eager bridegroom. The king drank horn after horn of ale. He seemed to have forgotten all about Thorgil's existence. He certainly did none of the thoughtful things Schlaup did when he was courting Mrs. Tanner. There were no flowers or little treats, though to be honest, Thorgil would only have thrown them in the king's face. But he should have tried, Jack thought.

"I have a knife strapped to my leg," whispered Thorgil. "If Adder-Tooth gets close, I'll kill him."

That was one solution, Jack mused. No bridegroom, no marriage. Then the guards would kill them to avenge their king. Like most of Thorgil's plans, it had flaws.

It was clear that Seafarer had been sent with a message, but the bird had been distracted by the fish. *Fire*, he'd said. Was that a warning? It was impossible to tell. Seafarer's ability to describe things was limited.

Or perhaps *fire* was a command. Calling up fire was the first thing Jack had learned as an apprentice, and he was very good at it. He looked around the hall and noted that the floor was covered from end to end with straw. A mountain of peat blocks leaned against a wall. The roof was made of dry turf.

What would happen if the hall burned down? Everyone would run outside. Most were outside already, doing chores near the cliff. The rest—and here the plan made sense—

would head for the only source of water, the fountain in the courtyard. Not only would fire distract the warriors, it would divide Adder-Tooth's forces.

"Stay close to the iron door. Be ready to run," he murmured to Thorgil. She nodded, instantly alert. She casually drifted toward the door. The guards glanced nervously at Adder-Tooth, not wishing to rouse his anger again. Thorgil sat down just close enough to make them uneasy and far enough away so that it didn't look as though she was being friendly.

Jack drifted in the other direction. A warrior barked at him to stay away from the door. He sat down next to the peat pile and closed his eyes. He cast his mind down to search for the sunlight of summers past that had sunk into the earth.

The ground below resisted at first, but suddenly it gave way to mud and water. Jack found himself floating in a warm sea, an *ancient* sea. Long ago this rock had been water, and the surprise of it made Jack stop and look around. Sunlight fell into green, murky depths. Strange fish with large heads and scales like leather armor swam around him. Ancient shores appeared and disappeared. A ripple hung frozen in the gloom, and when he put his hand out to touch it, he found it hard as stone.

He sank down again until light vanished altogether, but he felt the questing life-forms all around him, except that they were not alive. They were the memories of fish. Even here was a host of spirits. They lazily followed Jack, nibbling at his heels.

And then he felt the familiar fire, like a beating heart. He reached for it. *Come to me*, he called. *Come forth*. The fire swept upward and Jack fled before it. The fish swam away with red light flashing on their scales and the sea glowing like a sunset cloud. He reentered his body, dripping with sweat. A flame shot out of the mountain of peat and licked across the ceiling.

"Bloody Hel!" roared Adder-Tooth. "The peat's caught fire! Get water! Get rakes! Push that stuff outside!" But the fire was too intense and the guards couldn't approach it.

"We must go," begged Little Half.

Adder-Tooth knocked him sprawling. "Don't tell me I have to do anything! I'm a king!" Little Half's brother ran to pick him up.

The fire had by now engulfed the roof and the servants had fled toward the cliff. Next, the warriors bolted. Thorgil tried to reach the iron door, but they grabbed her and ran in the opposite direction. Bits of flaming peat fell all around them.

"Go to the water! Go to the water!" yelled Jack. The warriors were too panicked to listen. Big Half fled past with Little Half in his arms. By now the floor was aflame and there was no possibility of crossing the hall. Jack gave up and followed them.

Black smoke billowed into the sky, but the sea breeze fortunately carried it away from the cliff. Women gathered their children into little groups and men waited by the barns to beat out any flames that might reach there. Last of all King

Adder-Tooth burst from the hall, his body covered in ashes and his beard smoking. Behind him the roof collapsed.

The only sounds then were of crying children, bleating animals, and the crackle of flames. The destruction had happened so fast, everyone was too shocked to speak. The fire died down almost as quickly, because anything flammable had gone up like tinder. It was over in only a few terrifying minutes. But the stone walls still radiated so much heat that no one dared approach them. After a while Thorgil said brightly, "Who wants to go to the village?"

Chapter Twenty-eight

FULL MOON

"You—! You—!" Adder-Tooth was so enraged, he could hardly get the words out. "You aren't going anywhere!" He took a deep breath. "Someone is responsible for this! Someone didn't dry the peat, and it went up like a haystack. Was it you?" He grabbed a terrified servant by the neck and shook him until the man passed out. Adder-Tooth dropped him onto the ground.

The king raged around the cliff, raining blows on anyone he encountered, even children. "Someone did this, and when I find out who it is, I'm going to feed him to the hogboon."

Everyone was silent, and Jack thought the warriors looked slightly ashamed of their leader. It was one thing to lose your temper—Northmen did it all the time—but to blame people for natural catastrophes was foolish. Ships sank in storms, rats ate grain, haystacks burst into flame. These things happened. The warriors were not to know, of course, that this time someone *was* responsible.

"It's fate," one of the men said.

The king whirled around and fetched him a blow that knocked out teeth. "How dare you contradict me!" He drew his sword. "Was it you? Have you been plotting against me?" The man had fallen to his knees and his mouth dripped blood. Other warriors pulled him away and several more formed a barrier with their hands on their swords.

The king suddenly realized he'd gone too far. "Thor's thunderbolt!" he cried, clutching his head as though struck by a sudden pain. "I was overcome with battle fury. For a moment I saw enemies around me and thought I heard the hoofbeats of Valkyries riding through the sky. Please forgive me! I know you are loyal men."

The warriors relaxed their grip on their weapons, for they all understood battle fury. Jack knew it was a favorite Northman excuse for bad behavior, but sometimes the fury was genuine. Some berserkers were born that way and couldn't help running mad. Jack didn't think Adder-Tooth was one of them.

"We can't stay in this ruin tonight," the king said. "Gather the livestock and we'll go to the village."

"Is that safe?" one of the men said, keeping distance between himself and Adder-Tooth.

"The hogboon has never bothered the village," the king said scornfully, and the man flushed. Adder-Tooth was hinting that the man was a coward. "Personally, I think it is a stupid creature, always returning to the place it fed. I, of course, shall return here after I've seen you to safety. This is my hall, burned though it is, and I will not abandon it." The warriors murmured, but what they said was unclear.

Everyone began gathering emergency supplies from the barns and kitchen. Sheep were driven out and a few of the chickens were packed in baskets, to be cared for in the village. The rest would have to stay behind. Even the skald was given a sack of oats to carry. By now Little Half had recovered his wits, though the side of his face was turning purple. Big Half squatted beside him and said cheerfully, "You know what, little brother? You look just like I do after a game of Bonk Ball."

During the long afternoon the ashes cooled, until the warriors were able to enter the ruined hall and poke around with their spears. "It's hot, but I think we can get through," one of them said.

Another cursed when he tried to open the iron door. "Wrap your hands in cloth before you touch this," he called.

Jack saw to his amazement that the stone walls had changed. The sandstone slabs had melted together into one mass, like clay in a potter's oven. He felt them cautiously and found the surface smooth. What kind of fire had he called up?

Once the door was opened, groups began to move through. Nightfall was not far away and they had to hurry. They dragged the sheep, bleating and complaining, through the still-smoking embers. With the sinking of the sun, the anger radiating from the outer wall increased, and Jack heard the whisper of fell voices in his ears. A cold wind blew a plume of ash into the late-afternoon sky.

A group of villagers was waiting outside and rushed to help family members and friends. They had seen the smoke from afar. The rest were at home, arming themselves in case it had been a raid from across the sea. "It was a magic fire," the skald told his goggle-eyed audience. "I swear I saw a dragon breathe on us and turn the stones to glass. I'll write a poem about it."

Their shadows stretched eastward as they walked through the heather, so that they appeared to be a party of giants going for a stroll. The sheep ran back and forth distractedly as sheep do, and the children ran back and forth to herd them. After a while Jack saw the village. Beyond it, floating on a green sea in the late light, was Skakki's ship.

"Skakki may be badly outnumbered," whispered Thorgil, "but if I were Adder-Tooth, I would not trust the loyalty of some of these men."

Jack agreed. Many of them had served Bjorn and no one seemed to have much respect for Adder-Tooth. He wasn't the kind of man who inspired devotion. Jack had noticed that the king kept a personal guard of twenty men close to him and guessed that these were his original crew. They hung back from the main body of travelers and insisted on keeping Jack and Thorgil with them. "The Bard will have a plan to rescue us," Jack said quietly to Thorgil. "He always knows what to do."

"The hogboon awakes! Run for your lives!" Adder-Tooth suddenly shouted.

The villagers panicked. Mothers snatched up children, men thrashed the sheep with sticks, the sheep bleated and bounded forward. The warriors ran behind, urging them on.

Big Half slung Little Half over his shoulder, but the extra weight slowed him down and they were quickly left behind. "You! Come with us!" commanded the king. Big Half reluctantly obeyed.

What rotten luck, thought Jack. *Now we'll have to spend the night on that wretched cliff*. But to his surprise, instead of returning to the ruined hall, the troop turned aside. They went south and followed a faint trail at the bottom of a valley.

It was that time of evening when everything blurs together in a twilight, and very quickly Jack lost all sense of direction. Round and about they went through a confusing jumble of low hills. The sky was a bright gray and tendrils of mist drifted up from ponds gleaming like mirrors in the dark heather.

At last they reached a wide bowl in the midst of the hills with a single, solitary bulge rising in the middle. The men were huffing and puffing by now, and they stopped to catch their breath. A sunset glow still shone in the western sky. To the east a glorious full moon was rising. "What are you doing, master?" wailed a voice Jack recognized as Little Half's. "We must flee to the hall as fast as we can!"

"Not this time," Adder-Tooth said. "This time the debt will be paid in full."

There was an immediate intake of breath among the men. The light was muted, but Jack was able to make out the shape of the bulge. It was far more regular than a natural feature and at the top was a solitary standing stone. Jack was willing to bet it had Pictish carvings on it.

"How will it be paid?" someone said.

Something struck Jack then: The king had said "paid in full." Was it possible that Little Half had lied about Adder-Tooth not sacrificing to the hogboon? And that visitors to the king's hall had conveniently disappeared?

"I never told you lads the whole story about the man buried in this barrow," Adder-Tooth said. He sounded completely relaxed, as though he had nothing to worry about from whatever lurked in this hollow. "He was a Pictish king called Nechtan. It was rumored he'd been fed roasted wolf hearts as a child to make him savage. And savage he was," Adder-Tooth said approvingly. "He made a pact with one of the old gods to sacrifice one of his own sons every ten years in return for long life. Eventually, he slew nine. One was left.

"Nechtan needed a wife to give him more sons and so, when he was a hundred and fifty years old, he arranged to marry a young princess. But on the wedding day his surviving son let an army of enemies into the hall. They slew Nechtan and carried off the princess. Ever since then his spirit has searched for her. If he accepts Thorgil in her place, he may leave the rest of us alone."

"You won't buy safety with this coward's trick," said Thorgil. "My brothers will avenge me!"

"I thought you wanted a princess for marriage," objected Little Half.

"So I do," Adder-Tooth said with a cold smile, "so I do. But not for me. You were willing enough to help me on other occasions, my treacherous friend—the odd visitor, a runaway slave. Your sleeping potions have been most useful."

"Little Half, what have you been doing?" cried Big Half, aghast.

"Looking after you, you poor, stupid ox," the dwarf said. "Do you think anyone would have hired you with your pitiful skills? You can't even catch a ball. *I* was the one the lords wanted, the intelligent one who came up with entertainments and battle strategies. I served them for whatever purpose they wanted in return for tolerating you."

All this took place while the moon's rays had been strengthening, and the standing stone now stood out starkly with a long black shadow flowing behind it. "The hogboon will emerge when the moon stands directly overhead," said Adder-Tooth. "By then we must be long gone. Bind them both and leave them on the barrow."

"Take Thorgil with you," said Jack. "She can't replace Nechtan's bride because she isn't really a princess."

"I am so!" said Thorgil.

"You aren't helping a bit," Jack said.

The king laughed. "Children, children, now isn't the time to start squabbling. Save your energy for the hogboon."

"At least give me a sword and let me meet my fate like a true warrior," said the shield maiden.

"Ah, but you are not a warrior now, little princess," said Adder-Tooth. "You are the bride Nechtan has been waiting for these long years. But don't be afraid. He will not consume you, though I could not say the same for your friend. He will take you into his barrow to feast on earthworms and drink the cold dew that trickles inside."

"Master, it isn't right—," began Big Half. Jack heard the man grunt as someone, possibly Little Half, punched him in the stomach.

"Shut your mouth," snarled the dwarf. Big Half began to whimper, a terrible sound from such a large man.

The warriors tied Jack and Thorgil up and carried them onto the barrow, after which Adder-Tooth called for a swift return to the hall. When their footsteps had died away, Thorgil said, "They took my knife, but if we can get off this barrow, we might find a sharp rock."

How like her! Jack thought with admiration. She never gave up. He rolled across the grass and was pulled up short. "Something's stopping me," he said.

"Me too. Oh, curse it! Those wolf droppings have tethered us to that standing stone!" Their legs were bound and their hands were tied behind their backs, but with much effort, they managed to wriggle close enough to reach each other's ropes. The cold made their fingers too clumsy to accomplish anything.

Thorgil declared she would sink her teeth into the hogboon's throat like Sigmund when the wolf came for him. Jack didn't point out that even Bjorn had been unable to harm the creature, and he'd had a sword.

The moon rose slowly, fading from gold to white. Its chill light flooded the hollow containing the barrow. "It must have been the Man in the Moon," Jack said.

"What?" Thorgil had drifted asleep.

"That's the kind of god who would ask you to sacrifice your sons," Jack said. "Nechtan was in the service of Unlife."

Thorgil shivered.

"That's why the hogboon comes out when the moon is directly overhead. He's still in thrall to it." Jack twisted himself to look at the standing stone. It was clearly illuminated now, and he wasn't surprised to see a crescent moon crossed by a broken arrow. Thorgil slept again, and Jack, though he fought to stay awake, found his eyes closing involuntarily. The next time they opened, the moon was almost overhead.

"Thorgil!"

She stirred. "I can't understand this drowsiness. I'm so cold! How can I fall asleep?"

"It's the standing stone," said Jack. "It wants to lull you so you become easy prey. Last time a honeybee woke me. Too bad we don't have one now."

"The only thing that comes out after dark is bats," she said.

Jack tried to think of something good, something that might protect them from the helplessness creeping over them. "Remember the Valley of Yggdrassil? Remember Mimir's Well?"

"That *was* nice," Thorgil said sleepily.

"Honeydew rained out of the upper branches of the Tree and the bees gathered it in midair. The Tree was pure life force, forever being destroyed and forever renewing itself. Valhalla, the Christian Heaven, and the Islands of the Blessed were among its leaves, along with other places we can only guess at. But of one thing I'm sure: The Man in the Moon was a leaf that shriveled up and fell from the Tree."

"Was he?" said the shield maiden. Her voice was thick.

"Wake up!" Jack kicked her as well as he could with his feet tied together. "He's more dead than the stupid hogboon who worshipped him. He isn't even a wandering spirit. He's a *nothing*! And the hogboon is nothing too. I don't believe in him and neither should you."

"Oh! What's that?" cried Thorgil.

Something was beginning to take shape in the moonlight. At first it was a blur and then it was a mist. It lengthened out until it was as tall as a man, with gray cobwebs trailing from its body. *I like that, calling me nothing,* said the hogboon. *Who do you think sucked the life out of Bjorn Skull-Splitter and the other morsels Adder-Tooth brought me?*

"You only have power over people who believe in you," said Jack, who desperately hoped this was true. "To the rest of us you're a tiresome old bore."

You will think otherwise soon. But what have we here? The creature hovered over Thorgil. *A princess! By the dead moon, Adder-Tooth has outdone himself this time. I may even forgive his debt, though probably not.*

"She isn't really a princess," said Jack.

Oh, but she is, sighed the creature in a voice like the wind fiddling at a door on an October night. *She is a daughter of the horse lords. Hengist was her ancestor.*

"I *told* you," said Thorgil.

"You aren't helping," Jack said. He was dismayed that the hogboon knew so much, and it made his hope that the creature was only an illusion waver. "Whatever you think, she isn't the bride you lost."

Istolis, fairest of the fair, murmured the creature. *Yet this child of Hengist is also fair, and I have been alone so long.*

"It won't work out," Jack said stubbornly. "You see, Thorgil is a shield maiden dedicated to Odin. She's never going to get married, so you're wasting your time. My suggestion is to hunt up Adder-Tooth and make a meal out of him."

Food that fights back, said the hogboon with a hint of humor. *It has been long since I fed upon such courage, but first I must see to my bride.*

"You'll have to go through me first," said Jack. With enormous effort, he wrenched himself up and fell across Thorgil. His head lay at an awkward angle over her shoulder and his back felt horribly exposed. He couldn't see the hogboon.

Foolish boy, whispered the dust-clogged voice. *You force me to slay you.*

Jack waited in an agony of fear. Instinctively, he reached for the life force deep in the earth—and found it just below his heart. A warm sensation, at first no larger than a rose leaf, spread out and brought feeling to his entire body. *It's the rune of protection*, he thought, filled with wonder. It burned anyone who tried to take it by force—but he hadn't tried to take it by force. It lay between him and Thorgil.

Why aren't you dying? complained the hogboon, and Jack became aware of a hand pressing on his back. He cringed inwardly. *Faugh! I'll deal with you later.* Jack was flung sideways and the warmth vanished. He gasped for breath. It took a moment for his senses to clear, and then he saw the tall, gray hogboon bending over Thorgil and reaching for her throat.

The creature screamed a long, shuddering cry that shook the air. The moon became very bright, but it was a dead light and had no power against the rune. The hogboon began to come apart, peeling away like the filth one finds in an abandoned cellar: cobwebs, dust, corruption. Shreds of it came off and were blown away by a breeze rising in the east. The last fragments swirled around the standing stone and disappeared.

Jack lay stunned on the cold hillside. The damp of early dew soaked into his clothes. Equally stunned, Thorgil stared up at the round, white moon, now turning west to drown itself in the sea. After a while she said, "We really need to find something sharp to cut these beastly ropes."

Chapter Twenty-nine

THE DEAD WALL

They did find something sharp—several things, in fact. Bones, white with age, were scattered about as though they had been tossed there by a careless hand. Among them lay a throwing axe, a sword with a pommel inlaid with jewels, and a dagger. They used the dagger to cut the ropes, and if the bones were ancient, the dagger was as keen as if it had been forged yesterday.

Jack freed his hands, and after that things became easier. "Don't cut yourself," warned Thorgil as he sliced through the rope tethering them to the standing stone. "Some old weapons are smeared with poison."

Once they were free, they scrambled off the barrow and

climbed to the top of a nearby hill. "I didn't see those bones and weapons earlier," Jack said.

"Neither did I." Thorgil leaned against him.

The thought occurred to Jack that those things had been wrapped up inside the hogboon, and he wiped his hands on the damp grass. "The sword is beautifully made. Do you want it?"

"Do you?" she asked.

Jack liked her leaning against him, and not just for the extra warmth. They had decided against traveling in the dark, for neither of them was sure of the way. "The Bard told me of swords that should only be drawn when you want to kill someone," he said. "There's a kind of charm on them. If you pick one up, you *have* to kill the next person you meet, even if it's a friend."

"Olaf told me that story too," she said. They sat quietly until Jack saw a faint light in the distance. It wavered back and forth, sometimes disappearing altogether, but coming steadily nearer.

"Thoooorgilll! Jaaaack!" called a voice.

"It's Skakki," cried Thorgil. "We're heeere!" She jumped up and down, but of course no one could see her at that distance.

They shouted back and forth until Jack could see Big Half at the head of the group, with the Bard holding out his staff to provide light. Big Half's face was mottled, as though he'd lost a game of Bonk Ball. Behind him came Skakki and Sven the Vengeful. Thorgil hoisted up her skirts and ran down the hill to fall into Skakki's arms. "You have no idea what happened here!" she said. "The hogboon came out and tried to take the rune of protection. And the rune ate him all up! It was glorious!"

"Whoa! Little sister, start at the beginning. When Big Half came galumphing into the village, he said you were going to be sacrificed. We came as quickly as we could. Big Half was afraid to go out again, but he agreed to guide us with a little encouragement."

"I helped," said Sven the Vengeful, smacking a big fist into the palm of his hand.

"We must be grateful to him," the Bard chided. "He didn't have to tell us anything. My stars, lad, it's good to see you! I should have known better than to drink that tea Little Half served us. I must be getting careless in my old age. I see you managed the fire at the hall."

Jack and Thorgil told him everything that had happened, and the old man said that when Adder-Tooth and his men had almost reached the hall, Big Half bolted and ran for the village. "It was very brave of him. He was absolutely terrified the hogboon would get him."

"I couldn't let anything happen to the pretty princess. Besides"—Big Half's voice quivered—"Little Half called me a stupid ox."

"There, there," said the Bard. "You were very clever to run away. Now we must hurry back to the village. Others are waiting, and we have unfinished business with Adder-Tooth."

"What about those weapons on the barrow?" Jack said, pointing.

"Leave them for the sun to find," the old man said with an expression of disgust. "Ill fortune clings to weapons found in darkness."

It was now nearing dawn. The voices of lapwings and larks arose, and a hen harrier hawk gave its whistling cry. As the light strengthened, the moon sank into ever-deepening shadow over the western sea.

A mob of villagers and warriors had gathered just before the cluster of turf houses. "Adder-Tooth betrayed us," a man shouted.

"He's been doing human sacrifices," a woman cried. "My cousin disappeared, and we all thought he'd drowned."

"He went down the hogboon's throat," another woman moaned. "Who knows how many others did?"

"We will no longer serve such a master," a warrior swore. "We were aware that he used *seiðer*, which no honorable man resorts to, but we knew nothing of the sacrifices."

"You've stirred things up a bit," the Bard said to Big Half.

Jack saw that the villagers were armed with scythes, hoes, and axes. The warriors had swords and spears. It seemed a decent enough army. They had dragged the third-rate skald with them, and the poor man was almost fainting with terror.

"Warriors always do that," the Bard said privately to Jack. "They don't want to miss out on a chance to become deathless poetry, though what that poor creature writes won't last a week."

By now the sun had risen. The creatures of the day had emerged in the wilderness beyond the village, completely unaware of the war brewing in their midst. A haze of midges hovered over a marsh. Bumblebees crept into the sunlight and waited for its warmth to permit them to fly. Caterpillars crawled along leaves. Flowers opened their petals. It was a world unnoticed by the angry humans, but Jack was keenly aware of its presence.

"Adder-Tooth will expect us to join him," said the warrior who had spoken before. "Instead, we'll kill him and those filthy pirates who came with him."

"Hear! Hear!" roared the villagers, brandishing their farm tools.

"We march! Are you with us?" the warrior asked Skakki.

"Of course," said the young sea captain, "but I think strategy is called for. Adder-Tooth's wall is too strong for you."

"Piss on the wall! We'll tear it down!" The villagers were really getting into it.

"Listen to me," Skakki urged. "Those stones are haunted, and you shouldn't touch them. Adder-Tooth himself will open the gate if you pretend you've come to rebuild."

"That's the coward's way! The thrall's way! The worm's way!" sang the warriors. "We take the path of honor!" They had worked themselves into such a frenzy that they refused to listen to anything Skakki had to say and set off at once.

"That's the idiot's way," grumbled the Bard.

"*I* wouldn't do that," Big Half said.

"No, you wouldn't. You have far too much sense." The

old man patted him on the back, and the man blushed at the praise. "Those fools will guarantee that Adder-Tooth keeps his gate closed. They'll bluster and threaten outside, and Adder-Tooth will bluster and threaten from within. Afterward, when everyone's worn himself out, I'll solve the problem of the wall."

They had a leisurely breakfast. Eric the Rash got a peat fire going, and Eric Pretty-Face toasted fish on skewers. The other crew members gnawed on rusks and onions, washed down with ale. Because Schlaup was so terrifying, he had been confined to the ship and wasn't there. Rune kept him company so he wouldn't feel lonely.

"Schlaup doesn't know Adder-Tooth tried to kill Jack and Thorgil," the Bard warned everyone, "so keep the story to yourselves. When Schlaup gets really, really upset, he shape-shifts, and that's the last thing we need now. You can call them, Eric Pretty-Face."

Everyone automatically covered their ears. "HEY, RUNE AND SCHLAUP! WE'VE GOT GRUB! COME AND GET IT!" bellowed the Northman. This was followed by a loud splash, and soon they saw Schlaup swimming with Rune sitting on his back. He came ashore and shook himself like a huge dog.

"Thank Freya I've got my feet on solid ground again," said Rune, hobbling over to the fire. "I was frozen into position sitting on that ship." Schlaup enthusiastically greeted everyone.

"WHAT WASN'T I SUPPOSED TO TELL HIM? I CAN'T REMEMBER," said Eric Pretty-Face.

"Just don't say anything," the Bard said.

The encounter with the hogboon had taken its toll on Jack. His head kept nodding, and finally the Bard told him and Thorgil to take a nap. It was late afternoon before he awoke.

"Where is everybody?" he asked, sitting up and brushing sand out of his hair. Only the Bard and Schlaup were sitting by the fire.

"I thought it best to let you sleep," said the Bard. "The others have gone ahead. Don't worry. With Schlaup's help, we'll catch up with them."

"What's been happening?" Jack said, with a glance at Schlaup.

"Seafarer has been drifting back and forth with messages," said the old man. "As I predicted, there's been a fine show of temper on both sides, and nothing has been accomplished. When it gets dark, we can start working on the wall."

"When it gets *dark*? But—"

"Night is the very best time to find unquiet spirits," the Bard said heartily. "Well, Schlaup my lad, do you think you can carry both of us?"

The giant grinned. He perched Jack on his neck, cradled the Bard in his arms, and set off, falling into the long stride trolls were famous for and could keep up for hours. Jack had heard of trolls following giant Jotunheim elk until the animals fell down with exhaustion. Schlaup had no trouble finding his way through the village, either, for he was tall enough to see over the roofs. When he came to a wall blocking his way, he simply kicked a hole in it.

They traveled at a great rate and soon saw the villagers and warriors gathered outside the wall. By now long shadows were stretching across the heather. Thorgil ran out to greet them, dressed in men's clothes again, followed by the stallion she had tamed.

"Schlaup! I'm so glad to see you! You'll never guess what happened—"

"Not a word!" the Bard said sharply.

The giant crouched down to let his passengers alight. "Nice horsey," he said.

"Isn't he?" exulted Thorgil. "I'm going to name him Skull-Splitter in memory of—"

"Thorgil!" roared the Bard. "Send that beast back to his herd and stop causing trouble!"

She laughed, totally unrepentant. "They want to leave before dark," she said, pointing at the villagers and warriors. "Skakki has been arguing with them."

There was a shouting match going on, and Skakki appeared to be on the losing side. The villagers had already picked up their makeshift weapons and were starting back down the trail. The warriors soon followed, with the skald hurrying to keep up with them. "No deathless poetry today, I see," said the Bard.

Skakki threw up his hands in exasperation. "I can't talk sense into them. You'd better go along to protect them, Eric." Eric the Rash gratefully trotted after the fleeing villagers. The Northmen all knew he was afraid of the dark and would be useless anyhow once the sun went down.

"It's not much of an army," observed Jack. The remaining

warriors, minus Eric the Rash, numbered twelve. Or eleven, because Rune was too crippled to fight, though he would certainly try. Ten, when you subtracted Thorgil, because she was small. Nine, because Jack wasn't really a warrior, and eight, because Big Half was quaking with fear. But there was also Schlaup, who might count for four or five warriors on his own.

"It will do," said the Bard. He sent Seafarer on one last mission to look over the wall.

Two-legged beasts hiding, the albatross reported. *Air feels nasty.*

The wall is awakening, the old man said. *You must go and sleep now, my friend.* Seafarer soared out to sea, aiming for a distant rock covered with seagulls. "Now our work begins. Jack and I will tackle the wall. The rest of you stay back where it's safer."

Are you joking? Jack thought. *Us? Alone?* He could already feel the rage radiating from the stones. It made him sick, this hopeless anger and despair. He felt dizzy.

"It's all in a day's work for a bard, or perhaps I should say a 'night's work,'" the Bard said cheerfully. "And yes, it's nasty, but far less terrible than what these poor spirits endured. Put your hands on the wall."

Jack, after a moment's hesitation, obeyed. The rage flared up. He collapsed against the stones.

"Good. You've made contact," said the old man. "Now tell them about the hogboon's destruction. I'd do it, except they wouldn't believe me. You were there."

Jack didn't know how to begin. All around him he felt unending pain, loss so extreme that it surpassed his ability to comprehend. He heard voices, terrible voices that called to loved ones who couldn't hear them. They were all at the bottom of a pit, bound and helpless. Earth fell on their faces. The light of the sky vanished. They couldn't breathe.

"Steady, lad. You're seeing their memories." Jack felt the Bard's hand on his shoulder.

"Nechtan," he said weakly. Instantly, the attention of the spirits was drawn to him. "Nechtan has been destroyed. I saw it." He told them of the barrow and of the hogboon. He described the moon standing directly overhead and of what happened when the hogboon grasped the rune of protection. "It was life," he said. "Nechtan could not bear the presence of life. He has utterly disappeared."

Dimly, Jack heard a voice say, *Is this true?*

"Yes, I was there," he replied. He felt the presences crowd around him, reaching into his mind.

It is true, the voice said. *He does not lie.*

"Now your long vigil is over," said the Bard from somewhere close by. "You must go into the west, there to be restored and in time to return with the sun."

But it seemed that the spirits could not let go of their sorrow. They continued to rage and cry out against their fate. Jack lay against the wall and felt himself pulled down into their desolation.

"Men of the sea, do you remember the feel of a deck beneath your feet," said the Bard, "when waves stood high and the ship flew before them like a bird returning to her nest?"

Voices sighed. *We remember.*

"Never were there more seacrafty men or mariners surer of strength under sky than you. You returned to your halls, bright with hearth fire and filled with friends, your wives waiting onshore for first sight of sail."

We remember.

Gradually, the Bard awakened their memories, and gradually, the anger dimmed, to be replaced by a great longing for all that had gone before. "It is time to take ship again," the old man said, "to fare forth to the islands where winter never comes and the sea is as clear as sky. You are young again, worthiest of warriors, and your wives and children stand beneath the apple trees."

Jack heard distant shouting and the sound of wind crackling in a sail and a thump as an anchor was hauled up. The voices, now joyful, faded until there was only the hiss of wind over stone. Jack found himself lying in an uncomfortable heap at the bottom of the wall. The air was cold with the first bite of fall, and the night was empty of fear.

Chapter Thirty

THE WATER OF LIFE

The moon was at zenith, painting the earth with a pale radiance, but a small slice had been taken out of its side. Jack saw Schlaup, Skakki, and the others clustered together for warmth. He was so cold, he couldn't move. "You've done extremely well," the Bard said. "Talking to the dead is one of the most difficult tasks a bard has, and one of the most dangerous. In my opinion, you're ready to take on a *draugr*."

No thanks, thought Jack. *No* draugrs. He was unable to speak. His arms and legs were numb.

"I'll raise a fire," the old man said. Someone must have gathered firewood earlier, because there was a large heap of it near the gate. The Bard thrust his staff into it and a flame shot up.

"Thank Freya," groaned Thorgil. "Dragon Tongue wouldn't let us have a fire earlier. What were you doing over there, mumbling all that time?"

"N-N-Nothing," Jack managed to say, annoyed that she didn't appreciate his bravery.

"Certainly looked like it. Someone kick Schlaup. He's got his head on the cider keg."

Jack slowly came back to life. He took a grateful swig when the cider keg was passed. "We freed the spirits in the wall," he said. "What's next?"

"Cleaning out the hall," said the Bard. "Are you up for a little gate-pulling, Schlaup?"

"Sure," said the giant, taking an enormous drink of cider. He went straight to the gate and began tugging on it, his large legs firmly planted on the ground. Jack could hear each lock as it popped out of its holder. With a dreadful splintering of wood, Schlaup wrenched the gate from its hinges and threw it to one side. Excited voices came from the ruined hall beyond. Torchlight shone from the gaping hole where the hall's roof had been, but no one ventured outside.

"Good. They think the wall's still haunted," said the Bard.

"Should we storm them? Or wait for the villagers to arrive?" said Skakki.

"They'd only get in the way. Schlaup, attend to the iron door," the old man said. The giant went to work and tore it out easily. This time there was a reaction from inside as arrows flew through the opening.

"Hunh! Bee stings," said Schlaup, picking an arrow from his arm.

"Come back," the Bard told the giant. "I want you to hear what happened to Thorgil last night."

"Wait a minute," said Jack. "I thought we weren't supposed to tell him anything. You said the last thing we needed"—he glanced at the giant—"was a shape-shifting half-troll."

"Perfectly true. That *is* the last thing we need. We've done everything else. Thorgil, proceed."

"Excuse me, sir," faltered Big Half. He had said nothing until now, and everyone had forgotten about his existence. He stood up in the flickering light and bowed to the Bard. "I know my brother's been bad and I should hate him. But I can't. He's always looked after me, you see. I was wondering . . . before you do things in that hall . . . could Little Half come out?"

There was silence for a moment. Then Skakki said, "Your brother is responsible for many deaths."

"I think he did it for me," said Big Half. "I'm the one who always got us thrown out of places. I *am* an ox-brain, like he says. I forget to feed animals and they die, or I leave doors open or set things on fire. He could have abandoned me many times, but he didn't. Sometimes he did bad things so he could take care of me."

Skakki looked to the Bard for guidance. The old man shook his head. "There is always a choice between good or evil," he said. "You chose to save Thorgil and Jack, showing that your heart is wiser than your brother's. He chose, not once but many times, to drug travelers, knowing full well their fate. The answer is no."

Big Half didn't argue. "Then I want to join him."

"You don't have to. We'll take care of you," said Jack.

The big man smiled. "That's awfully nice of you, but I've been with Little Half all my life. It wouldn't feel right to leave him now that he's in a tough spot."

"You don't know what's going to happen," Skakki said. "No one is going to survive in that hall."

But Big Half couldn't be persuaded, and eventually they gave him a burning branch from the fire. "Hold it up by your face so they know who you are," said Thorgil. They watched him go through the ruined gate, cross the courtyard, and go inside.

Thorgil unfolded the saga of what had happened in Adder-Tooth's hall as they sat around the fire. As she spoke, a change began to come over Schlaup. First, he panted like a man who has run many miles. Then he moaned and drummed his feet on the ground. The Northmen moved away from him. "My sister, my little sister," he kept groaning.

"Everybody give him space," said the Bard in a low voice. Jack had seen a half-troll fall into a snit only once before, when he'd made Queen Frith's hair fall out. Frith's body had bulged in a dozen places. Her features had rippled and twisted until he couldn't guess what she was turning into—only that he didn't want to find out. Northmen had fought one another to get through the door, whimpering in a most unheroic way.

Now Schlaup changed in an equally alarming manner. He swelled up, and his body turned lumpy and dark. He no longer looked remotely human, or remotely troll, either. Instead, he resembled a giant wave full of rocks. He towered up and up and up until he crashed over—*SCHLAUP!*—and flowed through the gate like an avalanche. On he went across the courtyard and into the hall, where they couldn't see him anymore. But they heard the rumble of boulders dashing against the walls and saw flickers of light where rocks ground together.

The noise died away. Jack's ears rang and his heart pounded. He found that his fists were clenched so tightly, his fingernails had drawn blood. Skakki, Rune, Sven the Vengeful, and the others seemed turned to stone. The Bard leaned on his staff, intently watching the hall.

"We really . . . must . . . let Mrs. Tanner see him do this sometime," breathed Thorgil.

A figure stepped into the courtyard. It was Schlaup. He was slightly hunched over, a habit he'd acquired to apologize for his size. "The hall's clean," he said.

Jack didn't want to see what lay inside. He'd seen terrible scenes before when Olaf One-Brow destroyed a village. He'd seen the Forest Lord demolish Din Guardi. He sat down next to the fire, hugging himself and shivering.

"You need to rest," the Bard said. "We all do." He raised his staff and murmured something Jack found familiar. It was a spell the old man had cast long ago when he'd pushed the boy too hard. Something dropped over Jack like a soft blanket. It felt safe and warm. He wanted to wrap himself up in it and never come out.

Others lay down close to the fire. Skakki stretched out his long legs as though he were on the most comfortable bed. Eric Pretty-Face curled into a ball with his thumb in his mouth. Thorgil pulled her cloak over her face. "I'd give anything to learn how you do that," said Rune, yawning.

The Bard smiled. "It is the *lorica* of Amergin, the founder of my order—a warding-spell against harm. The words come when they are needed and cannot be spoken at any other time. They may not be memorized."

And that was true, Jack thought, slipping into welcome sleep. He couldn't remember anything about the *lorica* now, though he'd just heard it.

He woke wonderfully refreshed. Not only had the spell relaxed him, it had kept him warm. The ache that had crept out of the wall the night before was gone.

The sun was still hidden by hills, but the mist lying between sea and sky to the west had turned pink. Sven the Vengeful had risen early and returned with brushwood to replenish the fire. It was crackling cheerfully now, and Jack savored the heat. "I can't stop thinking about poor Big Half," said Thorgil. "His courage shames me, for I despised him as a fool."

"Everyone did," Jack said. He dreaded going into the hall. In the morning light it looked a complete ruin, like something that had been abandoned for a hundred years. Jack was very thirsty and suspected that everyone else was too, but the closest water lay in the courtyard. No one went near it. Finally, when the sun had cleared the hills, Skakki rose and led the way.

Jack was surprised to see the courtyard covered with

tendrils of grass, with here and there a tiny clover leaf pushing its way through the soil. The channel by the spring was
bright with reflected clouds. He cupped the water in his
hands and found it cold and refreshing, with the hint of
something green in it. "This is like water from the land of
the yarthkins," he said.

"Yarthkins?" echoed Skakki.

"*Landvættir,*" translated Thorgil. "Spirits of the land. We
encountered them on the way to Din Guardi."

"Yarthkins are the first to arrive when Unlife is driven away,"
said the Bard. "They are repairing the land, and for a time this
water will be full of life. We should drink deeply of it." So they
did, and all declared that it was as good as a feast. Schlaup lay
on his stomach and sucked up enormous quantities of it.

Jack approached the hall in better spirits, though his mind
still recoiled from what lay inside. But when he got there,
he found the place had been scoured clean. With the stones
melted together, it looked like a hall-shaped rock formation.
"I've never seen anything like this," said Skakki, running his
hands over the walls.

Everything on the cliff overhanging the sea was gone except
for one small shed. Jack approached it warily. Inside, a pit had
been filled with straw to house chickens, and when Jack opened
the door, a hen scurried past him. More hens clustered against
the far wall, squawking and climbing on top of one another. Big
Half was lying on the straw, blinking at the sudden light.

"You're alive!" Jack cried.

"I didn't want to hurt the nice chickens. Or him," admitted Schlaup from behind him. He looked vaguely guilty, as though expecting to be scolded.

"You did exactly the right thing," said Jack. "Sir! Skakki! Thorgil! Big Half's alive!" Everyone crowded around, trying to see into the dark interior. The man rolled to one side, and they saw that he had been concealing Little Half. But the dwarf looked completely witless. He stared into space and showed no awareness of anything around him.

"Don't hit me!" cried Big Half, cringing away from Sven the Vengeful.

"I'm only trying to get you into the fresh air," grumbled the Northman. "Phoo! The chickens have been roosting all over you." Sven pulled both men out and laid the dwarf on the ground.

"I don't know what's wrong with my brother," said Big Half. "He won't talk."

The Bard knelt down and felt the dwarf's neck. "His heartbeat is strong. What happened last night?"

"Everyone got mad when I returned," Big Half said miserably. "Adder-Tooth told me to go away. Little Half said I was a big dummy and he was sorry he'd ever known me. Then I heard thunder. Rocks and stuff poured into the hall. Little Half screamed, but I held on to him tight and said, 'Little Half, we'll get through this. See if we don't.' The next thing I knew, we were in the henhouse." Big Half tenderly smoothed his brother's hair. "He hasn't said a word since."

"Is he injured?" Jack said to the Bard.

"Not in his body. His mind has been unhinged by terror."

"Then how did Big Half escape the same fate?"

The Bard smiled slightly. "There is sometimes a point to having an uncomplicated mind. Little Half's brain swirled with many ideas. Every scheme gave rise to further schemes and every fear called up more fears. Such an imagination is easily overwhelmed. Big Half sees things simply. A rock is a rock, a tree is a tree, an avalanche is an avalanche. He doesn't waste time imagining what they might do to him."

By now the villagers and warriors had arrived and were amazed at the utter destruction. They had seen the torn-off gate, the glassy walls, and the absence of their enemies. They treated Skakki with extreme respect, considering him to be the man responsible for it.

"We are your subjects now, King Skakki," one of the men said, bowing low. "Please accompany us to the village for a celebration."

"King Skakki! I like that," said the young sea captain.

"Don't let it go to your head," said the Bard.

Thorgil called up the wild horses and rode the stallion, which she had named Skull-Splitter in honor of Bjorn. She persuaded a mare to carry the Bard. This greatly impressed the villagers, especially when the Bard informed them that she was a descendant of King Hengist. But when Seafarer arrived and Thorgil spoke to him in Bird, their admiration knew no bounds. "It's like living in a saga," a woman gushed. And the third-rate skald, who had shown up when it was clear the fighting was over, said he would write a poem about it.

The excited voices died away in the distance. Jack had chosen to stay behind with Schlaup and the two brothers. Schlaup was too frightening to invite to a feast and Little Half too despised. Some of the villagers had wanted to throw him off the cliff, but when they saw his vacant eyes, they left him alone.

Jack found the silence soothing. There was something to be said for people who spoke seldom and had uncomplicated thoughts. He was tired of dealing with things that wanted to kill him. It was enough to listen to the wind and watch the seabirds coasting the air above the cliff. He could understand why St. Columba and St. Cuthbert had had a fondness for lonely islands.

Schlaup sat down next to him and watched the clouds drift by as if they were the most interesting things in the world. "I was thinking," the giant said.

"Yes?" Jack was pleasantly diverted from his thoughts.

"Dragon Tongue said the stream was full of life."

"The yarthkins have that effect on water," explained Jack. "It has something to do with how things grow."

"*Landvættir,*" said Schlaup, showing that he not only knew the word, but that he might know a great deal about such beings. The boy reminded himself not to underestimate the giant. "*Landvættir* heal things," said Schlaup after a moment. He paused to call up the words. "If we put Little Half into the water, he might get better."

"Why didn't I think of that?" said Jack.

They found the brothers next to the chicken house. Schlaup picked Little Half up and carried him off to the spring. "Please don't hurt him," begged Big Half. "Don't *drown* him! Please! I beg you!" The giant plunged the dwarf into the channel and held him down. Big Half fought to loosen Schlaup's hands to no avail.

"That's enough!" cried Jack.

Little Half's eyes flew open and he began to struggle. Schlaup hauled him out, coughing and spluttering, and patted him on the back gently—gently for a half-troll, that is. Little Half vomited up water, straw, and a few chicken feathers. "Better," said the giant.

"Brother," Big Half said, weeping, "are you all right?"

Little Half blinked and looked around. "Who are you?" he asked.

Reason had returned to the dwarf's mind, but his memory had entirely vanished. He spoke well enough and he remembered what was said to him, yet his behavior was that of a small child. A nice child, Jack decided. It was Little Half before all the plotting and scheming had happened.

After a while villagers appeared with baskets of supplies, and one of them asked whether Jack would like to join them for the festivities. The man pointedly avoided asking the others. "No thanks," Jack said. "I'm perfectly happy here."

And he was. They feasted on oysters, smoked haddock, bannock cakes, and buttered cabbage. For drink they had ale and cider, but all agreed that the water from the spring was better. "That's an oyster," Big Half said patiently. "You don't eat the hard part."

"Oy-ster," repeated Little Half.

Afterward they napped under the sky, except for Schlaup, who found his way down to a beach. Unlike true trolls, he wasn't afraid of water, and Jack saw him in the distance, floating and spouting water like a whale.

Chapter Thirty-one

VOYAGE TO NOTLAND

"Spending the winter here is an excellent idea," argued Skakki the following morning. "The weather is changing, and Egil and I might not have time to reach the Northland before the fall storms arrive." The puffy clouds of the day before had changed into high, feathery wisps that spread out across the sky.

"Are you sure you don't simply like the idea of being a king?" the Bard said. "You already have an excellent hall and fields. You have horses, cattle, and thralls to care for them. You're a king in everything except the title."

"I must bend the knee to Ivar the Boneless, an utter fool, and you know why we leave our fields to go pillaging, Dragon Tongue. The lands of the north are barren. This land is fertile and the seas abound with fish. My family will love it here. So will Egil."

Skakki stood in the doorway of Bjorn's ruined hall, gazing out to sea. Jack thought he looked every inch a king with his broad chest and noble face. He was certainly better than any ruler Jack had seen. Skakki wasn't prone to insane rages. He didn't spend his days lying in bowers, ignorant of what went on in the outside world. Nor did he demand that praise-songs be sung about him day and night. He was a sensible, intelligent young man who would rule well, whatever land he found himself in.

"Speaking of family, won't they worry when you don't show up?" said the Bard.

"Olaf sometimes wintered elsewhere. He always left the family well supplied before sailing, and I have done the same. I'll fetch them in spring."

The Bard accepted Skakki's decision and, personally, Jack was delighted. Tomorrow they were supposed to sail north to Notland, or to where the Bard *thought* Notland lay. Then he, the Bard, and Thorgil would sail on in a coracle that was hardly bigger than a washtub to a place full of sea hags and Pictish beasts. Now Skakki could wait for them as long as necessary on Horse Island.

Jack went outside. Rune was standing on the cliff, shading his eyes as he studied the sky. "What do you see?" the boy said. He didn't really expect an answer, but the old warrior had as complete a memory of the sky as he had of the sea.

"Rain is coming," Rune said. "It will last three days."

"It doesn't look so bad to me," said Jack, peering up at the bright, feathery clouds.

"Those are called 'sky silk.' They are spun in the hall of mists by Odin's wife. Stand here with your back to the wind," ordered Rune. "Now tell me what direction those clouds are moving."

Jack watched carefully. He had often observed storms approaching or retreating. It had never occurred to him that the filmy sky silk had any importance. "They're going that way." He thrust out his right arm.

"Very good. When you have the wind at your back and sky silk moves to the right, it means a storm is coming. It isn't going to be a big one because the air doesn't smell like metal and the gulls aren't agitated. I'll tell Skakki to delay the voyage for three days."

That pleased Jack even more. He was in no hurry to leave. He wandered around the cliff, trying to imagine all of Skakki's relatives living here. It was clearly a better place to farm, and they would have Thorgil's horses to ride. The animals had become much tamer. They allowed Skakki to command them, though of course they were too small to carry the tall sea captain. Olaf had had the same problem.

Egil would find good pastures for his *merini* sheep. He'd never been an enthusiastic warrior, much preferring to farm and trade. Schlaup could build a separate hall for Mrs. Tanner—but here Jack's imagination failed. The half-troll was never going to be accepted by the villagers. In the Northland, where people were used to trolls, he would be tolerated. Perhaps Schlaup could find another island.

By afternoon the sky was covered with a flat, gray layer of clouds that gradually lowered until it was almost on the ground. Then the rain began in earnest, and they had to shelter in the largest house in the village. It had originally belonged to Bjorn, then to Adder-Tooth, and now King Skakki was its owner. It was a dark, musty place, hardly more cheerful than a cave, but it had a hearth. With food and song, Skakki and his followers passed a reasonably pleasant time.

On the third day Jack woke to find the sky covered with high clouds that resembled the scales of a fish. He thought Rune had been wrong about the three-day rain, but soon the fish scales turned into more storm clouds. This time the showers were brief, with fierce winds that blew up suddenly and disappeared just as rapidly. By afternoon they had been replaced by another layer of wispy sky silk.

"Does that mean we've got another three days of rain coming?" Jack asked hopefully.

"Not at all," said Rune. "Stand with your back to the wind. See? The sky silk is moving *left*. We shall soon have outstanding weather for a voyage."

But where will we go? thought Jack. So far no one seemed to know, and that was because Notland wasn't always there. It came and went at the will of the fin folk.

They went north at dawn. The Bard said Pictish beasts were more common there and that autumn was their mating season. "If we find a swarm, the fin folk are sure to be nearby," he said. They left Schlaup behind, in the interests of speed, for he weighed the ship down and was useless as an oarsman. He,

Big Half, and Little Half made camp on the cliff, and Schlaup was given the task of cutting turf for the new hall.

They passed several bodies of land, all smaller than Horse Island. They camped on deserted beaches, and once Jack thought he heard strange cries in the night. On the third day, when it seemed they had run out of islands, Seafarer returned with news of a fog bank to the west. Or as he put it, *Big cloud. Sits on sea. Place where sun dies.*

"Go west," said the Bard.

"Are you sure?" said Skakki. "Rune says there's nothing out there."

"Perhaps not when he was there. Notland is always surrounded by fog, and it may mean the fin folk have encountered a swarm of Pictish beasts. Battles will be fought and blood spilled. The fin folk harvest the losers."

The ship changed direction, but by late afternoon they still hadn't found the fog bank. The sun burned like a fire on the western horizon, and on either side of it were pillars of light. They were rainbow-colored and very bright, making it seem almost like there were three suns in a row. "That's what I've been looking for," said the Bard. "Those lights are the gateway to Notland. Sail toward them, and with luck, we will reach its borders at dawn."

No one spoke. The gateway was too otherworldly. The Northmen, who would cheerfully have waded into battle with bears or trolls, were utterly spooked by the strangeness of the vision. They clutched the talismans they wore around their necks—amber beads for Freya; boar's teeth for Frey, the god of plenty; and Thor's hammer. As the ship approached, the sun set and the gateway faded, but a single red ray shot upward to mark where it had been. "Strike the sail," ordered Skakki. "I enter no gateway I cannot see."

The air was breathlessly calm. The surface of the water was as still as a lake, and this worried the Northmen even more. "I'd give anything to weigh anchor," Sven the Vengeful said. "I saw a sea like this once. It rose like the back of a dragon, and Ran and her nine daughters nearly dragged us down."

"There's nothing to anchor to. The water is too deep," said Rune. When the last streaks of light faded, the cries began— long, mournful howls that turned everyone's blood to water. From below the sea came low rumbles that rattled the timbers of the ship and made Jack's ribs vibrate with their power.

"The howls are made by male Pictish beasts," the Bard explained. "Remember my description of the *huushayuu*, Jack? Imagine a hundred Pictish war trumpets making that noise. It's no wonder Roman soldiers deserted and ran into the woods. Of course, that wasn't a good idea either, with the Forest Lord waiting inside."

"It sounds like there's at least a hundred of them out there now," said Thorgil.

"The rumbles are the females coming up from the depths," the old man said. "When they reach the surface, they'll attack one another. There are always more females than males, so they have to fight to get a mate. The victorious sink down to the bottom again."

"And the fin folk?" said Jack.

"Oh, they won't come out until dawn. No one in his right mind would sail into a mating swarm of Pictish beasts."

"Now he tells us," groaned Skakki.

They heard vast splashes, like whales surfacing, and the sound of water being expelled from vast mouths. A roar exploded from not far away, followed by a heavy *whump* as two creatures came together. Soon the whole sea was seething with cries, roars, gnashing of teeth, and the screams of the losers. A half-moon rose, making the great bodies dimly visible. They curved up and over in the dark water like obese snakes. The females were a ghostly white with long, fleshy horns and pointed muzzles that opened to show rows of teeth. Their flippers battered at their rivals and their tails lashed as they propelled themselves into battle.

The males were much smaller. It was difficult to see what color they were in the moonlight, though Jack guessed they were a delicate green. Their heads were horselike and their bodies were slim and graceful. When a female vanquished a foe, she grabbed the chosen male in her flippers and gave a terrifying bellow before plunging into the depths.

As time passed, the battles became less frequent, until finally the sea was calm except for the thrashing of dying beasts. A heavy smell like the odor of butchered fish hung in the air.

Chapter Thirty-two

THE FIN FOLK

Not surprisingly, no one on the ship got any sleep. When the gray light of dawn seeped over the water, Skakki and his crew discovered the bodies of a dozen whale-size creatures. They floated belly-up, with their long tails uncurled in death.

"Are they . . . edible?" said Skakki. Like all Northmen, he was always on the lookout for supplies.

"No! I mean, yes, they are edible. But no, you mustn't come between the fin folk and their prey," said the Bard.

"There's surely enough to go around," Eric the Rash said.

Eric Pretty-Face offered his opinion. "I ATE SEA SERPENT ONCE. IT DIDN'T KILL ME."

"I said no and I meant it," the Bard said crossly. "The fin

folk can make a ship-destroying rock appear to be an open patch of sea and send you to the bottom. They are masters of illusion." The old man sent Seafarer out to explore. He warned the bird to ignore the dead beasts in the water, but Seafarer needed no warning. They aroused an instinctive terror in the albatross. He soared upward to get away from them until he was only a tiny dot against the sky. He returned with the news that the fog bank was close.

The Bard unwrapped the mysterious parcel Brother Aiden had given him weeks before. Jack was amazed to see the polished bronze mirror belonging to the chief. It was the most valuable item in the village and something the chief wouldn't have given up willingly. "How did you get it?" the boy asked.

"Aiden borrowed it," said the Bard, "though I fear it will not be returned. It's a small price to pay for the safety of the village. Aiden and I made a plan in case things didn't turn out well in Bebba's Town, and as you know, they didn't." Next, the old man unwrapped a beautifully made comb. A row of teeth was set into a bone handle carved with designs stained purple, green, and vermilion. Jack recognized Brother Aiden's famous inks.

"That's deer antler. Aiden carved it himself," the Bard said.

Jack had an eerie feeling he'd seen a comb like that recently, and then he remembered. When he was trapped by the *haar* outside Edwin's Town, the stone on which he lay had been etched with designs. He'd seen a crescent crossed by a broken arrow, symbols of sacrifice to the old gods. There'd been male and female Pictish beasts, and next to them had been a comb and mirror. At the time Jack had wondered why anyone would carve such odd things.

"Aiden knows quite a bit about mermaids," said the Bard. "He's a Pict—don't wrinkle up your nose, lad. Picts are no worse than the rest of us. They merely have an unfortunate history. Do you know the story of how they lost their women?"

"The hobgoblins told me," Jack said. "When the Picts first came to this land, they angered the old gods by cutting down forests. The Forest Lord took a terrible revenge against them. He asked his brother, the Man in the Moon, to drive their women mad, and the women threw themselves off cliffs or drowned themselves."

"The Picts never quite recovered from that tragedy," said the Bard. "Later they found wives among the Irish, but first they married fin wives."

"Mermaids?" said Jack, surprised. Perhaps that was why they preferred mist and shadows.

"Exactly. Fin blood runs through the veins of most Picts. Now we must gain permission to enter Notland, and for that we need a gift for their king. He's called the Shoney. Aiden says there are two things he absolutely won't be able to resist: mirrors and combs. Fin folk love gazing into mirrors, which they call 'endless water.' They believe they are portals into another world."

"What about the comb?" said Thorgil, turning the lovely

artifact over in her hand. She ran it through her hair. "This certainly beats fingers," she declared.

"Mermaids have long, beautiful hair of which they are justly proud," the Bard said. "Unfortunately, they are plagued by barnacles that find their heads an ideal place to grow. If a mermaid doesn't comb her hair regularly, she becomes so encrusted with barnacles, she can't swim."

By now sunlight had flooded the sea, and in the distance they saw what appeared to be a gray mountain range. Long, slim boats were moving away from this in their direction. Each one bore a tall figure plying a pole.

"How can they pole?" Skakki said. "The seabed is beyond their reach." Yet the figures continued to push themselves along as easily as if the boats were on a shallow pond. Several surrounded a dead Pictish beast, and then the poles were shown to have hooks at the end. The beings snagged the beast and began towing it back with them at the same measured pace.

They were manlike and yet otherworldly. Taller and thinner than any human, their skin gleamed with silver scales. Their arms and legs were skinny like the legs of herons, and their faces were shadowed by broad-brimmed hats. They wore gray robes that drifted about them like shreds of mist. The fin men went about the business of gathering dead beasts with not a glance at the ship. They made no sound at all, not even a splash.

"SHOULD I CALL THEM?" said Eric Pretty-Face. Everyone jumped, yet not even Eric's bellow caused a disruption in the methodical harvesting.

"I have a better plan," the Bard said. He lifted the bronze mirror and directed a beam of sunlight straight into the middle of a group of boats. The reaction was instantaneous. The boats swung sideways, vanishing as fish do when they turn to avoid sunlight shining on their scales. Jack couldn't make them out at all, but he knew, somehow, that they were coming nearer. The Northmen reached for their weapons.

"Draw no sword. Fire no arrow," said the Bard. "They come to barter."

When it seemed impossible that boats could still be out there, one suddenly appeared directly beneath the prow. The tall figure within pointed at the mirror.

"This is a gift for the Shoney," said the Bard. "I request safe passage into Notland for myself and two companions."

The ship may not enter, said a voice that was there and yet not there. Jack felt it in his mind and remembered that trolls also communicated silently.

"The ship does not ask to enter. I shall travel in a coracle," said the Bard. He held up the comb, and several other boats with eerie owners appeared. And now Jack had a good look at their faces. They were long and thin, with round, fishy eyes. Their mouths were shaped like an upside-down *V*, giving them a humorless, disapproving expression.

A beautiful comb, fit for the long hair of our daughters, said the first fin man. *It is colored with the fine dyes of the Picts. A master hand has made it.*

"With this gift, I request passage out of Notland as well. Answer now or we shall turn away."

Such things lie in the hands of our king.

"Then we must go." The Bard began wrapping up the mirror again.

A sigh ruffled the air. *Wait.* A conference seemed to take place among the shadowy figures on the water. Jack couldn't make out the words. *You may enter,* said the first fin man after a moment.

"And my request? Do you swear to let us leave Notland as well?"

We swear.

"You can't do this," Skakki said as the Bard signaled for the coracle to be launched. "They changed their minds far too quickly. Everyone knows the fin folk are treacherous."

"That's true, but it's the best we're likely to get," said the Bard.

"You can't go blindly to your death!"

"The lives of many depend on the success of this adventure," said the Bard. "Remember Beowulf and his final battle with the dragon. He knew he would die. He was old. His arm no longer had the strength it'd had when he killed Grendel, yet he went forth to battle for his people."

"Fame never dies," murmured Thorgil.

"When he was dying, having slain the dragon," Skakki remembered, "he asked his companion to bring out the jewels from the dragon-hoard so that he might feast his eyes on them."

"Aye, it was a hero's death," said Rune, his eyes dreamy.

"Excuse me," said Jack. "Aren't there any tales about

heroes who go home after slaying the monster and live happily ever after?"

"Of course there are, lad," the Bard said heartily and unconvincingly. "We may yet find ourselves drinking cider in the old Roman house. But first we must solve the problem of the *draugr*. I accept your offer, fin man. We will sail to the Shoney's palace and lay before him our gifts. There we will tell him the reason for our visit."

The fin man vanished along with his boat, and Jack felt the creature moving away. By now all the dead Pictish beasts had been hauled off. The sea was clean, as though no savage conflict had taken place in it, and only the gray mountain in the distance still remained.

Chapter Thirty-three

THE CITY UNDER THE SEA

Jack had learned to like sailing, but the coracle was another matter. It rocked perilously when Eric Pretty-Face lowered him into it. There was barely room for three people plus the meager supplies they would take with them. And when Jack looked up at the sleek, handsome *karfi*, he regretted with all his heart that he had left it.

"How will we find you again?" Skakki called.

"You won't," the Bard replied. "We'll make our own way to the mainland."

"What? I'm not going to abandon you!"

"You'll have to. Notland comes and goes as it will. You won't be able to see it." The Bard stood tall in the coracle, his ash wood staff in his hand. He didn't seem the slightest bit worried about sailing home in a craft that was barely adequate for a lake.

"You planned this all along," Skakki shouted, for now the distance between them was increasing. "You tricked my sister into a quest she can't possibly survive."

"I chose this adventure!" Thorgil yelled back.

"Then you're an idiot! You're all idiots!"

Now they were picking up speed, though Jack couldn't see what was propelling them along. He was too busy holding on to the side. The last thing he heard was Eric Pretty-Face bellowing, "WE'LL BE BACK!" when the ship suddenly disappeared and all that was out there was empty sea.

"What happened to them? Where are they?" Jack cried.

"We must save them!" exclaimed Thorgil, grabbing an oar and attempting to turn the coracle. The current, or whatever they were caught in, was too strong.

"They're all right," the Bard said, sitting down amid the sacks of cargo. "We've merely crossed the border of Notland. I would guess they've seen us disappear, too, and are searching. They won't find anything."

"You've been here before, haven't you?" Jack said. There was nothing left to do but sit down and make the best of the situation. The mountain range was drawing nearer.

"I've wheedled a child or two out of the Shoney's clutches," the old man admitted. "Sea hags sometimes steal toddlers who wander too close to the water."

"So you're . . . enemies?" guessed Thorgil.

"More like well-matched opponents. I tell him what to

do, and he eventually does it. But never underestimate the Shoney. He's intelligent, devious, and dangerous. Oh, and if he offers you ocean meat tonight, don't accept it. Pictish beast has the most disagreeable flavor imaginable."

The mountains rose up before them, peak after peak of the same uniform gray. Jack looked for the surf that should have been breaking at their base and found nothing. "Shouldn't we slow down?" he said nervously. The rocks were very near.

"It's only a fog bank," the Bard said.

"Look out!" screamed Thorgil, throwing herself to the bottom of the coracle. Jack raised his arms as the gray mass rushed at them—and then they were through. They floated over a fair, green land covered with fields and houses. Above them arched a bowl of cloud. The land below was bathed in a gentle light, like the glow that brightens a mist just before the sun breaks through. The air was as warm as summer.

"As I said, a fog bank," said the Bard.

"It looked so solid." Thorgil picked herself up and leaned over the side. "Is this one of those illusions that go *poof* and you find yourself in some horrible dungeon?"

"The fin folk aren't like elves," the old man said. "They can't create something out of thin air, but they can hide themselves with borrowed colors. They bend light around their realm and blend into a background as fish do at the bottom of a stream. The trolls of Jotunheim also do this."

"I remember," said Jack. "When we walked away from the Mountain Queen's palace, it was as though the palace had folded itself away. All I could see were icy mountains."

Below, the fin folk went about the chores of villagers. They herded cattle, tended crops, and even built fires, though Jack could have sworn there was water beneath him. The coracle floated along as though it were on a lake, and the fin folk swam rather than walked over their fields. Yet their small, white cattle walked along the bottom like normal beasts.

The houses were adorned with towers and fanciful arches that seemed to have no purpose but were pleasant to look at. They were pink and orange, purple and gleaming white, the colors of the seashells one found on a beach. In the distance was an impressive castle. Processions of fin men bearing the horrid carcasses of Pictish beasts were making their way along the road to this castle. Mermaids swam behind them, their long hair streaming like living gold. These were followed by creatures so hideous, Jack wondered for a moment whether they were stalking the mermaids like a pack of wolves. Then he realized they were sea hags.

No wonder mermaids wanted to marry humans, he thought, if they were in danger of turning into such repellant creatures. The sea hags were as shapeless as seals. They stumped along on spindly legs that looked hardly strong enough to support their blobby bodies. Their arms and shoulders, by contrast, were as powerful as a blacksmith's. They were in varying stages of going bald. This might not have mattered if their heads had been shapely, but they weren't. They were simply blobs at the end of too-thick necks. With the loss of beauty came a lack of personal hygiene, and more than one of the sea hags had a severe barnacle problem.

The fin folk seemed to be enjoying themselves, though. They danced ecstatically as they carried the flabby Pictish beasts, and an honor guard of merchildren swam beneath the tails so they wouldn't drag on the ground.

"Look! Human children," said Thorgil. Jack saw that she was correct. Four sturdy little boys were scattered among the troops supporting the tails.

"Mothers should never let their toddlers wander on the beach," the Bard said sadly.

"What will happen to them?" said Jack. He remembered that elves discarded toddlers in dark forests when they were no longer cute.

"They'll grow up to marry mermaids. The sea hags will spoil them rotten because they want them as husbands for their daughters."

This was something Jack hadn't considered, and it put the sea hags in a better light.

All this time the coracle had been keeping pace with the celebrating crowds below. Now, as the revelers entered the front gate of the castle, the coracle floated over the wall to a large courtyard where fire pits had already been constructed. The little craft began to sink.

Jack braced himself for water to come flooding in, but nothing happened. The air only seemed to get thicker and richer. It made him feel extraordinarily good, as though he could run a mile and not get tired. He raised his arm and felt the air pushing back. "It feels like swimming," he said.

Thorgil propelled herself upward with a kick. "It *is* like swimming," she cried, delighted. "How wonderful! You can swim and breathe at the same time." She set out with a strong stroke and came to a stop halfway up a tower crusted with coral. "Try it, Jack!" He followed her to the tower and did a couple of somersaults in the air to show off. They clung to the coral, smiling at each other.

"If you're quite finished larking about, come down," the Bard said crossly. "We have work to do." He was already on the ground, sea bottom, or whatever it was. The fin folk, as they had done before, paid no attention to the newcomers. They set about cleaning the innards out of Pictish beasts.

But as Jack floated down he heard their voices in his head. *Who invited them? Is that Dragon Tongue? Oh, bother, it is! Hide the humans.* The voices became more distinct the closer he got to the ground, until there was such a babble that he could hardly make sense of it. But he heard, *I wonder if we can keep the new boy and girl.* And: *The boy is adorable. I want him.*

"You carry Fair Lamenting," the Bard instructed Jack. The ruined bell was wrapped in cloth, and Jack wondered what the old man planned to do with it. Thorgil was given the mirror and comb, also wrapped. The Bard had his own parcel, the contents of which he didn't reveal. "You must be on your best behavior. The fin folk have said we can speak to their king, but nothing is certain until it happens. And please don't call anyone a 'sea hag.' The correct term is 'fin wife.'"

No one had greeted them yet, but the Bard said this was normal. "It's considered bad manners to force your attention on people," he explained. "We'll hang around for a while until they're used to us." He led the way to a platform where a gang of fin men were flensing a Pictish beast. They expertly stripped off the skin, exposing vast strips of blubber. "They'll lay the skin out for fish to nibble clean. The blubber will be used in cooking," said the old man.

An indescribably foul odor filled the air. Jack swallowed hard; he didn't want to disgrace himself by throwing up. Thorgil also looked as though she was struggling. "You might as well get used to it," the Bard said. "Beast blubber deadens the sense of smell, and if you can endure it for a few minutes, you'll be all right." He breathed deeply as though savoring a rare perfume. Jack didn't say anything. He was working hard to keep his breakfast down.

"Good hunting, eh?" the old man said.

Good hunting, replied one of the fin men. Several minutes passed. Gradually, Jack's nausea subsided and he was able to pay attention to the activity before him. Long strips of yellow blubber were peeled off and put into giant pots. Here it was rendered into a bubbling, oily liquid. The beast's green flesh was carved and put on skewers over a fire pit. A large, leathery bag—the stomach?—was emptied of its contents, a mess of kelp and half-digested fish. Jack clamped his teeth shut again.

The bones were interesting. Jack had been expecting something like the skeleton of a fish, but this was entirely different. A series of flat paddles flared out from a central column, somewhat like branches of a pine tree. They were large enough to lie down on in the middle but grew smaller and smaller toward the tail. A fin man was cutting and stacking the paddles. "What do you do with those?" Jack asked, and then scolded himself for being pushy.

We make dishes, said the fin man.

All right so far, Jack thought. He hadn't annoyed anyone. He put down his bundle and watched for a while longer. "How can a Pictish beast swim with such a long, straight pole in its middle?" he said.

The fin man grasped Jack's arm and walked him to the end of the tail. The boy almost panicked. The creature's fingers gripped him with frightening strength, and Jack didn't know what he intended. The fin man pointed at the tip of the tail. *Bend it,* he said.

Jack touched it cautiously. It wasn't as nasty as he'd expected, and he found that it was amazingly springy. He used both hands to pull it up as far as it would go, when the tail suddenly whipped back into position. Jack was flung head over heels into a wall. Fortunately, the thickness of the air saved him from real harm. He slid down with the sound of clicking in his ears. The fin men's *V*-shaped mouths had reversed so that they resembled smiles. *I'll bet anything that clicking is laughter,* Jack thought.

He walked back with as much dignity as he could manage. "Good for you. You've broken the ice," approved the Bard. *I could have broken my neck, too,* Jack thought resentfully. The fin folk seemed to have the same sense of humor as Northmen.

We play that trick on all youngsters, the first fin man said. *My name is Whush. You are—?*

"Jack," said Jack. He introduced Thorgil and the Bard.

We know Dragon Tongue. He shows up now and then to lecture us.

"Merely looking for stolen property," the Bard said. "And that reminds me, I saw four human children in the victory procession."

They've been here for years, said Whush. *You would do them no service by taking them from their new families.*

"You're probably right." The old man sighed. "I just wish you wouldn't steal toddlers."

Their mothers were careless. Without us, the toddlers would have drowned.

Now other fin folk shyly approached the flensing platform to inspect the visitors. Mermaids and merlads swam around them, darting away like frightened fish when they were noticed. Jack hadn't thought about the existence of merlads, but of course fin men had to start out somewhere. Like the maids, the lads were much handsomer than their adult counterparts, though they didn't deteriorate to the level of sea hags. *Fin wives,* Jack corrected himself. He saw a few creatures that seemed to be halfway between the two stages. Their hair was falling out and their mouths were broadening into a *V* shape.

The merlads were showing a great deal of interest in

Thorgil, swimming in to touch her and speeding away. "The next time one of them does that, I'm going to smack him," said Thorgil.

"No, you aren't. We have enough problems," the Bard said.

The mermaids were just as interested in Jack, but shyer about it. He was uncomfortable with them because they weren't wearing anything from the waist up. At least they kept their distance. *Pretty boy, come with me,* one of them called.

I saw him first, said another.

You! He'll never look at you, barnacle-face.

He will so, seaweed-for-brains! The two mermaids fell into a squabble, poking and pinching each other until a sea hag came over to separate them.

Maids! Maids! If you don't behave, you won't go to the banquet tonight, scolded the sea hag—*fin wife,* Jack amended. He had to keep himself from bolting, the creature was so overpowering close-up. With her brawny shoulders and big hands, she looked stronger than Whush.

She was cloaked in a gown that shimmered with color like the inside of a shell. Hundreds of pearls were looped around her thick, scaly neck. It was such a contrast, Jack couldn't take his eyes off her.

You're a bold one, giving me that fish-eye look, said the sea hag.

"I—I—was admiring your dress," he stammered.

Silver-tongued, too, the creature said approvingly. *You'll make a fine husband for one of our mermaids.*

"He's only visiting, Shair Shair," the Bard said. "You'll have to look elsewhere." Shair Shair smiled in the fin folk way, as if to say, *We'll see about that.* She lumbered off, for like all the sea hags, she was graceless. Jack caught a glimpse of her toes, long and scaly with claws at the tips, beneath the beautiful, shimmering robe. In spite of her unsettling appearance, Jack rather liked her, as he had liked the troll-maidens Fonn and Forath once he'd gotten used to them.

"At first everyone was standoffish and now they're too friendly," Thorgil complained, swiping at a merlad who was attempting to grab her hair. "Who was that monster? She had enough pearls on her to sink a ship."

"Do not insult her," the Bard said sharply. "She is Shair Shair, wife of the Shoney. She's the *draugr*'s mother."

"Oh, bedbugs," said Jack, using Pega's worst swearword. "What's going to happen when we tell her about her daughter?"

Chapter Thirty-four

THE SHONEY'S FEAST

Nothing happened quickly in Notland, Jack discovered. The fin folk were masters of indirection. They knew that the Bard had come to see their king and did nothing to bring it about. Shair Shair had looked the visitors over and gone away. Whush invited them to follow him around. He seemed to have no particular goal in doing this.

"Can't we just ask to see the Shoney?" Thorgil said. Both she and Jack were tired of wandering around aimlessly.

"That's not how things get done here," the old man said. "If we try to hurry the fin folk, they'll simply melt away. They have a saying: 'The longest way around is the shortest way there.'"

"It's already long enough," said Thorgil.

Whush, for reasons known only to himself, led them on a tour of the farms. They observed the white cattle, the barley fields, and the chicken-of-the-sea coops. They endured a long and exceedingly boring description of kelp harvesting. They were introduced to sea goats, or capricorns. These were handsome creatures with long horns and flowing hair, and Whush informed them that the hair could be used to spin cloth. Instead of hind legs, the goats had fish tails. They could both swim and leap, and were altogether charming in the way they frisked around.

But even capricorns got tedious after a while. Jack was tired and thirsty, and when they came to a dark stream, he asked whether it was all right to drink from it. *Not that stream*, said Whush. *It comes from the* oueems. *It wouldn't be good for you.*

"*Oueem?*" Thorgil said. "That's the Pictish word for 'tunnel.'"

Yes. Tunnels of the dead.

Jack looked across the stream and realized that what he'd taken for small hills were in fact barrows. They were covered with thick grass that had turned an autumn yellow and were humped up like cats waiting to be stroked. "Tunnels going where?" he asked.

"Remember what I told you about mirrors," the Bard said. "They are called 'endless water' because they are believed to be a portal to another world. The dead swim through them to a long, dark *oueem* that leads to a bright new sea where winter never comes and the water is as clear as sky. Departed fin folk are buried with mirrors for that reason."

I'll bet the draugr's *barrow doesn't contain a mirror*, thought Jack. *That's why we've brought one.* He wished they could simply drop the wretched thing off and go home, but that would have been too simple. The longest way around was the shortest way there.

Fortunately, Whush next took them to a farmhouse, where they were offered food and drink. The water was salty and the oatcakes had too much seaweed mixed into them. The farmer's wife, a sea hag with so many barnacles that it looked like she was wearing a helmet, tried to interest Jack in one of her daughters.

Rest here. The banquet will begin late, said Whush. It was the first time anyone had suggested that they might attend the banquet. The sea hag—*fin wife*, Jack reminded himself— showed them into a courtyard. Kelp was heaped up for beds. It was unpleasantly clammy, but Jack was too tired to care.

It was dark when a pack of small merlads sprang upon him like so many puppies and rousted him out of bed. The dome of cloud over the courtyard flickered with lightning. A distant rumble told Jack that a thunderstorm was taking place in the outside world.

"It's so *humid*," groaned Thorgil, who had been awakened by a group of little mermaids bouncing up and down on the kelp. "I'd give anything for a swim."

"You can swim in the air," Jack said. He leaped upward, much to the delight of the merlads, and did a somersault.

"It isn't the same. I feel hot and sticky."

Jack realized that he hadn't felt a breeze since arriving in

Notland. Thick, muggy air pressed down on him, and he felt a sudden longing to be on a ship with a crisp wind at his back.

The Bard was still asleep. Jack knelt down to wake him. "What? What's that?" said the old man, instantly coming alert.

"It's nighttime," Jack said. "I think we're supposed to get ready for the banquet."

"I don't know how much readying we can do," the Bard complained, rising painfully from his bed. "Drat this seaweed! It always makes my joints ache." He walked around the courtyard to get the stiffness out. "I'd give anything to miss the banquet, but we won't get anywhere with the Shoney if we don't attend. He'll insist on showing us his wealth and power. When we're suitably awed, he'll ask for our gifts. Then the bargaining begins."

The fin wife showed up with two sturdy merlads bearing torches and invited them to dine before leaving. The Bard thanked her graciously. Jack wondered why they would eat before attending a feast. "She's being polite," explained the old man. "She knows humans don't like ocean meat, and that's all the Shoney's going to serve. There are twelve huge Pictish beasts to get through, and the fin folk won't leave until they've devoured every scrap. They'll wash it down with buckets of kelp lager, a kind of beer. Stay away from the lager. You'll be running for the bushes all day tomorrow, and there aren't any bushes in this place."

The fin wife had laid a table with dishes Jack recognized as Pictish beast bones, and they were each given a hard-boiled seagull egg and a bowl of oyster stew. A single roast salmon graced the center of the table. The cow's milk, served in hollowed-out whale teeth, tasted strongly of seaweed. "The flavor comes from what they eat," pointed out Thorgil, who didn't mind the taste at all. "During famine years the Northmen feed their cows with seaweed, and the milk is just like this."

Afterward the entire farm family, numbering at least twenty, set out for the castle, with merlads going before and behind with torches. Everyone was excited, and Jack found it impossible to sort out the babble of voices in his head. The sky lit up with distant flashes of lightning, and dull rumbles ran around the horizon, yet the air was perfectly still. Farm smell—hay, manure, chicken-of-the-sea coops— seemed trapped next to the earth. The air seemed thicker at night.

Jack was queasy from the seaweed-flavored milk, and he glanced up at the cloud cover with longing. If only he could be out there with a wind throwing cool spray into his face!

The path took them past the black stream. Jack realized that although the water had seemed to rush past earlier, it had made no sound. Now he could see only the dark gash where it lay. Beyond, the barrows lay in a lightless land. They had melted together into one shadow.

With, of course, the *oueem*s snaking around underneath like the roots of a midnight forest.

"Will you look at that!" exclaimed Thorgil. Jack looked up to see the castle outlined in light. It seemed that the very air had come alive and twinkled with a thousand tiny sparks. They surrounded the partygoers, who were streaming in from all sides. Even the currents the fin folk made in passing glittered briefly before fading.

Presently, the glittering sparks found Jack and the others and illuminated them. He tried to see what they were, but the sparks winked out before he could focus on them, to be replaced by others. "They're sea mites," said the Bard. "They come out on warm, humid nights, somewhat like our fireflies. I suspect they're attracted by the smell of kelp lager. Thousands of them manage to drown themselves in it—another reason to avoid drinking the wretched stuff."

Once inside the walls, Whush appeared and led the Bard, Jack, and Thorgil up to a dais overlooking the courtyard. Torches blazed everywhere, making the air even warmer and more breathless. Fire pits smoked with dripping blubber. Buckets of lager were lined up against the walls, and Jack noticed that they glowed brightly with drowning sea mites. Fin men, fin wives, mermaids, and merlads descended on giant platters of roast beast, dipping down to bite off chunks and swimming away, the heavy fin wives moving more ponderously than the others.

Until then Jack had accepted the fin folk as odd almost-humans, just as he had once accepted the trolls. Now they seemed utterly alien. They resembled nothing so much as crabs tearing apart a dead seal. No emotion except ravenous hunger showed on their faces as their V-shaped mouths tore at the beast flesh. Between bites, they plunged their heads into the buckets and sucked up both lager and mites with mind-less ferocity. Even the beautiful mermaids seemed devoid of intelligence.

Imagine being married to one of those, Jack thought. *You'd have to live in this dank kingdom under the sea, knowing that your bride is not really human.* That was why Father Severus had never considered marriage with his mermaid. For the first time Jack felt a slight sympathy for him.

"Pay attention," murmured the Bard. Jack had been so riveted on the scene below, he hadn't noticed what was on the dais. At first he thought he was looking at a jumble of rocks, but their brightness and color told him he was wrong.

"I've never seen so many jewels," Thorgil said in an awed voice. Like all Northmen, she had a huge respect for wealth. "I don't even know what most of them are."

"Emeralds, rubies, sapphires, diamonds, and pearls," said the Bard. "Amber, tourmalines, and jade. You name it, the Shoney has it. Everything's available at the bottom of the sea. The gold and silver coins have been taken from sunken ships."

"Do you suppose he'd miss—," began Thorgil.

"Don't even think of it. He knows to the very last emerald the contents of his hoard."

The shield maiden frowned. "If he pillaged it, others have the right to do the same."

"The Shoney *found* it," the old man emphasized. "All things that fall into the sea are his, including the gold dust he's using for a floor down below." Mermaids diving to retrieve shreds of meat caused the gold dust to spurt up and fall down just as quickly. It was very heavy.

"Well, what's the point of heaping all this wealth in front of us?" demanded Thorgil.

The point is to make you desire it and know that it is beyond your reach, a voice suddenly said. A tall, shadowy figure had materialized on the dais. It was cloaked in shimmering silver that reflected the torchlight. The creature threw back his hood.

"Shoney!" the Bard said heartily. "What a pleasure to see you!"

The Shoney regarded him from yellow, slitted eyes like those of a snake. He was larger and older than any fin man Jack had seen before. *No visit of yours is ever an unmixed pleasure,* he replied. The creature waved his hand, and merlads swam to the dais with chairs. These were made of dark wood inlaid with ivory. Thorgil ran her fingers over the beautiful patterns before she sat down. *Do you covet my chairs, shield maiden?* the Shoney asked. Jack felt uneasy. How did the creature know she was a shield maiden?

"Indeed I do," Thorgil said enthusiastically. "I've never seen such fine work."

They were made in a land to the far south where the seas are ever warm. The ship that carried them was swift and strong. It had eyes painted on the prow to find the way, yet it did not see the rocks that slew it. Do you truly, truly covet them, shield maiden?

"Absolutely! And I can't tell you how much I want to pillage all the gold and jewels you've got lying around here. I don't know when I've been so jealous of a wealth-hoard."

Ahhhh, sighed the Shoney, half closing his eyes. *That's what I like about Northmen. You can always count on them for heart-warming envy. Not like you, Dragon Tongue. You care nothing for earthly wealth.*

"That's not true," the Bard said. "I love beautiful things, and these chairs are certainly beautiful. I'd welcome them in my house."

Bah! You'd be just as happy with a chunk of driftwood. What of you, apprentice? The Shoney turned to Jack. Again the boy was uneasy that the creature knew so much about him.

"Well . . . I like silver." He struggled to say something that sounded sufficiently greedy. "I don't have experience with jewels, you see, so I don't know how to crave them. Not that yours aren't wonderful. I once had a silver-hoard, but I gave most of it to my parents."

Gave it to your parents! cried the Shoney, almost making Jack's heart stop. *You have corrupted the boy with morals, Dragon Tongue.* He stood up as if to leave.

"My heart-father, Olaf One-Brow, was the most covetous man in Middle Earth," announced Thorgil. "Shall I tell you how he burrowed into a dwarf forge and stole thirty-seven gold rings?"

The Shoney sat down again. *I have often longed to get my hands on dwarf rings. Alas, I am chained to the sea. Tell me more, shield maiden.*

And so Thorgil related many fine tales of Olaf's cunning and greed. She began with the thirty-seven dwarf rings and went on to Olaf's pillaging of an entire shipment of wine meant for a Frankish king. She told of how he tricked a jeweled goblet away from a troll by using loaded dice and of how he made off with the Mountain Queen's scepter, although she got it back.

After each exploit, the Shoney sighed with pleasure. *He sounds like a man well worth knowing. I hope to meet him in the halls of Ran and Aegir someday.*

"He has already been taken into Valhalla," Thorgil said.

Jack was fairly certain she was stretching the truth about Olaf, but you never knew. Olaf had been willing to pillage anything, though brute force rather than cunning had been his specialty. And Thorgil was an excellent storyteller.

After a while the Shoney ordered a bucket of kelp lager brought to him and drank deeply from it. *You please me, shield maiden. Ask for a boon and I shall grant it.*

"Actually, the Bard has a request," she said. "My wish is that you grant it."

Oh, bother! More tiresome morality, grumbled the Shoney. *Very well, Dragon Tongue, but if you want the four human children, the answer is no.*

"I have something more serious to discuss," said the Bard. "First, I would like to show you the gifts we have brought. Thorgil, unwrap the mirror and comb."

I have heard of them, the Shoney said, and his eyes glinted with desire. The shield maiden first presented the magnificent mirror, and the creature looked into it with undisguised delight. At last he wrenched his eyes away and covered it with the cloth. *Enough! If I continue gazing, I shall find myself swimming to the other world. I wish my daughter had been granted such a portal.*

Jack didn't dare look at the Bard. The Shoney was far too intelligent and might guess his thoughts.

Thorgil held out the comb. *Deer antler from a buck in his seventh year,* said the Shoney. *The carving is masterful and the dyes will not fade for a millennium. This was made by the librarian on the Holy Isle.*

"You know of him?" said Jack, astonished.

I had reason to watch for a certain monk on the Holy Isle. I kept hoping he would go for a swim, but he never did.

Jack felt cold. That had to have been Father Severus. Fortunately for him, he considered swimming a sinful waste of time and never did it.

The little librarian swam often, said the Shoney.

"His name is Aiden," Jack said.

Aiden. A good name. It means "yew tree" in Pictish. I could tell he had fin blood by the way he took to the water. Once he went out too far and was too tired to return to shore. I held him up so he wouldn't drown. I don't know why I did that.

"It was kindness," said the Bard.

The Shoney glared at him. *It was for my own pleasure. I liked to see Aiden paint pictures by the water. None of the other monks did that. His colors were as brilliant as the colors of my jewels.*

"He isn't a half-bad ale-maker, either." The Bard unwrapped the parcel he'd been carrying.

That wouldn't be—that can't be—heather ale!

"The same." The old man placed the heavy bag into the Shoney's hands.

The creature stood up, and at once two merlads swam over. *Call Shair Shair. Tell her we have a rare treat. Tell her to hurry.* The Shoney seemed hardly able to wait. Soon Shair Shair came speeding across the courtyard and sprang with a great leap onto the dais. Her eyes were feral, like a wolf's when interrupted at a kill. Her dress was flecked with bits of meat. A shudder passed through her body.

This had better be good, she said.

Heather ale, the Shoney said, holding up the bag. Immediately, she reached for it, crooning and wheedling, and he poured ale into her *V*-shaped mouth before taking some himself. The two of them entirely forgot they had company. They circled each other, uttering wild cries. They bounced around like capricorns, offering each other sips or teasingly holding the bag out of reach.

Thorgil turned her back and sat with her legs dangling over the side of the dais. "I don't know about you, but I find this somewhat embarrassing."

The Bard and Jack sat beside her. "It's really good ale," the Bard said. When they eventually turned back, the royal couple had gone and Whush was there.

The Shoney says you are to have the best bedroom in the castle, he said. *He asked me to bring you man food and anything else you might require. He will discuss your request in the morning.*

They gratefully followed the fin man through a door and

down a winding hall to a large, round room with a domed ceiling as smooth and pink as the inside of a shell. It was lit by lamps made of a frail, transparent substance that cast a soothing light without adding heat. Whush brought them a platter of grilled eel, fried oysters, and clams. With it was a keg, surely salvaged from a ship, of fresh, sweet water.

"It *is* possible to have a good meal in this place," said Jack, tucking into the eel.

"Yes, but the beds are still made out of kelp," complained the Bard.

Chapter Thirty-five

THE *DRAUGR*'S TOMB

In spite of the damp, rubbery kelp, they all slept extremely well and woke feeling refreshed. Whush staggered in with bowls of clam chowder and ship's biscuits, a hard, dry bread carried on voyages. He looked decidedly hungover.

They had to soak the bread in the chowder to render it soft enough to chew. "Where do you suppose they got this?" said Jack, gnawing on his chunk. "If it was from a sunken ship, wouldn't it have fallen apart in the water?"

"Adult fin folk can leave the sea, though they prefer not to and dare not go far," said the Bard. "Sometimes they take revenge on humans fishing in what they consider their part of the ocean. They snap fishing lines and make holes in nets.

They also steal food for the human children they are raising. A toddler can't survive without land food."

When they were finished, Whush staggered back and led them through the halls to the Shoney's audience chamber. On the way Jack distinctly heard the fin man muttering *ow . . . ow ow . . . ow* as he walked along. He seemed to have a thundering headache. Here and there in the hallways, fin folk were collapsed on the floor. "Kelp lager," said the Bard, poking at one with his staff. "They never know when they've had enough."

"Will the Shoney also be—?" Jack began.

"He doesn't allow himself to get drunk. I wish he did, because he'd be easier to deal with. Let me do the talking. He's going to be angry enough when I tell him why we're here."

The Shoney's audience chamber was filled to overflowing with chests of jewels and coins. Odd treasures stood everywhere—statues, furniture, goblets, Christian crosses, vases painted with flowers, and bolts of cloth that shimmered like pearls. Thorgil touched one of the bolts, and her fingers came away shining with gold dust.

One statue was of a man with the head of a long-nosed dog. Another was of a dancer standing on one leg. He had four arms fanned out on either side of him. "Are there truly such people?" Jack whispered to the Bard.

I've never been sure, said the Shoney. He was sitting in a chair so surrounded by treasures that the boy hadn't seen him. *I haven't seen anything like them, but my knowledge ends at the edge of the sea.*

Jack thought each of the treasures was beautiful on its own, but when they were jumbled up together, it was hard to appreciate them. The chamber reminded him of the chief's root cellar, with basket upon basket of apples, turnips, and onions, stacked with firewood and cider kegs.

"I am here for a serious purpose," the Bard said.

You always are. What is it this time? The Shoney seemed unimpressed.

"I wish to speak of your daughter."

The Shoney sat straight up as though he'd been stabbed. *What right have you to ask about my child? It was your kind who slew her, your people who left her spirit to wander.*

"I know. That's why I'm here."

I hunted for her murderer. I watched the Holy Isle, and he did not come within my reach. When the isle was destroyed, I rejoiced, but he was not among the bodies that fell into my realm. Long years have I searched for Father Severus. Have you come to deliver him into my hands?

"I can't do that—hear me out!" The Bard raised his staff as the Shoney loomed over him. For the first time Jack felt a breeze in Notland. It came through the door and blew a film of shimmering dust from the treasures stacked around the room. The dust flowed along the floor, piling up in a shining border against a wall. The breeze died.

"Your daughter's plea was brought before the councils of the nine worlds, and I gave my oath that I would free her spirit." The Bard then described what had happened in the village. "In her rage and sorrow she slew innocent beings. For this she has lost the right to demand Father Severus's death."

The Shoney bellowed like an enraged bull. The ground shook and the vases and goblets rattled. Several fin men rushed into the chamber.

"Anger won't save your daughter," the Bard said in the shocking silence that followed. "If you truly care for her, you'll listen to me."

Be gone, all of you, the Shoney ordered his men. *But don't go far. I may need you to throw these humans into the giant eel pit.*

"Threats won't help either," the Bard said calmly. "Really, Shoney, I expected more sense from you. You're too old to throw tantrums."

Jack thought the Bard had gone too far this time, because the Shoney raised a jeweled goblet as if he intended to bring it down on someone's head. But after a moment he lowered his arm.

"Very good," said the old man, as if he were lecturing an unruly child. "If your daughter starts killing again, her spirit will never find peace. She'll be trapped like a hogboon in an unending round of destruction. Eventually, like a hogboon, she will vanish utterly from the living stream."

The Shoney moaned softly.

"The comb and mirror I have brought are for her tomb. I know these are the traditional grave gifts for mermaids and fin wives."

Shellia. Her name was Shellia. The creature hunched over with his face in his hands.

"Take me to her tomb at nightfall," the Bard commanded.

"Let me lay the grave gifts inside. Then it will be time to summon Shellia and send her to the farther sea."

For a long while the Shoney sat. *She was so beautiful the last time I saw her,* he said at last. *So young and happy. Her bones were carried by the dolphins to Notland. They had not seen her drown or they could have saved her, but they knew what had happened to her. And who was responsible. I will call Shair Shair to go with us, though it will break her heart.*

When night fell, Whush led a troop of fin men carrying flaming torches, and the Shoney and Shair Shair walked behind. In the middle were Thorgil with the mirror and comb, Jack with Fair Lamenting, and the Bard. As they went, though no one had spread word of this expedition, fin men and wives, mermaids and merlads came out of their houses to pay homage. They seemed to know it was a solemn occasion, for they were entirely silent.

The procession came to the dark stream, now only a shadowy gash dividing the realm of the dead from the rest of Notland. Somehow Jack knew the water rushing by was very cold. He didn't have any desire to touch it. They crossed a bridge to a path that wound through the barrows until they came to the outer edge of Notland.

The fog came down like a wall, with only a small gray circle lit by the torches. And before it Jack saw a tomb unlike any of the others. It wasn't made of earth, but of stones so cleverly fitted together that it resembled a wave frozen in the instant before it breaks. In the middle was a door. On either side were slabs of rock to seal the opening.

Shellia's tomb, said the Shoney. His wife moaned and collapsed on the ground. Several fin men ran to help her. The Shoney didn't move.

The Bard took the mirror and comb from Thorgil. "I remind you, Shoney, of the promise your men made before we entered Notland," he said. "We must be allowed to leave once Shellia is laid to rest."

You may go if you are successful, the Shoney said.

Jack didn't like the implied threat in this reply, but the Bard accepted it. He carried the grave gifts inside, lighting his way with the pale glow from his staff. Jack could see shadows moving as the old man walked around. "The tomb is beautifully done," he said when he had emerged. "You have carved her history into the walls and filled it with her toys, but the mirror you left her was broken."

I know. She would not rest until she was given a life for a life.

"Let's hope it doesn't come to that," said the Bard. "Jack, hand me Fair Lamenting."

The boy quickly unwrapped it. The old man removed a lump of iron from his carrying bag and fastened it to a string inside.

So that is Fair Lamenting, the Shoney said. *It has long called to my kind under the sea. I should hate it, but it is too beautiful. I should desire it for my wealth-hoard, yet greed dies when I gaze upon it. I must be getting sick.*

"There's nothing wrong with you," said the Bard. "Fair Lamenting is beyond earthly concerns."

"Where did the clapper come from?" asked Jack.

"I found it," Thorgil bragged. "I went to every blacksmith in Bebba's Town until I found the one Ythla had traded with. He had six or seven similar lumps, but this one still had a pattern of scales on one side."

Jack felt depressed. It had been such a marvelous work of art.

"You should look after your wife, Shoney," the Bard advised. "The sight of a *draugr* can be upsetting."

Jack waited in fear and anticipation as the old man swung the bell. He remembered the golden chime rolling through the hazel wood and the rapture that swept over him. It was the most sublime sound he had ever heard, yet it was frightening as well—too intense, too alive and overwhelming.

The bell rang.

It was . . . nice. *More than nice,* Jack told himself, wanting to believe. The Bard frowned and rang it again.

The Shoney bent down to inspect it. *Is this the music that called my daughter from the sea? I expected more.*

The Bard impatiently rang it again, and now Jack heard a tinny note, not unlike a rock rolling around in a brass cauldron.

"I'm sure I found the right blacksmith," protested Thorgil. "It was the only lump with a pattern of scales."

The old man laid Fair Lamenting on the ground and leaned heavily on his staff as though he were exhausted. "I don't doubt you, child. It isn't your fault. It's simply that the magic of the clapper lay in its art, and now that's gone. I had hoped there was enough magic left to summon the *draugr*, but I dared not try until we got here."

You mean you can't call back my daughter? demanded the Shoney. *I've suffered and Shair Shair has suffered for nothing?*

"Believe me, I would do anything in my power to save your child. I have vowed to do it. I *will* do it, but I don't know how." The old man tottered to a rock and sat down. "Where do I go first? Return to the village? Do I wait until Shellia emerges of her own accord and starts killing? It will be too late then."

Jack tipped the bell on its side and removed the clapper. It did have a faint fretwork of scales in one section, but this was battered until it was almost unrecognizable. A memory hovered just out of reach in his mind, something important, but he couldn't bring it into focus. Each time he tried to capture it, it slipped away like a fish diving into deep water.

Fish. Why that image? But of course the original clapper had looked like a fish, the Salmon of Knowledge that knew the pathways between this world and the next. And then he understood. "Your flute, sir," Jack said. "The flute of Amergin is the right shape."

"You're right," murmured the Bard. "It was made by the same hand." The old man quickly found the instrument and attached it to the bell. One chime and everyone knew instantly that this was the real Fair Lamenting. The fin men sank to their knees. Shair Shair collapsed into the Shoney's arms. Thorgil grabbed Jack as though they were on the deck of a ship in a stormy sea. The chime went on and on, fading slowly and sweetly until it seemed impossible that one note could endure so long. Then it was gone.

Chapter Thirty-six

A LIFE FOR A LIFE

I did not understand my daughter's longing before, said the Shoney. *I want something and do not know what it is. The gold, the jewels, the wealth I have accumulated are as nothing, and my life has been wasted in useless pleasures. It is a cruel thing, this bell, yet fair beyond reckoning.*

The Bard rang Fair Lamenting again and waited. The silence grew. Jack listened for the sounds that were always present, even on the darkest night, on land—the crickets and frogs, dogs barking at a passing fox, leaves sighing in the breeze. There was nothing except the rustle of the torches. What a melancholy place Notland was, Jack thought, without the bustle of life. Even the mermaids, and he had heard they could lure sailors with their beautiful singing, were voiceless here. Everything was silent except—

Jack heard a woman sobbing in the distance. It went on and on, as though there could be no end to such sorrow. It came gradually closer, and a foul stench arose. The air turned cold. A darkness among the barrows grew thicker, taller, more terrible, and a mist rose from the ground.

Who calls? said a voice full of death.

Shellia, groaned Shair Shair. *Oh, Shellia, what has happened to you?*

Deep was my love. Bitter was my fate. I was left to perish and may not rest until life has been given for life.

"Now, that's something we have to discuss," said the Bard. "I agree that Severus deserves punishment, but he's stupid rather than evil. And you haven't been exactly innocent either. You can't ask for his life."

I disagree, the Shoney said. *Lure him to the water's edge and we'll see what's what.*

"No, no, no!" said the Bard impatiently. "You can't keep heaping up revenge, or we'll never see the end of souls asking for justice. Severus doesn't deserve death."

Deep was my love. Bitter was my fate. I followed his ship until the waves overcame me. I may not rest until life has been given for life.

"See, that's what happens with unquiet spirits," said the Bard. "They get locked into an idea and it's hard to shake them loose. Shellia, believe me, Severus will pay for what he did to you, but you can't afford to wait for it. The longer you spend in this world, the more you will be tempted to kill. Soon you will be unable to stop."

I am owed his death. I will take him in my arms, and together we will swim to the sea where winter never comes.

He's not worth it, interrupted the Shoney. *He's a dried-up old stick and will make you as miserable in the next life as this one.*

Father, the *draugr* said with a sigh. The voice was no longer cruel and full of jagged rocks.

Shellia, cried Shair Shair. *There is a new mirror in your tomb, the finest that has been seen in this land, for your long journey. There is a comb for your beautiful hair.*

The *draugr* turned to her mother, and the darkness shrank until it was no larger than a young woman. *I may not go until life has been given for life. Deep was my love. Bitter was my—*

"You're getting into a rut," the Bard said. "If you do any more killing, you won't be able to leave this world. You'll be stuck like a wretched hogboon."

I have already killed.

"What?" shouted the old man. "Are you an idiot as well as a spoiled, self-centered mermaid? Don't give me that 'deep was my love' garbage. You saw something you wanted and didn't get it. Well, boo hoo! We don't always get what we want."

Jack was shocked, and both the Shoney and Shair Shair looked extremely upset. This had to be one of the Dragon Tongue scoldings that made Northman kings cower in fear. He was afraid that the *draugr* would revert to her giant, menacing shape, but she did nothing of the kind. If anything, she became smaller.

You said you were going to ring the bell. I waited ever so long, the *draugr* said in a sulky voice. *You shouldn't promise things if you aren't going to do them.*

"I know. I apologize. Events happened beyond my control," said the Bard.

The bell did ring and I followed it through the earth. After a while I came out into a sty that smelled worse than a rotting whale. A man was there.

"Mrs. Tanner's brother," cried Thorgil. "She must have found her way to his hut."

I asked him where Severus was, but he wouldn't answer. He cowered before me. I breathed into his face and went back into the earth.

"Would that . . . kill him?" faltered Jack, thinking it was no great loss if it had.

"Worse," the Bard groaned. "*Draugr* breath contains flying venom. She has infected him with a fatal illness, but it doesn't end there. Whoever comes in contact with him will get sick too."

"I hunted for Mrs. Tanner's brother when I was looking for the bell's clapper," said Thorgil. "His house had caught fire in the night and had burned to ashes. No one had seen him since. I think it likely he died before he could spread the disease."

"Dear Freya, I hope that's true," said the Bard.

The sky above showed the faintest glimmer of light. It

was no longer dead black, but a deep gray. On land such a change would have meant birdsong and a breeze. Here nothing heralded the coming of dawn. The air was as still and stagnant as before.

"You must enter the tomb before the sun rises, Shellia," the Bard said gently. "Do not be afraid. Remember the bright seas of your youth and the sound of waves and the birds calling your name. You will find that joy again, but only if you let go of this world."

We love you, daughter, said the Shoney and Shair Shair. They held out their arms but did not dare touch the darkness their child had become.

No! I won't go. Why should I? cried the *draugr*. *Deep was my love. Bitter was my fate. I will return to the village and spread such death that it will be talked of for a millennium.*

"I command you by root, by stone, by sea to enter that tomb!" roared the Bard, raising his staff. The *draugr* laughed and began to drift away.

You can't stop me! she jeered.

The old man snatched up Fair Lamenting and rang it with such force that Shellia was dragged back against her will. "Ha! Got your attention that time. I *will* stop you," said the Bard. He rang the bell again, softly. Jack thought it was like the first voice he had ever heard—his mother? His grandmother? The midwife who had taken him into her arms on the night of his birth? Whoever it was, the voice was infinitely gentle and compelling. He couldn't think of turning away from such love.

I am still owed life for life, the *draugr* said with a sigh.

"You shall have it." The Bard walked toward the tomb, carrying Fair Lamenting, and the *draugr* followed. She was almost visible, no longer a dark stain against the night, but a young woman.

"You can't go in there!" Jack cried as he realized what was happening.

The old man turned and smiled. "Remember the story of Beowulf, lad. He knew he would die when he fought the dragon. Yet the lives of his people depended on it and he embraced his fate gladly. One old man is a small price to pay to keep plague from our land."

"A death worthy of Valhalla," murmured Thorgil.

"Don't *you* start with your Northman stupidity," Jack shouted at her. "The *draugr* doesn't deserve mercy, sir. She's a selfish brat. You said so yourself. I won't let you go in there."

The Bard rang Fair Lamenting again. The same gentle, compelling voice held Jack back.

"I won't let you," the boy said weakly.

"I'm proud of you, lad. Never forget that, but you cannot go against fate," the old man said. "Remember your promise, Shoney. These two are allowed to leave Notland."

I remember, said the Shoney.

"Thorgil, I lay upon you this oath: Save my daughter. I don't need to ask Jack because he'll do it anyway."

"I give my oath," said the shield maiden, deathly pale.

"Now I must go before dawn breaks in the outer world.

Come, Shellia. We have much to do." The old man rang the bell one last time and disappeared into the depths of the tomb. The young mermaid followed him obediently.

At once the Shoney commanded fin men to restrain Jack and Thorgil and to seal the mouth of the tomb.

"You can't do this!" shouted Jack, struggling against the fin men. "The Bard doesn't deserve to die! The councils of the nine worlds will hold you responsible!"

They will not hold me responsible. Dragon Tongue went willingly, said the Shoney.

"Shair Shair, you know this is wrong," the boy pleaded.

Great was her love. Bitter was her fate. She could not rest until life was given for life, said the sea hag, and Jack saw again the mindless face of the creature feeding at the banquet. She wasn't remotely human. She had no more regard for the Bard's fate than she had for a fish she was planning to eat.

By now the tomb was completely sealed, and the procession began to move away. Both Jack and Thorgil fought their captors, but it did them no good. They were carried back to the palace courtyard, bound with ropes, and deposited in the coracle. Whush presented himself for orders.

Take them away. You know where, said the Shoney. There was nothing they could do to stop him. The coracle sailed off, and Whush pushed them along with a pole. They came to the wall of fog and broke through to the open sea, with the wind blowing and cold spray lashing over the side of the boat. Somewhere they crossed the outer border of Notland, but Jack couldn't be sure when. He looked for Skakki's ship. The ocean was a vast wilderness of gray waves with not an island, a bird, or a boat anywhere on it.

Whush poled along steadily with his gray hat pulled down over his gray face. His robe billowed out behind him like a sheet of rain.

Chapter Thirty-seven

GRIM'S ISLAND

"The Bard couldn't give up that easily," said Jack. "He must have a trick up his sleeve." They had been sailing for what seemed like hours. The sun had climbed to zenith, bringing welcome warmth, and now was descending to the west. Clouds were beginning to gather.

"His fame will never die," Thorgil said dully.

"If you say that one more time, I'm going to kick you over the side."

"We shouldn't fight among ourselves," she replied, and Jack was immediately repentant.

"I'm sorry. It was a stupid thing to say."

"And if you tried, you'd find that I can kick harder than you can," the shield maiden said.

They were lying in the bottom of the coracle, and now Jack noticed that the quality of the wave sounds had changed. He struggled up, to look over the side. They were approaching land. It was a rocky, uninviting place with a tall mountain in the center. The only greenery was a forest of trees at the top of this mountain; the rest of the island was barren. Whush was poling toward it at great speed, and presently Jack felt the bottom of the coracle scrape over sand.

"What's happening? Are we going to be thrown into the giant eel pit?" cried Thorgil.

Jack heard a clicking sound in his head, which meant that Whush was laughing. *Much as I hate to deprive our eels of a treat, the Shoney has decreed otherwise. Pity. He is becoming sentimental in his old age.*

"The Shoney gave his word that we would be allowed to leave Notland," said Jack, realizing that a fin man's word didn't mean very much.

So he did and here you are.

"Where's here?" demanded Jack.

I need not tell you, except that it gives me pleasure to do so. Whush's *V*-shaped mouth tilted up into a smile. *This is Grim's Island, where our princess met her death. It seems fitting that you should be abandoned here.* The fin man hoisted Jack and Thorgil under one arm and carried them onto the beach. He dropped them onto the sand and continued on to the base of the mountain. *You won't be climbing that anytime soon,* he said with satisfaction when he returned. He cut their bonds, but before they were able to wriggle free, he was pushing off in the coracle.

"Wait! That's our boat!" shouted Thorgil. "How do you expect us to leave?"

Whush paused, well out of reach. *Swim, I suppose. One word of advice: I'd find shelter quickly, because the weather is about to turn bad. It does that often here.* And he sped off, poling vigorously, until he was lost among the tossing waves.

"It's so cold! What do you remember about Grim's Island?" Thorgil said.

"It's dark all winter, and in summer it's either shrouded in fog or lashed by storms," said Jack. "Let's see, the mermaid built Father Severus a hut shaped like a giant sea snail. We should look for that."

They were both extremely stiff from being tied up, and they hadn't had anything to eat since the day before. "I could look for shellfish," Thorgil offered.

"Water and shelter are more important. Look at that sky!" Jack's courage almost failed him when he saw the storm rapidly approaching from the north. They ran along the beach, and large drops of freezing rain began to pelt down. Soon it was difficult to see more than a few feet ahead. Jack shouted when he tripped over a lump of rock and fell onto the sand.

"It's a doorway!" yelled Thorgil over the rising wind. "I think it's that snail house." They wriggled into the entrance and found that the inside chamber was spacious. The walls were as smooth as glass and the floor was of fine sand that was surprisingly dry. They burrowed into it for warmth. After a while they took turns crawling to the door and holding their hands out to gather rain to drink.

"It's already dark," said Thorgil as she nestled into the sand again.

"Then we should sleep," Jack said.

"Shouldn't we, you know, write a praise-poem for the Bard? Like we did when Olaf died."

"The Bard isn't dead!" Jack didn't want to think about it.

"Not yet," said the shield maiden with relentless honesty, "but he soon will be, sealed into that tomb."

"Why don't you shut up and leave me alone!" the boy shouted. "It's one of those things you don't talk about in the dark. Go find some other barrow to haunt if you can't keep quiet." Afterward he felt ashamed of himself, but not enough to apologize. He didn't want to open a discussion. He didn't want to think. Unfortunately, he couldn't sleep either. He kept waking up all night, and all the periods of sleep were full of dreams he didn't want to remember.

The morning was cold and clear. They trudged around the island and found a stream flowing out of the mountain. "At least we won't die of thirst," said Thorgil.

"Who cares?" said Jack. "We'll either starve or die of cold. It only prolongs the misery."

"You're the one who's always telling me to cheer up."

"You're the one who has something to be cheerful about. You've got the rune of protection. I have nothing to remember the Bard with," said Jack.

"Yes, you do," said Thorgil. "You have his lore. He could have chosen anyone in the world to be his apprentice, but he chose you. He said he was very proud of you."

"What good was that?" the boy cried. "I couldn't save him from—from—" Jack walked off before he could break down, and Thorgil wisely left him alone. Instead, she waded out to some rocks to gather winkles. Her feet were blue with cold by the time she got back, and she had to jump up and down to get the feeling back. She heaped up a stack of driftwood. Jack was sitting on a rock, looking out to sea.

"Could you call up fire?" Thorgil asked him.

Jack tried, but his mind wouldn't settle.

"Never mind," the shield maiden said. "Winkles are good raw. Olaf used to eat them all the time. You dig them out with your fingernail, see?" She had found sea tangle and dulse, two kinds of seaweed, and rinsed them in the little stream to get the sand off. Little by little she induced Jack to eat, and gradually he felt better. But only slightly.

"I wish we could climb that mountain," said Thorgil, looking speculatively at the thick grove of trees at the top. "I'm sure there's food up there."

"Father Severus tried," Jack said. "He couldn't even get up there when he was trying to escape from—" His throat closed up and he couldn't say more.

"Well, I'm going back for the ropes Whush left. They might come in handy." The shield maiden walked off along the beach, and after a while, reluctantly, Jack followed her. She had found the ropes and something else they hadn't noticed in the rush to find shelter the day before. Next to the mountain, where Whush had walked the day before, was a small chest about a hand-span wide and a hand-span deep. It was made of the same dark wood as the chairs in the Shoney's audience chamber. Like them, it was inlaid with ivory.

Thorgil opened it and gasped. It was filled with jewels. Red, blue, yellow, green, and clear as ice, they sparkled in the sunlight. And among them were pearls as large as hazelnuts. "The Shoney must have sent them," she said. "But why, if he means us to perish?"

"He liked you," said Jack. "You were envious of his wealth-hoard and that made him feel good. And you told him stories about pillaging. I guess he thought you'd like to feast your eyes on a wealth-hoard of your own before you died. He can always send Whush back later to collect it." Jack spoke bitterly, wanting in a perverse way to destroy Thorgil's pleasure. How dare she be happy when the Bard was dead. *If* he was dead, the boy amended. He wasn't ready to believe it.

But Thorgil was too delighted to care. "This is what Beowulf asked for after he slew the dragon. I remember the words from the saga: 'Run quickly, dear nephew. Despoil the dragon and bring me a banquet of jewels to feast my hungry eyes.' He sure knew how to die!"

"You're both crazy," said Jack, turning away. Then he noticed the sky. It was full of the kind of clouds the Northmen called sky silk, and he remembered Rune's words. *When you have the wind at your back and sky silk moves to the right, it means a storm is coming.* These were certainly moving to the right. And swiftly. Even as he watched, the clouds thickened to a milky haze.

"Uh-oh," said Thorgil, shading her eyes.

"It's a storm, isn't it?"

"Look at the gulls. They're fleeing before it," she said. The seabirds were coming in from the sea. They screamed to one another as they circled distractedly before landing in the forest at the top of the mountain.

Jack remembered something about the smell of the air before a really big storm, something about metal. He could smell it now. The clouds had already changed from milky white to gray.

"We have to get to higher ground," Thorgil said urgently. "Storms like this produce giant waves."

"What about staying in the snail house?" said Jack, beginning to catch her alarm.

"If you want to drown. It's too close to the sea. Hurry!" Thorgil handed the rope to Jack, hefted the chest, and ran for the mountain.

They looked for a way up, but all of the apparent paths ended only a few feet above the beach. By now the sky had deepened to an ominous slate blue, and wind began to buffet them, threatening to knock them over. "Drop that cursed chest!" Jack shouted. For Thorgil, always somewhat clumsy because of her paralyzed hand, was dangerously so with the heavy box under one arm.

"Don't touch it!" she screamed when he tried to yank it

away. They both slid down the boulder they were attempting to scale and into a deep crevice in the side of the mountain.

"Put that down, or you won't be able to climb up!" Jack ordered.

"It doesn't matter. We can't get out anyway," said Thorgil, panting and hanging on to the chest.

Jack looked up. It was true. They had fallen down much farther than he had realized, and the rock was perfectly sheer. The wind howled over the top, and waves had begun to crash so violently that the spray reached them even where they were trapped.

"I guess this is it," said Thorgil. "You can tell the sea enters here because of the barnacles. It's certainly going to be flooded during this storm." A wave hit a rock and the ground trembled.

It was growing dark although it was only midday. The sky—and Jack could see only a small slice of it—was boiling with evil-looking clouds. The speed at which the weather had changed was astounding, and the far end of the crevice was so deep in shadow, it might as well have been night. He edged toward it, hoping to find a way up. He put out his hand to feel the rock and found—nothing at all.

It wasn't a shadow after all. It was the mouth of a cave.

Chapter Thirty-eight

ST. COLUMBA'S CAVE

"A cave? Let's go inside," said Thorgil.

Jack had an instinctive dislike of dark holes in the ground. So far he hadn't found anything good in them. "What about knuckers?" he said, remembering the spiderlike creature that had almost trapped him and Pega.

Thorgil paused. She had met them too. A wave shook the ground and cold water splashed over them. "If we stay here, we'll surely drown. We don't *know* that there are knuckers inside."

"There could also be wyverns, hippogriffs, manticores, basilisks, and krakens," said Jack, naming a few of the things they might find in dark tunnels. He wasn't sure what all of them were. More water sprayed over their heads.

"Those things eat you quickly," pointed out Thorgil, who seemed to have more information. "That's not so bad. Knuckers kind of *suck* at you for a long time."

"Wonderful," said Jack. They both stared at the dark opening, unwilling to move. "The Bard once said . . ." Jack swallowed and forced himself to go on. "The Bard once said that caves with no air movement are the most dangerous. This one has a breeze." He could feel a steady flow of warmer air blowing in his face.

"So . . . only wyverns, hippogriffs, and the rest to worry about," said Thorgil. A really big wave sent water swirling around their feet.

Jack slung the rope over his shoulder. He used one hand to feel the wall and the other to hold on to Thorgil. "If I disappear, you're to go back," he said.

"If you disappear, I'm going with you," she retorted.

Jack went first, slowly and cautiously. It had occurred to him that the cave could fill up with water and they'd be no better off, but the ground went up. The roof of the cave went up as well. "I say! This is lucky," Jack said. "It's a regular tunnel." The farther they went, the better he liked it, although he had no reason for this.

"Is that light?" said Thorgil.

Jack had been so absorbed with avoiding rocks, he hadn't noticed. There *was* a faint light coming from a side cave. *Side cave,* he thought, remembering the knuckers. Yet even here a breeze stirred. It was cold and smelled of the sea. When he got to the entrance, he could see that the light came from a small hole on the farther side. The ground trembled as a wave crashed nearby.

He thought he saw a man crouching in a white robe. *The Bard,* he thought, for one frozen moment. But it was a cloth draped over a rock. He expected to feel sorrow and disappointment. Instead, he was unaccountably happy, as though he'd turned aside from a dark road to find a house with a cheerful fire on the hearth. The cave was brimming with the life force.

"Why is it so nice here?" said Thorgil, coming up behind him.

"You feel it too? I don't know. It seems like a good place to rest." Jack saw other articles around the room. Yes, room. This was no ordinary cave, but the dwelling place of someone long gone. He saw a three-legged stool, cooking utensils, a cauldron, a goblet with a pattern of vines inscribed on it, and a staff. Everything was coated with fine sand that must have come in through the hole.

"Do you know what this place is?" Jack said, with dawning excitement. "This is where Father Severus found Fair Lamenting. His cave is on the other side of that hole. It was a small cave, remember, and he enlarged it with his knife until he broke through to here. He didn't realize this place was so large. He thought it was simply a hiding place."

"It would have looked dark from that side," said Thorgil.

"He reached inside and found the bell wrapped in the robe St. Columba had worn when he was head of the School of Bards. Brother Aiden said it was very fine and embroidered with gold."

"It never occurred to Father Severus to look farther," said Thorgil. They stood together in the room, caught in the wonder of it. After the total darkness of the tunnel, this place seemed bright. The walls were decorated with wonderful scenes. Swans floated sedately on painted lakes, deer gathered in a meadow, dogs leaped and barked for the pure joy of it.

"St. Columba must have made these," Thorgil said. "What was he doing here?"

"Brother Aiden said he was giving up his magic to become a Christian," said Jack. "It looks like it took him a while to make up his mind."

Thorgil sank gratefully onto the sandy floor. "I'm tired," she admitted. "There must be another way out or St. Columba couldn't have lived here, but I'm too tired to look. It wouldn't hurt to take a nap."

Jack looked around instinctively. In his experience falling asleep in a strange place was always dangerous. They could find themselves in a hogboon's barrow, for example. But if there was any place in the green world that felt safer than this cave, he couldn't imagine it. He sighed deeply. Even sorrow was forbidden here, or was unimportant.

He shook the sand off the white cloth and found that it was a well-made woolen cloak. He spread it over himself and Thorgil, for the damp wind coming through the hole was very cold. They fell asleep, burrowed into the soft sand.

"Smell that!" cried Thorgil, sitting bolt upright.

Jack was still comfortably half asleep. He hadn't rested this well since leaving the village and was unwilling to move, until the odor wafted into his nostrils too. He sat up abruptly. "That can't be what I think it is." His mouth filled with saliva and his stomach knotted.

"Wild boar," Thorgil said reverently. "Beautiful, succulent, greasy wild boar roasted over a fire."

"But how . . . ?" Jack knew from Brother Aiden's description that Grim's Island was too desolate for such large animals.

"Who cares? I know what it is and I want some." Thorgil stood up and swayed on her feet. "By Thor, I'm weak with hunger!"

"Is the smell coming from outside?"

"No. From there." The shield maiden pointed at the dark tunnel. "Do you suppose St. Columba is still hanging about?"

"The Bard said he sailed for the Islands of the Blessed long ago," said Jack. Strangely, he wasn't sad thinking of the Bard now. He felt slightly guilty about it, but almost instantly that regret vanished as well. It was impossible to be depressed here. Jack went out into the tunnel and sniffed. The odor was coming from somewhere above them. "Whoever it is, I hope he's generous."

"We should take the cloak," Thorgil said. She rummaged around and found a carrying bag with straps that fitted over her shoulders. "This is perfect! I can put my wealth-hoard in here."

"I don't know," Jack said doubtfully. "St. Columba meant to abandon these things. Look what happened when Father Severus carried off Fair Lamenting."

"That's because Father Severus didn't understand magic," the shield maiden said reasonably. "You do. You're a bard."

"Not really," said Jack.

"Well, you're the closest thing we've got. Now put on that cloak and pick up that staff. It will make a decent weapon if we run into trouble. I'd take the cauldron except it's too heavy—now what's wrong?"

Jack had turned very pale. "You can't take a bard's staff."

"Don't be silly. St. Columba isn't going to want it back."

"You don't understand. Such things have to be earned." Jack had never, ever dared to ask the Bard to borrow his. It was one of those things you didn't do. A lifetime of experience went into crafting the magic. Life itself gave power to a staff—all the minutes and hours and days of a person, all the memories, hopes, triumphs, friendships, sorrows, and mistakes. They went into the wood to be called up at need.

Jack had only begun to build this lore when he used his staff to free Din Guardi. It had crumbled into dust.

"You used to have a staff. How did you earn that one?" said Thorgil.

It was when they were in Jotunheim, he told her, crossing the frozen waste to the Mountain Queen's palace. Thorgil's ankle had been broken and Jack went in search of wood to make her a crutch. He found an ash tree, a most unusual plant in such a cold place, with two branches exactly suited for his needs. One had a fork at one end for Thorgil to lean on. The other reminded him of the gnarled, blackened wood the Bard used. He decided to make himself a walking stick from it. It was only later he realized that the ash had been an offshoot of the great tree Yggdrassil.

"You see?" Thorgil said triumphantly. "The gods meant you to have that staff, and now you are meant to have this one."

Jack wanted to believe it, but he was afraid. "I'm not worthy," he said.

"Probably not, but you have to start somewhere," Thorgil argued. "It's like learning to be a warrior. You get knocked around a lot at the beginning."

Jack's hand hovered over the staff. He could feel a thrum of power in the air. "If it burns me to ashes, you'll be sorry."

"If you don't do something soon, I'm going to die of hunger, and *you'll* be sorry."

Jack grasped the staff, and it was as though a sheet of light wrapped him from head to toe. He saw the entire island in a flash: the seas battering the shore, the stormy clouds, the dark mountain and forest on top. He saw men fighting one another with swords. Then the vision was gone. He slumped, still holding the staff.

"Well? Are you burned to ashes yet?" the shield maiden demanded.

"I'm not sure. I think the problem will be to avoid burning up other things," said Jack. He felt dizzy. "I hope I'm strong enough to control this."

"You'll be fine. You're Dragon Tongue's successor."

"Don't say that!" A flame licked out of the end of the staff and left a black mark on the ceiling. "Oh, Freya! Don't make

me angry," Jack begged. "I need time to get used to so much power. I meant to say that I'll never be Dragon Tongue's successor. I'm only his apprentice."

Thorgil shouldered the pack carrying her wealth-hoard and went outside. "I'd say if we don't get to the end of this tunnel fast, there won't be anything left of that boar except bristles."

Chapter Thirty-nine

ODIN

Jack slung the cloak over his shoulders, and to his surprise it fit perfectly. It had seemed larger when he'd used it as a blanket for himself and Thorgil. The staff, too, was exactly the right height. The dizziness passed and Jack was able to walk steadily. The tunnel turned pitch-black only a few paces from the side cave. He called up a spell in a language he did not consciously know. He could not have repeated the words, but the meaning stayed with him:

> Keep foot from fall,
> Hold head from harm.
> Drive dark from day.

A gentle light radiated from the staff to reveal the gray walls of the tunnel. A path of white sand went up before them.

"Now, that's a trick worth learning," said Thorgil, who had been about to walk into a wall.

"It's not a trick, and I don't know how I did it," Jack said. "We'd better hurry, because I don't know how long this spell will last."

The smell of roast pork grew stronger the higher they went, and soon it was mixed with the odors of many other good things. "I wonder what they're celebrating," said Thorgil. "They're certainly making a lot of noise."

"That's not a celebration." Jack stopped her from going farther.

"By Thor, you're right! I can hear swords."

"I should have told you earlier—when I touched the staff, I had a vision of men fighting on this mountaintop. I thought it was only my imagination. How could a troop of men climb up here and still have the energy to fight?"

They heard cries and oaths. A man screamed as he was wounded. "Perhaps there's another tunnel," suggested Thorgil.

"That still leaves the question of why anyone would do such a stupid thing," Jack said. "It's so brainless, it could almost be berserkers."

He expected Thorgil to argue—she always championed berserkers—but she grabbed his arm. "I know that voice!"

"*Gaaaahhh!* That's the third time I've cut your head off today, Bjorn!" someone roared. "You've gone soft!"

"That's Olaf One-Brow," cried Thorgil. "I know it is! What's happened to us? Are we dead and don't know it?"

"Olaf! Watch your back!" shouted someone else whose voice was familiar.

"*Arghh!*" bellowed Olaf. "You think that's going to stop me? You'll need at least three spears to slow me down."

Jack heard the sound of something being messily plucked out of flesh. "Pick up your head, Bjorn, or I'll use it as a football," said the voice he now recognized as Eric Broad-Shoulders's. Eric, Jack remembered, had been eaten by trolls.

"If you want to kick something, you'll need *two* legs," jeered Bjorn. Everyone laughed heartily at the joke. Someone blew a horn and the sounds of fighting ceased.

Thorgil had collapsed against the wall, trembling violently. "I don't know what's going on, but I'm sure we're alive," Jack said, kneeling beside her. He guessed that she was terrified of meeting the dead, and he wasn't all that thrilled about it either. He'd run into a lot of unquiet spirits recently, from the *draugr* to the men trapped in the wall to the hogboon.

"I'm so afraid," she moaned. "It's like the night of the Wild Hunt. Olaf wouldn't take me along because Odin wouldn't let him. Oh, Jack, what if we go out there and he—he—rejects me?" She burst into tears.

Of course, thought Jack. Thorgil wasn't afraid of a host of dead berserkers who, by the sound of it, had spent a happy day slicing one another to bits. She was afraid they wouldn't let her join in. He could see the opening at the top of the tunnel. Night had fallen, but a bonfire nearby cast flickering light. A large figure suddenly eclipsed it.

"Don't hang back now," a man called. "We have food aplenty and the party's just beginning." He lumbered down the tunnel and picked up Thorgil. "You're too dainty for a Valkyrie," he rumbled. "Get on the outside of a haunch of boar and we'll see you right."

"Don't touch her!" Jack cried, pointing his staff, but nothing happened. No fire sprouted out of the end, and the man was completely unaffected. He laughed good-naturedly, and Jack could see a line of red where his head had been reattached. So this was Bjorn.

"You come too, little skald," said Bjorn. "I haven't seen your kind since Dragon Tongue scorched the fur off Ivar the Boneless for marrying Frith. Plenty of boar to go around."

"It's all right," said Thorgil, tucked under the warrior's arm. Jack followed them up, feeling somewhat foolish. The cloak and staff of St. Columba ought to have earned him *some* respect. Little skald indeed!

They came out to a completely wild scene. The whole mountaintop was covered with warriors wandering among the trees to find parts of themselves that had been hacked off. They fitted hands back on to wrists, feet onto ankles, heads on to necks. When reapplied, only a line showed where they had been joined, and the scars faded quickly. Bjorn's neck was already completely healed. Other men stuffed intestines into gaping holes in their stomachs, and the skin grew back.

Horses huddled in clearings, their eyes glinting whitely.

Above the trees the clouds rushed by in a mighty, soundless storm.

A giant boar was roasting over a fire pit, and dozens of warriors were hacking off bits to devour. Tables were laden with all manner of food, including pots of nauseating *graffisk*, codfish that had been buried underground until it smelled of the graveyard. Beefy Valkyries in leather armor served horns of drink to the feasting men.

In the middle of a clearing a Valkyrie sat behind an enormous, surly-looking goat. She monotonously pulled on teats the size of grain bags and liquid thundered into a washtub.

"The goat's name is Heidrun," said Bjorn, putting Thorgil down. "She feeds on the leaves of Yggdrassil and produces an endless supply of mead. *Good* Heidrun," he said, patting the beast on the head. The creature snapped at him.

"Don't Valkyries have names?" Thorgil said faintly. The women were moving around the forest, finding men who were too injured to move. They reattached missing parts and dragged the warriors to the tables, where they fed them morsels of food. "Dotti and Lotti used to baby Olaf like that when he came home drunk."

Jack had once made fun of Valkyries, claiming that they were no better than servants in Valhalla. He had driven Thorgil into a fury, but he felt no wish to do so now. She looked stricken. This was the ideal she had always held in her mind, to fall in battle and join her comrades in Odin's realm. Only now it seemed she would be consigned to waiting on tables and milking goats.

"I want to see Olaf," she said in a tearful voice.

"You mean Olaf One-Brow? He's my best friend," said Bjorn proudly.

In spite of cutting your head off three times today, thought Jack. "You wouldn't happen to be Bjorn Skull-Splitter?" he asked. The warrior was almost as big as Olaf, with legs like tree trunks and a chest as broad as a door.

Bjorn grinned. "I see my fame has not died in Middle Earth. Tell me, little skald, am I sung about wherever brave men gather?"

"Your tale has certainly spread," Jack said evasively. Einar Adder-Tooth had been wrong in one regard: Bjorn wasn't roaming the icy halls of Hel. "Would you like to know what happened to your—" Jack had been about to say *enemy* when he saw a familiar figure emerge from the forest and snatch a horn of mead from a Valkyrie. "That can't be Einar Adder-Tooth!"

"He arrived recently," said Bjorn. "Said he'd been caught in a landslide. I killed him twice last week, and he only got me once." The warrior showed not the slightest resentment toward the man who'd arranged for him to be devoured by a hogboon.

I'll never understand Northmen, Jack thought.

Thorgil swayed and almost fell. "I want to see Olaf," she repeated. But by now Bjorn had been distracted by the appearance of Adder-Tooth and went over to deliver a friendly punch to his head.

"Sit down," Jack said. "I'll find him."

This proved difficult, for dozens of men were careening around, stuffing themselves, drinking, and bragging about their victories. One patted a Valkyrie on the behind, and she snarled, "Try that again and I'll rip out your windpipe."

"Haw! Haw! Haw!" laughed the warriors all around. One voice sounded familiar.

Jack saw him seated at the foot of a throne. He was wearing his helmet, which was probably why Jack hadn't recognized him before. It had a ridge across the top like a cock's comb and two panels at the sides to cover his cheeks. The front was a metal mask like a hawk's face and the beak came down over Olaf's nose. His eyes peered out of holes and made him seem otherworldly. *He is otherworldly,* Jack thought.

But the figure that towered over Olaf, the one sitting on the throne, was so terrifying that Jack almost sank to his knees. He wore a helmet similar to Olaf's, but only one eye glinted through the holes in the mask. The other was an empty socket. Jack knew who he was.

Odin's missing eye lay at the bottom of Mimir's Well. No one could drink from the well without sacrificing something of great importance. Jack had given up his rune of protection. Thorgil had given up her status as a berserker. In return they had gained the knowledge they needed most. Odin, in payment for his eye, had acquired the lore necessary to rule the nine worlds.

The god's single eye blazed like a star as he considered the boy. Wolves—Jack noticed them now for the first time—lounged at the god's feet, and ravens perched on his shoulders to bring him news of the wide world. *You are not one of mine*, said a voice like distant thunder.

I am not one of yours, Jack agreed, clutching St. Columba's staff. *I serve the life force. I do not believe in a world of endless killing.* He was very afraid, but at the same time, he knew it was important to stand up to this being.

The figure laughed. Both air and earth shook with it. *You sound like a puny Christian,* or *perhaps one of those harp-strumming skalds always yowling about trees.* One of the wolves stood up and yawned. Its tongue lolled out between its fangs.

A single leaf unfurling in springtime is worth more than all your realm, said Jack, surprising himself. He hadn't planned to say that. It was one thing to resist the awesome power before him and quite another to pick a fight.

War is inevitable, Odin thundered. *All exists to kill and be killed, and only courage in the face of death is beautiful.*

What good is this courage when you fear life itself? said Jack. *If you are deaf to the laughter of your children or cannot under-stand why your wives rejoice when you return from a voyage, are you not already dead? What courage does it take to leave a world when you are blind to its wonders?* Jack was pretty impressed with his poetry, but he was also afraid of how Odin might react. He didn't seem able to stop arguing. The words simply rolled out.

In the end night covers all, said the war god. *The bonds of this world will break, and Garm, the hound of Hel, will be freed from his leash. The frost giants will make war upon light. The ship of death, made from the finger- and toenails of corpses, will set sail to bring destruction upon the living. Ragnarok is coming, the final battle. None can escape it.*

Jack gazed at the being looming up and up and up until it brushed the racing clouds. His blood sang in his ears as it had on the Northman ship with the waves foaming beneath the prow and a fine breeze following. *Your world is only one leaf on the Great Tree*, Jack said. *It is already falling from the branch. I do not believe in Ragnarok.* Warmth spread from St. Columba's staff to his hand and on to the rest of his body. A light radiated and fell on the throne.

It was empty.

It wasn't even a throne, but an outcropping of gray stone that had weathered until it was pitted and broken. Lumps of rock at the side had been the wolves.

Olaf One-Brow was sitting on one of the lumps. He removed his helmet and squinted at the boy. "Jack!" he cried delightedly. "How did you get here? Don't tell me you fell in battle."

Jack's ears still sang with blood. It took him a moment to realize where he was. "I'm not dead, Olaf. At least I don't think so. Thorgil's with me, but she's afraid you don't want to see her."

Chapter Forty

A JOYFUL REUNION

They found her eating at one of the tables. She dropped the chicken leg she was holding and held out her arms.

"What a treat, heart-daughter!" bellowed Olaf, swinging her into the air. "The very idea, thinking I wouldn't welcome you! Nothing could cheer this battle-scarred old heart more. It's too bad you didn't see me earlier. I killed five warriors and maimed a dozen others."

"I heard the last part of it, when you cut off Bjorn Skull-Splitter's head." Thorgil was laughing and crying at the same time.

"Between you and me, he got soft sitting around on Horse Island," Olaf confided. "But he acquitted himself well at the end." He put the shield maiden down.

Her knees buckled and she had to hold on to him. "I'm sorry, heart-father. I've been on short rations for a while."

"That's easily fixed," her foster father said. He went to the fire pit and tore off a rib blackened with smoke. Jack was surprised to see that so much meat was left after the scores of warriors who had been feasting. Perhaps the boar, like Heidrun, was a never-ending supply of food.

"Is it safe to eat?" Jack said, though the smell was driving him mad. "I mean, for the living."

"Who cares?" said Thorgil, tearing into the meat. Soon her face was smeared with grease and soot. Olaf fetched her another rib, as well as one for Jack. The boy ate carefully, mindful of St. Columba's white cloak, and wiped his fingers on the grass. He was still somewhat dazed from his encounter with Odin. How could he have dared to challenge such a foe? It seemed that St. Columba's staff had a will of its own.

They helped themselves to pickled herring, grouse, leeks in cream sauce, baked apples, and many other wonderful dishes from the tables. Olaf thrust a bowl of purplish lumps floating in a slimy gray liquid in front of Jack's nose. "*Graffisk*. Have some," he urged.

Jack almost threw up at the odor of rotten teeth and bilge water. "No, thanks."

"HAVE SOME," roared the Northman.

But Jack was no longer a frightened slave in fear for his life. "IT'S THE NASTIEST STUFF I'VE EVER SEEN. YOU EAT IT," he roared back.

And to his very great surprise Olaf did. "I don't understand why people don't enjoy this," the giant said as he mopped up nauseating gobbets of *graffisk* with bread. "I had to sit on Dotti and Lotti to force it down their throats. They never did get the hang of it." He shook his head over the perversity of wives.

By the time they were finished, most of the men had passed out. Valkyries were dragging them into orderly rows near the fire pit. The warrior women settled around Heidrun and dipped their drinking horns into the tub of mead. "Do you remember that battle where I picked up the wrong hero by mistake?" one of them remembered.

"Oh, yes!" another said. "You had to drop him and go back. It was someone who'd converted to Christianity, and they had a claim on him."

"It's getting harder and harder to sort them out," the first one said.

Jack and Thorgil found a stream near the clearing and washed their faces and hands. "I'm confused," Thorgil said to Olaf when they had returned to the table. "Is Grim's Island a corner of Valhalla?"

"No, Valhalla is much more glorious than this," said Olaf, leaning back and gazing at the storm clouds rushing past. "Its walls are made of thousands of spears, and its ceiling is covered in shields as thick as shells on a beach. It has hundreds of doors, enough for all the berserkers in the world to rush out at once, when Ragnarok is declared."

Ragnarok, thought Jack. What an evil destiny, for warriors to slaughter one another endlessly until the final battle, where they each got slaughtered for the last time.

"You have no idea how magnificent everything is, and yet . . ." A look of regret crossed Olaf's face. "I mean, I'm honored to be there with the gods, but sometimes it's just a little too grand for me. I miss honest dirt. And trees. And rolling in a meadow. That's why some of us get together for a Wild Hunt."

"So this is a Wild Hunt," said Jack.

"Grim's Island is where we rest up afterward," the giant explained. "It's a fine place. Good forest, plenty of kindling, no nosy neighbors."

The boy suddenly remembered the blacksmith's slaves, Gog and Magog. "Exactly *what* do you hunt?"

"Our old piggy. Sæhrímnir is his name." Olaf pointed at the fire pit where the boar was still roasting.

"But he's . . . dead."

"So are most of us at the end of the day," said the giant. "We pull ourselves together and go on. Tomorrow morning Sæhrímnir's bones will cover themselves with flesh and he'll be pawing the ground, ready for another run."

It didn't sound like fun, getting roasted every night, but maybe the boar liked it. He was probably as dim-witted as the berserkers. What bothered Jack most was that Thorgil valued this afterlife. "When you came through our village," he said, "there was a pair of brothers called Gog and Magog. They liked to sit outside during storms and watch the sky. After you left, they were gone."

"Gog and Magog. I didn't know they had names," said Olaf. He went over to the mead bucket, shoved a Valkyrie aside, and filled his horn. "They're around here somewhere. They were so pleased to see us that we brought them along. They've been as happy as a pair of ticks on a fat dog ever since. They stay on this mountain all the time, keeping the campsite tidy, gathering kindling, and so on. Very restful companions, Gog and Magog. Never bother you with conversation."

Jack was aware that Thorgil had said nothing for some time. He glanced at her and saw that one of her gloomy moods was building up inside, not unlike the storm clouds boiling overhead. He knew the reason for it, of course. Olaf had chosen Gog and Magog over her. "Why did you leave Thorgil behind?" Jack said.

She looked up, her face pale with emotion.

"Leave her where?" Olaf belched richly and wiped his mouth on his arm.

"When you went over our village, she begged you to take her with you."

"She did?"

"Yes, I did," cried Thorgil. The paleness was being replaced with a rosy flush of irritation. "Only, I didn't beg. I *asked*, and you looked down and pretended you couldn't see me. And then you rode off. It's because I have a paralyzed hand, isn't it?" Jack was almost relieved. Anger had replaced sorrow, and with Thorgil, this was a much easier thing to deal with.

Olaf looked puzzled. "Believe me, daughter, I didn't know you were there. We'd just picked up Gog and Magog, and

Sæhrímnir was running for all he was worth. I had my eye on that pig and my spear was ready to bring him down. Are you sure you saw me?"

"Of course!" shouted Thorgil.

"Put it down to the heat of battle, then. There's a blindness that comes over you when you're really involved. At any rate, an injury doesn't disqualify you from entering Valhalla. Tyr had his hand chomped off by Fenris. Hoder is blind and still leads men into battle. He sometimes hits the wrong target, though," Olaf said thoughtfully. "They have special privileges because they're gods, but I've seen a number of men missing body parts. What keeps you out of Valhalla is being alive."

Olaf drained his mead-horn, oblivious to Thorgil's simmering emotions.

"I suppose I could throw myself off this mountain," the shield maiden said sarcastically.

"There you go. You'd find yourself in Valhalla in no time. Hey, Brynhilda! Stir your stumps and fetch us another horn of mead." A Valkyrie stood up from the group clustered around Heidrun and obeyed.

"But I've sworn an oath to save Dragon Tongue's daughter. I can't die until I fulfill it," Thorgil said sulkily.

"Oh, well. I guess you'll have to wait," said Olaf, who didn't sound particularly disappointed. "How is old Dragon Tongue? Is he still making Northman kings run for cover?"

Jack stepped in before Thorgil could completely lose her temper. He described the visit to Notland, and sorrow weighed heavily upon him as he recalled how the Bard had walked into the tomb with the *draugr* following. But Olaf listened with only half an ear. Perhaps that was how it was with the dead. Being shut into a tomb wasn't the devastating thing it was to the living.

It was clear something else was on Olaf's mind, and after Jack was finished, the giant said shyly, "You wouldn't mind . . . I mean, it would please me very much . . ." He blushed deeply. "I'd really like to hear that praise-poem you wrote for me again."

And so Jack recounted the poem he'd sung in the court of King Ivar the Boneless, and again on Olaf's funeral pyre:

Listen, ring-bearers, while I speak
Of the glories of battle, of Olaf, most brave.
Generous is he, that striker of terror. . . .

When he was finished, Olaf sighed with pleasure. Jack saw, to his delight, that Gog and Magog had crept out of whatever shadows they'd been hiding in. He was never sure how much they understood, but the joy on their faces showed they had liked the music.

Thorgil was nodding with exhaustion, and Jack longed to lie down and sleep. Olaf told the silent brothers to carry them to the beach. "Isn't it too stormy?" said Thorgil, stifling a yawn.

"The storm is over," Olaf said. "We ride for Valhalla in the morning."

She was so tired, she didn't have the strength to grieve at their final parting. She fetched the pack with her wealth-hoard and kissed her heart-father on the cheek. He ruffled her hair. Then Gog and Magog picked up Jack and Thorgil, and climbed down the sheer rocks of the mountain as easily as a pair of spiders coming down a wall. They laid them in front of the snail house and were gone.

Jack and Thorgil fell asleep on the sand. They didn't awaken until the sun was high in the sky and the storm clouds had been gathered away into the utter north.

Chapter Forty-one

RESCUE

"Did it really happen? Was it a dream?" said Thorgil, staring out to sea the next morning. A mild sunlight had brought warmth to the beach and gray-green waves lapped gently against the shore.

"I still have St. Columba's cloak and staff," said Jack.

Thorgil shivered. "Then it's true we ate the food of the dead. What will it do to us?"

"Keep us from being hungry for a while." Jack thought longingly of roast salmon, grouse, and leeks with cream sauce. Certain parts of the previous night still seemed unbelievable to him. Had he really stood toe-to-toe with Odin? Other parts—the warriors slashing at each other—were depressingly familiar.

"Did you see how those Valkyries were treated?" said Thorgil. "I would never, ever let anyone order me around like that. 'Get me a horn of mead. Fetch me some bread.'"

"'Put my head back on for me,'" Jack said, stifling a laugh.

"That too," the shield maiden said, completely without humor. "All my life I've wanted to go to Valhalla. Now . . ."

"The Bard said people get to choose their afterlife. He's probably on the Islands of the Blessed right now." Jack blinked back tears. The wonderful calm he'd felt in St. Columba's cave didn't extend to the beach. "I'm a Christian, so I guess I'll wind up in Heaven eventually."

"What do people do there?"

"I'm not sure," Jack admitted. He felt listless after the turmoil of the past weeks—the battle with the hogboon, the trip to Notland, the loss of the Bard. It was enough to sit here on the pale sand and listen to the lapping of the waves. But of course he couldn't do it forever. Today was only a brief pause between storms. They'd have to find food and they had to build a boat. *Out of what?* Jack thought. *Driftwood? Seaweed?* Perhaps Gog and Magog could fell trees, if he could get to the top of the mountain and ask them.

Thorgil had opened her treasure chest. She ran her fingers through the gems, letting them fall back into the box with a soft patter. "I must be coming down with a cold," she said. "I don't find any pleasure in this."

"Perhaps like the Shoney, you need someone to covet a wealth-hoard before you can enjoy it," Jack said.

After a while they explored the foot of the mountain, hunting for the way into St. Columba's cave, but they didn't find it. Later the weather turned cold, and it rained for three days. They scoured the rocks for shellfish. Jack was able to call up fire in the fragments of driftwood they found, so they had cooked food. They were never warm enough. They huddled together under St. Columba's robe in the snail house. As before, it was large enough for both of them at night, and small enough to fit Jack perfectly in the morning.

A dullness crept over them, an unwillingness to do anything unnecessary. Jack stared at the water for hours without actually seeing it. Thorgil sorted her gems into different-colored piles and mixed them up again. Neither spoke.

But on the fourth day things changed. A flock of seagulls fled screaming over the island, and Jack shaded his eyes to look for signs of a storm. Thorgil dropped an armload of sea kale she had gathered and yelled, "It's Seafarer! It's Seafarer!" She jumped up and down, shrieking in Bird. The distant dot changed direction and came toward them.

Seafarer! Lord of the sky! Widest of wing! Thorgil screamed.

Pecks-from-Afar! Great happiness! Long searching! the albatross screamed in answer. He landed on the sand, and the two of them danced around each other in ecstasy. When the excitement died down, Seafarer told them Skakki had been hunting for them. *Sea-nest coming,* he said, giving his word for *ship. I bring.* He was off again.

Very soon they saw the striped red and white sail and the

oars flashing as they dipped into the sea. Jack could see Schlaup looming amidships. When the craft came near to shore, the giant jumped overboard and towed it onto the sand.

"At last!" cried Skakki, hugging Thorgil. "I thought we'd never find you. We couldn't find a trace of the coracle after we dropped you off, so I went back to Horse Island to fetch Schlaup. He kept sniffing for you, but he couldn't find a trail until today. Where's Dragon Tongue?"

Jack had to repeat the story of Notland and the *draugr*. "I knew something bad would come of trusting the fin folk," said Skakki. "Can you find the location of their kingdom? Perhaps I can deal with them."

"We could always invade," Sven the Vengeful suggested. "My hands are itching to put a spear through one of those bog worms."

"No one can find them if they don't want to be found," said Jack. All the anger and regret came flooding back as he remembered the swiftness with which the fin folk had turned on them. "The only comfort is that the Bard chose his fate willingly."

"Aye, he would," said Rune, with tears trickling down his withered face. "If I had a tenth of his courage, I'd count myself lucky. The oddest thing happened, though. When we were still far off this island, I thought I saw him standing on the shore. But it was you, Jack, in that new white cloak. Where on earth did you get it and that staff?"

"It's a long story," the boy said wearily.

They made camp on Grim's Island that night, using rations

from the ship because little else was available. Jack unfolded the saga of St. Columba's cave and the tunnel leading up through the heart of the mountain. When he got to the part about Olaf, everyone cried out in disbelief.

Thorgil shouted them down. "He was there! I saw him!"

"If you could see the dead," Eric the Rash said, his eyes rounded with fear, "then you must be dead too—ow!"

Thorgil had poked him viciously with a branch from the fire. "Does that feel like a ghost?"

"I don't know. Maybe." The warrior rubbed the burn on his arm.

"My little sister is not a draugr*!"* roared Schlaup. His body got larger and lumpier, and everyone got ready to flee.

"Of course she's not a *draugr*," Rune said quickly. "Dragon Tongue used to say there were paths between the nine worlds for those with the eyes to see them. You don't have to be dead to use them."

Schlaup's shape settled back to normal.

Jack told them of Bjorn Skull-Splitter and Einar Adder-Tooth, and no one was surprised to find bitter enemies in the same afterlife. "IT'S MORE FUN TO SLICE UP ENEMIES THAN FRIENDS," Eric Pretty-Face explained.

Everyone listened rapturously as the boy described Heidrun, whose udders gave never-ending mead, and Sæhrímnir, who was devoured each night and sprang to life again in the morning. "Mead and roast pork forever," Sven the Vengeful said with a sigh. "You can't beat it."

Jack spoke of Valkyries and—with a glance at Thorgil

to see how she was taking it—of how they cared for heroes after a day of fighting. Most of all, he spoke of Olaf, but he kept secret the encounter with Odin.

"I wish I could have seen Father," said Skakki wistfully as they sat around a driftwood fire rippling with blue and green flames. "It's so like him not to be satisfied with Valhalla. He never stayed in one place long and used to spend one winter out of three with the Mountain Queen. Speaking of which, I'm giving Father's hall to Schlaup once I've moved the family to Horse Island. I think he'll be happier there."

Jack thought so too. Both he and Thorgil congratulated Schlaup.

"You can visit. Everyone can visit," the giant said. "When winter comes"—he paused to organize the words—"my sisters, Fonn and Forath, will stay. They like snow."

And a jolly time they'll have too, thought Jack. He could see Mrs. Tanner roasting elks in the fireplace and the troll-maidens smiling, or at least baring their fangs, at Ymma and Ythla.

In the morning, before they set sail, Skakki and Schlaup looked for a way onto the mountain. Even the half-troll couldn't haul himself up the sheer cliffs, nor were they able to find St. Columba's cave. When Jack wriggled into the small cave where Father Severus had spent a winter and reached through the hole at the end, his hand met rock only a few inches away.

It's like the hazel wood, Jack thought. *The paths open only when it's time for them to open.*

❖ ❖ ❖

Summer was over and the wheel of the year had turned toward fall. They sailed back along the coast to Bebba's Town. There was need to hurry, for trees were changing color and the few fields they passed were yellow. They reminded Jack of the barrows in Notland, and he felt a sadness that would not lift. For the first time in his life he had no direction.

First, he had been a farm brat chasing sheep. Then he became the Bard's apprentice. He had been carried off to the Northland with his sister and had won their freedom. He'd had to set forth again when she was kidnapped by the Lady of the Lake. Each adventure had led to new adventures, with periods between to rest up. Now he had only one task left: to rescue the Bard's daughter. What would he do when that was accomplished?

He wasn't ready to be a bard. True, he could do a few tricks and remembered some of the recipes for elixirs. But it was depressingly clear to him that he wasn't much better than the third-rate skald Adder-Tongue had hired to sing praises. Would that be his fate—to go from hall to hall like Big Half and Little Half until people got tired of him and threw him out?

Thorgil, too, was immersed in gloom. She wouldn't recite her bloodthirsty poetry even when Eric Pretty-Face asked her nicely to sing about freezing to death. She was closed in, not accessible to anyone except Seafarer. The bird sat by her constantly, crooning softly. "He is mourning his lost flock," she translated on one of the few occasions she consented to talk. "They are lost in the far south and he will never see them again."

Jack knew she was thinking about her shattered dream of becoming a Valkyrie.

The ship sped before a swift wind, and soon they had passed Edwin's Town and were approaching the Holy Isle. Jack saw a few campfires on the isle after dark and guessed that monks were trying to rebuild the monastery.

They arrived at Bebba's Town in the middle of the night, the only safe time for a shipload of berserkers and a half-troll to dock. "I wish I didn't have to leave you," Skakki said as they silently rowed to shore. "I'm afraid to wait. I can smell ice on the wind. As it is, we'll be lucky to get Egil to Horse Island before winter sets in."

"Don't worry about us," Thorgil said listlessly.

"I do worry, little sister. Why don't you come with us?"

"I've given an oath to save Dragon Tongue's daughter."

"But what will you do afterward?" Skakki asked.

"If the snows hold off, we'll go on to the village," said Jack. "If not, we'll spend the winter with King Brutus." The boy had no enthusiasm for either path. He would be an embarrassment to the village, not skilled enough for a bard and too educated for a farm brat. King Brutus would put up with him for a while, but the Lady of the Lake was obviously more to the king's liking. Eventually, Jack would have to move on.

"I don't like this," said Skakki.

"It is our fate," Thorgil said. "In the spring look for us

again, or if you don't find us, we'll meet in Valhalla." She looked away. Jack knew she had no real hope, or desire, now to go to Valhalla.

"Little sister," rumbled Schlaup, planting a large kiss on the shield maiden's head, "you can stay with me."

"Perhaps I will," Thorgil said sadly. Jack knew she didn't belong there, either.

The ship pulled into the dock, and Schlaup lifted both of them out. "Be careful. I'll look for you in spring," said Skakki. The ship pulled away, and Jack watched it disappear in the darkness. Gone were his friends Rune, Sven the Vengeful, Eric Pretty-Face, Eric the Rash, Skakki, and Schlaup. For a moment he felt as though he had been sealed into a tomb. Then he scolded himself for self-pity.

Chapter Forty-two

FLYING VENOM

"I told Seafarer I was going to look for a nesting site," said Thorgil. "He understood that. His kind do it every year. Skakki will take him to Horse Island, where there are dozens of rocks covered with seabirds for company. Perhaps a lady albatross will be blown there someday."

They carried their belongings along the dock, and Jack noticed that there were no ships in the harbor. He found this odd. Bebba's Town wasn't as important as Edwin's Town, but it was still a thriving port. Even in winter, there should have been a few vessels waiting out the storms.

They found a secluded beach and made camp under some trees above the high tide line. But they slept fitfully, for in places with many people, thieves were possible. "I suppose it's safe to build a fire," said Jack as the wet fog surrounding them turned pale with dawn. In spite of St. Columba's robe, both of them were cold and damp. The wood they gathered was damp too, but Jack was able to call up fire with the new staff. "Does that work better than your old staff?" Thorgil asked. She spread her travel cloak out to dry.

"It's different." Jack had used it to call up fire, drive away annoying flies, and summon a wind—things he'd already learned. But sometimes St. Columba's staff had a mind of its own. On the way to Bebba's Town, Eric Pretty-Face had complained about a hangnail. Jack had impulsively grasped the warrior's hand. Warmth had spread from the staff to both of them, and when he let go of Eric's hand, the hangnail was gone.

The Northman was spooked by this. So was Jack. He didn't like powers he couldn't control.

Thorgil unpacked a bag of dried fish and berries. "It's awfully quiet here," she remarked.

Jack raised his head to listen. She was right. They weren't far from the dock, and normally there would be a hubbub of noises at this time of the morning. "Perhaps it's a holiday."

"Or perhaps a dragon landed and ate everyone up." Thorgil sucked on the fish. It was too tough to chew.

"There aren't any dragons here."

"Until now." The shield maiden smiled with a trace of her old malice. Jack thought she must be feeling better.

They ate and listened to the drip of fog and the whisper

of the sea advancing and retreating. The beach was sheltered from large waves by outlying islands. Finally, the fog began to lift and a wan sun appeared in the east. It didn't bring much warmth.

"It's a long walk and we should begin," said Jack, lifting his carrying bag and taking up his staff. They made their way to the dock. From there they took a path to the main road leading to Din Guardi. Even now, they saw no one and the harbor was entirely empty. A light mist fumed from the ground. The silence and muted light made everything seem remote, as though they, Jack and Thorgil, were walking through another world.

"This had better not be glamour," said Thorgil, kicking at a stone.

"I don't know what it is," Jack said uneasily. "It's too quiet." But at that moment a company of Saxon men suddenly loomed before them. They didn't look as dangerous or as well trained as the Northmen, but they were armed with the crude weapons available to villagers.

"Halt! No one goes farther!" shouted their captain. "Where've you come from?"

"The harbor," said Jack.

"Then go back to your ship. No one enters Bebba's Town."

"Why not? Has there been an invasion?"

The captain laughed bitterly. "Aye, you could say that. Flying venom has struck this town."

"Flying venom!" echoed Jack. "How bad is it?"

"It burns you with fever. Or it enters the lungs and you drown. No matter what it does, in the end you die. So far it has been contained in the monastery, but Father Severus has ordered us to keep all folk indoors and all travelers away."

"What about King Brutus?" Thorgil asked.

The captain spat. "Don't worry about him. He feasts every night with his courtiers. We can smell the food and hear fine music, but none enter or leave. It is said the Lady of the Lake keeps him company."

Jack's mind was whirling with possibilities. This had to be the disease the *draugr* breathed into the face of Mrs. Tanner's brother. "We must see King Brutus at once," he said.

"Not likely! His gates are locked."

"What about Father Severus?" Jack said.

"The monastery is the last place you want to be," the captain said. He crossed himself and his men followed suit. "When the disease spread from their infirmary to the monks, Father Severus ordered the monastery doors sealed. They will not be opened until spring."

"But the monks will die!" cried Jack. *Ethne will die*, he thought.

"Aye, and find welcome in Heaven. Go back to your ship, young travelers, and thank God for such saints as Father Severus. There hasn't been a case of flying venom since he sealed their doors."

"We'll take our chances," said Jack, with more courage than he felt. He stood as tall as possible, with the white robe of St. Columba about his shoulders and the staff at his side.

"You will not," the captain replied. "We've been given orders to slay those who disobey." His men fanned out across the road. They grasped their knives, clubs, and axes.

Orders from Father Severus, no doubt, the boy thought. He wondered how many hapless travelers had been killed with those crude weapons.

"Return or die!"

Jack began to speak. He didn't know where the words came from, or even what language they were. But the meaning hovered briefly in his mind:

> *I arise today through the strength of Heaven,*
> *Light of sun, brilliance of moon,*
> *Splendor of fire, speed of lightning,*
> *Swiftness of wind, depth of sea,*
> *Stability of earth, firmness of rock.*
> *I summon today all these powers*
> *Between me and this evil.*

A light filled the air around him. He placed the robe of St. Columba around Thorgil, and the light covered her as well.

"Where are they? What happened to them?" shouted the captain of the Saxons. The men scattered along the road, probing bushes with their clubs.

"It's wizardry!" one of them cried. "Satan is after us!" At that, all the men panicked and fled, with the captain following and bawling orders at them.

They aren't like Northmen, Jack thought with grim humor. Northmen would take on Satan without thinking twice. And that was because they didn't think in the first place.

"What just happened?" whispered Thorgil.

"Walk with me," Jack said. They continued along the road, and presently the captain passed them without his men. He was shading his eyes and trying to find any trace of the fugitives. Jack had to credit him with bravery.

The road took them into town, and they saw another group of watchmen patrolling the market square. When anyone appeared, he was stopped and escorted to his destination. People were still being allowed to trade, but their movements were controlled. *What incredible authority Father Severus must have*, Jack thought, *to make the townsfolk so obedient.*

They walked past houses with gardens and chicken pens. Farther on, the dwellings were humbler, but the farms were more extensive. All was orderly, if very, very subdued.

The fortress of Din Guardi sat on its stone shelf over the sea, but there was little about it to strike fear into the heart of enemies. No army of berserkers would be dismayed by the pretty pink towers or stonework carved to resemble vines. Still, it was solidly built and the gate was closed. You couldn't just walk in, as the Bard had before.

Jack felt the light around them drift away. He took a deep breath.

"Now will you tell me what happened?" demanded Thorgil. "You cast a spell in a strange language and turned us invisible. I didn't know you had that kind of magic."

"Neither did I," admitted Jack. "I think that was a *lorica*, a warding-spell. I saw the Bard do it, but he couldn't teach it to me. He said that the words came when needed and that you couldn't remember them afterward."

"*I* could," boasted Thorgil, and then stopped. "By the Aesir, I can't! What good is a spell you can't call up at will?"

"I think it's something you can't own," said Jack. "Anyhow, we're visible now, and we should ask for help from King Brutus. I'm very worried about Ethne."

Not only was the gate closed, but the windows on the landward side appeared to have been bricked up. A sheer cliff prevented them from looking on the seaward side. "Do you think they're dead?" said Thorgil.

"Listen," Jack said. Above the waves they heard singing and laughter. A breeze brought them the smell of roasting meat.

"Nidhogg's fangs!" swore the shield maiden, naming the dragon that gnawed at the roots of Yggdrassil. "Brutus is feasting while his people suffer! No Northman king would sink so low. Even Ivar at his most foolish looked after his folk in winter."

"I wonder if Brutus even knows what's going on out here," Jack said.

"Can you use your new powers to knock down the gate?"

"Perhaps," Jack said doubtfully. He stood in front of the massive wooden doors and tried to draw up fire, but nothing happened. Only the sounds of merriment floated out to mock him. "I don't know how to use St. Columba's staff," he admitted. "Sometimes it obeys me, but mostly it does things I don't expect."

"We'll have to go on to the monastery," Thorgil said.

"I had hoped . . ." Jack trailed off as he gazed unhappily at the lovely green stonework at the top of the wall. The Lady of the Lake had decorated it with jeweled flowers. How much of the fortress was real and how much was glamour he couldn't tell. It was still a barrier he couldn't cross. "I had hoped to find Ethne inside. The Bard wanted King Brutus to rescue her and make her his queen."

"I don't think there's much chance of that." Thorgil hefted her pack, and they set off in the direction of St. Filian's. Jack resigned himself to a long walk, but when they passed a field containing a few stray ponies, the shield maiden whistled sharply. Two of the ponies looked up and cantered toward them.

"How did you do that?" Jack said with admiration.

Thorgil shrugged. "It's like the *lorica*, I guess. It just happens."

The shield maiden's pony accepted her gladly, but Jack's danced around so much, she had to calm it by whispering into its ear. Even so, it hunched its back and made every effort to make the ride uncomfortable. "Let's stop for a few minutes," said Jack when they got to the pine forest overlooking St. Filian's. "I need to think." He gratefully slid off his pony and found a comfortable patch of grass.

The walls below were beautifully whitewashed, but Jack thought the gardens and orchards looked neglected. The lake had invaded some of the fields, and a long tongue of water lapped at the monastery door. To one side was the small white convent. "We should go there if we can't get into St. Filian's," Jack said. "Perhaps the nuns weren't infected."

"Or they might all be dead." Thorgil, as was her way, faced the possibility directly. "We don't know how long the disease has been raging."

Jack felt a dull anger at Father Severus. If he hadn't been so pigheaded, none of this would have happened. If he'd shown pity for the mermaid, the Bard would still be alive. If he'd had even a tenth of Brother Aiden's kindness, he would never have allowed Ethne to wall herself up. If, if, if! One thing led to the next, and now all had fallen apart.

"I hate to admit it, but I'm afraid to go down there," said Thorgil. "Eventually, flying venom burns itself out like a fire, but until then we might easily catch it. Northmen who die such honorless deaths go to the icy halls of Hel. They are forever condemned to wander in darkness with thralls and oath-breakers."

"Northman religion is so cheerful," said Jack. "The best you can expect is Ragnarok. Odin was positively gleeful about Garm being let off his leash and the ship of death bringing destruction to the living."

"*What did you say?*"

Too late Jack remembered he hadn't told Thorgil about the encounter with the war god. "Oh, bedbugs," he muttered. "I saw Odin on Grim's Island. He was sitting on a huge throne with Olaf at his feet. We didn't hit it off."

"You saw Odin and I didn't?"

"You wouldn't have liked him. He would have made you fetch him a horn of mead."

Thorgil looked ready to throw herself into a fight when she suddenly stopped. She began to laugh, a real, heartfelt laugh that Jack hadn't heard from her in a long time. "Oh! Oh, that feels good! Of course he would have ordered me around. And I would have obeyed him. You don't say no to a god. But I would have felt rotten afterward." She laughed until the tears ran down her face, and Jack watched her with surprise and admiration.

When she had finished, she wiped her eyes with her sleeve. "I feel all light inside," she said, "as though someone had thrown open a window."

Jack leaned over and took her hand. "You are Jill Allyson's Daughter," he said, using the name Thorgil's dead mother had given her at birth. "You are not meant for Ragnarok."

They gazed at each other seriously for a moment. A breeze rustled the branches of the pines and the smell of apples came to them from the orchards down below. Then Thorgil stood up. "We must go to rescue Ethne," she said. "May the gods grant that we find her alive."

Chapter Forty-three

SISTER WULFHILDA

They dismounted close to the walls. The apple orchard had been deserted for some time, for the branches were heavy with ripe fruit. It seemed to Jack that he had never smelled apples so fine. He picked one and held it to his nose.

"This alone tells us the nuns haven't prospered," said Thorgil. She, too, plucked one and began to eat. She stuffed several into her backpack.

They walked around the monastery walls, wading through areas where the lake had invaded. All the doors were bolted and the windows bricked up, but unlike Din Guardi, no sounds came from inside. "Curse Father Severus for being thorough," said Jack, trying to force his shoulder against a door. Even the lych-gate that led to the monks' cemetery had been reinforced. The walls were very high, like those of a fortress, and plastered so well that there was not a single foothold.

They shouted repeatedly. No one answered. Jack tried to raise fire to burn open the main gate. Nothing happened. "Why can't I get this thing to work?" he fumed. "I've drawn up fire before. Why not now?"

"Fate," Thorgil said simply. "It seems our path has been laid out for us. We were shown the entrance to St. Columba's cave, but you couldn't find it a second time. When it was time to leave Grim's Island, Seafarer appeared. When you needed the *lorica*, it came to your mind. But when we wished to enter Din Guardi, we were turned away. Also here. I think we should go on to the convent."

They found the gate open. Dry leaves blew across a small courtyard lined with doors. These, too, were open, showing small nuns' cells with little in them except bedding. At the far end was a chapel. A table was covered with a cloth and a pewter cross. A single window was made of small panes of glass fastened together by lead strips. The panes were milky white except for one in the middle, a triangular shard of ruby red. It hung in the middle like a drop of blood, and the sun shone through it with a glory that made Jack catch his breath.

"That must have come from the Holy Isle," he said quietly. "When the window there was shattered, the surviving pieces were fitted together at St. Filian's. One must have been left over." He didn't say—what was the use?—that berserkers had been responsible. Olaf One-Brow, Sven the Vengeful, Rune. Thorgil.

Someone groaned not far away. Jack and Thorgil ran from the chapel and looked into the cells they had believed empty. In the third one they found a woman lying in a heap of filthy straw. "Wulfie!" cried Thorgil.

Jack could hardly recognize the large, healthy nun he'd seen before. She had wasted away, and her skin was gray with illness and dirt. "Water," whispered Sister Wulfhilda. Thorgil grabbed her cider bag and dribbled a few drops into the woman's mouth.

Sister Wulfhilda coughed but managed to swallow. Thorgil gave her more. "We'll build a fire and cook you something," the shield maiden said. "All we have is dried fish, but if I can find a pot, I can make soup."

"Pots," croaked the nun. "Storeroom."

Jack and Thorgil pulled away the filthy straw and substituted fresh from the other cells. Thorgil cut an apple into thin slices and placed it in Sister Wulfhilda's hands. "Eat if you can. We'll be back."

They found the storeroom. It was an impressive structure made of stone with a thick wooden door that took both Jack and Thorgil to drag it open. Pots, cups, and wooden trenchers were stored on shelves. Firewood was stacked by the door. High on a platform were bags of grain and beans, while beneath were chests full of cheese wheels, bacon, and smoked fish. Crocks of honey and oil as well as a good supply of candles were in a side chamber. Eggs were stored in buckets of fine ash. A trapdoor led down to a cellar where they found onions, turnips, and kegs of ale and cider.

"Imagine!" cried Thorgil. "All this food and poor Wulfie was too weak to reach it."

"Where are the other nuns?" Jack said uneasily.

"One step at a time," the shield maiden said. "First, we have to get her strong enough to talk." They built a fire in an outside hearth, and Thorgil fetched water from a stream running into the lake. "I'll cook," she said. "You feed Wulfie cider mixed with honey. Not too much at a time. After famines in the Northland, people had to eat slowly or they would die."

Jack sat beside the nun and felt her head. It was cool. If she had suffered from flying venom, she no longer had it. He moistened her lips with the sweetened cider. "Good," Sister Wulfhilda whispered. She hadn't touched her apple slices. They had fallen into the straw.

Jack gave her cider until Thorgil returned with a cup of soup. She had boiled bacon in water to make a fragrant, salty broth with beads of oil on top. Sister Wulfhilda accepted this new dish with enthusiasm. "Goooood," she crooned.

Little by little they fed her, and little by little her strength returned, until she was able to speak. "Flying venom. All are dying or dead."

"All?" said Jack, fear quickening his heart.

"Father Severus ordered the nuns into the monastery," said Sister Wulfhilda. "He said we were doomed, but if we kept to ourselves, we could save the town from the disease.

God would see our sacrifice and forgive our sins." She had to rest a moment before continuing. "He made everyone fast."

"The idiot," said Thorgil. "Everyone knows starvation is the brother of death."

"What about Ethne?" Jack said.

"I wasn't allowed to go near her. I tried." Tears began to roll down Sister Wulfhilda's cheeks. Gradually, the story came out. As Thorgil had guessed, the first case of flying venom had been Mrs. Tanner's brother. He had fled to the monastery for help, and when Father Severus realized what a dangerous disease the man had, he sent monks to burn the tanner's hovel down.

First, the infirmary monks became ill and then the men who had contact with them. That was when the abbot brought the nuns in, for they had been exposed when they washed the monastery's clothes. To add to everyone's torment, fleas multiplied in the late-summer heat. It was much worse than the usual lice and fleas that pious people welcomed in order to offer their sufferings to Christ. Fleas infested everything, making everyone itch so much, their robes were spotted with blood from scratching.

That was when Father Severus had ordered the fast. After three days one of the monks, Brother Sylvus, came to Sister Wulfhilda and told her to bring food from the storehouse.

"Brother Sylvus is a good man," said Sister Wulfhilda, "not like most of the scum in there. He's genuinely kind, and it hurt him to see the weaker monks and nuns suffer. He let me out of the lych-gate and I ran here. I loaded up with as much as I could carry, but by the time I returned, the door had been locked." The nun wept silently for a moment. "I went round and round, begging to be let in. No one answered. Day after day I tried. Then my head began to hurt."

Sister Wulfhilda had come down with the flying venom. She had no idea how long she had been ill. At first she'd had the strength to crawl to the stream to fill her pitcher. Later her thoughts became too confused.

Jack saw the pitcher in a corner. It was dry, and a spider had spun a web over the mouth. "If you survived, others may have too," he said. "How can we get inside?"

"I don't know," said the nun, weeping. "Father Severus reinforced the doors and windows."

Jack and Thorgil walked around the monastery walls again. He attempted to call up fire again. He even—by now he was seething with anger—tried to create an earthquake, without results. It occurred to him, as he pushed fruitlessly at the bricks filling the windows, that the abbot really might have saved the town. Hundreds or thousands could have died if the flying venom had escaped. In that case, Father Severus was a hero. Or a saint. Could a man be a saint if he forced his companions to die with him?

"Let's eat some of that bacon soup," said Thorgil. "The smell is driving me crazy."

"Wait a minute," said Jack, halting in his tracks. He sniffed. The rich odor, even at this distance, made his stomach rumble. "That's it, Thorgil! You're brilliant!" He ran back to the nun's cell and roused her from a half sleep. "Which is the easiest door to open?" he asked.

"Why . . ." She struggled to remember. "The front and back gates are so heavy, it takes two men to move them. The garden door has been bricked up. The lych-gate, when it's unbolted, could be handled by a child."

"Thank you," said Jack, squeezing her hands. He ran back outside where Thorgil was wolfing down broth. "Find me a bigger pot from the storeroom," he ordered. "Bring cups and spoons. I'm going to make a stew fit for the saints in Heaven."

Thorgil fetched water while Jack went into the cellar for turnips, onions, rosemary, thyme, and garlic. He cut up an entire flitch of bacon. He built a new fire right outside the lych-gate. Watching Pega had taught him many things about cooking, and now he made a stew that not only tasted wonderful, but also smelled good enough to raise the dead.

"Wonderful!" said Thorgil, sniffing with appreciation. "I feel like diving into the pot."

"I'll take that as a compliment," Jack said. "Now, let's see if I can get St. Columba's staff to behave." He held it over the bubbling cauldron. Words came to him in a language he didn't know, but he understood their meaning:

Rise like the sun,
Bring warmth to world.
Bend like a branch,
Heavy with harvest.
Waken the woeful.
Heal heart with hope.

He repeated the charm three times, and the fragrant steam rose like a fountain and poured over the wall. For a few moments nothing happened. "Put your ear to the door," Jack said. "Can you hear anything?"

"I hear something dragging along the ground. And weeping," Thorgil reported.

"Someone's alive." Jack waited tensely. Presently, he heard feeble thumps against the door. A bolt was pulled back. After a long pause another bolt was slowly dragged out of its holder—*ih ih ih.* "If only we could help," said Jack, but there was nothing either of them could do. After four bolts the wooden door began to move.

"Stand aside. We'll do the rest," called Thorgil. But the person on the other side collapsed instead, and they had to push both him and the door back. The shield maiden managed to squeeze through the gap and drag the monk out of the way. Jack knelt beside him and felt his head. It was cool. He no longer had the illness.

"I've failed Father Severus," the monk moaned. "I smelled the food. I was weak. I opened the door."

"I'm sure Father Severus can come up with a penance," Jack said, irritated. The abbot had clearly meant his flock to starve to death, if they were lucky enough to survive the plague.

"Oh, no. He's already gone to God," the monk said. "In the middle of the night Sister Brecca saw his soul drawn up to Heaven by golden cords."

"Good for him. Where are the other people?"

"In the chapel," the monk said, gazing with undisguised longing at the cup of stew Thorgil carried.

She placed his hands around it. "You can have a little now and more later," she instructed.

Jack saw the graveyard clearly for the first time. Once it had been a grassy field with a few sad tombstones. Now it was filled with many, many fresh mounds. Some bore wooden crosses. Most didn't. The extent of the destruction appalled him. Jack braced himself to encounter unburied bodies in the halls, but there weren't any. The monks and nuns, feeble as they were, hadn't neglected their comrades.

The stench from the chapel hit him before he saw it. The sick must have fled here, he thought. It made sense, because none of them expected to survive, and what better place to die, for Christians, than at the heart of the church? Straw, now filthy and crawling with vermin, covered the floor. In the midst of this desolation, three emaciated monks and two nuns crouched around a body. *Is that all who've survived?* Jack thought. *Seven out of a hundred?*

The body was laid out more carefully than he would have expected, given the weakness of the survivors. She was lying on a deep bed of straw covered by a sheepskin, and she wore a crown of flowers on her head. The Bard's forget-me-nots. They had not withered in all this time.

Beside Ethne, the great cat Pangur Ban stretched out with one paw on her breast.

Chapter Forty-four

THE RUNE OF PROTECTION

"Oh, Ethne," whispered Jack, shocked to his very core. He saw the door of her cell beyond, chopped open. Someone had used an axe to get inside. Unable to speak, Jack automatically felt the heads of the monks and nuns for fever, and they gazed at him from somewhere far away, as though they couldn't believe he was real. None of them had a fever. They were going to recover. Next, he touched Ethne and recoiled. Her skin was hot!

"She's alive," he cried. Pangur Ban lifted his head and keened his sorrow.

"She is dying," one of the nuns said.

Thorgil came in, dragging the pot. She went back for the cups and passed them around to the survivors. She squatted next to Ethne and moistened her lips with sweetened cider.

Ethne's eyes opened. They were a beautiful blue, the blue of Elfland, and her face had the perfection of a white rose. Only the spots of red on her cheeks showed the fever that was raging within.

"I see you managed to comb your hair," the shield maiden said. "It's a definite improvement." Ethne wiped the cider from her lips with one delicate hand. "What's the matter with you?" Thorgil demanded.

"She has chosen to fast," the nun said. She paused from wolfing down stew.

"That's the stupidest thing I ever heard," said Thorgil. "I come all this way to save her, and she can't be bothered to eat?"

"She is giving her life for us," said the first monk, who had managed to totter from the lych-gate. "It's how Lady Ethne plans to gain a soul."

So it's "Lady Ethne" now, Jack thought. No one at the monastery had been fooled into thinking she was a real nun. He felt angrier than he could ever remember. Father Severus's foolishness had talked her into this mess, while the Bard had wanted her to go out into the world. Embracing life was the best way to gain a soul, the old man had said.

Now he was dead and his last wish had been for them to rescue his daughter. Well, Jack would do it—by all the gods, he would!—even if he had to cram stew down Ethne's ungrateful throat. St. Columba's staff thrummed and the earth trembled. The monks and nuns grabbed one another. "It's an earthquake!" one of them cried. Pangur Ban rose to his feet, came over to Jack, and sat down in front of him. The cat's wise blue eyes observed him, and the boy suddenly felt ashamed.

Never use anger to reach the life force, Jack heard in his mind, clear as clear. *It always turns on you when you least expect it.* And he remembered that Pangur Ban had been at the School of Bards, even though he'd failed the final exam.

Jack sat down on the vermin-infested straw. All the survivors were eating as rapidly as they could, something that might actually kill them. He found he didn't much care. "Please explain to me why Ethne has to die," he said.

The monk who'd opened the door was called Brother Sylvus—one of the good ones, according to Sister Wulfhilda. The nun who had said Ethne was dying was Sister Brecca. Between them, they unfolded the tale of what had happened after Sister Wulfhilda had been locked out.

When the ex-felons realized that they were trapped, Brother Sylvus said, they mutinied. They armed themselves with knives and raided the treasure room. Then they took hostages and threatened to kill them if Father Severus didn't give them the keys.

"They underestimated him," said Brother Sylvus. "Our abbot was like Samson, who brought down the temple upon the Philistines. He gathered the rest of us together and said that God would welcome us into Heaven if we died. Then he armed us and we fell upon the rebels. Our hearts were as strong as an army splendid with banners. Our blows were as the hooves of warhorses trampling a field. We slew them one and all." Brother Sylvus's face was filled with joy.

"I saw angels fighting on either side of Father Severus," added Sister Brecca, "and when he slew one of the enemy, a tiny imp came out of the man's mouth." The other monks and the nun nodded agreement.

"What happened to the hostages?" asked Thorgil.

"The evildoers cut their throats," said Brother Sylvus. "Father Severus said that was unfortunate, but you have to remember that all who live are doomed to die. Holy martyrs are assured a place in Heaven. He said you could argue that the hostages were actually lucky."

Jack rubbed his eyes. A sense of unreality crept over him. He could almost be listening to a group of Northmen explaining why it was good to die in battle and go to Valhalla.

"We had a grand funeral," said Sister Brecca. "The martyrs were buried in consecrated ground, and the evildoers were buried next to the privies."

"I suppose they'll go to Hel," said Thorgil.

"You can count on it," Sister Brecca said with shining eyes.

But unfortunately, things began to go downhill after the victory. The flying venom spread, and soon the dead outnumbered the living. Father Severus worked to the last, hearing the confessions of the dying and forgiving their sins. Then he, too, became a victim.

"He *chose* to fall ill so he could show us the proper way to die," insisted Sister Brecca. "He was always thoughtful. Always. That dear, kindhearted, saintly man."

Kindhearted except when he made Sister Wulfhilda carry a glowing piece of iron, Jack thought.

"I saw his soul pulled up to Heaven with golden cords," said the nun.

Brother Sylvus took up the tale. "He gave me the keys, all except the one for Lady Ethne's cell. He said that was not my concern."

So he meant her to die, thought Jack, with a return of his former rage.

"Father Severus ordered me to protect the sanctity of the monastery. Gradually, a few of us began to recover. This was not due to any goodness on our part, of course, but to teach us humility. We were not yet worthy of glory."

And, of course, they were very, very hungry. They had water from a well, but no food—unless you counted the rats. Rats they had aplenty, great, swaggering, confident beasts that came within reach of your hand. "But we never considered such unclean food," Brother Sylvus said hastily.

"Why didn't you just make a quick trip to the storehouse?" Jack asked wearily.

Oh, no. Never. They would never do that. Father Severus had told them *with his dying breath* that they were not to go outside until spring. Fortunately, Ethne came to their rescue. She called to them from her cell. She had food enough for all. Brother Sylvus didn't have the key, but he still managed to open her door.

Jack looked at the door, hacked and chopped in a perfect frenzy.

All the packets of dried meat, cheeses, and Pega's special scones that Thorgil had smuggled in had gone to feed this lot.

And when these were gone, the monks and nuns had begun to starve again. Ethne had never touched a morsel. She had continued to live on the watery, gray gruel handed through her window, though toward the end she ate nothing at all.

Once outside, she quickly fell ill. She sweetly refused any help, saying that it was her penance to gain a soul. She welcomed suffering. "She's giving her life for us," said Sister Brecca, reverently.

"Excuse me!" shouted Thorgil. "Excuse me, but you're all alive! She's already saved you! Why does she have to die now?" Jack had rarely seen her in such a towering rage, and he'd seen a lot of rages.

"She's an elf," said Brother Sylvus, cowering away from the shield maiden. "Father Severus explained it to us. Elves have to make their souls, and it isn't easy for them. They have no regard for anyone except themselves. They can see a child drowning and never think to stretch out a hand. Lady Ethne *did* stretch out her hand."

"Which you bit, thank you very much," snarled Thorgil. "I don't know anything about Christian souls, but I know ingratitude when I see it. She's proved her worthiness for whatever moldy afterlife you oath-breakers inhabit. I intend to see she inhabits *this* world." She bent over Ethne and tried to pry open her mouth. The elf lady turned her head aside.

"Thorgil, don't," said Jack.

"I'll pour cider down her nostrils if I have to!"

Jack grabbed the shield maiden's arm. "You'll drown her."

"Then *you* hold her jaws open. I can't do everything."

"Thorgil," said Ethne in that beautiful, musical voice only elves had. "I choose this path." Jack was startled. He hadn't known she was strong enough to speak, but apparently half-elves could endure starvation better than humans. "Thorgil," repeated the elf lady, "remember how you used to tell me about Valhalla? You longed to fall in battle so you could go there. This is no different."

At the mention of Valhalla, the monks and nuns drew away from the shield maiden in horror. They hadn't realized she was a Northman.

"It *is* different." Thorgil faltered. "Let me think why. It's because we like fighting for Odin." Jack saw uncertainty in her eyes and knew she was remembering Grim's Island. "And so, naturally, we want to keep on doing it until Ragnarok is declared." Except that she wouldn't be fighting alongside the men, Jack thought. She'd be putting warriors back together and milking goats.

"Dying, for me, is how I will achieve Heaven. Do you understand?" said Ethne gently.

"No, I don't! I was a berserker once. I wanted to die with a sword in my hand, but I lost that desire after I drank from Mimir's Well."

At the word *berserker*, the monks and nuns scuttled on hands and knees to hide behind Brother Sylvus. He began praying.

"No, that's not quite right." Thorgil was struggling to find the right words. "Things changed before I drank from Mimir's

Well. The well grants you knowledge, but only if you sacrifice something of great importance. I offered up my life, but the well rejected me. Apparently, my life wasn't good enough because I didn't value it. So in my grief I tried to stab myself anyway, and Jack—"

Jack could see where her argument was going; he wanted to stop her, but he wasn't fast enough. In a split second she had lifted the rune of protection from around her neck.

It was only visible in that short time when it was passed from one wearer to the next. It was a beautiful, bright gold that gathered light from the air. It was surpassingly lovely and desirable, but it had nothing to do with the sick desire for wealth or power. The rune was life itself made visible. And in the middle of the pendant was the shape of the great tree Yggdrassil.

Thorgil placed it around Ethne's neck, and it glimmered briefly before it disappeared.

"Oh!" said the elf lady, placing her white hand over it. Her skin deepened in color as blood flowed through her veins. Her breathing, scarcely audible before, became stronger. The fever faded from her cheeks. "What a nice chapel," murmured Ethne, gazing up at the grim ceiling. "I never noticed how many colors gray comes in. And what a good idea it is to cover the floor with grass," she said, looking at the filthy, discolored straw.

Ethne had always been a featherbrain, and the rune of protection would do nothing about that. But she was at least recalled to life.

Jack was more concerned about Thorgil, who looked devastated. It was how he'd felt after handing the rune to her. He'd never stopped longing for it, but no one could keep it forever. It had been passed from the Bard to Jack and on to Thorgil. Now it was with the Bard's daughter. It seemed fitting.

"Feed Ethne the rest of that stew," growled Thorgil, shoving the pot at Brother Sylvus. "If you don't, I *will* go berserk and tack everyone's hide to the wall." She stalked out of the chapel.

Chapter Forty-five

DEPARTURE

Jack found Thorgil outside in the orchard. She was gathering apples into a pile. "The monastery will need these for the winter," she said. "As soon as the monks and nuns regain their strength, they'll have to make preparations for the cold weather. There's food in the storehouse that will have to be moved to the monastery. The monastery should at least look sealed up until spring. We don't want trouble with those guards from town. We'll have to chop more firewood. And something has to be done about that filthy straw. I've already got flea bites."

She talked feverishly, laying out plans. Jack didn't interrupt. He knew she was trying not to think about the rune.

He helped her move the apples. Later she called up one of the horses and rode off by herself to go hunting. She had only one good hand, but that didn't diminish her ability to use a spear. She returned with a deer slung over the horse's back. Brother Sylvus skinned it.

For the next few days Thorgil snapped out orders as crisply as Father Severus himself. Jack noticed that the monks and nuns crossed themselves and avoided her eyes, but they obeyed her. They burned the straw and washed the floors with vinegar, a known remedy against flying venom. Ethne wrinkled her pretty nose and went outside to sit in the orchard. She did little except look beautiful, but no one seemed to mind.

Sometimes Sister Wulfhilda sat with her, telling stories about her life before the terrible trial by ordeal. Ethne was fascinated. She knew almost nothing about Middle Earth beyond the monastery. Sewing, weaving, and milking cows were as fantastic to her as the jeweled wonders of Elfland were to the nun. As for husbands, Sister Wulfhilda had a struggle getting the concept across. "You can only have one? Truly?" said Ethne with her tinkling elvish laugh.

"Truly," swore Sister Wulfhilda.

When they got on the subject of children, Ethne knew all about how *they* were made, except that elves almost never had any. It had something to do with not having souls. Or perhaps it was because they were so careless with the ones they did have. Many an elvish infant was left behind at a picnic or placed on a high shelf and forgotten. "I would like to have a baby," said Ethne.

"For that you must be married," Sister Wulfhilda said firmly. "To only one man."

Jack saw that the nun, who had never had children of her own, had adopted the Elf Queen's daughter.

Thorgil ordered everyone to kill rats. The monks had grown up on farms, so they knew all about hunting with slings. The nuns merely hit the creatures with clubs. They set about the task with a relish that wasn't altogether holy, but Sister Brecca swore she'd seen an imp turn into a rat and Brother Sylvus declared the slaughter a Christian duty. Pangur Ban helped.

Three nuns, four monks, and Ethne. That was all who were left out of a hundred. The enormity of the disaster kept preying on Jack's mind as he helped the monastery recover. If they had been allowed to flee, most would probably have survived. They weren't all sick in the beginning. Yet if they had run, the flying venom would have gone with some of them like sparks blown from a forest fire in a high wind.

Was Father Severus a saint, as the survivors insisted, or a monster? Jack's opinion was weighted on the side of *monster*, but the same scales held Olaf One-Brow, who was certainly no one's idea of a good neighbor. Yet he towered above ordinary men with his openheartedness. Olaf would never have rejected a lonely mermaid on a beach.

Jack didn't take part in the killing of the rats. He felt their death screams in the air and the cries of their young left to starve. Instead, he called life into the apple trees, so that they would survive the winter to come. He blessed the monastery fields with the ancient call to earth that his mother had used.

And he thought he saw bodies as brown as freshly turned soil nestled together. The silky strands of autumn grass above them bent before the wind.

Thou art a good lad, Jack, to bless the fields, whispered the yarthkins. *We will not forget thee.*

"Brother Aiden will have to come here," Thorgil said one chilly morning.

Jack looked up from the oatcakes he was toasting on a griddle. "Why?" he asked. It surprised him how much Thorgil cared about the monastery, for someone who had helped destroy the Holy Isle.

"The monks and nuns need a leader. They're like children on their own. Father Severus gave them tasks for every hour of the day, and without him, they don't know what to do."

Jack nodded. He remembered how Father Severus had organized things in the dungeons of Elfland. *You must always have an hourglass*, he had said. *It tells you when to go about your chores, when to meditate, and when to pray. Without direction, men fall into sloth. And from there they degenerate into other sins.* But perhaps such unrelenting control wasn't good for people either.

"Brother Aiden won't like it," Jack said. "He had a rotten time when he tried to run St. Filian's before."

"All the troublemakers are dead," Thorgil said bluntly. "In my opinion, Sister Wulfhilda would make the best leader, but they won't accept her. She's a female."

"You're female."

"I'm an ex-berserker," Thorgil said with a wolfish smile.

"I told them I'd tell my brothers, one of whom is a half-troll, where the monastery was if they didn't obey. At any rate, I'm sick of telling Christians when to pray and when to go to the privy. I want to start for the village before the winter storms."

Jack looked out at the lake. It was pale under the autumn sky and some mornings there was a crust of ice around the edges. He wouldn't mind leaving either, although he dreaded seeing the Roman house empty. "Brother Aiden won't be able to come before spring. Can the monastery survive until then?"

"With Sister Wulfhilda's help. You'll have to bring him back without me, though. I won't return."

Jack knew she didn't want to see Ethne with the rune of protection. She couldn't actually see it, of course, but a brightness around the elf lady told her it was there. "Fair enough," he said.

They found Father Severus's hourglass and showed Sister Wulfhilda how to use it. She would tell Brother Sylvus what to do each day—humbly, of course. The nun knew very well how to make others think they were making the decisions. And Brother Sylvus would pass the orders on to everyone else. The monastery was stocked with food meant for a hundred. They had ample firewood.

"I'm leaving this with you, Wulfie," Thorgil said, handing over the small chest of jewels from Notland. Jack was astounded. Nothing separated Northmen from their wealth-hoards except death. Even Beowulf, as he lay dying, had asked to feast his eyes on the gold he had wrested from the dragon.

"Are you sure?" he murmured.

"It was bought with Dragon Tongue's life," she said simply. Jack saw that a profound change had come over the shield maiden.

Sister Wulfhilda admired the dark wood inlaid with ivory. "I've never seen anything this fine, not even in the treasure room of the monastery. Is it a saint's relic?"

Thorgil laughed. "I'll never understand why Christians keep bones in boxes. No, Wulfie. It's not a relic. You'll have fun looking at the contents, but for Freya's sake, don't let Brother Sylvus or anyone else see it. Keep it hidden until Brother Aiden arrives. He'll know what to do."

They left very early the next morning while the ground was covered with frost. Only Sister Wulfhilda saw them off, for they wanted to slip away without long good-byes. "If I don't return by spring," Jack said, "send a message to Brother Aiden. Send it in my name. You and he can decide whether to introduce Ethne to King Brutus. The Bard thought she'd make a good queen, but I'm not sure he'd make a decent husband."

They kissed good-bye and rode off on a path that Sister Wulfhilda said would skirt the town and join up with the road to the village. The horses blew mist from their nostrils, and the morning star blazed in the eastern sky. "Why did you say that?" said Thorgil. "I mean, about not returning by spring."

"I don't know," Jack admitted. The air was cold, but St. Columba's robe was proof against any weather. The staff was slung on his back, and the horse's saddlebags contained provisions for the long journey.

They rode west for a while and then south. The town was barely visible, even in the pearly light of dawn, and they met no one until they came to a stream. A creature sped out of the bushes and sat down on the road ahead of them.

Well met, Pangur Ban, said Jack.

You sneaky wizard. You tried to go off without saying goodbye, accused the cat.

I'm sorry. I didn't mean to be rude.

"What language are you speaking?" said Thorgil. "And why is Pangur Ban yowling?"

She doesn't understand the Blessed Speech, said the cat. *You should use Saxon.*

"All right, I will," Jack said, surprised that he'd been using anything else.

"Will what?" the shield maiden said crossly. "It's cold as a troll's backside out here. If we're going to be entertaining cats, we should build a fire."

They dismounted and gathered firewood. Jack set it alight with the staff without any trouble, although the wood was damp. "Nothing like a fire on a cold morning," he said, warming his hands.

"Sister Wulfhilda packed venison pies," said Thorgil. "I can heat one up if you're hungry."

"Do you want one, Pangur?" Jack gave a friendly scratch

behind the cat's ears. The creature was stretched out to get maximum warmth on his stomach.

Save them for the trip, he advised. *It might be longer than you think.*

"He says we should wait," Jack translated. By now the sun had risen over the eastern sea, but it was still veiled in mist. It shone like a pale gold moon.

"You can understand him. That's new," said Thorgil.

"Yes, it is," Jack said uneasily.

"Ask him what he ate all that time Ethne was starving herself."

So Jack asked, and Pangur Ban said he'd been eating rats. He preferred lamb chops and roast goose, of course, but one made do with what one could get. He'd slain any rats that tried to get into Ethne's cell and taken them outside to devour because she was so tenderhearted. *She's turned into a decent human*, he said. *Dragon Tongue would be pleased.*

"You do know what happened to him?" the boy said sadly.

I know everything, replied the cat. They spoke of this and that, and Jack invited him to come along, but Pangur Ban preferred to stay in the monastery. *They spoil me rotten*, he said, purring loudly. *Besides, I want to keep an eye on Ethne. Now you should go, for the way is difficult.*

They put out the fire and called the horses, and Thorgil gave a last stroke to Pangur Ban's fur. He sniffed her hand and made an excited chattering sound. *Forgive me. She smells like Bird and I always lose control.*

"What's he saying?" Thorgil said suspiciously.

"Nothing you need to know. Farewell, old friend," Jack said to the cat. "May the life force hold you in the hollow of its hand."

And you as well. Pangur Ban stretched luxuriously and then trotted off. After a moment he turned aside and vanished into the bushes.

Chapter Forty-six

THORGIL SILVER-HAND

Up until then the weather had been cold but dry. Now storm clouds blew in from the northeast, and by afternoon the first raindrops began to fall. "Balder's backside," grumbled Thorgil, wrapping herself in a heavy, woolen cloak treated with oil. The rain increased until they could hardly see the way forward. The road became awash with streams pouring out of the forests on either side. The ponies' hooves slipped in hidden holes, and finally Jack said they would have to camp.

They had only gotten as far as a small beech wood, a half-day's journey from town. In the teeming rain they saw a well with a copper cup attached to a chain. "We won't be needing that for water," said Thorgil. "All we have to do is look up and open our mouths."

The beech trees were completely leafless and offered no shelter from the storm. Jack and Thorgil had to huddle next to the well, where an ancient wall, half tumbled down, gave some protection. The ponies stood together with their backs to the wind.

"Maybe we should return to the monastery tomorrow," said Jack.

"Never! I shall never go back," Thorgil said. Jack knew there was no point arguing with her yet. By morning she might be miserable enough to change her mind. He put St. Columba's robe over both of them, and as before, it gave them ample cover. It not only made them feel warmer, but drier. The wool didn't smell of wet sheep either, but of green leaves and summer.

"I wonder whether I could magic up some kind of shelter," Jack said, looking at St. Columba's staff.

"That would be very welcome," said Thorgil. She might be warmer, but she was still shivering.

Jack held the staff out, trying various commands such as "Walls, arise!" and "House, appear!" but nothing happened. Even to him the words sounded lame. He needed a *lorica*, and that only came when needed.

I really, really need one now, Jack thought, hoping that someone was listening. The water kept thundering down. Next, he tried to stop the rain, but he had only ever been good at calling it up. "The staff has a mind of its own," he conceded at last.

"We'll get through this," said Thorgil. "I remember once, when I was very small, being stuck on a cliff with Olaf while he was hunting wild sheep. A storm came up and we couldn't move. The wind was so strong, I thought it was going to blow us over the edge, but Olaf said, 'Hang on by your fingernails, child. That's why Northmen never cut them. They're as good as eagle talons.' He was so cheerful about it, I lost all fear."

Jack unwrapped one of the venison pies, and they took turns nibbling it. Darkness fell with no letup in the storm. The ground where they lay was full of stones and a tree root meandered through the middle, but eventually exhaustion brought them sleep.

It was still raining in the morning. "We have to return," Jack said.

"Never," said Thorgil flatly.

"I've seen these storms go on for a week. Besides, what's the harm in staying at the monastery until spring? You can stuff wool in your ears if you don't want to hear Christian prayers."

"I won't go back!" cried Thorgil, with more than a little hysteria in her voice.

Jack decided it was better to eat breakfast before pushing the argument further. He unpacked a round of cheese and cut her a chunk with his knife.

"I'm not hungry," she said.

"You need to eat." He made the mistake of trying to put the cheese into her mouth, and she struck him. The whole round went spinning into the mud. "What's the matter with you?" Jack shouted, retrieving the food and holding it out in the rain to clean it.

"I said I wasn't hungry and I meant it! I want to get moving! I'll go mad if I sit here and do nothing!"

"Go mad, then." Jack turned his back on her. He ate slowly while staring at the teeming rain. Even on the high ground where they were, the water sat in pools. It seemed likely that the road ahead was flooded. He heard a slight noise over the relentless storm and turned to see Thorgil crying.

She was trying not to make a sound, but her body shook with sobs and a few gasps escaped her. "Thorgil, I'm so sorry," cried Jack. He was used to her rages. Crying was much more alarming. He slid over to put his arm around her and found that her skin was hot. "Oh, Thorgil. Oh, no," he murmured. She had caught flying venom. It had simply taken a while to surface.

When they had arrived at the monastery, the monks and nuns no longer had it, but Ethne was still ill. Thorgil had bent over her when she transferred the rune of protection. The elf lady had breathed on her.

Jack held Thorgil closely. He was aware that she could infect him, but he didn't care. "You know you're very sick, don't you?" he said. There was no point avoiding the truth. Northmen preferred to face a problem head-on.

"I don't feel good," Thorgil admitted. "My head aches horribly, and I keep having chills. My eyes are blurry."

"It might be flying venom."

"It might. Wulfie said she felt like this."

They sat for a while longer. "You know that we can't go to my village now," said Jack. "We'd carry the disease to them."

"I know," she said.

"The only place in the world where we'll be welcome is the monastery. They've already had the disease. They won't catch it again." Jack smoothed her wet hair. Even that was too hot.

He helped Thorgil to her feet, and she called the ponies in the way that only the heirs of Hengist knew. They came readily, but he had to help her climb up. "Put your arms around its neck," Jack advised. "That way you won't fall off."

Far too slowly, they began to retrace their journey. The road was cut by streams and sometimes disappeared altogether. Jack had to keep checking landmarks to be sure they were going the right way. Without the sun, he had no sense of direction. Thorgil slipped into a kind of trance as they plodded on. She no longer raised her head and depended on Jack to find the way. Unfortunately, his pony wasn't at all cooperative. It balked at going down the road and turned around frequently to be sure its companion was following.

Jack had to fight the animal constantly, and it soon became clear that they wouldn't reach St. Filian's before dark. He was looking for a place to camp when suddenly the way before them was blocked by a tangle of bare branches. He halted. "Where are we?" said Thorgil in a drowsy voice.

"Almost there," Jack lied, his heart thudding with fear.

Somehow, while fighting the pony, he'd gotten off the road. He looked back and found the trees completely unfamiliar. He couldn't remember which way they'd come, and now they were surrounded by the confusing jumble of a hazel wood.

Paths led off in all directions, most of them roofed by branches so low, a horse and rider couldn't get through. The light was dim and getting dimmer. Jack looked around desperately for some kind of shelter. "Must lie down," said Thorgil in a muffled voice.

"No!" cried Jack, but she had already slipped to the ground. She landed in a mush of dead leaves, and he dismounted quickly and ran to her. His pony, freed of its burden, wheeled and galloped off through the trees. Thorgil's pony followed. "No! No!" shouted Jack, waving his arms, but they paid not the slightest attention to him.

"Call them back, Thorgil," he begged.

"Throat sore," she whispered. Jack didn't dare try to track the ponies. He'd get lost, and anyhow, they would obey only the shield maiden. Perhaps in the morning she would have recovered enough to speak. Right now, though, they were in a terrible situation, because the ponies had gone off with the food and supplies. All they had left was what they were wearing and, of course, St. Columba's robe and staff. Jack never let go of these.

Now is the time for a lorica, implored Jack to whatever powers were listening. But apparently, it wasn't. "Curse this staff!" he cried, flinging it away. He wrapped himself and Thorgil in the robe, and it not only became large enough for both of them, it insulated them from the ground. Inside, it was warm and dry, so apparently some of the magic was working.

After a while Jack crawled out and retrieved the staff. "I smell flowers," murmured Thorgil. He sniffed. Incredibly, so did he. Outside, the winter storm raged and water poured past them on either side, but inside it was spring. "If I die . . . ," the shield maiden said. Her voice was so low, Jack could barely hear it.

"Hush. You're going to recover," he said.

Thorgil swallowed. It was evidently very painful to talk. "I'll go to Hel."

Jack was shocked. He knew that Northmen who died of illness were supposed to be condemned to the same afterlife as oath-breakers. It was dismaying that Thorgil still believed it after learning the truth about Valhalla. "You are absolutely not going to Hel," he said. "The Bard said we get to choose our afterlife. If it were up to me, I'd choose the Islands of the Blessed. That's where your mother went."

"Mother," whispered Thorgil.

Jack racked his brain to think of something that would comfort her. "You know, I never told you the poem I wrote about your battle with Garm, the hound of Hel," he said. "It's called 'Thorgil Silver-Hand.'"

She stirred in his arms. "Truly?"

"It's the best thing I ever did and will be sung in halls forever after. It goes like this. . . ." Jack hadn't the slightest idea what words would come out of his mouth, but he needn't have worried. The same marvelous feeling came over him as when he'd recited the *lorica* in Bebba's Town. In fact, the poem was a *lorica*, only a very long one. And it *was* the best thing he'd ever done, right up there with the Bard's "Beowulf."

There wasn't a single word that was not beautiful and inspiring. It told of Thorgil Silver-Hand, who was put out for wolves to devour when she was born, but the royal dog Maeve rescued her. Many were the battles and adventures of Thorgil Silver-Hand. She fought a dragon even as it was carrying her to its nest to feed its young. She slew a giant eagle when it attacked her on the ice bridge to the Mountain Queen's palace. She fought the hound of Hel to save her comrades and sacrificed her hand, just as the god Tyr had when he confronted Fenris.

Tyr became the star that never moved, the one they called the Nail, that guided ships to their safe harbor. Thorgil, too, would shine in the night sky, and her fame would never die.

By the time Jack had finished, Thorgil was asleep. He felt shaky, as though he'd run for miles, and his head throbbed. His throat hurt so much that he was amazed he'd been able to speak at all. Very soon he fell into the same stupor as Thorgil and gradually drifted into unconsciousness. The winter storm raged on around them, and water poured through the hazel wood like a river.

Chapter Forty-seven

THE ISLANDS OF THE BLESSED

The sun was shining when he awoke. More than that, the sky was a glorious blue and the air was fresh and sweet. Jack sat up. He was on an island in the middle of a great river with the hazel wood lining its banks. The storm must have been mighty indeed to carve out such a channel. St. Columba's robe lay on the ground, and he picked it up hastily, but there was no mud on it.

He picked up the staff, too, and then realized Thorgil wasn't with him. "Thorgil!" he cried, terrified. She must have fallen into the water and been swept away.

"I'm here, silly," she answered. "We've been waiting for hours." She was in a little coracle tied to a branch overhanging the water. And with her was—

Jack was so overcome with emotion, he couldn't speak.

"Come on," the Bard said briskly. "We have a long journey, and you've made us late." As if in a dream, Jack stepped into the coracle. It was unsteady and damp, as such boats always were. Thorgil untied the rope, and they sailed away down the river, going west.

"Are we dead, sir?" Jack asked as the hazel wood moved past.

"Of course not," the old man said. "You've passed the qualifying exam for the School of Bards. You don't think it's easy getting in, do you? Not just any farm brat can knock on its doors and expect to be made welcome."

"But you're . . ." Jack wanted to say *you're dead*, but it seemed impolite.

"Learn to ask questions when you want answers," the Bard snapped. "Self-imposed ignorance does no one any good. I *was* shut into a tomb with Shellia for a while—and believe me, listening to her complaints made one want to be dead. I had to chase her all the way to the farther sea. But when Severus died, I was released from my oath."

"You know about Father Severus?" said Jack, astounded.

"I know everything. Pangur Ban is the world's biggest gossip." The old man smiled at something he didn't choose to share. "It took me a while to find the path back to Middle Earth. I just missed finding you at St. Filian's, but no harm done. Ethne is positively blooming, for which I am most grateful to you and Thorgil."

"It was Thorgil's doing," Jack said honestly. "Will Ethne marry King Brutus?"

"Perhaps. If Brutus is very lucky. Now admire the view a while, lad, because I want to think." The old man sat in the stern of the coracle and turned his thoughts inward. Jack went to sit with Thorgil in the prow.

The hazel wood had given way to oaks, and blue mountains rose to the north and slowly passed. "Do you want an apple?" said Thorgil, reaching into a basket. "The horses ran off with the venison pies, but the Bard brought these from the monastery." She expertly cut one of the fruits in two with her knife.

Jack stared. "Your hand—"

Thorgil laughed merrily. "I forgot to tell you. When I woke up, it was as good as new. I guess I can't keep the name Silver-Hand." She passed him half of the apple and lowered her eyelashes. "I really liked your poem, though."

Jack felt his face grow warm. "Thanks," he said.

The coracle swept on and the river widened until the blue mountains withdrew to the north. The channel deepened, and a skein of geese passed overhead, calling to one another.

"What's that?" cried Thorgil, pointing. A large fish with sun-bright scales swam just below the surface, going against the current. It passed the coracle, stroking the water with powerful fins.

"I think it's a salmon," said Jack, filled with wonder. "It's the biggest one I've ever seen."

"It's the Salmon of Knowledge returning to the pools of its youth," said the Bard, stirring from his reverie. "It goes to feast on hazelnuts. Hobgoblins aren't the only creatures besotted with them. Look ahead. We've come to the sea."

And so they had. Long waves rolled out of the west and changed the river's color from blue to gray-green. "We're going out there?" said Jack, looking with dismay at the waves.

"It's the only way to the Islands of the Blessed," the Bard said. "That's where St. Columba moved the School of Bards." They continued outward just as steadily as they had on the river, though they had no sail.

Jack looked back to see the land disappearing in the distance. "Will I ever return?" he said, suddenly close to tears.

"Of course. I have done so many times," said the Bard. "Once you learn the paths in the hazel wood, you can go to quite a lot of places, not all of them nice."

"But what of Mother and Father, Hazel and Pega? I can't just abandon them!"

"You can watch over them. That is part of the high calling of a bard, but there is always a price to pay for such power and responsibility. It is to serve all life, not just a little corner of it. Don't grieve, lad. If it puts your mind at rest, the Blewits have moved into the old Roman house and Hazel won't have to leave the village. They decided it was better to be mud-struck than risk losing her. Pega has found the love she always deserved with your family. I think you'll find that most of the time people get along just fine on their own."

The sun passed zenith and turned toward the west. The Bard brought out hard-boiled eggs, bread, and a bag of cider.

They talked of many things, and the time passed quickly. Little by little Jack's sorrow lifted.

In late afternoon they saw the islands shining in the distance. A breeze brought them the scent of apples and land birds began to circle the coracle. As they approached, the sea became clear, as though they were sailing through the sky. They passed one island, then another and another. One had a green hill on which horses grazed.

"Look! Oh, look!" shouted Thorgil. A woman and a dog were standing on the shore. The woman raised her hand in greeting. "It's Mother," cried Thorgil, bursting into tears. "She looks so young. And that's Maeve, who saved me from the wolves. Oh, can't I stop? Can't I stay here?"

"Another time." The Bard waved back at Allyson and Maeve. "You can visit after you've studied awhile at the School of Bards. Don't worry. They'll understand."

"*Thorgil's* going to the School of Bards?" said Jack, outraged. She hadn't learned nearly as much magic and poetry as he had.

"Jealousy is not encouraged here," the old man said severely. "She may not be the same kind of student as you, but she's just as qualified."

"So there," said Thorgil, sticking out her tongue. She wiped the tears from her eyes. "I feel torn up inside, miserable and happy at once. I don't like it."

"It's one of the things that happens when you serve the life force," the Bard said. "Ah! We've arrived at the school for apprentice bards." They had come to a large island with mountains and valleys and forests, but at the top of a small hill close to shore was a gray building every bit as grim as St. Filian's Monastery.

"Apprentice bards?" said Jack, somewhat upset. "I thought I'd got beyond that."

"You've come a long way, lad, no mistake. I'm very proud of you. But the study is difficult and you don't accomplish it in a few years. As you improve your skills, you will move deeper into the island."

Jack suddenly became aware of the cloak and staff he carried. "Is St. Columba going to be angry with me for taking his belongings?"

"Not in the least. He moved on long ago," said the Bard. "The Islands of the Blessed are what Brother Aiden calls the doorstep of Heaven. It is for those of us who are not finished with the affairs of the world. St. Columba's cloak and staff were meant for you, but don't look too pleased about it. You'll have to work three times harder than anyone else to understand them." The old man unfolded a cloth in the bottom of the coracle and took out Fair Lamenting. It had not been left in the tomb after all. In place of its clapper was the silver flute of Amergin. The Bard rang it.

The chime rolled through the evening air as golden and sublime as Jack had remembered, but this time it brought only joy, for it had come to its true home. A door in the gray building opened.

"They're expecting you," said the Bard, beaching the coracle and waiting for Jack and Thorgil to step onto the sand. "I'll look in on you later." He pushed off, sailing away tranquilly without a backward glance.

"Oh, bedbugs," said Jack, looking up at the forbidding school. A group of men and women in white robes had come outside. They looked even grimmer than the building.

"I'm not even sure what a school is," said Thorgil.

"Neither am I," admitted Jack. The late sunlight had turned the hill a deep green, and a cat came out of the building, meowing for attention. One of the bards leaned over and picked it up. That was encouraging.

"It's probably no worse than the dungeons of Elfland," Thorgil said doubtfully.

"Or getting pulled into a knucker hole."

"Or being eaten by a hogboon," said Thorgil.

"Come on, Jill. We can get through this." Jack took her hand, and together they walked up the hill.

Appendix

THE *CARNYX*

This war trumpet was as tall or taller than a man. Its origin is unknown, but the best-preserved example of it was found in northeast Scotland. The wide end was shaped like the head of an animal, but which animal is anyone's guess. Some say it is a boar. I think it's a Pictish beast. The mouth of this trumpet contained a hinged, metal tongue that made a particularly nasty sound.

A Greek historian, Diodorus Siculus, described "the dreadful din (of battle), for there were innumerable horn blowers and trumpeters and, as the whole army were shouting their war cries at the same time, there was such a tumult of sound that it seemed that not only the trumpeters and the soldiers but all the country round had got a voice and caught up the cry." The Romans were so intimidated by this that they made the *carnyx* the official emblem of their enemy.

A team of Scotsmen—Dr. John Purser, archaeologist Fraser Hunter, silversmith John Creed, and musician John Kenny—recreated a *carnyx* in 1992. John Kenny played it in Smoo Cave, a wonderfully creepy place in northern Scotland where the Vikings used to hide out. You can hear it and get an idea of what a Pictish beast sounded like, at this very long website: bbc.co.uk/scotland/music/scotlandsmusic/episodes/episode_02.shtml.

Or you can go to YouTube and look for "John Kenny + *carnyx*." There are a couple of YouTube clips of other people blowing *carnices* (the plural of *carnyx*), but they don't really know how to do it.

FATHER SEVERUS

Some may find it amazing that Father Severus had so much authority that he was able to keep his monks from fleeing the plague. Such an event actually happened in 1665–66. Bubonic plague was sweeping the port cities of England, but the disease had not reached the countryside. In particular, the town of Eyam in Derbyshire had been safe. Unfortunately, someone in London sent a sample of cloth to a tailor in Eyam, and out hopped a few plague fleas. The tailor sickened and died.

The Anglican rector William Mompesson and the Puritan preacher Thomas Stanley both realized that if the villagers panicked and ran, they would spread the disease. They forbade anyone to leave the town. This bottled up the plague and made its effect much worse. Two hundred sixty-seven people died out of the three hundred fifty who fell ill. This included Mompesson's devoted wife, Catherine. But the villages around Eyam were spared. Mompesson survived, and as soon as Eyam was plague-free, the villagers locked him out of his church and forced him to leave town.

THE FIN FOLK

The fin folk lived in the Orkney Isles north of Scotland. Fin men were tall, thin, gloomy shape-shifters with no love of humans. They punished anyone who tried to fish in their domain. They dealt in illusion and were able to render themselves invisible. They propelled their boats along by magic.

Fin wives started out as beautiful mermaids, but if they were unable to win a human husband, they deteriorated into sea hags and had to make do with fin men. Both spent the summer on an island called Hildaland, which was sometimes invisible. Winters were spent in a fabulous city at the bottom of the sea called Finfolkaheem. In the book I have combined these into one place, Notland.

The Shoney was an ancient sea god, possibly a Pictish god. Until recently, islanders won his favor by pouring a keg of ale into the sea. Most of my information comes from this website written and maintained by Sigurd Towrie: orkneyjar.com.

FLYING VENOM

Until recently, people didn't know how disease was communicated, but they did have some ideas about avoiding it. Medieval monasteries (where the hospitals were) usually separated contagious patients from those with physical injuries. Doctors (also called "leeches") knew that the medicines they made should be prepared with clean ingredients, using clean tools.

Flying venom (*onflygge*) was how they explained a disease that could move swiftly through an entire community. The source was described in various creative ways, such as dragon breath, evil winds, and small winged creatures. We know today that small winged creatures (flies and mosquitoes) *do* carry disease. Sneezes, too, are a favorite way for a germ to get around, and that isn't so far from dragon breath.

The old British and Irish historians kept records of plagues. It isn't always easy to know what they were describing, but some of the diseases were probably bubonic plague, smallpox, and cholera. A few might have been relapsing fever, polio, rabies, and anthrax.

And there was the yellow plague. No one knows what the yellow plague was, but it was devastating. It began (so the story goes) with "a vaporous column sweeping over the land, one head in the clouds and the other trailing along the ground." All who breathed of it fell sick and died. People fled in all directions. Maelgwn the Great, king of north Wales, hid in a church, but when he peeked through the keyhole to see what was happening, the sight of the yellow plague killed him.

My personal favorite among disasters happened in Ireland in 896. Vast numbers of "vermin-like moles with two teeth" fell from the air and ate everything up. They had to be driven off with prayers.

I don't give a name to the disease in this book.

LORICA

Lorica is the Latin word for *breastplate* or *body armor*. It was also an incantation used by early Christian monks to protect themselves from enemies. The most famous *lorica* is "The Breastplate of St. Patrick" with which the saint hid himself and his followers in the shape of deer. The style of St. Patrick's spell is very similar to ones used by Amergin, the founder of the druidic order in Ireland.

MERMAIDS

Two of the most common symbols carved by the Picts were mirrors and combs. They occur together. People have guessed that these indicate the death of a woman, but there might be a larger explanation. Mermaids are often shown holding mirrors and combs. They could be later memories of Pictish sea goddesses. At any rate, mermaids were generally bad news to the sailors who encountered them. One of the oldest versions of the Scottish ballad "Sir Patrick Spens" has the following verse:

Then up there came a mermaiden,
A comb and glass all in her hand,

"Here's a health to you, my merry young men,
For you'll not see dry land again!"

At which point the ship sank to the bottom of the sea.

ST. COLUMBA

Columba, according to his biographers, was the saint equivalent of a rock star. He was "a tall, striking figure of powerful build and impressive presence, who combined the skills of scholar, poet, and ruler" (*Oxford Dictionary of Saints* by David Farmer, Oxford University Press, 2003).

Columba was born into a royal Irish family and may well have had connections with druids. He certainly knew how to calm rough seas, dispel fog, and call up winds going in *opposite* directions at the same time. Even more interesting, Columba argued for the preservation of the bardic order. This was at a gathering of newly Christianized Irish kings who wanted to suppress the old religion. Columba convinced them that the future of Irish culture depended on preserving it.

Among his many achievements, Columba converted King Brude of the Picts to Christianity and scared the Loch Ness Monster away from an intended meal. But there is one disturbing story about him in connection with the building of a church on Iona. Whatever was built during the day was thrown down at night. Columba set guards to watch, but in the morning these men would be found dead. Columba, being the hero he was, stood watch himself.

And in the darkness he saw a creature come out of the

sea. It was half woman, half fish, and very old. When she shook herself, the whole island quaked and she emitted a tinkling sound like pots rattling together. She was terrifyingly ugly. From this we can tell that Columba had encountered a sea hag.

He asked why she was killing his guards, and she replied that she did nothing but that the sight of her gave them all heart attacks. Columba then asked her why she had knocked down his church. The sea hag said that it wasn't her fault but that the building could not stand unless someone agreed to be buried alive under it.

One of Columba's followers, Odhran, volunteered. Columba promised him that he would be taken into Heaven. Odhran was put into a deep pit with a roof over it, and after twenty days, Columba lifted the roof to see whether his friend was still alive. When Odhran tried to climb out, the saint ordered that he be covered up with clay.

Now this, however you look at it, was a human sacrifice. Such "foundation sacrifices" are found from earliest times in Britain and Ireland, although later a dog, horse, or cat was substituted.

SEAFARER

Seafarer's species, the black-browed albatross, lives in the south Atlantic near Antarctica, but occasionally storms can blow one thousands of miles from its homeland. In 1967 a single male arrived in Scotland and has been there ever since. Bird-watchers have named him Albert.

Albert has been unable to find a mate, although he has tried to woo gannets less than half his size. Not surprisingly, they drove him away. Albert has a seven-foot wingspan, and some albatrosses can reach nine feet. Now he lives on a tiny rock between the Outer Hebrides and Shetland Islands. Albert is at least forty-nine years old and may live to be over seventy (BBC News, May 9, 2007).

Sources

Aebi, Ormond, and Harry Aebi, *The Art and Adventure of Beekeeping* (Emmaus, PA: Rodale Press, 1983).

Brondsted, Johannes, *The Vikings*, Kallie Skov, trans. (Middlesex, England: Penguin Books, 1967).

Byock, Jesse L., trans., *The Saga of the Volsungs: The Norse Epic of Sigurd the Dragon Slayer* (London: Penguin Books, 1999).

Cummins, W. A., *The Age of the Picts* (Gloucestershire, England: Allan Sutton Publishing, 1995).

Davidson, H. R. Ellis, *Gods and Myths of Northern Europe* (Middlesex, England: Penguin Books, 1964).

Fry, Timothy, ed., *The Rule of St. Benedict in Latin and English with Notes and Thematic Index* (Collegeville, MN: Liturgical Press, 1982).

Griffiths, Bill, *Aspects of Anglo-Saxon Magic* (Norfolk, England: Anglo-Saxon Books, 1996).

Guthrie, E. J., *Old Scottish Customs* (Glasgow, Scotland: Thomas D. Morison, Co., 1885).

Hagen, Ann, *A Second Handbook of Anglo-Saxon Food and Drink: Production and Distribution* (Norfolk, England: Anglo-Saxon Books, 1995).

Kennedy, Charles W., trans., *An Anthology of Old English Poetry* (New York: Oxford University Press, 1968).

Leahy, Kevin, *Anglo-Saxon Crafts* (Gloucestershire, England: Tempus Publishing, 2003).

Lindow, John, *Handbook of Norse Mythology* (Santa Barbara, CA: ABC-CLIO, 2001).

Matthews, Caitlín, and John Matthews, *The Encyclopedia of Celtic Wisdom* (Dorset, England: Element Books, 1994).

Pollington, Stephen, *Leechcraft: Early English Charms, Plantlore, and Healing* (Norfolk, England: Anglo-Saxon Books, 2000).

———, *The Mead-Hall: Feasting in Anglo-Saxon England* (Norfolk, England: Anglo-Saxon Books, 2003).

Pretor-Pinney, Gavin, *The Cloudspotter's Guide: The Science, History, and Culture of Clouds* (New York: Penguin Books, 2006).

Ross, Anne, and Don Robins, *The Life and Death of a Druid Prince* (New York: Simon & Schuster, 1989).

Serraillier, Ian, trans., *Beowulf the Warrior* (New York: Scholastic Book Services, 1968).

Sturluson, Snorri, *The Prose Edda*, Jean I. Young, trans. (Berkeley, CA: University of California Press, 1964).

Sutherland, Elizabeth, *The Pictish Guide* (Edinburgh, Scotland: Birlinn, 1997).

———, *In Search of the Picts* (London: Constable, 1994).

Taylor, Paul B., and W. H. Auden, trans., *The Elder Edda* (New York: Random House, 1970).

Whitlock, Ralph, *In Search of Lost Gods* (Oxford, England: Phaedon Press, 1979).

Wilson, David, *The Anglo-Saxons* (New York: Penguin Books, 1981).

NOTE: The complete text of the oldest book on this list, *Old Scottish Customs* by E. J. Guthrie, is available online.